Praise for I Am Livia

"It humanizes historical figures that had, for me, just been names on a timeline. I can't recommend it highly enough."
—Susan Coventry, author of *The Queen's Daughter*

"*I Am Livia* is a wonderful journey to ancient Rome . . . The historical backdrop of Rome becomes more accessible, less academic, when seen through the lives of Smith's characters."
—*Historical Novels Review*

"[A] highly polished and compelling story of ancient Rome . . . Seamlessly written, this novel will appeal mightily to fans of historical fiction."
—*Publishers Weekly*

"Readers who seek out fiction about intelligent, powerful women of the past will find a great deal to enjoy here—I definitely did!"
—Sarah L. Johnson, author of *Historical Fiction: A Guide to the Genre*

THE DAUGHTERS OF PALATINE HILL

Also by Phyllis T. Smith

I Am Livia

THE DAUGHTERS OF PALATINE HILL

PHYLLIS T. SMITH

LAKE UNION
PUBLISHING

Published by Lake Union Publishing, Seattle

www.apub.com

Amazon, the Amazon logo, and Lake Union Publishing are trademarks of Amazon.com, Inc., or its affiliates.

ISBN-13: 9781503952485 (hardcover)
ISBN-10: 1503952487 (hardcover)
ISBN-13: 9781503952478 (paperback)
ISBN-10: 1503952479 (paperback)

Cover design by Rex Bonomelli

Printed in the United States of America
First edition

To Sheila Levine

Leading Characters

》》》》》》》》》》》

Julia

Livia Drusilla, Julia's stepmother

Caesar Augustus (called Tavius by intimates), Julia's father, ruler of Rome, adopted son of Julius Caesar

Cleopatra Selene, Mark Antony and Cleopatra's daughter

Scribonia, Julia's mother, briefly married to Caesar Augustus, then divorced

Tiberius, Livia's older son by her first marriage

Drusus, Livia's younger son by her first marriage

Marcus Agrippa, Rome's foremost general, Caesar Augustus's friend since boyhood

Gaius Maecenas, another boyhood friend of Caesar Augustus, now a political advisor and patron of the arts

Octavia, Caesar Augustus's sister, once wife of Mark Antony

Marcellus, Octavia's son by her first husband who died before she married Antony

Marcella, Marcellus's sister

Antonia, Octavia's daughter by Mark Antony

Jullus Antony, Mark Antony's son by an earlier wife, raised by Octavia

Juba, prince of Numidia

Vipsania, Agrippa's daughter

Phoebe, Julia's maid

Sempronius Gracchus, senator of democratic views

Mark Antony and Cleopatra, Caesar Augustus's great rivals for empire, now defeated and dead

Part I

Julia

My father, Caesar Augustus, celebrated his victory over Mark Antony and Cleopatra when I was nine years old. By defeating them in a great sea battle, he had become ruler of the Roman Empire. I watched the triumphal procession from a stand built for the occasion on the Sacred Way in Rome. My stepmother, Livia, sat beside me, wearing her red hair in a severe, old-fashioned style, a stola of plain yellow wool draping and obscuring her body. She did nothing that day to emphasize her beauty but exuded dignity and propriety.

She had told me I must be careful how I behaved, for many eyes would be on me. And indeed, the people who packed the other side of the roadway gawked at my stepmother and me. So I sat up tall in my cushioned chair and tried to look dignified.

My aunt Octavia also had a seat on the stand. Her mouth turned down at the corners, and she had an empty look in her eyes. I wondered if this was because Mark Antony had once been her husband.

The air smelled of roast meat and spices. A great outdoor feast awaited us, not far from where we sat. Some people in the crowd drank from wineskins, and many joked and laughed. It was a holiday, and even slaves had been released from their work.

Trumpeters led the procession. They did not play the martial tune I expected, but a cheerful air. Just behind them came hundreds of men in purple-edged senatorial togas. My tutor had told me who would be marching, and I realized this could only be the whole Senate, here to do my father honor. A row of fat oxen, led by priests, came next. When the procession ended at the Temple of Jupiter Capitoline, they would be sacrificed to the god.

My heart hammered because I thought I would soon see my father riding his triumphator's chariot. But I was wrong. I had forgotten that war prisoners came next.

The street filled up with Egyptian soldiers, row after row of them, chained together. They had on identical gray tunics, and their faces all looked the same to me—grim and dark. I understood why they were so somber. Prisoners were put to death at every triumph, strangled in the dungeons under the temple. I had not been allowed yet to attend the gladiatorial games, so this was the first time I ever looked upon men about to die. A few of them stumbled because of their chains, but for the most part, their strides did not falter, which made them admirable in my eyes. I hoped my father would spare some of them, as was his right. I looked up at my stepmother to ask if she thought he would. But the moment I opened my mouth, she shook her head, indicating I was to remain silent.

My tutor had prepared me so well that none of what had transpired so far truly surprised me. But what came next—no one had prepared me for that. A gilded cart appeared, pulled by a single black horse. The sides were cut out so you could see the occupants, a girl and boy about my age and another boy a few years younger.

They all had curly dark hair and pale faces, and they were bound in chains, their wrists manacled, the chains draped across their small bodies. But the chains were not iron like those of the captive soldiers. They were made of gold.

People on the roadside roared their approval at the sight of the chained children. My eyes went to the little girl because I was a little girl too. She had begun to shake like a willow in the wind. I knew that the spectators' shouts filled her with terror.

"Who are they?" I asked my stepmother. I could not hold back the question.

"The children of Antony and Cleopatra."

As soon as she uttered those words, she touched her lips, a sign to me to be quiet. So I did not ask the other questions already formed in my mind: *What will happen to the little girl? Are they going to kill her?*

The cart proceeded down the road, and next came the sight I had been waiting for, my father in his chariot. The crowd of spectators gave one great shout, like a thunderclap. Father rode in a chariot pulled by four white horses. Red dye stained his face—this was tradition. He wore a long robe, purple like a king might wear. A laurel wreath adorned his golden hair. He was Rome's First Citizen; the offer of a monarch's crown would have filled him with disdain. He looked neither left nor right, but forward, always forward—toward the temple of the god. To me he might have been a god himself. I did not shout like the people in the crowd. I just gazed at him in adoration.

Two boys rode on the trace horses of his chariot—my father's nephew Marcellus and Livia's son Tiberius. They were fourteen and twelve years old, respectively, and with all my soul, I envied them. It seemed so unfair that I must sit and watch them ride by in glory and could not ride one of my father's chariot horses too. I never wished I had been born a boy more than I did at that moment.

It was only later, as I watched the soldiers of Father's army marching past, singing a song of victory, that I remembered the children in the gilded cart. The thought came back to me: *Will they kill the little girl?* I almost whispered the question to my stepmother, but I was afraid she would say yes, and that answer would have been unbearable.

For months, long after I learned the fates of the three children, the image of a small girl in chains recurred again and again in my dreams. In these nightmares I somehow became the girl. I felt what she had felt; I quaked in fear. I was not the daughter of Rome's First Citizen but a helpless captive, bound with chains of gold.

My childhood could be split into two parts—the times lit by the sun of Father's presence and the months and years of missing him. I thought of him as my only true parent and, as a small child, even pretended to myself that I had been born like the goddess Athena, who sprang fully formed from Jupiter's forehead.

Athena and I—we were motherless beings. Of course my mother, Scribonia, was alive, and I even saw her from time to time. My stepmother, Livia, had married my father soon after my birth, and she oversaw my upbringing. But I never thought of her as my mother.

I can't say for sure when the path of my life was set. But the year I was fourteen looms large in my memory. Father was away then, fighting a war, and because he was gone, the world around me looked colorless. That autumn the war in Spain filled my thoughts. As powerful and invulnerable as Father always seemed to me, I still feared he would meet injury or death on a battlefield. I wanted the war finished, and him home. And my wedding day was approaching. I hoped against hope he would be there to give me away.

One morning, as I sat at my books, I heard the household steward in the next room talking to a messenger. The word *Spain* was mentioned. "Oh, I must see what it is," I said to my tutor and, without even waiting for his permission, went rushing into the steward's office. An official-looking leather case lay on his writing table. It went without saying that it was for my stepmother, and only she would open it. "Where is she? Where is Lady Livia?" I demanded of the steward.

"Why, she went out—I don't know where—"

I whirled and raced into the atrium. I had to speak to the messenger before he left. I caught him in the entranceway—a legionary in full military regalia, a white plume on his helmet.

"Soldier, wait! Please—do you have news from Spain?"

He was young and olive-skinned. "I just delivered a letter from there," he said, almost warily.

"But my stepmother isn't here to open the letter. If you would only tell me what is happening in Spain. My father . . . is all well with him?"

The soldier was silent. Lines of exhaustion were etched in his face, and I sensed how tired he was. *He must have rushed all the way here from Spain,* I thought. *Carrying what news?*

Fear clutched at me. "There hasn't been a disaster, has there? No terrible defeat? My father—"

"Are you the First Citizen's daughter?"

"Yes," I said, and watched the soldier's face change as he took in the fact that he was talking to the child of the ruler of Rome.

"My lady, please understand, we messengers are supposed to keep silent no matter who we speak to, just deliver the letters and dispatches, not talk about what's in them. Those are strict orders."

A part of me could have wept. I so wanted news of the war. But I was the daughter of an imperator. I nodded.

"Orders are orders," the soldier said.

I nodded again. "I'll wait for my stepmother, then. I just wish she were home."

The soldier let out a weary sigh. He looked about to drop. I imagined him bravely fighting the enemy, then riding days and days to bring us news.

I said, "Please sit down and rest here for a while before you go. I'll have food and drink brought to you."

"I can't do that. I have dispatches to the Senate to deliver. Thanks for the kind thought just the same." For a moment, the soldier seemed to be studying me. Then he said, his voice low, "You spoke of disaster? There's no disaster. The barbarians who set their filthy paws on our territory are in full flight like the pieces of—the miserable cowards they are, and we've won new ground for Rome. When we met them in battle, it was like the gods themselves fought on our side. Oh, my lady, it was like . . ." He paused for a moment, then added, "But don't let on that I told you, or I'm liable to be flogged."

"I won't," I promised, my heart leaping with joy. A victory. Father was alive and safe, and soon he would be home for my wedding. "Thank you—thank you so much for telling me."

The soldier thumped his clenched fist on his chest, and he was out the door. I went back to my tutor, Krito, who gave me a reproachful look for deserting him—and also twenty more lines of arcane Greek philosophy to translate.

Later, in the afternoon, my stepmother arrived home, and soon after that she summoned me into her study. To be sent for in this way by Livia was quite usual. She was always busy with Father's business, Rome's business, and she had little time to converse casually. Every so often she would call me to her study at an opportune moment so we could talk and she could be sure that all was well with me. But I knew today she wished to share the news she had received from Spain.

She rose when I came into the room. I smelled her faint perfume and felt her soft cheek brush against mine as she embraced me.

Documents on shelves or sorted into wooden cubbyholes threatened to overflow the study. Looking at it all, I had a sense of just how busy my stepmother was. The study was functional, much like a man's.

I noticed a tension in her shoulders as, unsmiling, she invited me to seat myself on the one couch, then sat down beside me. It puzzled me, in light of what the soldier had said, that she did not look happier. "Your father has written from Spain," she said.

"Yes? Is the war over?"

"For the most part, yes, and your father has won a great victory. But the situation is not completely resolved. And he has a slight indisposition."

I stared at her. "He's ill?"

"It's a slight illness, he says." From Livia's level voice, it was impossible to know if she was worried about Father.

"But what is wrong with him?"

"He didn't elaborate."

"If he is ill, we should go to him."

She shook her head impatiently. "He does not wish us to do that. Now, listen to me—"

"What if he is dangerously ill?"

"He will recover," she said flatly. "Your father always recovers." She was looking into my eyes, her face taut. "He always recovers. You understand?" She took a breath. "His health has never been robust, you know that. He falls ill from time to time. But then he gets better. It has been that way since he was a boy. It is worrisome, but we all live with it."

For a moment, I had imagined I saw something beyond her cool and flawless surface, that she fully shared my concern for Father. But now that moment had passed.

She said in a controlled voice, "Your father has written that he wishes us to go ahead with your wedding next month as we planned."

For four years, I had been betrothed to my first cousin Marcellus. "Why can't we wait a little longer—wait until Father is home? I don't want to marry until Father is here to give me away."

Livia shook her head. "I'm sorry. No."

"But—"

"No, Julia."

Tears sprang to my eyes. I could not help it. A feeling of being abandoned engulfed me like an ocean tide. To not be given in marriage by my father would mean being truly alone on that day, no matter who else was there. "I want Father here on my wedding day! Is that so much to ask?"

Without a word, she handed me a piece of papyrus. Unrolling it, I saw Father's handwriting.

My precious Julia,

I am so sorry that it will not be possible for me to be present at your wedding. What Rome asks of me is to remain at my post here until my work is finished. What it asks of you is to nobly bear the sacrifice of your father's absence and make me proud by your good comportment. I do not wish to delay you on this next step in your life's journey, especially when I cannot say at this moment how long you would have to wait for me. I will be there with you in spirit when Agrippa gives you in marriage in my stead. And be sure I will offer prayers to the gods on that day for your future happiness, which, my sweet child, I desire far more than my own.

Below the writing was his seal, the sign of the sphinx, pressed into a dab of wax.

Reading this letter, I felt just for a moment as if Father held me in his arms.

I rolled up the papyrus. I would keep it as I kept all his letters to me. There was a tightness in my throat. "Then Agrippa will give me away?"

"That is your father's wish."

"It's hard to talk to Agrippa." He had been my father's close friend since boyhood, and I had been taught to look upon him almost as an uncle. But he was a quiet man who treated me with formal courtesy.

"He is Rome's leading general. If anyone but he stood in your father's place, he would feel insulted. We can't afford to slight him."

I tossed my head. "Do you think he'll revolt against Father if someone else presides at my wedding?"

I intended these words as nothing more than a jest. But Livia gave me a long, serious look. "I think it is wrong to slight a man we rely on," she said, "and must depend on especially in your father's absence."

A little jolt of fear went through me. "Father will recover from his illness soon, won't he?" As soon as these words were out, I knew how silly and childish they were. How could Livia know how sick Father was at this moment in far-off Spain? He might have died since dispatching the messenger who had brought my letter. Livia could not predict the course of his illness any more than I could.

But she looked at me with an expression of grave certainty. "Yes, he will recover soon. I am sure of it. Your father has much he wishes to do. He won't let illness hold him back for long."

We were silent for a few moments. "Well, may I at least have my mother at my wedding? Is she to be invited?" I suppose I spoke less politely than I intended. I was still upset that Father would not be home.

There was no flicker of emotion in Livia's face, no sign that she had heard anything but the most courteously framed request. "Yes, of course, Julia," she said. "Of course we will invite your mother to the wedding."

Then she made a small dismissing motion with her hand. She had had enough of me.

I flushed and rose. *I am Caesar Augustus's daughter,* I wanted to tell her. *His only child. I know who you are. Do not forget who I am.*

I did not have the nerve to say this. I just walked out of the room.

>>>>>>>

On the day I was born, my father divorced my mother. Some suspected this was because he was angry that his first child was a girl, but that was not it. Passion for another woman gripped him. Livia was six months pregnant by her husband at that time, but it did not matter. He, acting out of fear and political prudence, speedily divorced her. Father married her immediately. He was twenty-four; Livia was nineteen. They married for love.

I was reared in my father's household, as is usual. But though he had no fondness for my mother, Father did not bar her from visiting me. She came quite often, I understand, when I was a baby. Then the visits tapered off. I always imagined that once she had determined that I was well cared for and thriving—that Livia did not mean to smother me in my cradle—she lost most of her interest in me.

My aunt Octavia lived in a house adjacent to ours that Father had bestowed on her, and I spent much more time with her than with my mother. She would look at me sometimes with an appraising frown. Marcellus, my betrothed, was her only son, the child of the husband who had died before she married Mark Antony.

Throughout my childhood, I was never free to go into the street on my own. Attendants accompanied me everywhere. I was strictly forbidden to talk with strangers. There was a sense that Father—despite his power—still had hidden enemies in Rome, that these enemies might try to harm me.

The only time Father was truly furious at me during my childhood was when at the age of ten, I evaded my attendants and went outside alone. I did not get far before I was caught, but Father had to be told. He did not strike me. He did not even raise his voice. He just said I had done a wrong and dangerous thing, and added in an emphatic tone that it must never be repeated. But the look on his face was so terrible that I trembled. For an instant, I thought he might murder me.

Though I wanted to, I never sneaked out again.

In truth, my childhood world consisted of two adjoining households—one presided over by Livia, one by my aunt. It was such a constrained world.

Is it a wonder that deep inside myself, I longed to be free?

>>>>>>>

I emerged from Livia's study into the atrium of our house. Ostentatious plainness was the motif of this receiving hall where Father welcomed important visitors when he was home. The couches looked well worn, the cushions flattened by years of use.

The frescoes on the walls—painted by mediocre artists—showed everyday Roman street scenes. On one panel, a woman sat under an arch, a baby in her arms; in another, children played with a hoop. A bust of Julius Caesar—Father's great-uncle who had adopted him—had been set on a marble pedestal and was the only good piece of art in evidence. Our house was no bigger than that of a typical senator, and no more luxurious. This was all calculated for political effect. I much preferred it when we stayed at our private villa at Prima Porta, where we could relax in opulent style.

I knew why we presented a modest face in public. Envy brought with it hatred; envy had gotten Father's great-uncle killed. I understood this, but I can't say the danger ever felt real to me. Father seemed to exist in a golden circle of adulation and glory. Two years ago, the Senate had given him the title Augustus, the revered one. No one had challenged him. I did not think anyone ever would.

To my surprise I found Cleopatra Selene—Selene as we called her—waiting in the atrium. Despite her natural grace, she looked at this moment out of place and ill at ease.

I had been told to treat Selene as my cousin, though she was not my real kin. I had been ordered to be kind to her, and this I found easy enough to do. Most people turn away from a young bird that has fallen from a nest. Others like to throw stones at it. I have always felt an odd tenderness for such pitiful, lost creatures. I could never forget the first time I had seen Selene, at my father's triumph. She was Antony and Cleopatra's daughter—the little girl bound in chains.

No one looking at Selene now would have found her pitiful. She was clothed as richly as I, in a tunica of fine linen that fell to her ankles. A large gold bulla hung from her neck. She wore ruby earrings and sandals trimmed with gold. She was neither a captive nor a slave but, by decree, a free Roman citizen. My father had given her to Aunt Octavia to raise as her own daughter.

She stood in the atrium now, grim-faced. "Are you waiting for someone?" I asked her.

"Lady Livia has sent for me." She tried to speak nonchalantly, but I heard fear in her voice.

"Oh? Well, don't worry. She won't eat you."

Selene said nothing. Did she know why Livia wanted her? If so, she did not tell me.

A silence hung between us.

"My father will not be home for my wedding," I finally said. "He won't be here to give me away." I had some silly notion that speaking of my unhappiness might distract her from her own misery.

"What a pity. I am sorry to hear that." Her voice had become cool and remote.

It struck me that when she married, her father would not attend the wedding—because my father had killed him. Killed him not with his own hands, but by defeating him in battle, making it necessary for him to take his own life.

She knew what I was thinking; I was sure she did. A little smile flickered across her face, so quickly I almost did not see it.

I do not know what that smile meant, but I hoped it was a sign of friendly feeling and understanding of my discomfort.

After a moment, she said, "I wonder if I will ever marry."

"I'm sure my father and Aunt Octavia will arrange a fine marriage for you."

She gave me a look that was not precisely mocking, but not kind either. Plainly she did not assume the benevolent intent of the adults who had her in their power. But she had heard the ring of sincerity in my voice and saw that I truly assumed she would be handed a bright future. I think she believed I was a fool.

>>>>>>>

I walked out to the garden. It was only a small patch of flowered greenery, as most city gardens were, separated from the outside world by high walls. I liked to come out here sometimes to look at the sky. Today it was a deep azure and contained no clouds. *In a little over a month, I will be a married woman.*

Everything would change with my marriage; I would be accounted an adult. Yet I felt strangely little excitement. I clutched Father's letter in my hand. My wedding day would be shadowed by his absence.

I thought of Marcellus, my betrothed, of his slender build, his boyish face. I neither feared nor adored him. He was nineteen years old and always seemed to be rushing off somewhere when I met him. I could remember only a single time he had showed any special interest in me. Three years ago when I was visiting at my aunt's villa outside Rome, I had gotten a splinter in my palm. Marcellus had fetched a needle and, trying to hurt me as little as possible, had bit by bit worked the splinter out of my flesh. I noticed how intent he was, how serious and competent. I also noticed his hands. He had large, beautifully shaped hands.

My cousin Marcellus had always been part of my life, and I felt a certain fondness for him. I supposed we would be happy.

Livia

There was a time, after the Battle of Actium, when I let myself hope that we were safe. My husband had defeated Antony and Cleopatra, his greatest foes, and then he returned to me. He forgave me for what he considered my lack of faith in his cause—the fact that I had tried to hold him back from waging civil war. I forgave him for his marital infidelities, and also for the Roman blood he had copiously spilt—for I hated the thought of my countrymen killing each other. We discussed frankly my failure to bear him an heir and accepted that I probably never would—our shared misfortune. My husband loved me; he wanted me for his wife even if I never gave him a child. And I loved him, despite the disappointments the years had brought.

I imagined for a brief moment that we—our family—had reached a secure harbor, that his Julia and my own boys would live easier lives than my husband and I had, and that the blood price for power had been paid. How I wanted to believe all this were true.

One autumn day, I sat in my study, my nails biting into my palms, listening as my stepdaughter pleaded for her marriage to be delayed until her father was home to give her away. A part of me understood—what girl does not want her father at her side on that day of all days, her marriage day? But I found it hard to be patient with Julia at that moment.

My husband—Caesar Augustus, Tavius to those who knew and loved him best—was in Spain, defending the empire's boundaries against savage invaders. The war was all but won, yet there remained delicate diplomacy to be conducted to bring about true peace. Tavius was living, I knew, in conditions of great hardship. And he was sick. He always minimized his illnesses. That he mentioned it at all in his letter to me meant that this illness was serious.

I could read his state of mind between the lines of his letter. He wished his daughter married in his absence because he was thinking of her security; he wanted her safely wed to the man of his choice. And though Tavius was not yet forty, he was contemplating his own mortality. If he died—I could hardly bear to think of the world without him, but I must—if he died, aspirants to imperial rule would be seeking to marry Julia to give themselves legitimacy. Tavius wanted to be succeeded by his only nephew—a natural choice, this boy who shared his bloodline. But it was plain to me that whatever he hoped, Marcellus could never hold the empire together. He was too inexperienced, too young. Tavius had been a like age when he began his climb to imperial rule, but the climb had taken twelve years. And he was Tavius.

If he died now, the empire would be plunged into renewed civil war. The gods alone knew what would happen then to Julia or any of us.

I did not tell Julia about this, for I knew it would terrify her, and I could not afford to be swept away by emotion, hers or mine.

Of course I wished to rush to Tavius's side. But my role now was to hold Italy for him. Tavius wanted his daughter and Marcellus immediately wed, and I would see to that. I would bolster our security in every other way I could. And I would wait and pray for my husband to come home.

After Julia left my study, I sat at my writing table for a few moments with my eyes shut. I was thirty-three years old, and at that moment I felt much older.

Now, after my talk with my stepdaughter, I had to have a conversation with another woman-child, a conversation that might prove difficult. That did not lift my spirits. But after a moment, I told the slave who stood outside my study door to show in Cleopatra Selene.

I received her seated, gestured for her to sit on the couch. I did not pretend an affection I did not feel. Not that I had any personal dislike for this girl; up to this point I had had little to do with her.

"Good afternoon, Selene," I said.

She averted her eyes. "Good afternoon, Lady Livia."

"Aunt Livia," I corrected her. "You should call me Aunt, as you do Octavia."

"Aunt."

Maybe men who write histories will give my husband credit for this someday; maybe the gods will. When his worst enemies' young children fell into his hands, he let them live. He did not kill them, as any Eastern potentate—Cleopatra included—would have done. He did not cage or enslave them. He accepted them into his own family, an extraordinary act of mercy.

His mercy was not indiscriminate. Antony and Cleopatra each had a son old enough to bear arms. These two young men—Selene's half brothers—Tavius executed. The threat they posed was obvious. The question that seared Tavius's soul was what to do with the three children born of Antony and Cleopatra's union. Their very existence was in a sense an insult, a reminder that Antony had deserted Tavius's sister, Octavia, for their mother. They also represented a danger, because of who their parents were. The allure of that couple persisted even after they lay in their shared tomb, and the disaffected within the empire might rally around their children.

Tavius told me he had spared the youngsters for my sake—for I had long counseled clemency as a general policy. So perhaps I was in some sense responsible for Selene's continued existence.

The two little boys—frail transplanted saplings—had died within a couple of years of their arrival in Rome. There was no foul play; young children often die in ordinary circumstances, and it is possible the great changes in their lives affected their health. Selene, however, had survived. And she alone carried on the line of Antony and Cleopatra.

I had seen statues of her mother, and the resemblance was strong—the aquiline nose, the full lips. I had known her father, and he had given me cause to hate him. She was Antony's daughter too. Her dark hair was unruly like his. She also had his jutting chin, not a lovely feature on a young woman. I compared Selene in my mind to Julia, who, a short while before, had been sitting on that same couch—Julia with her fair hair and fine features. Set these two girls side by side and Julia would draw all eyes, not Cleopatra's daughter. But Cleopatra had not been beautiful by Roman standards, and that had not detracted from her appeal. I wondered if this child would develop her mother's magnetism.

"Has Octavia told you that you are to come to live in my household, Selene?" I asked.

"Yes." Her voice was empty of emotion.

"Do you know why?"

She shook her head.

"I wish to know you better. It will help me to correctly advise my husband about your future."

"I am most honored that you wish to . . . know me." Her face had tensed, but she spoke in a level voice.

How careful she was being.

One would have to be made of stone not to pity this young girl's losses, and I was not made of stone. I thought of what had befallen her in her brief life. Both parents and four brothers dead. She had been brought to live with the family of the man who had driven her parents to suicide and killed two of her brothers. She lived by that man's sufferance.

"You will have a new tutor," I said. *One who will watch you.*

"I hope I will please him . . . and you."

I imagined Selene running off and marrying some ambitious fool—the two of them vying for supreme power the way her parents had. I envisioned the result—the return of the terror and bloody chaos I had lived through as a girl. "You are to behave with discretion, so as to reflect credit on our house. You are to defer to my judgment as a daughter would," I said. "I expect obedience from you. If I do not receive it, I will be very angry. Is that clear?"

"Yes, I understand."

Truly? Do you understand that your life hangs by a thread, and I will cut it if I have to?

"When I was sixteen, my father's side was defeated in war," I said. "Do you know by whom?"

"By Augustus."

"And by your father, Mark Antony," I said.

Selene's chin rose a little at the mention of her father's name.

"My father fought for the Republic," I continued. "After the Battle of Philippi, he took his own life. My mother did the same. As I said, I was sixteen."

Selene stared at me, as if my speaking of this amazed her. I too was surprised by my words.

I leaned toward her, met and held her eyes with mine. "The world in which we live is a very dangerous place. You realize this?"

"Yes."

"I mean the world as it exists for people like us. Those who move within the circles that we do, close to great power. It is as if we spend our whole lives in a gladiatorial arena, visible to all and always under threat. Few people around us can be trusted. Very few."

"I know," Selene said. And perhaps she did know. Her mother had executed her own sister, who seemed to pose a danger. Surely the girl had drawn some conclusions from this fact. One could only hope she had drawn the right ones.

"Octavia made no fuss about giving you to me," I confided. "That is because she does not like you."

Her eyes widened. "She has always been most kind to me."

"Of course. She is kind to everyone. My sister-in-law is the epitome of virtue. But even she has her limits. Your brothers reminded her of your father, and she became fond of them. You, however, remind her of your mother, who stole her husband from her. It is not your fault, but if you believe she could fight with her whole heart to protect you, you are wrong. She was glad when I asked for you. Truly."

Selene nodded bleakly. I don't think what I was saying surprised her, once she had a moment to think about it.

"You haven't a real friend in the world with the slightest degree of influence. Except for one."

"One?" Selene looked puzzled. Poor child, she probably did not believe she had any friend.

"One friend, who fortunately wields even more influence in Rome than Octavia does."

"Who is that friend?"

"Can't you guess?"

She shook her head, an anxious look on her face. She was, after all, only fourteen.

"If you are intelligent," I said, "if you are loyal—that friend is me."

With that, I sent Cleopatra's daughter off to her new tutor. She gave me a searching look before she went, the look one might give to a lifeline, wondering if it will hold.

The conversation left me drained. I had not told that child a single lie. A gladiatorial arena—that was how I saw my world. I usually did not speak of this, and it cost me something when I did so, as it might cost one to speak frankly of death.

Would I have climbed so high had I known what awaited me?

Of course I would have. To be with Tavius, if for no other reason. I would have faced down lions to be his wife.

I was in an unhappy, uneasy mood, but everything would be bearable once he held me in his arms.

I prayed to Diana, my patron deity, *Oh, goddess, let him come home.*

Cleopatra Selene

My mother . . . all I have left of her are bits of memory, like fragments of dreams. I can recall the scent of spices and musk that clung to her. I remember how she tossed back her head when she gave her throaty laugh. The last time I was in her presence, she wore a linen shift with rents in it, which she surely had torn herself in mourning for my father. The kohl on her eyelids was smeared and her hair disheveled. My two small brothers and I stood staring at her, and she—goddess on earth, pharaoh in a woman's form—knelt on the green marble floor of our nursery. She embraced each of us in turn—first my twin, Alexander Helios, then little Ptolemy, then me. When she held me in her arms, her nails bit into my shoulders and I whimpered. "Live," she hissed in my ear. That was her farewell before she killed herself, by means of a cobra's bite.

She would never wear the chains of captivity. How could she, being who she was? Better to join her ancestors, better to pass into immorality. We—Ptolemy, Alexander Helios, and I—were paraded down the Sacred Way before our enemies. We bore that shame in her place. It was fitting.

>>>>>>>

For us, Rome was a place of pestilence. My brothers and I came down with fever again and again. Octavia tended us, fretted, wept when Ptolemy died, wept again when Alexander Helios passed away. My mourning was silent and deep. My twin had been named for the sun, I for the moon. The sun was swallowed by darkness, but somehow the moon lingered in the night sky.

I obeyed my mother. I lived, dwelling among the enemy. No one received my complete trust. And yet I had one surviving half brother, Jullus, son of my father, Mark Antony. Blood called to blood. We grew to care for each other.

"Father forgot about me," he told me once. "Octavia raised me after they married. When he shed her, he shed me too. He left me behind with the family of his worst enemy. Just a forgetful man."

"Jullus, who was your mother?"

"Another wife our father cast off along the way."

"She died?"

"When I was three or four. Died pining for Father. Or so I've heard."

I was ten when this conversation took place, Jullus almost fourteen. We sat in the garden of Octavia's house, I on a marble bench, he on the ground, hugging his knees. The sun glinted on his dark, curly hair. The air smelled of marigolds.

I dared to whisper a question I would not have uttered in anyone else's presence. "Why hasn't Augustus killed me?"

"For the same reason he has not killed me, sweet Sister. He likes to make a show of benevolence."

"And any day he might decide . . . it is time for the show to end?" I felt ice in the pit of my stomach.

Jullus gave me one of the endearing lopsided grins he used when he wished to reassure me. "Oh, little moon, don't worry. If he kills either of us, it'll be me, not a small, harmless girl like you."

>>>>>>>

At the age of fourteen, I came under the tutelage of Livia, Augustus's wife. When I entered her household, I foretasted death. I saw Lady Livia looking at me warily and always imagined her thinking, *Isn't it time to be rid of this perilous burden?* She said she would be a friend to me, but I did not believe her.

Meanwhile Julia, Livia's stepdaughter, fluttered around like a butterfly, my age but happy, doted on, and safe—above all, safe. Her nuptials would be a grand occasion. I doubted I would ever be allowed to marry and bear my parents' grandchildren. I might have hated Julia if I had energy for that. But all my being was focused on survival.

I obeyed Livia in everything, and I deferred to all the other members of the household. I guarded my words and my expression. People called me Selene, and of course I did not correct them. My full name, Cleopatra Selene, I only whispered to myself at night.

Live, Mother had commanded me.

Sometimes I felt it would be less trouble to die.

Julia

> *Let us live, my Lesbia, and love*
>   *And value all the talk of strict*
>   *Old men at a single penny.*
> *Suns can set and rise again;*
> *For us, once our brief light has set,*
> *There's one unending night for sleeping.*
> *Give me a thousand kisses, then a hundred,*
> *Then another thousand, then a second hundred . . .*

I enjoyed committing these words by Catullus to memory while I awaited my wedding day. I had had to memorize so much poetry I did not care for—vast sections of the *Iliad* and many hymns to patriotism, full of martial fervor. It was a relief to memorize lines that spoke to my soul.

Krito, my tutor, told me often that I was fortunate to have a renowned scholar like him teaching me, and indeed he had a formidable reputation. Father wished me to receive an excellent literary education. That meant acquiring a good command of Greek and reading the works of literature and philosophy that Krito considered fit for the eyes of a girl. A diligent student, I generally did what Krito told me to do. But when he gave me the *Oresteia* to read in the month before my marriage, I balked. These plays concerned Orestes, a dutiful son who very properly took vengeance on his father's killer, who happened to be the boy's own mother. I was not in the mood for anything that grim.

I reached up and took another book from a high shelf in the library that served as my schoolroom. It was one I had peeked at when no one was looking. "Please, Krito, can't I read this instead?"

Krito's round face went pink under his bald pate. "Catullus is hardly proper reading for a young girl."

"But I will soon be a married woman! And you know that when I wed, my studies will be over. Don't you want our time together to end on a happy note? Please, Krito, can't you indulge me this once?"

He had begun, lately, to treat me less as a child. My future friendship would be valuable to him. And so he surrendered, and instead of reading a Greek tale of bloody vengeance, I read Roman poems about passion. Again and again Catullus begged for love and for an impossible, nearly infinite amount of kisses as love's expression.

"Is Catullus still alive?" I asked Krito.

"He died about twenty-five years ago."

"Was he old?"

"Just thirty, I believe."

"Who was Lesbia?"

"What does it matter?"

"Did she ever become his wife?"

Krito frowned and said, "No, she was his mistress, someone else's wife. And you see why this is not the sort of book a young girl of good family should be reading."

"But I like reading it," I said. "And after all, my father keeps it in his library."

"Your father has this volume here because Catullus has few equals as a poet. But Catullus spent his youth in thrall to an immoral woman—exactly the wrong person for him to have fallen in love with. If you must read this book, think of it as a negative example. It is a treatise on how not to conduct a reasonable life."

I have wondered who I might have become if Krito had snatched the volume of Catullus's poetry out of my hands. But he did not, and at an impressionable age, I was plunged into the poet's world of sensuality and longing. Clearly, Catullus was not Lesbia's only lover, not even the favored one. But in poem after poem, he burned for her.

At night I lay awake for hours in my small bedchamber, listening to the snoring of a maid who slept on a pallet in the anteroom in case I should need her. The room was perfectly dark except sometimes for a little bit of moonlight filtering through the half-closed shutters. I thought about my approaching marriage and asked myself if Marcellus and I might come to feel true passion. And I wondered how that would be—how it might feel to burn.

>>>>>>>

Livia invited my mother to my wedding, just as she had promised. It had been decided that both my stepmother and my mother would help me dress for the ceremony, which was usually a mother's role. So on the morning of my wedding day, Mother fussed with my hair while Livia saw to it that my white muslin dress hung properly and tied the traditional wool band—the knot of Hercules—around my waist.

There were deep lines in Mother's face that her thick chalk-paste makeup could not hide. She was much my father's senior; he had married her because it seemed politically convenient at the time. Livia was easily young enough to be her daughter.

When I was properly decked out as a bride, Livia looked at me with approval. Then something unfathomable happened. My mother began to weep. I could see she truly could not help it. Her shoulders shook with suppressed sobs, and tears rolled down her cheeks. "Oh, forgive me, forgive me," she said.

Livia looked stricken. "I see you are shedding tears of joy, Scribonia. I can well understand how happy you must be to have such a beautiful daughter, about to be wed."

At once, I suspected she was saying this not just to soothe my mother, but to avert an ill omen. I felt a stab of fear.

"Oh, yes, they are tears of joy!" my mother hastily agreed. "How beautiful you look, Julia."

But there was no true joy in her voice or her expression, only grief and regret. I wondered at first why she should weep in this way, and then I did not wonder. She had played no part in my rearing, and we were half strangers. I realized she felt loss, seeing me grown up, attired as a bride, and I wished I knew what to say to comfort her.

A maid fetched her a handkerchief. She dried her eyes, forcing a smile.

My mother's sorrowful tears. My father's absence. It was not how I had pictured my wedding day.

I donned a sheer red veil that completely covered my face and tinted the whole world red when I looked through it. Accompanied by Livia and my mother, I went out to the atrium, which was crowded with guests. Marcus Agrippa came and stood beside me. "*Feliciter*, my dear," he said to me, kindly enough, looking down from his towering height.

"Thank you," I said. "Thank you for taking my father's place today. You do me great honor."

"The honor is mine."

I had known Agrippa all my life, but we had little to say to each other at any time, and on my wedding day it was no different. I remembered that his wife had died in childbirth only a few months before, and imagined that a wedding brought back poignant memories. He looked as if giving me away was the last thing he wanted to be doing.

I longed for Father. He would have known just what to say to me, on this day of all days. He would have let me see his pride in me, and then he would have joked and gotten me giggling. Whenever I thought of him, my feeling of being abandoned revived. And I worried—had he recovered from his illness in far-off Spain? He was never out of my thoughts.

My cousin Marcellus came forward. He had the family look— that is, he was fair and blue-eyed, slim, and not particularly tall. His hair was darker than mine and my father's—the color like burnished bronze. He had high cheekbones, a long, straight nose, and a wide mouth. His lips were compressed now, and he looked determined to get everything right.

Priests offered the usual sacrifices. The examination of the entrails was followed by a proclamation that the signs were good. Agrippa took my hand and placed it in my cousin's. "Where thou art Gaius, I am Gaia," I said. Marcellus gave me a barely perceptible nod. All the guests shouted, *"Feliciter!"*

At the wedding feast, my bridegroom hardly looked at me as I perched on his dining couch. He said the correct things to the right people who came forward to congratulate us. I said little, demure silence being required of a new bride. Quietly, I took in the swirl of people, listened to the laugher and the conversation. The dining room and the atrium were packed, men and women squeezing in to attend the wedding of the First Citizen's daughter.

I ate roasted peacock, sipped honeyed wine. People paid me compliments. I smiled and thanked them, trying to act like a gracious lady. Meanwhile I anticipated my wedding night.

A virgin bride is supposed to be slightly fearful. But I wasn't. I imagined some great secret was about to be revealed to me that all adult women know. I was hoping that intimacy with my new husband would be, if not ecstatic, at least interesting.

Aunt Octavia, wearing a perfectly draped yellow stola and fine emerald earrings, approached and for a moment simply gazed at her son with joy and pride. Then she said to me lightly, "You must get Marcellus to work less hard than he does. Perhaps a wife will have more success with that than a mother."

Marcellus made a face. "Please, Mother . . ."

"He works and works," she said. "Studies rhetoric and law, attends every meeting of the Senate and of the city aediles. The program your father has laid out for him is rigorous. Too rigorous, I think."

We did not notice that Agrippa was standing by, listening. But he was, and suddenly asked, "Is there any military training mixed with all this rigor? Anything about how to fight?"

Marcellus said stiffly, "I practice with arms daily at Mars Field."

"Practice daily?" Agrippa looked as if he might laugh. "Well, that's impressive."

Marcellus's face reddened. "I wish to study strategy too."

"By all means, study strategy." With that, Agrippa walked away.

To my knowledge, it was completely unlike Agrippa to be rude.

My aunt made an anxious little gesture, patting Marcellus on the shoulder. Marcellus gave her a half smile and shrugged.

Later, Jullus Antony came forward to congratulate Marcellus and me. He brought in his wake Selene, holding her hand, as if she were a shy flower he must protect.

Jullus was notably tall and robust-looking, the tallest man in the room except for Agrippa. He had been put into my aunt Octavia's care before I was born, when he himself was very small. A kind stepmother, she had embraced the motherless boy, Antony's son by a dead wife. Jullus had stayed in her charge during what was supposed to be a temporary separation from Antony. That separation never ended. Even after my father and Antony went to war, Aunt Octavia had kept the boy and treated him as if he were her own child.

He and Marcellus had grown up together and were about the same age. "*Feliciter*, my friend, you are a fortunate man," Jullus said. He looked at me then. Of course we had spoken to each other many times before—but only as young people do in passing, when they are part of the background of each other's lives. This moment felt different. Jullus stared at me and held my eyes for several heartbeats. "Yes, Marcellus is very fortunate." I could not identify the emotion in his voice, but it seemed out of place.

I did not know how to answer. Selene spoke up quickly. "Julia, you are the most beautiful bride. May the gods smile on your marriage!" I caught the glance she gave Jullus, the hint of reproof.

He had let go of her hand, but now he took it again. They walked away then, to make room for other guests who wished to congratulate Marcellus and me.

>>>>>>>

My new husband and I had been given a suite of rooms in Aunt Octavia's house. When the last sounds of guests' revelry faded, I found myself alone in a flower-decked bedchamber that had been sprinkled with a pungent perfume. A scarlet coverlet, trimmed with golden threads, was spread over the bed. The wall mural looked freshly painted—a bucolic scene of pretty children at play. I sat on the bed, fully clothed, not knowing what else to do.

Marcellus entered. He had on just a tunic—he had taken off the toga he had worn for the ceremony and also removed the wreath of flowers from his head.

"This is . . ." He sounded partly amused, partly embarrassed.

He came and sat down beside me, untied the knot in the band of wool around my waist, did it quickly and expertly as a bridegroom should. Before this, we had shared the sacred cake, stood in the light of the wedding torch, been showered with nuts thrown by a crowd of children. Only one act remained to make our marriage complete.

"At least they didn't marry me to Marcella," Marcellus said half to himself. It was a joke. Marcella was his sister.

"Do you think I'm ugly?"

"No, you've grown up prettier than I expected."

He was almost five years my elder, and for much of our lives, we had lived in what could almost be called one vast household. He had glimpsed me as a baby learning to walk and as a little girl playing with cloth poppets. Just two years ago, I had been a gawky twelve-year-old with no more breasts than a boy. He no doubt remembered all that.

"Well, this has to be done," he said. To be kind, he added, "I'll be gentle."

He was gentle. There was only a moment's twinge of pain. And then there was something else, deep, exquisite sensation. And the weight of his body on mine, the warmth, the closeness. I liked it. It was as if I always had wanted this—a man's body—without knowing it. My hands stroked his shoulders, his back. I was surprised at how smooth his skin felt.

Too soon it was over. He pulled away.

I snuggled up against him, pressed my cheek against his shoulder, but he just lay there. I wanted him to put his arms around me, but he didn't, and I had no idea of how to entice him to do this. It didn't seem possible to ask him to hold me. Feeling bereft, I contemplated what had happened. I was no longer a virgin, but no man had ever kissed me with passion. Marcellus had not kissed me at all.

Catullus's words came back to me. *Give me a thousand kisses . . .* But I did not say them.

Livia

*I*t was awkward to spend time with Scribonia at Julia's wedding. We were civil to each other, as always the case when we met. Then she started weeping over Julia in her bridal finery.

When my first husband divorced me and I married Tavius, I lost custody of my sons. They were only returned to me when their father passed away. During those five years that we lived in different households, I wept many times, missing them.

I knew what Scribonia had suffered because I snatched her husband and daughter from her. I would have preferred not to see her tears.

Scribonia's crying was not the only unpleasant moment that day. At the feast that followed the ceremony, I happened to look across the atrium and see Jullus Antony and Selene standing together, waiting to congratulate Julia and Marcellus. I had never noticed before just how much Jullus resembled his father. He had Mark Antony's strong, regular features and powerful build, while Selene took after her mother. Gazing at the brother and sister, one could easily imagine Mark Antony and Cleopatra standing there.

A chill went through me, and the back of my neck prickled. I pictured two malevolent ghosts, here to curse the festivities and bring misfortunate to the living on the day their enemy's daughter was wed. I truly had a sense of an evil presence. Then that passed, and I felt foolish. I approached the pair with a smile on my lips.

"Are you enjoying the feast, Jullus?"

"We both are." He added in a low voice, "I count it as a boon that you have taken my sister under your wing. I know your goodness and that you wish her well."

I know your goodness. Those words were extravagant, yet he had sounded sincere.

Gazing at the fresh-faced young man, I saw hints of a sensitivity his father had completely lacked. He was not a ghostly apparition and neither was his sister.

I put my arm around Selene's shoulder. I had never touched her before. She gave a slight start, and I felt a small tremor go through her. But then she managed a smile.

The shades of Antony and Cleopatra at the feast—that was a product of my imagination. What troubled me more was the brooding look I saw on Marcus Agrippa's face. When I spoke to him, he was polite as always, but incommunicative. The victories he had won had been vital to Tavius's assumption of power. The army loved and admired him, perhaps more than Tavius himself. In Tavius's absence, he had command of the army in Italy. I tried to enjoy the feast, but worry about Agrippa tugged at me.

Later, I sought out Maecenas. He, his new young man, his wife, Terentilla, and *her* new young man constituted a cheerful foursome and were stretched out on adjacent dining couches.

I despised Terentilla because Tavius was her former lover and she never truly gave up her efforts to get him back. Maecenas, however, I liked very much. He had been Tavius's close friend since childhood days and had also become my friend.

So I did not hesitate to ask Maecenas a question. Sitting on the edge of his couch, I lowered my voice and said, "Why is Agrippa looking so unhappy? No, not unhappy . . . discontented?"

Maecenas's expression became thoughtful. "Is there a difference between unhappiness and discontent?" he asked, lowering his voice too.

"We suffer through unhappiness, but when were are discontented, we try to change things. Tell me Agrippa looks the way he does because he is still mourning Caecilia, and I'll believe you. I'd very much like to believe you. She deserves more than a few months' grief." Caecilia, Agrippa's late wife, had been my dear friend.

"I'm no expert on Agrippa's state of mind," Maecenas said, "but I think this wedding has put his nose out of joint."

"The wedding and all the preferment given to Marcellus?"

"I believe so."

"Agrippa thinks he should have been Julia's bridegroom?" I had never imagined him as a candidate for Julia's hand. "He wants to be Tavius's heir?"

Maecenas sighed. "Wouldn't you, if you were him?"

If there was a way to sweeten Agrippa's mood, I did not know what it was. I prayed, *Divine Diana, let Tavius come home soon.*

≫≫≫≫≫

Early in the new year, I had a talk with my son, Tiberius, on a subject unwelcome to me. "I am a man now, Mother," he said. "I want a military posting. Soon."

He had passed his seventeenth birthday only a few months before. "A year or two more with your tutors, perhaps study at Rhodes—"

"Rhodes!" he cried. "Do you think I want to be a philosopher? I intend to be a soldier!"

"Kindly lower your voice. I don't enjoy being shouted at."

Tiberius had large dark eyes like mine. I sometimes thought that was the only way he took after me. He was tall like his late father, and also had his love for all things military. As I looked at him, I could almost hear my former husband saying gleefully, *He's my boy.*

"The next time Rome fights a war, I'll go, Mother. I'd like an appropriate rank, but I'll go as a common soldier if I must."

"I hope there will not be another war."

His mouth twisted at my absurdity. "There is always another war."

We were standing in my study. As if to add emphasis to his words, at that moment we heard the clamp of military boots in the atrium. A messenger had arrived, carrying a letter from Tavius.

The steward brought in the letter. I calmly thanked and dismissed him. Inside, every fiber of my being seemed to have gone tense. I had not heard from my husband for three months. Was this the good news I hoped for?

I saw Tavius's bold handwriting as I unfurled the papyrus. The first words told me all I truly wished to know: *My Livia, All is well, and I will be home soon.*

After I read the letter, I turned to Tiberius, my heart racing with joy. "Your stepfather is returning to Rome."

"Good," Tiberius said flatly.

I'm so glad you share my happiness, I almost said. But it would be foolish to pick a quarrel when our quarrels were so slow to heal. I loved my son, but we irritated each other.

"Someday I will return from war too," Tiberius said. "And on that day, Mother, I swear to you, you will be proud."

There was a hint of a plaintive little boy in his tone—the small child I had protected during the many dangers our family had weathered. I still would have given my life to protect him. I patted him on the cheek. "I am proud of you now." It was pointless to say I would rather he stayed safe at home. He would be a soldier. His younger brother, Drusus, and my foster son, Marcus, would be soldiers too. We are a warrior race, we Romans. "In a month or so our family will be together. We can talk then about what you want to do."

"About what I *will* do," he said. "Don't try to hold me back, Mother. You can't."

I did not reply. Why seek out pain by anticipating it? Why brood now about future wars? One war was over, won. Tavius had recovered from his illness. My beloved was coming home.

>>>>>>>

Tavius would return to a changed household. I felt the absence of Julia's voice and her laughter. Selene, now living with me, did not begin to fill that void as she moved circumspectly on the edge of my vision, on the edge of my family. Tiberius and Julia had never gotten along—the way they goaded each other had irked me since they were small. But my son's eyes glanced off Selene, indifferent as if she were a slave. Drusus and Marcus were courteous to her, just as they were courteous to the servants. The girl antagonized no one. She kept her head down. It was exactly what I would have done in her position.

I called her into my study one day, waved her to a seat on the couch. "You have heard Augustus is returning to Rome soon."

"Yes, I am so glad. That must give you great happiness." She smiled, but her face had tightened. Of course she feared my husband and wondered what his return boded for her.

"I will be able to tell him your behavior has been exemplary. Your tutor says you work hard."

Selene had brown, almond-shaped eyes, eyes of great depth. Her father had not had eyes like that. I was sure they were an inheritance from her mother. I imagined Cleopatra looking at me through this young girl's eyes, for they were not those of a child. "I am glad I have pleased you, Aunt," Selene said. She always took care to call me Aunt as I had instructed her.

"One small thing that might be better . . . your Latin."

She looked startled. "People say I speak the language quite well."

"You do, for someone not a native of Italy. Your grammar is flawless, and your Greek accent is very slight and actually quite charming. Greek was your first language, was it not?"

"Yes," she said. "It was what we always spoke when . . ." Emotion flickered over her face but was gone in an instant. "I did not realize that was so obvious."

"I will provide you with another tutor who will concern himself only with your spoken Latin. I am sure that in a little time you can speak like a native-born Roman."

"That is what you wish . . . for me to speak like a Roman?"

"I think it would be better that people see you as Roman, and not be reminded of . . . well, your foreign birth." *Better for you if every time you open your mouth, Tavius does not think of Cleopatra, who wished to grind him—and Rome—under her pretty feet.*

"Is it that you think if I speak like a Roman, it would be better for my . . . my future?"

"Yes, for your future, Selene."

Her face lit with relief and gratitude. You don't bother to give a girl elocution lessons if you believe she will soon be executed.

>>>>>>>

I awaited Tavius's return at our villa in Prima Porta, outside Rome. It was here that he returned to me after he defeated Antony and Cleopatra, making himself master of the empire; and it was here, away from prying eyes, that we could be most fully ourselves. I invited no one to come with me—not my children, not Julia. For a day at least, I wanted my husband to myself. Before he once again belonged to all of Rome.

One might expect a blast of trumpet music when an imperator returns, but his homecoming was not like that. He entered the villa at a time when I was not expecting him and found me in my sitting room. Our first moments together resembled the quiet homecoming of any soldier—kisses, embraces, joyful murmurs. But a dagger went through my heart when I saw him. I knew then what this last war had done to him.

He had not yet reached his thirty-ninth birthday. He had been born with a weakness in his left leg, but the limp that had been slight when he was thirty had become more pronounced, and he moved like a much older man. His face was still handsome but also gaunt. He had driven himself all his life far beyond his physical strength. I knew at that instant he could not go on doing it forever.

"You are not going to war again," I said as I held him. "Never again. Send Agrippa. Send Marcellus. Even send my foolish son, he's so wild to wade through carnage. But not you—you must not go. And if you travel again to distant parts of the empire, I will accompany you. I am not asking, Tavius. I am demanding."

"Do I look as bad as that?"

"You look as though you almost died."

"Almost doesn't count."

"You must let me take care of you."

"Do you know that all the time I was gone, not one person dared say 'you must' to me?"

I kissed him. "I love you. To the point of madness, I sometimes think. That is what gives me the right."

Much later, in our bedchamber, he whispered, "You see, I'm in better health than you imagined. Aren't you reassured?"

We lay together under a coverlet of purple silk. I could smell the first buds of spring, flowering in the garden. The windows were only half shuttered. It was still light outside, though twilight was coming on. Tavius's skin looked amber where the sun illuminated it. My fingertip traced the new scar on his upper arm.

"That kind of wound is trivial," he said, "a common thing for any soldier."

I began to weep then—I who never cried anymore, certainly not where anyone could see me. That he had been wounded, that this wound was an ordinary thing, reduced me to tears. I did not try to explain myself. Rome's First Citizen held me and made soothing sounds as one might to a baby as I cried and cried.

Julia

My father came home. At last! He looked thin and tired, but he was still the iron pillar on which my own life had always rested. I hardly took in his frailty as I rushed into his arms. "Father! Father!"

He embraced me, then pushed me away so he could see me better. "Look at you! All grown up."

I wore a married woman's flowing stola, not a girl's tunica. "All grown up, Father," I said.

He had been home for an entire day before Marcellus and I were invited to join him and Livia at Prima Porta. I must have become more of an adult with my marriage, because I understood this, though I did not like it. The delay was Livia's doing, and she acted out of love not spite.

For as long as I could remember, I had known about Father wrenching Livia away from her first husband—doing this after shedding his own wife. But now I understood Father's actions, and also knew why Father refused to divorce Livia even though she did not bear him an heir. I was a new bride, with eyes suddenly opened, and I understood what bound my father and my stepmother. I saw it in their every glance, every small touch.

They were delighted to be with each other after their long separation, so delighted that I think after his first warm greeting, Father had to force himself to attend to my husband and me. Fourteen years into their marriage, he could barely make himself look away from her. At dinner that evening, she sat on his supper couch and ensured that his wine was properly mixed with water and the slaves placed the most perfectly cooked morsels of food before him, and she herself hardly touched either wine or meat. Instead, she ate up my father with her eyes. Gods above, maybe I should have been revolted. But I wasn't. I saw what they had, and I felt like weeping, because Marcellus and I did not have that love, that passion, and we never would; and it was the only thing on earth worth having.

Marcellus had eyes only for Father too. I am not suggesting he was in love with his uncle, now his father-in-law. He merely worshipped him. If Jupiter himself had dropped down from Olympus and joined us for dinner, Marcellus could not have been much more overcome with awe.

"Do you find attending the meetings of the aediles informative?" Father asked him.

"Extremely," Marcellus said. "It's been an education, sir, just as you said it would be."

"I think you should stand for aedile yourself next year."

"Next year? Truly?" He would have a place on the board of magistrates charged with the day-to-day government of the city of Rome.

Father smiled. "You're young for it, I know. But I think with my endorsement, the people of Rome will elect you." The elections of course were a matter of form. Father's candidates always won. "Be warned, it's not an empty honor. It's a lot of work."

"I'm willing to work," Marcellus said. "I've taken instruction in law, as you advised. I won't disappoint you, Uncle."

Father nodded benignly. "I've heard only good things about how you have conducted yourself while I was away. But you must show you're worthy of all I envision for you. I won't sacrifice the welfare of Rome because I love my nephew. I won't leave this empire to a man who can't rule at least as well as I have. Remember that—and prove yourself worthy."

"Sir, I promise you, I will." Marcellus stammered out the words.

Father grinned. "Good!" He looked at me, winked, then went back to eating his dinner.

>>>>>>>

Marcellus and I returned to Rome. I would have preferred to stay at the villa longer, but he was more eager than ever to throw himself into his work and could not wait to get back to the city.

Once back home, melancholy dogged me. I had spent hardly any time alone with my father, and it struck me this was often how it was, how it had been all through my childhood. It seemed I never got as much of him as I wanted.

Hardly anything was required of me. I helped my aunt Octavia in supervising the household servants, but she actually needed little assistance from me. I read poetry to divert myself, but it filled me with longing, for I wished to feel the exalted emotions the poets wrote about.

As days passed, my husband redoubled his effort to prepare himself for a role in government. During daylight hours, I hardly ever heard his voice except coming from another room when he practiced speechmaking with his rhetoric teacher. We coupled regularly;

Marcellus was conscientious in that regard, as in all else. But our lovemaking remained as perfunctory as it had been on our wedding night.

"For you, it's all about giving my father a grandson, isn't it?" I said to him one night after he had taken me in his usual dutiful fashion.

"What do you mean?"

"You want to get me with child as quickly as possible."

"Of course I want a son. Don't you?"

Someday, of course, I might have answered. A child was not a pressing desire for me at this time. I just shrugged.

"It's a problem for your father that he has no sons," Marcellus said. "The only way to preserve his work is to ensure the succession. And he's done such great work, Julia. He saved Rome."

"I know that."

"Well, then you see why it's important . . ."

Why it's important for us to couple.

"To produce an heir for the empire. Yes, of course." My mouth twisted.

My husband turned over in bed so he was facing away from me. "Marcellus—"

"I'm tired. I have a busy day ahead of me tomorrow."

When did he not?

Touch me, I wanted to say. *Touch me once with your whole being. Love me, at least a little. Hold me the way I know my father must hold Livia after the candles are out.*

>>>>>>>

Does an unborn chick, inside an egg, know a whole world awaits it when it begins to peck on the shell that encloses it? The chick surely does not know the egg will give way and it will emerge into

47

the light. Nature guides young living things, even when they are blind to the road ahead and also to who and what they are meant to become. So it was with me.

One evening after we retired, Marcellus sat on the bed, reading some official-looking papyrus scroll. *Oh, gods,* I thought, *he even takes public documents to bed!*

I stood there in my night shift, watching him for a few moments. "Is that interesting?" I finally asked.

He shrugged.

His hair, usually so carefully combed, hung down on his forehead as he read. He wore only a loincloth. He had broad, muscular shoulders, but the rest of his body was boyishly lean.

"What you're reading must be interesting since you can't tear your eyes away," I said.

He glanced up at me. "It's just a lot to absorb."

"And I'm not interesting at all, am I, Marcellus? Your boring little cousin, now your boring little wife."

"I never said you were boring."

"You've said it without words. And I don't blame you. I understand how you feel. You bore me too."

He just stared at me.

"You bore me to tears. You're so earnest about everything. Reading your musty documents in bed. You bore me, Marcellus."

He put the document on the little marble table at the side of the bed. "Well, that's unfortunate, isn't it? That we bore each other?"

"It's a tragedy," I said.

I was fourteen. I did not know what I was doing. Surely instinct guided me.

I walked to the bed, reached out, and tenderly stroked his cheekbone and his chin. "It's a tragedy. Especially when you are so handsome."

"Am I?"

"You have the handsomest face, and the most beautiful body. If only . . ."

"If only what?"

I laughed. "Don't you know?"

He shook his head.

I moved away from him. "If only you weren't such a bore, Marcellus."

He just watched me. He looked wary.

"Do you even see me?" I asked.

"Of course I do."

"Truly?" I pulled my shift off over my head, cast it to the floor. I had never before stood naked in his presence, never stood naked in front of any man. My heart hammered. A part of me wanted to flee. "Do you see me now?"

"Yes."

We stared at each other. It was strange, that moment. It was as if we had never met until then.

"You're very beautiful," he said, his face flushed.

Gods above, it was easy, so easy. I felt a power in my nakedness, a power I had never felt before. I walked to the bed, bent, and kissed his lips. It was the first time we had ever kissed. "Are you always so good and earnest and—"

"Not always," he said, and his arms went around me.

"Prove it," I said.

>>>>>>>

One night, not long after this, I murmured in his ear, "You ask how many of your kisses are enough for me. As many as are the stars."

He laughed. "I don't remember asking you that."

"It's poetry."

"Very pretty," he said and nuzzled my neck.

"Have you had many other women?"

"Of course."

I frowned. "A great many?"

"What does it matter?"

"I'm curious."

"For someone of my birth and with my prospects, women are . . . well, women are always available. It's been that way since I was twelve."

I did not feel that he was boasting, but telling me the truth.

"Oh. And did you love any of them?"

"Of course not."

"You made love to them and cared nothing for them?"

"Julia, it's never been as it is with you. You're my wife and . . . you're like a new country for me. That's the closest I can come to poetry."

We were young, and every night, we explored each other's bodies. In his arms I discovered sensations I did not know I was capable of feeling. I learned the meaning of ecstasy.

Did he love me as Catullus loved Lesbia, as my father and Livia loved each other? I asked myself that sometimes. And I wondered, did I love him that way?

His flesh was sweet. I knew that much. And when he held me, I felt warm and safe and no longer alone. I imagined years ahead in which our love would only grow.

Cleopatra Selene

*O*ctavia's house, the home of my brother Jullus, echoed with a girl's wailing. I had come—as I was permitted to—for a brief visit with my brother. "What is it?" I asked him. We stood in the atrium, the sound reaching us from down a corridor.

"Marcella," he told me. He explained that Octavia, her mother, had just informed her she was to marry Agrippa.

"He's so old," I said.

"Forty isn't ancient."

"She's only sixteen."

Jullus shrugged. "Augustus decided to reward Agrippa, so he's giving him his niece. Personally, of the two, it's Agrippa I pity. What a little bitch that one is."

Marcella, like Marcellus, was Octavia's child by a senator now long dead. She was pretty and arrogant. Octavia had three other daughters, two the children of my father, Mark Antony. I never felt the sense of kinship with my half sisters that I did with Jullus. They were Augustus's nieces after all.

"I wish Marcella would stop shrieking," my brother said.

"Augustus will be home in just a few days," I said abruptly. It was what I had come to talk about with Jullus. I could hear fear in my own voice. "He's with Livia at Prima Porta, but I hear they are returning to Rome. I will have to live under the same roof with him."

Jullus gave me a warning look. "That's a privilege, sweet Sister."

"Of course. I am so lucky."

He nodded approvingly, then said in a low voice, "Watch your words when you speak of him, even with me. We have to keep in mind that unseen ears might be listening. And when you're with him, smile. Let him know you're grateful for his kindness. Charm him."

"Charm him?"

Jullus smiled at me. "After all, you are Cleopatra's daughter."

>>>>>>>

As I lay on my sleeping couch, after snuffing out the candle, I often whispered the names of my mother and father. Cleopatra. Mark Antony. The names of my twin, Alexander Helios, and my little brother, Ptolemy, whom I had adored. I thought also of my two tall half brothers, the giants of my early childhood. *Say their names. Remember them. Caesarion. Antyllus.* Caesarion was seventeen, Antyllus sixteen, both accounted men when Augustus, the benevolent, put them to death.

In daylight I tried to drive all thoughts of the dead from my mind, to show myself cheerful and content, not sad nor angry and certainly not vengeful. This became especially important after Augustus returned home.

One morning I heard a not completely unfamiliar voice in the atrium. I peeked in from behind the curtain that led to the corridor off my bedchamber, and I saw him. He was of medium height and too thin, in no way the colossus you would expect to bestride the world. He stood talking to Livia, both of them examining a wall mural, which I guessed had been painted while he was at war. She touched his arm as she spoke, smiling up at him. He laughed. The two of them could not have looked more ordinary—a loving married couple discussing domestic matters.

I had seen him in Octavia's house, but fleetingly, from a distance. I had never before thought of him as in any way like an ordinary man, but rather as a monster, the stuff of childhood nightmares.

Later that day, Livia summoned me into a sitting room, and he was there. He stood when I entered. That surprised me because I anticipated no courtesy from him. Livia was standing also, but I did not look at her, only at him.

He had bright blue eyes and a thin, tense mouth.

He gazed at me for a long moment, and I thought I should avert my eyes, but I could not. It was as if I became my mother. Her pride entered me in her enemy's presence. I could not humbly lower my eyes before this man, even if my life depended on it.

"I hope you are happy living here, Selene." His voice was softer than I expected it to be.

"Oh, yes, I am very happy."

We had never spoken to each other before. I wondered if I was I supposed to call him Uncle as I called his wife Aunt. Fearful of making a mistake, I called him nothing.

Livia mentioned my studies, praising me, I think. I could not fully comprehend what she was saying, nor could I look at her. My eyes were locked on his. *Charm him,* Jullus had advised me. *Smile.* I could not do it. My heart pounded, and death's metallic taste filled my mouth. I was sweating, yet I felt terribly cold. A word, a flick of this man's hand, and I would be dead with my brothers.

Strangely enough, he looked sad. "Well, I am glad you are attending to your lessons. Knowledge is precious. I wish I had the time to read philosophy, history, as I did as a boy. You like your tutors?"

I nodded, unable to force out a word.

"That is good," Augustus said. "I'm happy all is well with you."

"Run along, Selene," Livia said gently.

I turned and walked away. I was out of the room, out of their sight, when I felt a churning in my guts. I ran and barely made it to the privy. Kneeling on the tiled floor, I leaned over the wooden seat, looking down at the stinking hole, smelling the sewers, as I vomited.

Julia

My cousin Marcella, Marcellus's oldest sister, was betrothed to Marcus Agrippa soon after my father returned from Spain. Sitting in the sewing room one morning with her mother, Octavia, and me, she did not hide her misery. "It is not that he is old—though he is—he's older than your father, Julia! It is that he is so disgustingly lowborn. Everyone knows his grandparents were nothing but freed slaves!"

"He has merits that far outweigh the circumstances of his birth," Aunt Octavia said.

An expression of distaste constricted Marcella's features. "Nothing can outweigh descent from slaves! Oh, Mother, if you spoke to Uncle Tavius—if you begged him—surely he would relent and not force me into this grotesque marriage!"

"The peace of Rome is at stake," Octavia said. "There cannot be a severance between Agrippa and your uncle and your brother. It is life and death, Marcella—can you understand that? Your uncle believes a marriage tie is necessary at this juncture. And Agrippa has many merits as a man."

"Merits!" Marcella had honey-colored hair and fair skin that took on a mottled look when she was angry or upset. It was mottled now. She had been doing some decorative embroidering—fine gold thread on a red coverlet. She snapped the thread in a furious gesture. "Oh, yes, and if Agrippa had no merits at all, if he were cruel and vicious as well as old and baseborn, I would have to marry him all the same, wouldn't I? For Uncle Tavius's convenience? As far as you're concerned, Mother, that's all that matters, isn't it? Oh, gods, what's the use of talking?" She got up and rushed from the room.

Octavia shut her eyes for a moment. "She blames me. Does she think I can change the circumstances of our lives? Doesn't she understand anything?"

"I think she only knows she is unhappy," I said.

"Agrippa is a great man. The greatest man in Rome after your father. It is not as if your father is forcing Marcella into some mean marriage." Aunt Octavia spoke in a calm, even voice, but she suddenly looked older, every line deeper cut.

She had married Mark Antony in order to seal the alliance between Antony and my father. The marriage had dissolved, and the peace of Rome had been destroyed. I imagined she was thinking of that—remembering her own unhappiness, fearing a similar fate for her daughter.

Poor Aunt Octavia—and poor Marcella, I thought. I felt so lucky when I compared my lot to theirs that I felt a prick of guilt. Why should I have good fortune when they did not?

I thanked the gods that I was married to Marcellus. For there was passion in our marriage; and looking toward the future, I could imagine a deeper bond, even the kind of partnership that Livia and my father had. In time Marcellus would fill my father's place. He wanted that grand destiny, and I desired it for him. I wanted to stand beside him. For the first time, I listened with true interest to political conversations. I thought of what it meant to get and retain power, and what was required of the wife of a ruler.

I had become ambitious, but that ambition was born of my feeling for my husband. What came first with me was the joy we found in our marriage bed, the way just looking at him could move me, the moments of tenderness that were incomparably sweet. *Give me a thousand kisses . . .*

Shortly before he turned twenty, he became an aedile, and Father also gave him a Senate seat. My aunt Octavia told me pointedly that a young man needed his rest. I suppose she had heard sounds coming from our bedchamber late at night. Father certainly worked him hard during the day. My husband seemed to thrive on this, however. I believe he was happy.

During the first year of my marriage, I came to a true understanding of my own role in the greater scheme of things. I might picture myself becoming a trusted partner in government, just as Livia was, but I knew that right now, one thing was required of me—that I give birth to sons. Father's imperium had brought Rome's peace. Marcellus and the children we had together must carry that imperium into the future.

However, as month followed month, my courses came with a disappointing regularity. Livia and Octavia took to asking me from time to time if there was any chance I was pregnant. Of course I had to tell them no. I sensed that they reported this news back to Father, and as months passed and I was not with child, I began to imagine that I saw a question in his eyes when he looked at me. When I contemplated what it would mean if I proved barren, it was Father more than Marcellus I feared failing.

Marcellus and I—we might have had high aspirations, but what good children we were. How hard we both tried to please Father. We were truly free only in the confines of our bedchamber—and even there we were doing exactly what Father most wanted us to do—performing the requisite actions for producing an heir.

Sometimes we appeared in public at Father's side—for example, at the chariot races or the theater. On these occasions, I wore my hair in exactly the same old-fashioned style Livia favored; it had been delicately suggested to me by Octavia that Father considered that most suitable. Marcellus always had his spotless toga perfectly draped. We smiled modestly at the people who gawked at us.

Our notion of a social evening was to attend staid dinner parties given by Father's allies in the Senate, and guard every word we spoke—lest some slip of the tongue embarrass Father.

We were of course just puppets. But we quickly became well liked. As an unmarried girl, I had been allowed to go almost nowhere. Now my life was not so secluded. I remember how odd it felt the first time I heard people shout my name at the racing course at Mars Field. As I entered Father's private box, I was gaped at by great hordes of people—some in ragged tunics up in the bleachers, others well dressed in the good seats. Many waved wineskins or sausages on sticks that the venders sold. All these strangers cried, "Julia! Julia!" They called to me as if they knew me, though they did not know me at all. Father smiled at me. "It's all right to nod at the people," he whispered. I nodded, and the shouts grew louder.

Father looked proud, and I felt a little thrill of happiness.

"The people gaze at you and Marcellus, and they see the future," Father said later. "It reassures them."

Father wanted my husband to be popular with the people and seen by them as a future leader. When Marcellus and I had been married a little over a year, he, as aedile, presented gladiatorial shows to the people of Rome. The games were in fact paid for by my father and arranged by men in his employ. But my husband officially sponsored them.

I remember the stench. *It is not blood you smell,* Marcellus informed me. *Blood has no odor. It is men's insides, the viscera torn open. The half-digested food, the voided bowels. And of course the sweat. The sweat of men fighting for their lives, the sweat of thousands of eager spectators. All that mixes together and causes a terrible odor.*

"You didn't enjoy the games much," Father said to me when they were all over.

We were at dinner. I looked down at a hunk of venison and shook my head.

"A philosopher I know wrote this about the gladiatorial games," Father said. "'Granted that many of those who fight and die are criminals who deserve their fate—what in the world have we spectators done that we must witness such butchery?' Would you agree with his point of view?"

"I agree," I said.

Father leaned across the space between our couches. "I'll tell you a secret," he said in a low voice, almost in a whisper. "I hate gladiatorial games. Not the fighting. The dying. As I've grown older, I've become queasy when I look at corpses." He smiled faintly. "Maybe because dying myself is less and less of a distant prospect."

"You won't die for a long time," I said.

"Truly, wonderful seer? Well, one can hope." He munched on a fig. "I'm glad these games were a success. That's important for Marcellus's standing. The people love the games."

I dared say, "Father isn't it up to you—as their leader—to show the people something better?"

"You have an exaggerated idea of my power. We—our family— are the people's rulers but also their captives. The day they want us gone, we'll vanish like that." He snapped his fingers.

"The army would protect you."

"The army is made up of common men—the people, in other words." Father paused for a moment, then went on. "You kept a good countenance all through the games. Really, you did well for the first time. But in the future, try to look as if you are enjoying yourself. The face we show in public matters a great deal—never forget it."

>>>>>>>

Marcella's wedding day came. Father gave her away. I could see he took no pleasure in it. Nobody seemed overjoyed by this marriage, not even the bridegroom. Watching Agrippa when he looked at Marcella, I guessed that he understood perfectly well that she hated the idea of marrying him. Covered with honors—the greatest general alive—he was also physically imposing and rugged-looking; surely many women would have found him quite attractive. But Marcella did not want him, and she carried herself so as to make that plain to the world. I thought I saw a look of injured pride on his face as she spoke the ceremonial words, "Where thou art Gaius, I am Gaia." Her tone was grudging. After that, the bride withdrew into sullen silence, hardly speaking to her new husband or anyone else at the wedding feast.

It troubled me. If, as Octavia said, the peace of Rome depended on this marriage, surely there was cause for unease.

Cleopatra Selene

When Livia decided I ought to lose my Greek accent, I applied myself to the task with all the zeal I could command. She was startled by how quickly I learned to speak like a Roman. The tutor told her I had a knack for languages. I almost said that my mother had spoken seven tongues flawlessly, and so perhaps I inherited her gift. But I caught myself. I wanted Livia to believe I was nothing like my mother.

I wore the mask that I thought would be most acceptable to Livia and to Augustus—and since I almost never removed it, I am not sure I could have said who I was apart from the mask. Was I truly who my tutors reported me to be—a mild little wren, eager to please, respectful, even bookish?

When my lessons were over, I spent hours alone in the household library. Sometimes a slave would come in asking for a book that a member of the family or even Augustus himself wanted, and the library clerk would hasten to find the papyrus scroll that had been called for. But except for these interruptions, the library was usually quiet and all but deserted, and I felt very safe.

Now that we were living in the same house, I had gotten used to seeing Augustus in passing and exchanging brief greetings and pleasantries with him. I did not become sick or tongue-tied when I found myself in his presence; my terror had subsided. But I never forgot who he was and that I was in his power.

One day my library sanctuary was invaded. I heard footsteps and looked up to find Augustus standing there.

At the sight of him, the clerk, Brumeo, leaped to his feet, all atremble in his eagerness to serve. Augustus gave a dismissing wave of his hand; the slave sank into his chair and went back to repairing a book.

I sat holding an open scroll.

"So this is where you spend your time," Augustus said. "What are you reading?"

"Callisthenes's history," I said. "About Alexander the Great."

"I've read that book. Callisthenes lied. But then, historians usually do."

I was silent. My mouth was dry.

"You have his blood in your veins," Augustus observed.

I knew he did not mean Callisthenes's blood but Alexander's. I felt a prick of fear, and hastened to deny all claim to greatness. "Oh, I doubt that story is true. My ancestor, the first of Ptolemy . . . who can say who he was? He was not born in wedlock."

Augustus shook his head. "He was the illegitimate half brother of Alexander. That's well known."

I said nothing. The last thing I wished to do was get into a debate with him about my long-dead forebears.

"Alexander died too young," Augustus said.

"Yes. He was only thirty-three."

Augustus nodded. "If Alexander the Great had lived longer, his empire would not have fallen apart. He might have brought about an age of universal peace. Then, I think, even his enemies would have forgiven him for all the blood he shed. Don't you think so?"

I doubted it. But I nodded my head up and down.

"When he died, everything devolved into chaos, and he left behind nothing. All that warfare was wasted."

"He left behind a glorious name." *As my mother did. As my father did.*

"True. For what it was worth, there was that." Augustus went to a bookshelf, removed a scroll. He started to leave with it but then turned. "Don't believe what Callisthenes says about Alexander's madness. That book is full of slanders. Some people hate the great." His eyes probed my face, as if he were asking a question.

I kept my eyes on his and said in a steady voice, "But greatness should be revered."

He smiled slightly. "You're right, it should be." With that, he walked out of the library.

>>>>>>>

Aristocratic Roman girls usually married when they were about my age, but there was no talk of a marriage for me. I tried not to envision a husband, children, the kind of life other young women had. I imagined Livia and Augustus thinking: Why let me breed? Wasn't it enough that I had been allowed to live?

No doubt by their lights, I was well treated, even indulged. I even had my own maid, who helped me bathe and dressed my hair.

A Greek woman named Chares, she was plump and white-haired, advanced in years, but energetic. She was also a chatterer. Sometimes I would have liked to have shushed her, but I was careful to accommodate everyone in that household. I wanted no enemies, even among the slaves.

Lowering her voice, she would tell me all the servants' gossip about Augustus's family. Marcella and Agrippa were miserable together. Livia's son Tiberius was none too happy about being betrothed to Agrippa's little daughter by his previous wife. Marcellus and Julia, however, had fallen in love. That was an unexpected, lucky circumstance since their marriage was a political arrangement. Not like Augustus and Livia's marriage, which had grown out of a scandalous love affair.

"They say Augustus and Livia are wild about each other," she whispered in my ear. "He can't keep his hands off her. Not that he's always been faithful, of course."

"No?" I said curiously.

"No, indeed, mistress. He likes women. Or at least he used to, when he was younger. He always came running home to Livia, though. She has him in a talon grip. I give her credit." She piled my hair on top of my head in ringlets. "Now, this style becomes you. Would you like to try it?"

"It will make me look older."

"But not too old," Chares said. She stuck a copper mirror in my hand. "Pretty, see? It's too bad you can't wear kohl on your eyes. You have beautiful eyes, and the kohl would draw attention to them."

I shrugged. "I can't wear it."

"Not until you marry, I know. It wouldn't be proper. But just imagine how fine you'll look, made up on your wedding day."

There will be no wedding day for me.

"Ah, mistress, you are getting to be a beauty. Just like your mother must have been, I think."

I was startled for a moment; no one ever mentioned my mother to me. But I could see Chares meant no harm. "My mother was far more beautiful than I could ever hope to be," I told her. My voice sounded unduly solemn in my own ears. I forced a smile. "You see, she was lucky—she didn't have my jaw."

"It's a strong jaw, mistress," Chares said. "I think it gives you distinction."

I felt rather touched. It was good to think someone in this household actually liked me.

I gazed at my reflection, not entirely displeased by my appearance. I did not have the soft, pretty features Romans favored. My jaw was too angular. But I did have my mother's eyes.

Then Chares spoke words that disturbed me. "I see Augustus looking at you sometimes. I don't think he sees anything wrong with your jaw."

>>>>>>>

"You look older," Augustus said a few days later. "Now why is that?"

He had stopped me in the atrium to ask this. He looked truly puzzled.

"My hair. My maid arranged it differently."

"Oh," he said. Then he smiled.

It was so important that he smile at me, so important that he not want me dead. I gave him a little smile back, and his smile broadened.

"I like your hair that way."

"I'm glad. I want to please you." As soon as I spoke, I felt myself blushing, as if there were a double meaning to my words.

He chuckled and walked away.

At a dangerous moment in her life, my mother enticed Julius Caesar into her bed. It allowed her to keep her throne and to save Egypt—for a while at least—from Roman rule. Why did I think of this? Why did such a revolting thought come into my head?

I had no throne to save. Only my life.

A few days later, I sat in the library, reading. Augustus appeared suddenly, held his hand under my nose, and said, "Look."

I raised my eyes to his, puzzled.

"My new signet ring," he said.

It was gold and surely very costly—graced by a small, perfect engraving of the head of Alexander the Great.

"My sign used to be the sphinx. But I thought—what message is there in that? That I'm a riddle? This is a better symbol. Tell me the truth . . . do you think it's presumptuous?"

"No." What else could I say?

"I mean it as a gesture of admiration. I have great respect for Alexander."

He stood close to me, so close I could feel the warmth of his body. And he was talking to me almost as if we were equals, almost as if we were friends. *Don't presume on it,* a voice in my mind warned. *Be careful.*

"It is only right that you should wear that ring. You are in a true sense his heir. Like him, you govern an empire," I told him.

"But you're his kin," Augustus said, his eyes sparkling.

I suddenly saw him as a man who wanted the admiration of a young woman—of a young woman who was royal as he was not, related to Alexander the Great. He held my life in his hands, but I would never feel completely helpless again in his presence. I had something to give him, didn't I? Something he wanted?

It was late. Oil lamps illumined the library. Augustus sat with an open scroll on his lap, reading what looked like a history volume. I walked in quietly. Several days had passed since we had last spoken.

"Selene, I'm surprised you're still awake."

"It's so warm these evenings. It is hard to sleep."

"We'll go to Prima Porta soon. It's cooler there."

"I've never come when you've gone to the villa, but I've heard it's beautiful."

"We'll take you along this time. Would you like that?"

"Oh, yes, that would be wonderful."

I walked closer to his chair. I felt strange—not myself. As if these moments existed in a dream. He looked at me, smiling faintly, a question in his eyes.

"I wonder if anyone else in the house is awake," I whispered.

They say my mother had herself delivered to Caesar rolled up in a rug. A gift. She made him a gift of herself and he gave her Egypt.

"What are you reading?" I asked. "About Alexander?"

"Nothing so interesting."

My soul seemed to split into three parts. A part knew what I was doing was mad and revolting—and told me that I should flee. I hated this man. I wanted him dead. He had injured me and mine in a way that was past all forgiveness. Another part of my soul cried out that what I did was right, that this could be the path to safety and more than safety. A life worth living. The third sliver of my soul—in that I felt a pull. An unfamiliar sensation, one of yearning. Every nerve in my body seemed alive. My heart pounded. *I am Cleopatra, you are Caesar.* I leaned closer to him, so that my breast touched his shoulder. He turned toward me, raised his head. In another moment, our lips would meet.

Then everything stopped.

"Selene."

Livia had entered the library. She did not look at her husband, only at me. I went hot and cold.

"Come with me, Selene. I have something to show you."

I followed her down shadowy corridors. My spine felt brittle. We entered her private suite where I had never been before—I saw we were in her dressing room. A slave woman sat sewing a garment and rose as we came in. "Leave us," Livia ordered. A note in her voice made the slave's eyes widen; she hastily put down her sewing and scurried away.

Livia turned to me. "Stupid child," she said, and then she slapped me. The blow to my cheek was hard but controlled. This was no wild striking out but a coolly administered punishment.

My legs felt as if they had turned to liquid. I almost sank to my knees.

"Even at your age, I would have been wiser. How could you be such a fool?"

Her distain seared me. "I did nothing wrong," I said. "Augustus and I were only talking . . . about books."

"If you want to make me angrier than I am already, go on in that vein. Tell me you two were chatting about philosophy. Go ahead. I'm waiting."

I knew I could tell no lie she would believe. "Since I was eight years old, I have lived always with the taste of death in my mouth. Do you know what that is?"

"Actually, I do know that taste," Livia said. "I tasted it in Perusia when it was under siege. We starved. We waited for the end. We waited for my future husband to come and burn the city to the ground. But the taste of death never made me stupid." She shook her head. "My husband is a strong man, but he is not proof against all temptations. It has been a great sorrow to me, but it would be foolish to see it as more than it is. We are joined. He can't get loose, and neither can I. You might be able to seduce him—who knows? But afterward he would still be mine, and you would have me as an enemy. Do you want that?"

"No," I whispered.

"Of course you don't," Livia said almost kindly. "Understand, I would not destroy you. Not in any active way. But there might come a day when a word from me in Augustus's ear would be life or death to you—and I would simply remain silent." She tilted her head and smiled faintly. "Believe me, sometimes silence can kill."

I shivered.

"Why were you acting like a trollop in there? Was it fear? Mostly fear?"

"Yes," I said. I was not certain if this was true, but it was all the defense I had.

"Poor child."

I did not know if she was mocking me. I could not tell from her voice.

"I will tell you something about my husband. He is an old-fashioned man. Very proper. Underneath his facade, I mean. Another thing about him—he is perceptive. He can see right into people's souls. If you give yourself to him, he might take what you offer. He has done it before. But if you did that—especially if you did it out of fear or ambition—do you know what he would feel for you? Contempt."

I could feel the blood rush to my face.

"Now aren't you better off with my friendship?"

"But I've lost that, haven't I?"

She shook her head. Her eyes looked into mine. "Just behave yourself." She touched the place on my cheek where her blow had fallen. "You're going to have a bruise, I'm afraid." She clapped her hands. A female servant came running. She had her fetch some face cream, good, she said, for covering blotches. "Use it for a few days," she advised me in a brisk voice. Her mouth quirked. "We can't have you going about looking like a beaten slave."

Livia

"A fifteen-year-old virgin? My ward? Please. You ought to have more trust." Tavius put his arms around me. We stood in our bedchamber, and the guttering candle flickered, casting dark shadows across his face. "Nothing would have happened."

"I'm sure," I said, ice in my voice.

"Livia, Livia . . ." He pulled me close and buried his face in the crook of my neck.

Cleopatra's daughter, I thought. Gods above. How had it ever seemed a good idea to me to have her in my house?

I moved away from Tavius. "The girl needs a husband."

"Of course," he said quickly. "The question is who. A loyal eligible man we would trust with Antony and Cleopatra's daughter . . . Off the top of my head, I can't think of anyone who fits that description. Can you?"

"No, but I will certainly give it more thought." After a moment, I added in an acerbic tone, "The only problem is finding a safe marriage for her? You have no objection to her leaving this house?"

"Livia . . . every other woman in the world is shadow and mist to me. You're the only one who is real. Don't you understand that yet?"

I said nothing.

He changed the subject. "Tomorrow I'll talk to Tiberius."

"Good." I had been wanting him to speak to him about his future. "I would appreciate that."

"Don't I always do my best to make you happy?"

I gave him a long, cool look.

The next day, as we prepared for a dinner party, Tavius told me how his talk with my son had gone. "He wasn't the least bit grateful. Do you know what he said? 'As you wish.' Anyone would think he were doing me the favor."

I grimaced. "But he seemed content?"

"Oh, yes, he was content. Content! Do you realize what I'm offering him? He can be a praetor by the time he's twenty-two."

Tavius intended to immediately make Tiberius a quaestor. Quaestors administered financial affairs in Rome and in the provinces and often served as a general's second in command. If Tiberius did well, the praetorship would be next—praetors acted as judges and also led armies. A path of enormous opportunity was being spread out before my son.

"Thank you," I said. "We both know Tiberius doesn't have the smoothest manners. But I'll wager you won't find anything lacking in how he performs his duties."

"Marcellus is always grateful for anything I do for him."

At all times, Marcellus did exactly what Tavius told him to do, and did it with a smile. Was I wrong to think he lacked some essential inner fire? Sometimes I feared the gods had stinted Tiberius on human feeling. He certainly could not match Marcellus at charming people at dinner parties. But there was iron in his soul. *For holding this empire together, I would take Tiberius.*

I could imagine my son maturing into the sort of man who could rule Rome. But Marcellus . . . ?

Marcellus was Tavius's choice. *Whether you know it or not, my boy is better than your boy.* I thought it, but I did not say it.

⋙⋙

I kept my eye on Selene. She had gone back to being shy in Tavius's presence, and was quiet and meek in mine. Had she learned her lesson? How could I know?

"What do you call my husband?" I asked her one day.

"Call him?" She looked confused and stupid. Maybe it was an act. I knew she wasn't the least bit stupid.

"How do you address him?"

"I do not know how to properly address him. Perhaps you could instruct me?" She spoke in a humble voice.

"You call me Aunt—call him Uncle," I snapped at her. "That makes sense, doesn't it?"

"Uncle, then," she said, dipping her head.

Strangely enough, I felt sorry for her.

The world would be safer for me and mine if you were dead, I thought. *Perhaps it would be better for my marriage too.* But the heart is a contrary organ. I did not want her dead. It was not just that I believe murder offends the gods—though I do believe that. For her own sake, I wanted no tragic end to Selene's story.

That I should feel solicitude for Cleopatra's daughter, of all people, struck me as distinctly odd. Then one day I realized the cause.

I had ordered her to spin wool with the maids one hour a day. Julia had once done the same, and I had had this chore assigned to

73

me when I was a girl. It is necessary for a young noblewoman who would eventually run her own household to have some acquaintance with domestic arts—but I think Selene took the imposition of this task as a punishment. One day I stood in the spinning room and watched her work, noting the deft motions of her hands. She had learned to spin well quite quickly. I saw, though, by her face that her thoughts were far away, her agile fingers faster than the revolving spindle. It struck me that I as a girl had been much like her—efficiently doing the domestic tasks my mother insisted on while my mind ranged far and wide.

Selene had lost so much, so young, just as I had. Like me, she had been forced at an early age to look at the world clear-eyed. She saw her danger. She knew what game she was playing; she knew she was playing for keeps. She would use what weapons life gave her. She intended to survive.

When we see ourselves reflected in another, we are sometimes repulsed by our own image and moved to hatred. But more often, I think, the recognition of likeness is the foundation of affection.

I had the sense, watching Selene at her spinning, that my own younger self was sitting there. "Come with me," I said. "I wish to speak to you."

I took her into my private rooms. She walked in looking tense. The last time I had summoned her in such a way I had rebuked and slapped her.

I gestured to a marble bust that stood on a pedestal. "Do you know who that was?"

"No, Aunt."

"That was my father, Marcus Livius Drusus Claudianus. You see, I keep his bust here. I honor his memory. When I was a girl, he was the person I loved most in the world."

Selene thoughtfully took this in. No doubt she wondered why I was speaking of my father.

"Who did you love most, Selene, when you were a little girl?"

She stared at me for a moment. Weighing whether to answer truthfully or not, probably. Finally she said, "My mother."

I nodded. I had somehow expected this answer. "When my father died I lost everything. Home, safety, my place in the world. But most of all, him."

"At six years old, I was a queen," Selene said. "My mother and father had me crowned queen of Crete in my own right. But that didn't last long."

"It can strengthen you to go through the fire when you are young," I said.

"I suppose so, Aunt. If you are not incinerated."

I saw my own younger self then indeed—bereft of home and safety, living in a forest, running from a fire that was setting all the trees aflame. "We have certain things in common."

"I see that we do."

I took her by the shoulders. "Not every choice I have made would strike most people as praiseworthy. But what you should know about me is this. I have never in my life abandoned anyone who gave me true loyalty. Not even a slave. The thought of such a betrayal is profoundly disgusting to me. I repay loyalty in kind, always."

"That is an admirable quality."

Did she intend mockery? I could not be sure. "You ought to try to trust me. Will you try?"

"Yes, Aunt."

What else could she say?

I dismissed her then, feeling I had said too much and too little. I doubted that child was capable of trusting anyone.

>>>>>>>

There is always another war. My son Tiberius had told me that with a certain amount of relish. Certainly the tribes in Gaul could regularly be counted on to provide bloody work for our army. An uprising occurred soon after he became a quaestor. Tiberius was chosen among those to be dispatched to deal with it.

One morning, he stood in our entranceway in his armor, the metal shining brightly because every inch of it was expensive and new, a delicate carving of winged victory on his breastplate. He towered over me now, this boy I had once cradled in my arms.

"I'll make you proud, Mother," he said to me when I embraced him in farewell.

"Come home victorious," I told him. Meanwhile my heart cried out, *Just stay safe!*

He hugged and kissed his brother, Drusus, before he left. They had grown up close, those two. His farewell to Tavius—indeed to everyone but Drusus and me—was so perfunctory as to be almost insulting.

Tiberius ought to have at least been happy that the gods and Tavius had handed him his dearest wish—a war to fight. The look on his face as he took leave of us showed satisfaction at finally getting his due, but nothing more than that. I tried to think when I had seen Tiberius outwardly joyful and could only remember moments in his early childhood. There were depths to him I did not begin to fathom.

"He is a fine soldier," Tavius said to me after my son had gone. He intended the words as comfort.

Tiberius had undergone the most rigorous training and had excelled in all feats of arms. But of course in every war, fine soldiers die.

That Marcellus would stay home stirred my resentment. He was too valuable to risk on a petty provincial war, in Tavius's opinion. Not that my husband had said that. "Those boys are our two great hopes for the future . . . better not to send them both to Gaul," he had muttered. "And you know Tiberius is so eager to go."

And Marcellus, your young hero, is not? I barely restrained myself from asking.

I wondered if Tavius eventually would see where Marcellus was lacking.

>>>>>>>

The fact that Agrippa did not lead the army we dispatched to Gaul troubled me. He preferred to stay home. Tavius did not argue with him, but sent another general. I thanked the gods that at least he did not choose to go himself, for his health would not have stood it. But I did not like Agrippa's disinterest.

"Achilles is sulking in his tent," Tavius said.

I remembered Agrippa when he had been married to my friend Caecilia. He had been a cheerful man then. She had known how to keep him content with the public role he played, along with everything else. Marcella, from what I heard, treated him as an unwelcome visitor in his own house.

One day Tavius came into my study, looking upset and drained. I knew he had just met with Agrippa.

"He is very unhappy," he said. "He says he's through. He wants to withdraw from public affairs."

"Just leave? And you'll let him do that?"

"He is not leading a mutiny, he is not turning against me. He just sees little future for himself, with Marcellus coming into such great prominence."

I let out a breath. "It will look bad if he deserts."

"I'll give him a sinecure. He can pretend to oversee Asia Minor—he doesn't even have to visit there. He'll go to his country estate and do what he says he wants to do . . . rest."

"And you think he'll actually do that? Not cause trouble, just retire?"

"He has been my faithful friend since we were children."

A thought occurred to me. "Will Marcella go off to the country with him?"

"He talked about leaving her in his house in Rome."

I nodded. The marriage was an utter disaster.

Agrippa's retirement represented a huge loss—the loss of a man who had been not only Tavius's leading general but his right hand in many other ways. He had rebuilt much of Rome from the sewers up—finally erecting a great temple dubbed the Pantheon. Marcellus could not in any way fill his place. And there was another personal aspect to losing Agrippa. The pinnacle of power was no place to make new friends. Everyone curried favor; everyone had an ulterior motive. Tavius had only two close, trusted friends—Agrippa and Maecenas. Now he was in effect losing one.

This was not a small thing. My husband carried enormous mental burdens. Agrippa, Maecenas, and I were the people he depended on most to make it all bearable.

As if to justify himself for preferring Marcellus over Agrippa, he told me again and again that Marcellus was the future. I disliked hearing this. "You are the future," I whispered to him one night. "The only future I want."

"To do what I have done—to seize supreme power—is only morally supportable if I exercise power responsibly. I have an obligation to try to shape the world after I am gone. An obligation, Livia. Otherwise, what am I? I wish Agrippa understood. It is not that I love my nephew and have no affection for my friend. It is that I see Rome's future when I look into that boy's eyes. You see?"

"I understand you wish to act for the good of all."

But he was melancholy. In a simple, human way, he pined for his old friend.

>>>>>>>

That summer a fever swept through Rome. It began in the slums near the market district, but of course it did not stop there. People all over the city died.

I wanted us to flee, to get as far away from the contagion as we could go. But Tavius would not hear of it. The best I could persuade him to do was to take up residence at our villa at Prima Porta, a half-day's journey from the city itself. That was close enough to attend to official business. We often stayed there in the summer in any case.

When the whole household was busy with packing, Selene asked me if she was to come with us. I think she expected me to leave her behind in a city full of contagion. When I said she was to come, she gave me one of her rare smiles.

Marcellus and Julia came to stay with us, for he too insisted on remaining close to the city. We also had another houseguest, Juba of Numidia. He was the son of a king who had rebelled against Rome and been defeated, but Juba had won Tavius's high esteem. My husband insisted he not stay in disease-ridden Rome but avail himself of our hospitality.

"It will be good to have his company," he said. "He's brilliant and can talk intelligently about an incredible number of subjects. When it comes to the natural world, he is like a walking compendium of knowledge. Really, he is an extraordinary young man. Completely Roman in his outlook." This last was the highest praise.

Tavius had been toying with the idea of giving Juba a throne in North Africa, in compensation for his lost ancestral kingdom of Numidia. Numidia had such high strategic value it had to remain under direct Roman administration, but there were other places where he could play a useful role. He would be a vassal king, in a sense a Roman administrator, but would possess considerable autonomy. The question—always the question when it came to such matters—was whether or not he could be trusted. Tavius leaned to the view that he could be. My guess was that in the near future, this young man would wear a crown.

Cleopatra Selene

*I*t was cool at the villa at Prima Porta, far cooler than in Rome. We lived in the kind of luxury that brought back shimmering memories of how it had been in my mother's palaces. I saw beautiful murals and statuary wherever I looked and, outside, huge exquisitely cultivated gardens.

I had my lessons with my tutor in the villa's vast library, and often we had company. Juba of Numidia would sit quietly in a corner, reading from parchment scrolls and taking notes on waxed tablets.

One day, after my lessons were ended, I asked him what exactly he was doing.

He looked up from his work and did not seem irked by the interruption. "I am writing a book," he said.

"About what?"

"The behavior of elephants. Mainly I'm compiling anecdotes from various sources."

"Are you fond of elephants particularly?"

He smiled. "Not exactly fond. But I rode them when I was small. They are among the most intelligent animals that exist—perhaps as intelligent as apes."

"Are apes intelligent?"

"Oh, yes. Great apes are extremely canny. But I have not been able to find much information about them."

I liked the way Juba's eyes sparkled as he talked. He had a quick, lively way of speaking. His eyes were black, his skin light brown. On first impression, I thought he looked rather like an Egyptian.

"There is a lot of information about elephants, but it's rather scattered. What I intend to do is bring it together in one book. Elephants are worth knowing about. They care for and protect each other. In many ways they are more civilized than men."

"I see." A prince writing a book about elephants. How odd.

He read my thoughts. "Does it seem strange to you that I should be spending my time this way? I suppose it must—a king's son writing a natural philosophy book."

"I would not think to judge what you do. I'm sure it's a very useful occupation." Some impulse made me add, "You talk just like a Roman, with no accent. And the way you dress, everything about you—you behave like a Roman too."

"I could say the same about you."

"My father was Roman," I said, bristling a little. "A great Roman general. Perhaps you have heard the name Mark Antony?"

"My father was a general too, as well as a king. He was defeated, just like yours, and died by his own hand, just like yours. He was not a Roman like your father, but they ended the same way."

"And how do you suppose you will finish your life?" I asked him, an edge in my voice.

"Not like that, if I can help it."

"You've accommodated yourself to the world as you find it," I said.

"Do you think that wrong?"

I gave a low chuckle. "Gods above, I am the last one on earth with a right to reproach you."

We looked at each other in silence for a few moments, and in those moments, much was said without words. It was as if months of acquaintance were compressed in that short space of time.

Then Juba spoke in a low voice. "I am Augustus's friend, and he has discussed giving me a kingdom to rule. Just now he is hesitating, but I believe he will do it in the end. And I won't act as my father did—I won't revolt. I know the Romans will always be stronger. I will accept circumscribed power, and that will be enough." A glow came into his eyes. "I'll be a good king. In whatever land I'm sent to, I'll cause commerce and the arts to flourish, just as Augustus has done here. And scholarship too. There is nothing more important for a man to do with his life than to add to the sum of human knowledge. As a king, I will be well situated to do that."

I had thought he looked Egyptian. But now another image came into my mind. I had seen Assyrian wall friezes, portraits of their ancient kings, faces fierce and beautiful. He had a face like that, I thought.

"You have your life all planned," I said.

"It's important to plan."

I said almost in a whisper, "And do you never think . . . of vengeance?"

"Whom should I avenge myself on? Julius Caesar, who defeated my father in war? He is quite dead. As for his adopted son and heir, Augustus—if I were to kill him, would it bring my father back? Would it help anyone on this earth?" He paused, then asked abruptly, "Do you think I'm a coward?"

He had fought in war—two wars—at Augustus's side. He had acquitted himself honorably by all accounts. Beyond that, I did not hear a weak man shrinking from danger in the way he spoke. Every word had the ring of conviction.

"I know you're not a coward," I said.

We were quite alone in the library, but his voice sank to a whisper. "Do you imagine taking vengeance for your parents?" he asked gently.

If anyone else had asked, I would have denied it. But I said, "Sometimes." Then I stood aghast at the weapon I had given Juba to use against me if he wished.

He had been sitting at a writing table all during this talk, but now he stood up. "Don't be afraid," he whispered. "I don't carry tales." He did something very strange then. He reached out and stroked my cheek.

"I don't know why . . . I feel I can trust you," I said.

"Sometimes it's necessary to talk openly with someone. It's only natural and human. People are not like tigers, who are happy to hunt alone, but more like lions with their prides." He laughed. "And really, who better for you to confide in than a deposed prince whose head is full of elephant lore?" Then his expression sobered. "You mustn't think of vengeance, though," he whispered. "It would accomplish nothing. It would cost you your life—and what a waste that would be."

I felt a fluttering in my chest, like a trapped bird trying to get free. And then I remembered he had opposed my father at the Battle of Actium, fought for Augustus, and helped to destroy my father and mother.

I moved away from him. He looked gravely at me for a long moment, then made a humorous face of mock sorrow and went back to writing his book.

>>>>>>>

Later that day, I sat spinning wool—this daily chore that Livia had me do. I saw that she did not intend it as chastisement, rather as a fitting occupation and training for a girl. I still hated it.

Livia entered the room and watched me for a little while. "If nothing else, spinning wool will teach you patience," she said. "Patience is an important virtue, especially for a woman."

I felt more at ease with her here at the villa than I had before. After all, she had taken me away from the contagion in Rome. That meant something, surely?

My thoughts were still in turmoil after my conversation with Juba. I said carefully, "You told me that you loved your father more than anyone else when you were a girl."

"Yes."

"And yet Augustus . . . was not his friend."

"Augustus was his deadly enemy," she said.

I wanted to ask, *How could you marry him, then?* I did not dare speak the words, yet the question seemed to hang between us.

After a moment, she said, "Do you think I should have slit his throat one night when he slept?"

"Oh, no, Aunt, I would never suggest—"

She hushed me with a gesture. "I thought of it once or twice. But I love him, you see. And I know that both my father and my husband were caught in a net of necessity. My father, for the most virtuous reasons, allied himself with Julius Caesar's murderers. And my husband was tied to Caesar by every bond of kinship, loyalty, and affection. Of course he became my father's enemy. How could he not?" She gave a small shrug. "You have to adapt to life as it comes, Selene, in order to live at all. Little in this world is just as it should be. You look at the choices the gods present to you, and then you choose."

But how, I wondered, could you ever know if your choice was the right one?

>>>>>>>

I began to go walking in the villa's gardens in the afternoons with Juba.

He would talk to me about the natural world, about the different kinds of birds we saw, the varieties of plants. I felt comfort in his presence. He had a serenity about him, and he was kind—even to animals, even to slaves. I took care to treat the slaves who served me well, because I feared their malice. Juba's motives were different. "I was a slave once," he said to me.

This statement profoundly shocked me. "You're a prince!"

"When I was a small boy, I rode down the Sacred Way in chains, in Julius Caesar's triumph. No one misused me after that. I was given tutors and educated. But it was Augustus who freed me and made me a Roman citizen. That happened when I was seventeen."

I too, of course, had been exhibited in chains in a triumphal procession. But I had been made a free Roman citizen immediately afterward. I was different from Juba because I was the acknowledged daughter of Mark Antony, who had held the highest offices in the Roman state. Never had I been called a slave, never had I thought of myself as one. It might have been understandable to put me to death, but to enslave Antony's daughter would have been viewed as grotesque and infamous by all Romans.

Juba was ten years older than I. And he seemed to have everything worked out, to look at the world without fear—always through his own eyes, making his own judgments. There was a sureness about him, even about the way he walked. I thought of a word for his stride, fittingly derived from one of the animals he spoke of and loved—leonine. He moved like a young lion.

For several days, all we did was talk during our walks in the garden. We did not speak of weighty matters. Still, it was wonderful to me to have someone it felt safe to speak with. If my mind sometimes questioned my trust in him, my heart did not. One day, we stood in a shaded glade, shielded from all eyes, Juba put his arms around me. Tenderly, he drew me to him, and then he kissed me. It was so warm, so sweet, that kiss.

I had never expected to experience such a moment. I had expected precisely nothing from life, except perhaps mere survival. Certainly to love and be loved had seemed impossible for me. That made this kiss especially precious. For I was coming to love Juba, and I believed he returned my feeling.

After that, we would often embrace and kiss when we could be sure we were out of the sight of others. "I want more of you," Juba said one day. His voice was husky. We stood in a little garden glen where no one could see us.

"I am afraid. It is not that I don't care for you. It is prudence."

"Prudent little moon goddess," he said, "don't you want me?"

I had tossed in my bed at night, wanting him. "If we were to . . . if I became pregnant, I don't know what they would do to me," I stammered. "Livia and Augustus would be enraged. It would be terrible."

"Don't you think I'm capable of protecting you?"

I stared at him. "Protect me? How? If they knew you were the father, it would ruin you."

I whirled away from him and swiftly walked back alone to the villa.

We continued on as we were, not acting on our desire, but walking every day in the gardens together. For a time, no one seemed to notice. Livia and Augustus were occupied with other worries. The sickness in Rome was very bad, and then one of the slaves at the villa took ill, which drove a knife of terror through all our hearts. But even though Livia's attention seemed focused elsewhere, I tried to avoid her seeing me when I was with Juba. If I happened to be with him and heard her coming, I would walk away.

I was not so careful about not being seen by Julia. One day when she and I were alone in the courtyard of the villa, she said, smiling, "I saw you and Juba walking out to the garden together."

"We weren't together. We just happened to be there at the same time."

"I'm sure," she said with a little laugh. "Oh, don't worry. I won't tell."

"There is nothing to tell." I felt stung by her laughter, and frightened that she would go babbling about us, whatever she said.

Hearing my dismay, Julia looked troubled and said in low voice, "I won't say anything, really. I like Juba. And you're well matched, aren't you?"

"How do you mean?" I asked warily.

"Why, you're both royalty."

Royalty brought to Rome in chains. "He is pleasant to talk to, but there is nothing between us."

"Things are so awful and frightening with people falling sick. I think it would be good if you and Juba could find some happiness at such a time. Oh, Selene, I would never try to stop you being together—in fact, I would cheer you on."

I said nothing. I wished the conversation over.

But she went on talking. "If you feel for Juba what I do for Marcellus, that would give us something in common, wouldn't it? We do have more in common with each other than with anyone else here. I've always felt we could be friends."

No, I thought, *we can never be friends. Friends must understand each other, and you can't begin to understand how it feels to be me.*

"You have always been most kind to me," I said. "I would appreciate it if you would put any thought of Juba and me out of your mind. There is nothing between us at all."

"All right." She sounded more perplexed than irked and, after a moment, just walked away.

How could I ever be Julia's friend? Certainly, we were both surrounded by peril at this time and in some way bound by it, like people adrift on a boat in stormy seas. Still, she was her father's beloved daughter, the wife of his heir. She was so fortunate. She could be carelessly kind to me and never have to think twice about it. And she and Marcellus could go walking together openly anytime they wanted. Their joy in each other could only earn them approbation; indeed all of Rome looked forward to Julia conceiving and bearing Marcellus's child.

My and Juba's situation was so different. It was all I could do to keep from hating Julia for what she had and I lacked.

>>>>>>

As the days passed, the world around us darkened, for the pestilence that had been largely confined to the city now spread fully into the countryside. We heard of many people dying in nearby houses. And in our villa, the days were punctuated by the wailing of slaves—for although they could not lawfully marry, they did form families, and they mourned when their family members died.

Livia saw that all was kept clean, the floors and even the walls scrubbed. She ordered that the sick servants were separated from the others, that they have doctors to tend them. Augustus offered sacrifices to the gods, but it did no good that I could see. People kept sickening and dying. I feared for Juba; I feared for myself.

Then illness struck the one person who seemed most invulnerable to me.

Julia came running up to me one afternoon, when I emerged from the library after my lessons. "Oh, Selene, it must not be, it must not be. Oh, gods above, he has fallen ill. Selene, what will we do?"

She looked like a frightened child, her face flushed, her hair in disarray.

"Who is sick? Is it your husband?"

"No," she cried. "Oh, no, not him. It's my father." She sobbed. "My father!"

Her hands were raised, fluttering, like butterflies trying fruitlessly to escape the net. I grasped her wrists. "Julia, it will be all right. Calm yourself."

I felt ages older than her at that moment. I had already suffered the loss of father and mother, had seen those I loved die, and I had gone on living. All she had known were life's blessings.

It did not seem odd to me when she threw her arms around me then and wept on my shoulder. I held her, feeling her body shake.

"Augustus will recover," I said.

"Selene, you're right, he must. People do recover, don't they? One of the slaves has, hasn't he?"

"Yes. The blacksmith is up and well."

"But he's a big, burly man, and my father isn't. He's sickly, really. We're not supposed to say it, but that's the truth. Do you think he'll really get better?"

"With the gods' help."

Later, I saw Livia coming out of her husband's sickroom, not glancing at me or at anybody, only conferring with the doctor, a small, sinewy Greek. The doctor tried to reassure her, and I saw by her face she did not believe his words.

"The world will fall apart if that man dies," Juba said to me later. "The empire will seethe with disorder."

"Marcellus—"

"If he were older, maybe there would be a chance. He is twenty-one, barely. There will be civil war."

And what would happen to us?

"Selene," Juba said, "even if you hate Augustus, pray that he lives."

⋙⋙⋙

No one died quickly from this illness. Rather they went through days of torment. Their fevers would rise and fall. They would cough incessantly and suffer terrible headaches. Some developed spots on their chests and bellies. Some fell into delirium before they died. Occasionally the sickness ebbed away, leaving the sufferer exhausted but alive. But most died.

Meanwhile the great one, the one on whom the whole world depended—in his bedchamber, out of sight of the household, Augustus lay battling for his life. Livia usually stayed in the room with him, fearless of contagion. When she briefly emerged, the look on her face showed me he was losing his fight.

I could fall ill and die too, I thought. *Or Juba might. We could both be gone in a few days. Or whoever succeeds Augustus might well decide to execute me.*

"My father is dying," Julia said to me one morning. She was calmer now. "I know it. We all do."

"Then Marcellus—"

I meant to say *Marcellus will become First Citizen.* But Julia interrupted me. "I'll tell you something, Selene, but you must promise not to repeat it to anyone."

"I promise."

"Marcellus is frightened. He is not prepared to take my father's place. One day he will be. But not yet. He lay in my arms last night and whispered the truth. He is not ready. He is so afraid he will fail us all."

I felt a sinking in my belly.

We can count on nothing, I thought. *There will be no safety now for any of us.*

>>>>>>>

I was sixteen, and since I was little, all my actions had been geared to survival. But that evening, as the twilight came on, I made no calculations. Juba and I walked through the gardens, hand in hand. Finally we came to a little downward cleft in the land. We were completely alone, hidden on all sides by shrubbery.

"What do you truly ask of life?" I murmured. It is perhaps strange I would pose this question at such a moment. But I wished to fully know him, to grasp who and what he was.

"I want to be both a scholar and a ruler. I want to be one who leaves something of value behind for those who come after."

I nodded. "Is there anything else you want?"

"I want a beautiful queen. A queen descended from a line of god-kings. Who smells of jasmine. Whose mouth is like pomegranates."

I laughed. "Where will you ever find a queen like that?"

"She stands here before me."

"Do you think they will ever let us marry?"

"I doubt it very much," he said soberly. "The thought of you with a royal husband would fill even brave Romans with fear. We can only count on this moment."

"Only now. So we must fully seize this day that may never come again."

He studied my face for a moment to be sure he understood me. Then he said, "You realize what you are risking?"

"I am my mother's daughter. I am no coward."

He pulled me close. It surprised me how suddenly and forcefully he did it, but I did not resist. We sank to the ground. I let him take me there, under the open sky.

Afterward, I thought of my mother in my father's arms. I remembered them without grief. While they lived they had each other, though the whole world might have cursed them for it.

Juba's face loomed above me. "Cleopatra Selene . . . you're not sorry?"

"Oh, no." *Not even if I die for it.*

Livia

The doctors had tried bathing him in icy-cold water brought with great effort from snowy mountain peaks. It did not cool his fever. He lay back against pillows of purple silk, propped up so he could breathe better. His eyes were blazing, his face damp with sweat. But the illness had not touched his mind. "Send everybody else out," Tavius whispered.

We had three doctors in attendance at this time. I ordered them to leave the bedchamber and sat down on the bed beside my husband.

He pulled at the coverlet. "I'm burning up."

I turned the coverlet back so his upper body lay bare and struggled not to wince at the rose-colored marks on his chest. "Is that better, beloved?"

He nodded slightly. "Marcellus . . . what is your opinion of him?"

I did not reply, but took his hand, cradled it in mine, then raised it to my lips.

His eyes bore into mine. "You know what I'm asking. Answer." His voice, though weakened, was that of an imperator.

He wanted me to transform myself now from wife to political advisor; I played both roles with him of course. But at this moment I was all wife. Still, I tried to meet him where he was and give him what he needed.

"Marcellus is a good young man. He's not you." I reached over and stroked back a lock of golden hair from Tavius's forehead. "He is not strong, the way you are strong. How could he be? Everything has been handed to him. You know this."

I saw by Tavius's expression that not a word I said surprised him. I was just confirming what he thought himself.

It is a fine thing, I suppose, to be favored by the gods from the moment you are born. Tavius had not been so favored. He had barely survived his first years. His whole boyhood had been a struggle to overcome physical weakness, and he had emerged from it with resources that his nephew—whom the gods had granted every natural gift—did not have.

"Time may well temper Marcellus," I said. "Time and experience. He is talented and willing. In ten years . . ."

"Ten years." Tavius gave a terrible shuddering cough. "Ten years . . ."

"Tavius, don't dwell on this now. You need to rest your mind as well as your body." He stared at the ceiling for a long time. I knew he was incapable of rest at such a moment. He was imagining all his work destroyed, Rome once more plunged into anarchy and civil war.

Only one man had a chance of holding the empire together if Tavius died. We both knew who that man was.

Finally Tavius said, "Send for Agrippa."

Julia

*D*awn had painted the sky a pale pink. Marcellus and I stood in the portico outside our bedchamber. We had barely slept.

"It will be all right," I told him. "I have faith in you."

He gave me a wintry stare.

My father lay dying, and instead of being comforted by my husband, I felt impelled to comfort him. In the night, he had whispered his fears to me. Father held the empire in his hands. The Senate, the people, the army all bowed to his will. Would they allow Marcellus to rule because my father had designated him his heir? Or when Father drew his last breath, would civil war break out?

I knew I must swallow my own grief and fear for now, to be the wife Marcellus needed. I don't think I could have done it for anyone else, or even for Rome. But I loved Marcellus and ached to make his load lighter. "Whatever happens, I'll be at your side," I said.

"I ought to have insisted on a military appointment. I ought to have been making friends in the army, not in the Senate. What a fool I was. I didn't think I had to. Not yet."

"Men will follow you," I said. "You are my father's choice and married to his daughter, and you are the male heir closest in blood. You *will* be First Citizen. It is your destiny." I put my arms around him. "It's all right to show doubt with me—but only with me, my darling. The gods give us the power to do what we have to do. I've heard Father say that again and again. Please believe me, Marcellus—you will be able to do all that you must."

"You don't understand," he said quietly. "If your father were given time, he could arrange an orderly succession. But now, if I want to be First Citizen, I will have to raise an army and wade through rivers of blood, just as your father did when he was my age." The look on his face chilled me. He was gazing into the future and recoiling. *Rivers of blood . . .*

"Do you want to be First Citizen?"

"Yes. I want it."

"Then if need be, we must fight for it," I said.

I told myself I was the daughter of Caesar Augustus, and therefore I would not shrink from what lay ahead. But I was full of fear.

Later that day, when the physicians and Livia allowed me to visit my father, his appearance shocked me. He did not speak, but his eyes met mine, and I knew he was aware of my presence. "Father, don't leave me," I whispered, struggling to keep from sobbing. The physicians hurried me out of the room.

The next day Agrippa arrived. No one told me he had been sent for. But he had been—and he had come from his country estate, galloping the whole way to reach Father while he still lived. Corvus, head of Father's bodyguard, greeted him in the atrium with a salute, and then the two embraced. "I thank all the gods you're here," Corvus said.

"Is he still alive?"

"Barely."

"I was afraid I'd be too late."

The two spoke like old friends, which I suppose they were.

I walked forward to greet Agrippa, Marcellus beside me. "Thank you for coming," I said. My eyes welled up. "It means so much . . ."

Agrippa patted my shoulder with a large, clumsy hand.

"I will be depending on your help," Marcellus said.

I suppose he spoke his first thought. It was the wrong thing to say at such a moment. Agrippa gave him a contemptuous look. "Your father-in-law is not dead yet."

"Of course not, I didn't mean—"

I saw the situation plainly. If Father died, Agrippa and no one else would command the army's allegiance. He could make Marcellus First Citizen—or ruin him.

"You have been the pillar on whom we have all relied," I said. "Whatever befalls us, I hope you will always be our friend."

Agrippa's face softened. "My dear Julia, you can always count on my friendship."

Livia, informed of Agrippa's arrival, came and embraced him. "Tavius will want to see you at once." She looked at Marcellus and me. "You come too."

We—Livia, Agrippa, Marcellus, and I—entered the bedchamber. Father lay under a silk coverlet, propped up on pillows. His eyes were sunken in his head, and his flushed skin glistened with sweat. He looked worse than he had the day before, and inside myself I cried out with pain at the sight. I was losing him.

"I'm here, Augustus," Agrippa said, his voice husky with emotion.

Father tried to speak, but instead he let out a series of weak coughs.

He gazed at me. I felt he was trying to tell me something with his eyes. Then he looked at Marcellus. It was utterly silent in the room.

Father's lips moved, but he made no sound. Slowly—as if the task cost him great effort—he removed his signet ring. It was the ring he always wore, a symbol of his imperial authority. I understood what was about to happen. He would give the ring to Marcellus, to designate him as his successor.

But Father's eyes shifted away. "Agrippa," he whispered.

Agrippa came closer and leaned over him. Father extended his hand, holding out the ring, and grave-faced, Agrippa took it. I heard Marcellus's sharp intake of breath.

No words were spoken. None needed to be.

Father shut his eyes, completely spent. Only the slight rising and falling of his chest told me he still lived.

There was no gloating in Agrippa's manner. Wordlessly, he took off his own signet ring and slipped Father's on his finger.

Marcellus's face had gone white. I clutched at his arm and stared back at Father. I felt utterly betrayed. I wanted to scream, *What have you done? What have you done to my husband and me?*

Marcellus, Agrippa, and I walked out of the room, leaving Livia with Father. The outer hall was now filled with soldiers— members of the bodyguard and Father's personal staff. Agrippa did not speak, only held out his hand, on which he had placed Father's ring. There were no boisterous congratulations, nothing like that—just expressions of solemn assent on men's faces. No one even glanced at Marcellus.

It was as if a dagger had been thrust into my husband's heart, and my father had been the one who wielded it. My father, the man he worshipped, the man he lived his whole life to please. I did not know what to say to Marcellus, and he said nothing to me. He just turned and walked away, out of the house, out into the night.

I went into our bedchamber and wept.

Oh, I understood Father's decision. The army loved Agrippa, and Marcellus was nothing to them but an untested young man. Even I could more easily imagine Agrippa holding the empire together than my husband doing it. But Marcellus was Father's nephew. And I was Marcellus's wife. I felt as if Father had thrown Marcellus away and me with him.

Father loved Livia and he loved Rome. Those two great greedy loves crowded out all else.

In the end, how little Marcellus had mattered to him. And how little I did.

>>>>>>>

When Marcellus came back, it was already morning. There were welts on his arms and legs—he had stumbled in a patch of bramble, wandering in the darkness. And he was shivering. "You should have taken your cloak," I said. "The nights have been turning cold."

He did not reply. There was an emptiness in his eyes.

"You are young, Marcellus," I said. "Agrippa has twice your years. No one could expect you to equal him now. But you have years ahead of you, many years to—"

"Be quiet."

"Don't turn away from me. Please."

"My head aches," he said. He rubbed his temple. "Here. It throbs."

"Well, then lie down. You have been up all night."

"I think I caught the fever." He gave a little grimace and a small chuckle, as if he could not take in what he had just said.

"Oh, no. You're just tired and cold." But I knew—in the center of my being, I knew the truth even as I spoke.

He was twenty-one years old and strong. And yet the fever progressed more quickly with him than it did with many others. On the second day, he fell into a delirium. We had to tie him to the bed, but he kept struggling, exhausting himself. "Don't you understand?" he told me. "The Senate is meeting now! Important matters are being discussed. What will your father think of me if I'm not there?"

I swore to him that the Senate was not meeting and tried to explain that he was ill. But he shouted, "No! Why are you deceiving me?"

I wiped his face with a wet cloth. "Hush, hush, my darling. Please. You are sick and you must rest." It was useless. He kept on raving. It was as if his own mind had turned against him and he had become his own enemy. He could not rest. When the doctors tried to give him a sleeping draught, he choked on the liquid and spat it out.

My kiss, my touch—they meant nothing. Again and again, he cursed me for keeping him from his important work.

Everything that could be done was done. The physicians tried all their cures, dribbled elixirs in his mouth, bathed him in cold water. Nothing helped.

Livia

I held Tavius's hand. His eyes were shut, yet I sensed he was still conscious. But he was dying, Tavius was dying. The heart of the world would soon cease to beat, and my own heart would break. I held his hand, felt the warmth of his touch, knowing soon I would be alone in the cold.

We were twin souls. How could I live without him?

"You did the right thing," I said. "The boy could never get the army to follow him. But even Agrippa is not you. Rome needs you. I need you."

I felt a slight pressure on my hand, and then a letting go. It was like a farewell. But I tightened my own grip on his hand. "Tavius, I do not give you permission to die. I forbid it."

One side of his mouth quirked up in a half smile.

"I'm glad I amuse you," I said.

I leaned forward and stroked his hair—soft, fine hair, always pleasant to the touch. His hair was now moist with the sweat of his fever.

"Elysium must be very restful. I can understand if it exerts a pull. But, beloved, you must resist." I kissed his forehead. "I forbid you to die, Tavius."

He made no sound.

"Listen to me, beloved," I said. "Your will is different, stronger than that of an ordinary man. An ordinary man does not seize an empire. You are not ordinary, and you do not have an ordinary will."

He did not show any sign he was aware of me. But I somehow knew he was. With his eyes closed, he was listening as a tired child might to a story told to send him to sleep.

"You must exert that will now, Tavius. Fight. I know what you are capable of. Fight and you will win."

His eyelids fluttered. He tried to speak, but it took too much effort.

"I don't understand," I said.

He said something else. I made out the word *sleep*.

"Of course," I said. "You need sleep. I'll sit here and watch by your side, and I'll be here when you wake up. Go to sleep now."

I did not let go of his hand.

Silently, I prayed to Diana, my patron deity, and to Apollo, whom Tavius venerated before all other gods. I prayed to them to spare him for Rome's sake and for mine.

As the night wore on, I continued to sit beside him, immobile. I had had little rest myself these last few days, and my body ached with fatigue. It did not matter.

Two small oil lamps illuminated the room. I would glance at them sometimes, watch the flames dance, but always my eyes returned to Tavius.

His face was relaxed. The sleep was a deep one. But I felt that inside himself, he was waging a mighty battle. Once he told me if there were a great shipwreck and only two people survived, the two would be us. We were determined survivors. He said the sea would not drown us. But I knew the sea was mightier even than Caesar Augustus, certainly mightier than me. We were adrift on a great sea now.

All night long, I tried to reach him with my mind, to give him some of my health and strength. I told him again and again, *I forbid you to die.*

>>>>>>>

He seemed slightly better the next morning. Another day passed before he was strong enough to speak. "Can it be that I'm alive?"

When he struggled to sit up, I said, "No, don't tax your strength," and eased him back down. I did not realize I was weeping until I felt tears on my cheek.

"Agrippa will have to give the ring back," he said. "Life is a wonder, isn't it, Livia?"

"You are a wonder."

By then, Marcellus was already gravely ill. I kept the news from Tavius.

When the boy died, though, I had to tell him. By then he was strong enough to take the news.

For Tavius, this was like losing a son. He kept talking about how young Marcellus had been and shaking his head over how illogical it was that the boy had been taken when he himself was spared. It was the kind of loss that one never truly gets over; he would carry the pain of it for the rest of his life. His way of dealing with it was to keep a stern countenance and soldier on.

He insisted, though he was still weak, on speaking Marcellus's eulogy himself. And he talked about public buildings he would dedicate in his name. I doubt if any of that comforted Julia. She went through the funeral in silence, did a wife's duty, gathering the ashes and placing them in an urn. What I saw in her face was not just grief. Plainly, she blamed Tavius for not giving Marcellus his signet ring and, in some odd way, even thought that blow had played a part in his death.

I wished I could shake her, get her to understand that Tavius had no choice—that grim duty had compelled him to give Agrippa the ring. But I could only hope that her resentment would not fester and that she would get over it in time.

Cleopatra Selene

I think of the pestilence as a great wave that changed all in its
path, then swept out to sea again. One day it ceased to take
more victims, and we who had survived looked around at
the altered landscape. Our lives were irreparably changed. Marcellus
was gone; Julia was bereft of a husband and Augustus bereft of an
heir. Agrippa had emerged from his brief retirement—and though
he returned Augustus's signet ring, he had been lifted to even greater
prominence than he had had before, for all of Rome soon knew that
in a time of dire need, Augustus had dubbed him his successor.

And me—my life had been altered for good and all.

We had been reckless, Juba and I. Certainly our meetings had
been secret. I believe of the whole household only Julia suspected
we were lovers, and she told no one. But the fear of death—the fear
that the illness would rob us of all chance of love and happiness—
had overcome prudence. Whenever we could manage to steal off
together, we made love like starved creatures, as if nothing mattered
but those brief moments of joy. Only when my courses failed to

come at their expected time did I understand how far I had trespassed. I felt terror, not only for myself but for Juba.

It was a grave matter. I would bring into the world the grandchild of Augustus's greatest enemies. Juba and I had formed an alliance of the flesh, behind Augustus and Livia's back. We two, children of the defeated, only lived at all by Augustus's sufferance. I expected to be punished, and I feared Juba would be punished too. And the child—the child of our love, the child I longed for—would it suffer the fate of unwanted, illegitimate infants, be left on some roadway, abandoned to the elements?

We were still staying at the villa. Augustus was recuperating from his illness. Juba continued to work on his book in the huge library—his presence welcome, the scholarly work an apt reason for staying. He was thrown into Augustus and Livia's company, and this only fostered trust. One day he came to me in the garden, deeply troubled. "Augustus has decided to send me to Mauretania."

"You mean, you are to be the king of that country?"

"Yes, king."

"That is wonderful." I forced out the words.

"Selene, how can I leave you?"

I had not told him yet that I was with child.

The thought came to me that perhaps he would be better off if I were dead, and my baby with me. Love for me could only be an encumbrance. It might keep Juba from his destiny.

"Do you wish to be my wife?"

"Of course I do."

"Then I'll ask Augustus for your hand. I will tell him I'll refuse the throne, without you."

"No! Don't do that. Where we see love, Augustus will see political alliance. The son of a dead rebel king, and Antony and Cleopatra's daughter . . . He will be suspicious the instant you suggest marrying me. Juba, you know this is true."

"But I can't go to Mauretania and leave you."

A wonderful gift had come to me—this fine man loved me. And I carried his child. I was so blessed . . . and so cursed.

I knew I had come to a fork in my life path, a moment that had been waiting for me all along. I did not want a half life. I wanted to be Juba's queen and bear our child in honor.

It will be life or death for me, I thought. *But if I face destruction, I will not bring Juba down with me.*

I said softly, "Sometimes the most direct road is not the best one. Often men do not know this, but it is something girls learn young. I don't want you to talk to Augustus. Please. Leave matters to me."

"But what do you intend to do?"

"I'll speak to Livia, and see if I can move her heart."

"You think she would help us?"

"Perhaps. If I approach her in the right way."

>>>>>>>

My mother had known the stakes, and she had gambled. When she lost, she paid the price never flinching. The price was her life, not her honor. So too my father. He fought for imperium and faced defeat as a great Roman general must, salvaging honor.

I was a daughter of the Egyptian royal house and a daughter of Rome. I was not made for a life of degradation. One throw of the dice, win or lose; that was better.

I told Livia I wished to speak to her alone about a matter of importance. She looked puzzled by this formal approach, but set a time. I dressed carefully for that appointment, as carefully as might a girl preparing for her bridal day. I had my hair becomingly arranged, and I wore a fine linen tunica and my best jewels. When

I looked at my face in the mirror, it was with a feeling of saying farewell.

I saw the shadow of my parents' faces in my own visage, my mother looking out from behind my eyes.

Live or die, I thought, and my heart pounded. I tied a small drawstring pouch to my belt, the kind women carried coins or cosmetics in. Among my possessions was a small, sharp dagger I used for such homely tasks as cutting thread. I examined it, decided it suited the task at hand. There was a metallic taste in my mouth I recognized. I slipped the dagger into the pouch on my belt and prayed my courage would not falter.

Livia

*I*t was early in the morning. I had yet to begin my day. I wondered what Selene wished to talk to me so urgently about and in private, but I had made time for her. I sat in a cushioned chair in the small room off my bedchamber, and when Selene arrived I told her to close the door and gestured for her to sit across from me. She, however, remained standing. "We are quite alone," I said. "Now what is this great matter you wish to discuss with me?" I spoke with a forced lightness. The tension in her face had put my nerves on edge.

She sank to her knees and stretched out her arms, grasped my knees in the attitude of a suppliant. "I am with child. Help me."

For a moment I was so startled I could not speak. "Who is the father?" I asked finally between my teeth.

"Prince Juba."

I took a breath. I had been terribly afraid she would say Augustus. "I love Juba. And he loves me."

In the aftermath of fear, I was furious. "Oh? How sweet. You little fool, couldn't you keep your legs together?"

Her face remained strangely calm. "Help me. You said you would be my friend. Now help me."

A memory came to me—my nineteen-year-old self, pregnant by the man I had been forced to marry, but wildly in love with Tavius, kneeling before my husband and begging his forgiveness, praying he would forgo vengeance and let me go. When we are young, we are passion's playthings.

"Help you how? Do you want a potion to rid you of the child? Anything that would work might just as easily kill you. Don't you know that?"

"I wish to bear the child. Juba has offered me marriage. I desire to be his wife more than I want anything else on this earth. Help me and I will be your loyal friend forever. I will take any oath."

I stared at her, feeling cold inside. Arrange a royal marriage for Antony and Cleopatra's daughter? What simpleton would do such a thing? The future threat such a marriage might pose to Tavius and me was palpable.

Selene read in my face denial of her plea. She gave a small nod, accepting my verdict. She let go of my knees, then said in a voice charged with urgency, "You understand Juba is not to blame. He did not force me. I offered myself, I tempted him. Such a thing is always the woman's fault, isn't it? And after all, I am Cleopatra's daughter." A faint, bitter smile flickered across her face. "If there is a price to be paid, it is right I alone should pay it." She reached into a small pouch that hung from her waist and took out a dagger.

I nearly cried in alarm when I saw it, thinking she meant to kill me. But her eyes met mine and she gave a little shake of her head, to reassure me.

"I will not bear my child in shame."

"This is not necessary," I said.

"But it is. If I cannot marry Juba, it is better that I die with honor as my mother and father did." She trembled a little, but her voice was clear and calm.

I have experienced only a few moments in my life when time slowed and seemed to creep. This was one of them. Still kneeling, Selene raised the knife in her right fist. It was a small dagger, the handle inlaid silver, the blade brightly gleaming. Selene no longer seemed aware of me, only of the knife. She gazed at it as if entranced.

She had just turned sixteen and was only coming into the beauty of young womanhood. Her skin was smooth and unmarked as that of a child.

Disjointed thoughts flitted through my mind. I thought of my father falling on his sword. I remembered finding my mother dead of poison. I recalled what I had been told of Mark Antony's botched suicide and long dying, of Cleopatra holding out her wrist to be bitten by a poisonous snake.

This is how we leave the world when we are defeated—we who have walked on the stage of history. In pride, by our own will, and by our own hand, we go.

I had never seen the act performed before. But I had imagined many times how it would be.

The moment was brief but endless. I had time for all these thoughts, time to feel horror. I knew by the resolve in Selene's expression that this was no ruse. She had come fully prepared to end her life if I would not help her.

Parting her lips, she took a deep breath. Then she touched the dagger to the side of her neck. I saw a tiny drop of blood as she began the slashing movement across her throat, and at that same instant, I cried, "No!" I hit out with all my strength and struck the dagger from Selene's hand.

I pulled her into my arms. She did not weep, but I did. I wept for my parents. I wept for all the terrible choices, all the pain that had touched my life. I held the girl as a mother holds a beloved child. She had conquered me. She had taken a great gamble, but she had won.

Somehow I would persuade Tavius to give her to Juba as his wife.

The girl had won. But I would set the terms of her victory.

She had put her dagger away. I had cleaned and put balm on the bloody scratch on her neck, and she had rearranged her hair so the mark did not show. She sat in a chair, still shaking a little, understandably. She had come very close to death.

I had one of my maids bring her a cup of wine mixed with water. Selene drank, and gradually her trembling stopped. I dismissed the maid, and when Selene and I were alone, I said, "Swear loyalty to me and to Rome. Swear by your mother's Egyptian gods that if you are allowed to marry Juba, I will have your lifelong fidelity."

Selene nodded, as if she had expected this. Indeed she came prepared with a great and terrible oath. "I swear by Osiris and by Horus that if I become Juba's wife, I will be bound always to you and Rome in loyalty. If I break my oath, may I be struck blind and deaf. May eternal misery be my portion. May I die in agony and burn in everlasting fire."

She spoke gravely. But would the oath bind her? Can we be sure of another person—or even truly sure of ourselves? We can only guess, and hope.

Tavius was still weak from the sickness's aftereffects. Beyond that, he was deep in grief. He grieved for Marcellus, whom he had loved almost as a son. He felt pain for Julia, who was so withdrawn in her mourning that she barely answered when she was addressed. He did not speak to me of his daughter's future—but I knew him well enough to understand where his thoughts must be tending. Those thoughts only added to his woes. He already foresaw that he could not do what was right for Rome and at the same time secure her happiness.

To make matters worse, Octavia, his beloved sister, had been utterly shattered by her son's death. This was beyond grief. She spoke only of the son she had lost, saying again and again he had carried burdens too great for one of his years. She looked at Tavius with stony eyes, as if he were her son's killer.

I felt true guilt at the prospect of harrying Tavius further at such a time, seeking his approval of Selene's marriage to Juba. But the situation would brook no delay. So I chose a quiet evening when my husband was in his study alone and sat down across from his writing table. "Tell me, beloved, why did you decide to give the crown of Mauretania to Juba?"

"Are you objecting to that? If you were against it, you should have said so before."

"I am not objecting. I just wondered about your reasons."

"He'll make an able administrator. And the people of Mauretania will respect him because of his royal birth. His ancestral ties in North Africa will help keep the region stable."

"You don't think he would rise in rebellion?"

"His loyalty to me was twice proven in war. He is not the kind to break faith."

I nodded. "I think he and Selene have similar qualities. She is not lacking in honor. And you like her, don't you, beloved? It seems to me you have shown that you do."

His expression turned wary. "What exactly are we discussing?"

"Juba has gotten her with child. And they would like to marry."

He stared at me. "Gods above . . . he dared touch that girl? He dared?"

I had anticipated Tavius's anger, for after all, Juba had meddled with a young woman under his protection. To soothe him, I launched into a virtual ode to young love. I reminded him of how it was to be young and passionate, spoke of our own early days. Then I restated his good reasons for making Juba a king, which still applied. I told him of the fearsome oath of loyalty that Selene had willingly taken.

I said, "Sometimes kindness is weakness in a ruler. One must be pitiless, in certain situations, for the sake of a greater good. I realize this. Still, I would rather you err toward kindness in this case. I like to believe the gods reward mercy."

"I know you do. All evidence to the contrary."

It was an old argument with us. We were both silent for a few moments. Then I said, "You can lavish Juba and Selene with kindness and, with any luck, secure their friendship. Or else . . . well, if Juba loves the girl half as much as she loves him, he will never forget that we deprived him of her. He may well become our enemy. In view of that, instead of giving him a crown, you'd better execute him now and let Selene take her own life. That is the safest thing to do . . . if you are so enamored of safety."

Tavius frowned. "I am not enamored of safety. What I am is prudent."

"Of course," I said.

Cleopatra Selene

I felt strange, different, as if I had already died and this was the afterlife. I carried out my daily tasks—studied with my tutor, spun wool—and yet it was as if I were gazing through a veil at ordinary existence.

Livia had said she would be my advocate with Augustus. She by no means promised that she would be successful in obtaining his permission for Juba and me to marry. My fear was that Augustus would see Juba and me not as erring lovers—though that might in itself enrage him—but as allies dangerous to Rome. He had thought my half brothers constituted a danger, at sixteen and seventeen, and executed them both. They had done nothing to earn his wrath but be who they were. But Juba and I—we had done something, hadn't we? Something he might be unwilling to forgive?

I had not told Juba yet that I was with child, or spoken of my conversation with Livia. Sometimes I thought of urging him to run away, telling him that I was pregnant and he was in danger. But I knew in my heart he would not run.

I prayed that even if Augustus put me to death, he would spare Juba.

In the morning, three days after my talk with Livia, Augustus summoned me. My heart hammering, I went into the chamber, off the atrium, where he sometimes held audiences with public officials. He sat in an ornate chair that looked almost like a throne. Behind him was a huge, vividly colored wall mural, showing battle scenes from the siege of Troy. Livia sat beside him. Another person was in the room—Juba, who stood like one accused before his judges. He shot me a look full of apprehension—apprehension and yet also a kind of helpless tenderness. I was certain he had been informed of my pregnancy.

Augustus showed me none of his usual punctilious courtesy. He did not rise when I entered. Nor did he invite me to sit. He probed me with piercing blue eyes and said, "You are with child by Juba, is that correct?"

"Yes," I said.

Augustus nodded toward Juba. "He didn't know."

"I did not tell him."

If Augustus wanted an explanation of this, he did not ask for it. "You two had better marry, then." Augustus glanced at Juba. "You agree?"

"Yes . . . ," Juba said. He sounded at first almost stunned by Augustus's words. Then he added strongly, "Yes, Augustus. I want Selene as my wife."

I looked at Livia. Her face was impassive. I searched in vain for some sign from her that Augustus would truly allow us to marry. I had a terrible fear that we were being played with, that this might be all a cruel hoax.

Then Augustus said, "I will give you the same dowry I would if you were my own daughter."

I groped for words. "You are beyond generous . . ."

He nodded, as if agreeing with my assessment of his generosity. "Juba will come to you king of Mauretania. You will be a queen. Rome must rule Egypt directly—that is strategically necessary. I am afraid you must give up all thought of your mother's throne. Will you surrender all claim to Egypt and accept Mauretania?"

Any claim I had to Egypt was shadow and air, for I had no means to enforce it. I was giving up nothing. I had been given the greatest gift in the world—life with the man I loved. My heart soared. "Yes." I blurted out the word.

Augustus smiled. I think at that moment I amused him. "Then it's settled." Without another word, he got up and left the room.

Livia remained seated. Her eyes went from Juba's face to mine. "You are happy? Both of you?"

We agreed that indeed we were happy.

"Good," she said. "Let me tell you something that perhaps comes better from me than from Augustus. He gives you these gifts in friendship. Juba, the kingdom you will rule is somewhat less than the territory your father held. Still you will be a king. Selene, Mauretania is not Egypt, but you will be a queen. And Augustus is bestowing great riches on you besides. You will have a grand dowry."

"They are great gifts," Juba said.

"Be satisfied with them, then," she said. "It is important in this world to know what is possible and what is not. Take my advice. Do not look for more than what has been given to you. If you take Augustus's gifts and show yourselves ungrateful . . . well, he would never forgive that."

"You don't have to say this. I understand." Juba spoke with an edge in his voice.

"I'm glad you do. But let me repeat myself." She looked at me, her eyes seeming to bore into my soul. "He would never forgive that. And neither would I."

>>>>>>>

And so we were betrothed, and given every inducement to keep faithful to Augustus, faithful to Rome. My good fortune almost frightened me—as if it might turn to dust in my hand. And yet it was real.

"I feel an enormous debt to Livia," I told Juba. "I could never break my oath to her."

"We will be loyal," he said gravely. "Not out of fear but because it is right."

At the dinner celebrating the betrothal, my brother Jullus sat on the edge of my dining couch, leaning close so we could speak privately. "The goddess Fortuna has blessed you, little moon."

"Come to Mauretania with us," I said.

"It would be wonderful not to be parted from you. But what life could there be for me there?"

"Juba and I have discussed it. There would be a place for you, I promise. A place of influence and importance."

"Yes, every king and queen need a poor relative as a hanger-on. I'm sure it would be pleasant, and I'm almost lazy enough to take you up on your offer, but, sweet Sister, my life is here in Rome."

"What sort of life can you have under Augustus's rule?" I spoke in a whisper. "You are Mark Antony's son."

"Before long, Selene, I may give you precisely the kind of pleasant surprise that you have given me."

"You are speaking of marriage?"

"An advantageous marriage," Jullus said. He went on soberly, "I'm not unambitious, you know. Far from it."

"Is your intended a Roman?"

He laughed. "I would say so."

"Who?"

"You promise not to tell?"

I nodded.

He whispered, "Marcella." I must have gaped at him, because he grinned and said, "Oh, Selene, does it seem as unlikely as that that she would have me? Augustus's niece and Mark Antony's son—don't you think that will make a delightful combination? I do."

"Jullus, she is married to Agrippa."

"There's a divorce and remarriage in store for Agrippa, I strongly suspect."

I let that pass without probing. "You don't like Marcella," I whispered.

"But she likes me."

If she did, it was no wonder. Jullus was taller than most men by half a head, had a strong, handsome face, arresting hazel eyes, and curly black hair. And he had another quality, hard to define yet palpable. People still spoke of our father's raw magnetism. Jullus had inherited it.

I thought of how unpleasant a person Marcella was, how selfish and haughty. "You truly wish to marry her?"

"Oh, she's not bad-looking. I'll be able to do my duty by her. And don't you see, I'll be a member of Augustus's own family. You've found a place in this world. Don't grudge me one."

"I grudge you nothing. You're too good for her."

In the future, I knew, my brother and I would see each other only on rare visits, spaced out over the years. An ambitious young man, his life in Rome would be full of pitfalls. No one, least of all Augustus, would ever truly forget he was Mark Antony's son. And if he married Marcella . . . ? She would bring him advancement, but at what personal cost?

I loved my only remaining brother. He had always done his best to protect me. Now it was I who wished to protect him. "Jullus, think again," I said. "You are my kin. It is only right that you have a share in my happiness. Please, come to Mauretania with Juba and me."

He shook his head. "Little moon, I'm a Roman."

My wedding day was not as grand an occasion as it might have been if the family of Augustus had not been mourning Marcellus. I had been grafted on, made a member of that family. How strange it was that Augustus of all men, who had been my father's deadly foe, should act in his stead and give me away in marriage. But he did— he was the benign paternal figure presiding over the celebration.

He placed my hand in Juba's. The guests all cried, *"Feliciter!"*

I saw Julia in the crowd, dressed in mourning white. Her face was empty and bleak. What must she be feeling now, looking at me, a happy bride, when her own husband lay newly dead? Did she feel, as I did, that for this moment at least our fortunes had reversed themselves? She had always been the soaring lark and I the fearful wren who kept close to the ground. I did not wish her ill; I would have brought back Marcellus if I could. Yet I could not help but take note of the moment—this moment when she had cause to envy my good fortune.

Beside her, also in mourning garb, stood Marcellus's mother, Octavia, who had played a part in my rearing. Today, not she but Livia had helped me don my bridal finery. Octavia could never muster warm feeling for me, though, to her credit, I think she tried. Beside her, solicitous as a good son, was my brother Jullus, whom she had raised almost from infancy. Him, at least, she had come to love. He smiled broadly when I caught his eye. He delighted in my happiness. Nearby I noticed Marcella and Agrippa, neither of them looking in a festive mood.

The seeds of the future were here, though no mortal could say how they would sprout. The past too was almost close enough to touch. I wondered if my father and mother somehow knew of my marriage. If they did, I hoped they were pleased. *Live,* my mother had commanded me. In my womb, I carried Mark Antony and Cleopatra's grandchild. *Yes,* I told Mother silently, *my babe and I will live.*

As we received the guests' congratulations, I looked up at Juba and I saw a hint of wonder in his eyes. Truly, it was cause for amazement that we should stand before this company hand in hand, king and queen, man and wife.

Julia

*I*t was perfectly obvious I must marry again and to a man of Father's choice, a man he would choose with politics in mind. If I had let myself dwell on the question of whom my next husband would likely be, surely I'd have been able to make a good guess. But there are times when the mind protects itself. Already dazed with pain, I avoided thinking of the future.

I had seen death in the arena and I had been in close proximity to death when the pestilence carried away servants and acquaintances. But no one I loved had ever died before. Losing my husband devastated me. It seemed so strange that people, even people who had professed to love Marcellus, could carry on with their lives. People such as my father. He gave Marcellus a grand funeral and pronounced a noble eulogy. A few months later, he joined in the somewhat circumscribed festivities for Selene's marriage; and if he still grieved, he hid it well.

I noticed Selene casting somber looks at me during the wedding feast. I think she was one of the few people present who sensed what

I felt on that occasion, who knew that I could not forget my own wedding to Marcellus and the hopes we had had on our marriage day. Perhaps the pain she had borne in her own young life enabled her to understand me. Maybe friendship could have grown out of that understanding, if she had stayed in Rome. But in just a few days, she left Rome with her glowing bridegroom to take charge of the kingdom Father had given them to rule.

When Juba and Selene said their farewells, I saw their delight in each other—and Selene seemed transformed. She stood before us, queen of Mauretania, dressed not as a Roman wife but in a long blue robe, trimmed with pearls. A gift, I heard, from Mauretanians living in Rome—a gift to their new queen. It suited her. Taking leave of us, she embraced my father and Livia in turn. She hugged me too. She wore some exotic perfume I couldn't place—a scent I imagined her mother might have worn. She did not have on much makeup, just enough to bring out her eyes. But for the first time, she made me think of paintings I had seen of Egyptian queens of long ago.

"I wish you happiness," I said.

"I wish the same to you."

Then Selene and her bridegroom were gone. Off to a life that held every prospect of joy.

>>>>>>>

I continued to live in my aunt Octavia's household after Marcellus's death. It was a bleak, cheerless place for a young woman of my age. Octavia's three unmarried daughters kept sober miens and did their best never to trouble their mother, for her sadness permeated our home. The servants had taken to speaking only in low, grave voices. My aunt would sit in a chair and simply stare at a wall for hours on end. I would sometimes sit beside her, hoping my closeness would comfort her.

"You are a good girl, Julia," she said to me once. "You truly loved my boy."

Generally, she spoke very little.

I think it was out of affection for me that she agreed to attend a poetry reading at my father's house. Poetry was one of the few things that still gave me pleasure after losing Marcellus. Octavia had always been fond of poetry too.

My father's friend Maecenas was Rome's most notable patron of the arts. He would bring artists and poets he favored to Father's attention. Often poets gave readings in Father's atrium, before select groups of his friends.

On this occasion, a poet named Virgil was to read. We all had heard he was working on a great epic poem that some hoped would equal the *Iliad*. His literary gifts were far beyond the ordinary. Some people called him the Roman Homer.

The grand epic was by no means finished, but Virgil proposed to read a short selection from it. I thought—foolishly—that listening to soaring poetry would distract Aunt Octavia from her pain.

Father, Livia, Maecenas, and several dozen guests attended the reading. "I'm so glad you have come," Father said to my aunt when he greeted her. She gave him a cool look, and a troubled expression flickered over his face. He quickly turned to introduce us to the poet, a ginger-haired man with a bland, forgettable face.

My aunt and I were ushered to seats beside Father and Livia. An anticipatory buzz rose from the crowd. Then without preamble, Virgil began to read from a long parchment scroll he held in his hand.

He kept his eyes averted from the audience, and he never gestured as some poets do. He had a flat, unimpressive voice. Despite this, I knew I was in the presence of greatness. His words transported us all to another time, another land.

The hero of Virgil's poem, Aeneas, a Trojan warrior, was said to be the forebear of us Romans. In the poem, he journeyed to the underworld to meet Romans that in his time were yet to be born. He saw famous generals like the two Scipios and great political leaders like the Gracchi passing by in procession. I glanced at Father and saw his eyes gleaming. Patriotic pride, Roman greatness—the stuff of Virgil's poem was meat and drink to him.

We viewed the grand panorama of Roman history. The poet lauded Father and Julius Caesar—how could he not, being here to curry favor? But he also referred to the cruelty of the late civil wars, even ventured to reproach those who had fought fellow Romans. This required no great courage. Father always allowed citizens to speak their minds in his presence.

What came next, however, jarred us all. Certainly it jarred me to the soul. The poet referred to a young man, standing out among those awaiting birth and god-given destinies:

*"The Fates will only show him to the world, not allow him
to stay long . . ."*

I felt a prickle along the back of my neck. Virgil went on in a low, mournful voice.

*"No boy of the line of Ilius shall so exalt his Latin
ancestors by his show of promise, nor will Romulus's
land ever take more pride in one of its sons.
Alas for virtue . . ."*

I knew he spoke of Marcellus. It was less a tribute to who he had been than who he might have become in time. And that only made it more heartbreaking.

"Ah, boy to be pitied . . . Marcellus! Give me handfuls of white lilies, let me scatter radiant flowers . . ."

Next to me, Aunt Octavia gave a wordless cry. She half rose from her chair, and then she fell forward. Then she lay on the floor, unmoving. The poet had fallen silent; we were all silent. Father went to his sister, knelt, and propped her up in his arms while we of the family crowded round. I saw that her eyes were shut and for a moment wondered if she had died.

"Sister . . . Sister . . . ," Father murmured.

She opened her eyes and looked at him, the most terrible expression of loathing on her face.

≫≫≫≫≫

No one blamed Virgil. He had expressed what the Roman people felt about Marcellus's death. They mourned a shining figure they had seen from a distance, they mourned the leader he might have become. But his mother and I—we mourned the flesh and blood young man.

My aunt had suffered many blows in her life and carried on bravely. She struggled to avert civil war between my father and Mark Antony by maintaining a shell of a marriage. She saw her hopes collapse and never wept publicly for Antony, whom I had always believed was the only man she ever loved. Our entire family looked to her for steady good sense. I have never understood why listening to Virgil rhapsodize about Marcellus in deathless poetry destroyed my aunt.

Father recoiled visibly at the awful look she gave him. Maidservants carried her to a nearby couch. Father summoned a physician who said she had suffered an emotional shock and made light of it. She was unable to walk, however, and was transported home in a sedan chair. We put her to bed in her own bedchamber. She clutched at my hand and would not let me leave.

"You mourn my poor boy truly, don't you?" she said. "But your father—I saw him shed tears at the funeral, but I tell you he wept for an implement, snatched out of his hand. Not for my son, his goodness, his sweetness. We should scatter handfuls of white lilies, just as the poet said. That good, dear boy . . ."

"Oh, Aunt, put that poem out of your mind," I said.

"Marcellus was young and strong. He might have gotten sick, but he would have recovered—he would never have died if your father had not driven him so mercilessly. Harried and pushed him, and never let him enjoy a moment of his youth."

"How can we know what caused Marcellus's death?"

"I am his mother and I know. I know! I know!"

All my life my aunt had been mild, dutiful, and restrained. This was another woman.

Her face softened. "But you were a good wife. You aren't hard like your father is. Marcellus was not a nephew to him, only a tool to be used. As I was, when he had me wed Mark Antony. As you are—not a daughter but a tool. Understand who and what your father is."

I told myself Aunt Octavia would not have spoken so if she had not been so gripped by grief and misery. And yet she was saying things I already partly believed. I could not forget how Father had given his signet ring to Agrippa, and what that had done to Marcellus. To Marcellus and me.

My aunt never spoke to me again in this fashion. All the strength seemed to go out of her after that night. She attended no more poetry readings, at Father's house or elsewhere. From that time on, she was a housebound invalid.

Livia

We sat in a little alcove that looked out at the gardens, Tavius, Maecenas, and I. The garden was not such a pretty sight as it had been only a month before. Many of the flowers had withered; the air had a chill in it.

We—Tavius and I—had invited Maecenas to Prima Porta ostensibly for a brief, pleasant holiday. In truth, we wanted his services as an advisor and sounding board.

Our friend Maecenas was a paradoxical man. He was first of all a lover of poetry and of art, and here his taste was unerring. He was plump and unimpressive-looking but always wore clothing of the finest wool or linen, and I never saw him in need of a haircut or a shave. His high voice sounded womanish, and he had soft white hands like a well-bred woman's, the nails always carefully manicured. He had been very kind to me when I was young and unsure, and I did not forget it. But he had another quality that seemed not to go with the rest of him—a mind that could cut through iron bars. I would not call Maecenas ruthless, but he could look at the worst without blinking, and if he trusted you, he would tell you exactly what he thought. It was this latter quality that Tavius most prized in him.

Tavius began to talk about Agrippa and how the army loved him. He told Maecenas that it had somehow or other become generally known that when Tavius thought he was about to die he had dubbed Agrippa his successor.

"It seems the army, as a whole, warmly approved my choice," Tavius said, a touch of asperity in his voice. "In fact, a good number are mourning the fact that I rose from my sickbed. They love me dearly, so dearly they'd like me in Elysium, and Agrippa leading them on earth."

Maecenas nodded as if he knew all this.

"Now Agrippa is loyal, absolutely loyal," Tavius said. "But still—I think he is being nudged, pushed in a dangerous direction—he has ambitious friends who say he has not gotten his just rewards from me. I gave him my niece Marcella—that has turned out not to be much of a gift. There's a tension between Agrippa and me now, and I don't like it."

"The simple solution would be to sweeten Agrippa by letting him divorce Marcella and marry Julia," I said. "In effect, confirming him as Tavius's heir. But I think remarriage is far from Julia's thoughts and may be for some time. And I do not believe this marriage would be at all to her liking."

Suggest another way, I almost said. Suggest some agreeable young man we can marry Julia to who won't vie for power. Suggest how we are to keep Agrippa content and the army content without giving him Julia. I felt for the girl, so young, so recently bereaved. I did not think Julia would be happy with Agrippa, a reserved and phlegmatic much older man.

Maecenas smiled at me. "My dearest Livia, you are looking at me as if you expect me to pluck pearls from the heavens . . . or perhaps levitate."

"Yes," I said. "A miracle would go over very well with me just now."

He shook his head. "I don't believe in miracles. In my view, we are all subject to natural law and stuck on this hard, obdurate earth." He looked at Tavius. "Surely you know how I'm going to advise you."

"Say it," Tavius said.

"It seems to me you must either marry Agrippa to your daughter, as befits your heir, or else you must kill him."

Tavius drew in a harsh breath. "Kill the darling of the army? Oh, please, why even talk about my doing that? I could no more bring myself to kill him than I could to kill you."

Maecenas smiled faintly. "I personally have always thought that was a splendid quality of yours—not going in for killing your old friends."

We had wine served. Maecenas raised his goblet and, looking at Tavius, spoke as though tentatively proposing a toast. "May Julia give Agrippa a fine brace of sons?"

"May it be so," I said.

Finally, Tavius echoed, "May it be so."

Tavius was not cruel or indifferent to his daughter's happiness. He sipped that wine with all the pleasure he would have taken in downing a cup of poison.

I prayed for Tavius to live many more years. And then for the best eventuality, Rome's best hope given our world's imperfections—for him to leave a sturdy grandson, son of Julia and Agrippa, ready to step forward to succeed him.

Julia

On a day in summer a little more than a year after Marcellus's death I was summoned into my father's study. Livia was present.

"There is something I must tell you," Father said.

I felt an odd chill. I sat down on one of the couches, near where Livia sat.

"It is important that you marry soon," Father said.

"I am still mourning Marcellus," I said. "I don't think I am ready to marry yet."

"There are burdens that come with being my daughter."

"I just want time, Father."

"I'm afraid it's out of the question."

"Then who . . . who is to be my husband?"

"The only man who could carry on in my place if I were gone—Agrippa."

I stared at Father, and then said stupidly, "But he is married. He is married to Marcella."

"They will divorce."

"But Father . . . he has been like an uncle to me, all my life. He gave me away at my wedding. I could never love Agrippa as I loved Marcellus. I could never . . ."

"It is what Rome requires of you."

I felt as if I were drowning. "After Marcellus, after all we were to each other . . ."

"Marcellus is dead," Father said.

I turned to Livia. Why was she here? Why could Father and I not at least have this conversation alone? She was no ally to me; she was present to bolster Father's resolve, that was plain. Still, I tried to reach her, to speak to her as one woman to another. "You must understand. You married the man you love. I will never feel any love for Agrippa. Never."

She said in a low voice, "This can't be helped."

"The marriage is necessary. That is all," Father said.

"That is all?" I don't think I ever dared to be truly angry at my father until that moment. I felt heat rising from the core of my being and struggled to modulate my voice. "Father, don't you understand? I will never be happy if I marry Agrippa. I will be unhappy my whole life. Don't you love me?"

He flushed. "You are my only child. Of course I love you!"

I heard my aunt saying that I was a tool to my father, no more than a tool.

It was shocking to me that Father demanded I wed Agrippa, shocking the way a betrayal is shocking, a terrible betrayal by the person one has always loved and trusted.

I had grown up knowing I would marry Marcellus. I had accepted it, not truly understanding what marriage was. Since then, I had learned about passion and about the meaning of love. In light of that, marriage to a man I could never love seemed a horror. I knew of course that fathers were always marrying off their daughters to suit their convenience, with little thought at all of the daughter's happiness. But somehow I felt I was different. I was Father's only child. I was special to him. I had never imagined him forcing me into an unwanted second marriage after Marcellus died. Even after he named Agrippa and not my husband, Marcellus, as his successor, I somehow harbored the belief that we stood apart from other fathers and daughters.

Despite all that, I should have expected exactly what took place. For I was not ignorant. What I knew of political events, what I knew of the lives of other women, most fundamentally, what I knew about my father—all that should have prepared me for this moment. And yet I was not prepared.

"Agrippa is a good man," Father said. "He will protect you, always. You will come to care for him. Believe me, my child, this is for the best. You will be content with him in time."

"Father, please, don't make me do this. Please. Please. If you care for me at all . . ."

He said nothing. His expression was obdurate.

"It is as if you are condemning me to death."

"In the name of all the gods, Julia!" Suddenly, he was shouting. "I must do my duty and so must you. It's time for you to grow up. Stop being a child!"

I felt an awful emptiness. I always had believed until that moment Father loved me.

A year before I had been bereft of a husband. Now I was bereft of a father also. The difference was I had had Marcellus for a time. I felt now that my loving father had never existed.

I thought of Iphigenia being sacrificed on an altar by her father, Agamemnon. Had she once imagined she had her father's love?

When she was forced down on the altar, did she hate him? Did she hate him the more because she had been a fool?

"Julia, if I were a poor man, I might hand you to some sweaty peasant and you would have to accept him and hope he could manage to feed you and the children you would bear. That is life as most people live it. All your life I have showered you with every good thing, and you will marry the greatest man in Rome after myself. And you feel misused?"

"You married for love, Father."

"I could afford to," he said, his voice ice-cold.

"I will never be happy with Agrippa. All my life. All my life, Father."

"If you've made up your mind to be unhappy, then you will be," Father said. "But you will marry him."

>>>>>>>

Was I selfish? Was I a young fool? Was I a bad daughter to rage inside myself at my father as I did?

I think if I had not seen Livia sitting there beside him, if I did not know that to be together they had flouted all convention, shed two spouses, scandalized all of Rome, I might have acquiesced more easily to Father's will.

What mattered more in life than a loving marriage? Father had shown me by the way he lived that nothing mattered more. He would have walked through flames to be with Livia. He would have waged wars. He would have battled the gods themselves. So I believed, and I do not think I was in error.

But he condemned me to a loveless desert when he insisted I marry Agrippa.

Livia

*P*erhaps if I had been Julia's mother, I would have wept for her when she was compelled to marry Agrippa. Or perhaps not. The person to whom my sympathies naturally flowed was Tavius. Tavius, whose actions were constrained by laws of iron necessity. He was not a sculptor chiseling stone. As First Citizen, he dealt with human beings, all of whom had their own aspirations and desires.

One must face reality as it is, not as one would wish it to be. There are human feelings, and there are the necessities of state. Sometimes they war with each other. How easy it would be to govern an empire if one did not have to somehow accommodate the disparate passions of human beings.

Agrippa had to be designated Tavius's heir in order to keep Rome whole. Therefore it was necessary for him to marry Tavius's daughter. I think Tavius was more upset by his daughter's misery than he let show. But if Julia had a just complaint, it seemed she ought to bring it not to her father but to the gods.

When I was a girl, my father betrothed me to Tiberius Nero. He thought it necessary in order to bind him close to the Republican cause. I had not liked the man Father chose for me. But I obediently went through with the marriage. I bore Tiberius Nero two sons. And then I escaped—only after the Republican cause was rubble, my father was dead, and the marriage served no political purpose. Tavius and I married when we could do it without bringing disaster on ourselves and the people to whom we were bound in loyalty.

I understood what a hard blow had been dealt to Julia; I understood it in the depths of my soul. And yet . . . I had suffered what I had to, and I thought she must do the same.

When Tavius contemplated marrying Julia to Agrippa, he had to give thought to another individual—his niece Marcella, Agrippa's current wife. The fact that she and Agrippa had no affection for each other smoothed his path. But Tavius worried about how his sister, Marcella's mother, would take the divorce. Octavia was still in deep mourning for her son—so deep that she was unwell, and distant and hostile in her dealings with Tavius and me.

As we anticipated, Marcella did not try to cling to her marriage to Agrippa. The surprise was that she had chosen another husband for herself.

She appeared at our house one day and demanded to see Tavius. Indeed she stalked into his study while he and I were alone talking about important matters. Tavius's sputtering secretary was unable to keep her out.

"Please, please, dear Uncle Tavius," she begged. "Please let me marry Jullus Antony!"

Tavius stared at her as if she were out of her mind.

"He is a wonderful young man, and he wants to be of service to you. Oh, Uncle—"

"He is Mark Antony's son," Tavius said flatly.

"Oh, but he has been raised in the bosom of our family!" Marcella cried. "He has worshipped you since he was a little boy . . . as I do, Uncle. As I do!"

I doubted that Marcella worshipped anyone at all, except the image she saw in her mirror. As for Jullus, he was an intelligent, charming young man who had every reason to be grateful to Tavius—but his father had been Tavius's worst enemy.

I don't think Tavius would have seriously considered marrying Marcella to Jullus, except that Octavia wanted the two wed. She had raised Jullus. With Marcellus gone, he stood in the place of a son to her. She dreamed of seeing her daughter Marcella and Jullus bound together in a loving marriage. She made her feelings clear not by speaking to Tavius personally but by dispatching a letter. I did not see this missive. Tavius refused to show it to me. He was white-faced after he read it.

"She is not well," he said. "She could not have written to me in such terms if she were herself."

"She is struggling with terrible grief," I agreed. "You must not take what she says now too seriously."

I had had different feelings toward Octavia at different times in our long acquaintance. She had disapproved of my marriage to Tavius, and I had thought her prim and overly moralistic. Then when she fought so valiantly to preserve her doomed marriage to Mark Antony, because a rupture meant civil war, I came to admire her. For some years, we were fast friends, but the fundamental differences in our approaches to life remained. Now—seeing the ravaged look on Tavius's face—I felt anger. He had an abiding love and reverence for his sister, and she was one of the few people on earth who could wound him in a personal way. She hurt him, and I did not easily forgive that.

In any case, he allowed Jullus and Marcella to marry. He acted against his better judgment, purely to soothe his sister at a time when she was half mad with grief.

The past lives in us, and blood is blood. We cannot escape, though we may wish to. Jullus was Mark Antony's son. Tavius had caused the death of his father and executed his elder brother.

My husband himself had not rested until every one of the men responsible for the assassination of his adoptive father, Julius Caesar, was put to death. It was a question of honor.

Could Jullus truly brush the past aside?

It is expected that we exact blood vengeance for the slaying of our kin. This fact had accounted for some of my wariness toward Selene. But the duty to avenge falls much more heavily on a son than on a daughter. Looked at in these terms, was not Jullus a greater threat than his sister?

The young man had been a member of our family from his earliest years—he had not set eyes on his father, Mark Antony, since he was a little boy. For that reason, I rarely thought of him with suspicion. Now, however, I suddenly saw what it would mean if he married Marcella, and I recoiled.

"He will be your nephew by marriage," I said to Tavius one night, shortly before the wedding. "He will expect to be treated as such. He will probably want high office."

The oil lamp that illuminated our bedchamber left half Tavius's face in darkness. "He is a capable young man."

"So you will trust him?"

"Only so far."

"There will be a line to tread with him. To keep him close and yet not leave yourself exposed to betrayal."

"Don't you think I realize that?" Tavius said.

Despite his lingering doubts, soon after her divorce, he gave his niece in marriage to Jullus. He made lavish gifts to the beaming pair.

He could have killed Jullus and Selene when they were small. I reminded the gods—I will go on forever reminding them—that he let them live. Surely that deserves recompense in the final accounting.

Caesar Augustus was a noble being. He spared them at the cost of great risk to himself. That should be remembered.

Julia

*I*n the eastern part of the empire at this time, a tiny vassal kingdom that bordered Parthia descended into chaos, while a king rose in Armenia who wished to throw off the Roman yoke. The Parthians' emperor encouraged this dissension, perhaps with aggressive intent. Therefore Father did not attend my wedding to Agrippa. He was off to the East.

Livia insisted on accompanying him on his journey. She wanted to guard Father's health; I think she also wished to make sure he did not take it in his head to personally lead any armies into battle should war break out. She brought along several highly skilled physicians and also many sealed jars of herbal remedies she brewed herself.

I had grieved when Father had been absent from my first wedding. This time it mattered little to me that Maecenas, his friend, gave me away in his stead. In fact, it seemed entirely fitting that Father was far from me in body as well as in spirit.

I still mourned Marcellus. But I had suffered another loss, more bitter than any clean grief. I felt a severance from the fount of my own being. It was almost as if Father had died, though of course he still lived.

I saw how little I mattered to him, except as a vessel for his dynastic hopes. I wished it were possible to obliterate that knowledge, but I never could.

There are wounds we do not recover from. I think I lost a piece of my soul at this time. I know I was desperately unhappy.

>>>>>>>

"Does it seem strange to you that we should be married?" I said those words to Agrippa on our wedding night.

The flower-decked bridal chamber was ablaze with candles. I saw a frown surface briefly on his face, then he shrugged. "Why would it be strange?"

"You've always been like a brother to my father. I remember you that way from the time I was tiny."

"We have no blood connection at all," Agrippa said.

We said almost nothing more that night. Was it possible that being married to Augustus's daughter had struck Agrippa dumb? People spoke of his brilliance as a strategist, his gift for commanding soldiers. He knew how to give orders in battle, but in our bedchamber, he lacked vocabulary.

He kissed me once and, after that, silently caressed me with his huge hands. His body was big, hard and muscular, the body of a strong forty-two-year-old man, thick but not fat, solid like an oak tree. He had a great hairy pelt of hair on his chest, though the hair on his head was thinning. Father had said Agrippa would take care of me. I did not doubt this. He would put his hard, strong body between me and any harm; he would consider this his duty. But would we ever come to know each other in any true sense?

He entered me like a ramrod. I did not feel pain, just a sense of invasion. And no desire at all, no hint of pleasure.

I suspected on our wedding night that all our times together would be like this. Agrippa would make use of my body regularly, at least until he got me with child. I must have a son for him, for my father, for Rome. What I felt did not matter to anybody. Nobody cared that inside myself, I was weeping.

I compared. I could not help comparing. I longed for Marcellus, his touch, his laughter. The music of our coming together. Instead, in his place, I had this taciturn soldier. There was no music to our lovemaking, no music and no joy.

As days passed, I noticed that when my new husband did address me, he was always careful to be polite. I told myself it was no fault of his that he grappled with words and did not know what to say to me. But he touched my body as if he owned it. His hands were calloused like a workman's, and sometimes when I felt his touch, I could not help remembering that he was descended from slaves.

Marcellus had been in some ways still a boy, so it was easy to excuse him when he was not as attentive as I would have wished him to be. We were both young and learning from each other. Agrippa was a mature man, and I was his third wife. I did not imagine myself transforming him into someone I could love.

>>>>>>>

After I had been married to Agrippa for three months, I became certain I had conceived. During my marriage to Marcellus, this would have elated me. Now I felt almost indifferent about the fact that I would bear my first child.

I entered the study, where Agrippa was reading military dispatches, and said, "I am with child."

He looked up at me, unsmiling. "That is good," he said.

He had no son, only one daughter, a meek little thing named Vipsania, who was betrothed to Livia's son Tiberius. Yet I saw no delight in his expression at the prospect of the coming child.

I thought, *He will be relieved when the baby comes, if it is a boy. Relieved as a man is when he has carried out his assigned task.*

I had heard that he and Vipsania's mother had been fond of each other. Not wildly in love, but fond enough that their marriage, arranged by Livia, had been viewed as a great success, and that when she died, he sincerely mourned her. He had next married Marcella, who made her distaste for him obvious to all—and now he had me as his wife. The sort of passion Catullus had written about—had Agrippa experienced it? Had he ever desired it? I could not imagine asking him and so had no way of knowing. But I felt a kind of sympathy for him. It was as if we had both been robbed.

Just days after I told him a child was on the way, he informed me that he was leaving to take charge of matters in Spain. There was constant trouble there, dissension among the tribes, and his guiding hand was needed. "Look after yourself and the child," he said to me in parting. I do not think he was sad to go.

>>>>>>>

For the first time, I was truly mistress of my own house. I was eighteen, young enough to take a pleasure in the feeling of independence this gave me. I could invite whomever I wished for dinner parties in my home, but at that time I had a narrow circle of friends—just people Father and my husband approved of. I did take the opportunity to invite Scribonia, my mother, to dine with me. She willingly accepted my invitations. "I have longed to be closer to you," she said to me one evening. "Now perhaps that will be possible."

I remembered, of course, her weeping at my wedding to Marcellus. I also recalled the many years of my childhood when she had rarely if ever visited me. "You felt it was impossible before?" I said.

"Do you think I wished to be in Livia's presence?" she said. "In any case, it was better not to intrude on your life when I could not truly be a mother to you."

"That's why you didn't come to see me?"

"I thought it best for your sake," she said.

"I thought—well, you have other children. I imagined they kept you busy." She had two sons and a daughter from two ill-fated early marriages.

She gave me a long, level look. "I did not forget you, Julia. Soon you will be a mother too, and you will see how impossible it is for a mother to forget a child."

Sadly, it was too late for us to develop the deepest natural bonds of mother and daughter. Likely that was my fault; I was not used to having a mother and never truly thought of Scribonia as a parent. Yet we did form a kind of friendship. I turned to Mother for advice on how to treat my thirteen-year-old stepdaughter, Vipsania. I found it rather odd to be charged with being a mother to a girl only five years younger than me. "Do not try to force a tie that is not there yet. Just be kind," Mother said. She gave me a small, wistful smile. I suppose she was following this very course of action with me.

The best I can say for myself as a stepmother is that I was never cruel to Vipsania. She was quiet and shy. Perhaps an older, more experienced woman would have known how to draw her out. As it was, we inhabited her father's stately mansion together. We shared meals. We passed each other in the corridors, and I would see her with her tutor or sitting for hours in the garden, doing the embroidery she enjoyed. I gave her presents sometimes. But my efforts to make a friend of her failed. That was rather sad, for this was a lonely time for me and, I suppose, with no mother and her father away, for Vipsania too.

>>>>>>>

I did find a friend at this time, under unlikely circumstances. I say unlikely because the boundaries between the mistress of a house and a slave are usually insurmountable. But that turned out not to be true when it came to me and Phoebe.

She was a young woman of about my age, and she had striking looks, black hair, finely arched brows over huge dark-brown eyes, a proud hawkish profile, and a tall, statuesque figure. She might have been a beauty except that she had a clubfoot and an awkward, lurching gait.

To me, in the earliest days of my marriage, she was just another of the maids in Agrippa's household. Then, one day, not long after Agrippa left for the East, she stumbled while bringing me a bowl of rose-scented water, with which it was my habit to wash before bed. The water mostly spilled on the floor tile, but a bit splashed me and my *ornatrix*, Becca, who stood behind me, brushing my hair.

"Oh, I am sorry, mistress," Phoebe said, dismay in her voice.

"What a pity Augustus's daughter must be served by a cripple," Becca said. "You should get rid of her, mistress."

Many noble households would not keep any servants who had obvious physical imperfections. Probably Phoebe knew this. Perhaps she feared being sold. I saw her face turn white. But she did not lower her eyes, did not allow herself to be shamed. The eyes she turned on Becca burned with defiance. She did not speak, though. It was I who spoke.

"Phoebe can't help her stumbling foot. But you can curb your spiteful tongue, Becca, and if you wish to serve me, you had better do it."

Phoebe looked at me then, in a way that warmed my heart. Not with humble gratitude, which I might have expected, but rather with respect.

Becca babbled apologies. I ignored her.

I made it a point to give Phoebe personal chores to do for me after that—and at times when Becca would see it. Phoebe would smile faintly. Oddly enough, she never tripped again, at least when she waited on me.

She had useful knowledge. When, due to my pregnancy, I was plagued by nausea in the mornings, she told me, "Women in my village boiled mint leaves in water. It helps with the sickness when you are with child, mistress."

I did not ask where her village was. I had learned it was better not to ask about the origins of slaves. The tale of enslavement was all one story—Roman soldiers arriving one day to enforce Roman order, the unequal battle, the dead men, the women and children carried off and sold. I never liked hearing this story, and slaves never liked telling it. It was enough to know about Phoebe that she was Greek, that she was utterly alone in the world, and that she was willing to offer me kindness along with loyalty.

The mint actually did help my nausea—certainly it worked better than anything my physician could suggest.

Phoebe became my personal maid and, in time, my friend.

I pictured at times the young woman I ought to be, one truly grateful for the life she had. For I knew that in many ways I was fortunate. I was rich and free, while many others were poor or enslaved. I was the First Citizen's daughter, married to his foremost general. Some women in my position would surely be happy. I tried to mold myself into the woman I imagined—a proper wife, a proper daughter—to act in the way it seemed all Rome expected me to act, even to feel what I ought to feel.

When I labored to bring forth my first child, I asked for a piece of leather to bite on, so I would not cry out. After all, I was Augustus's daughter. I told myself I should have no regard for the pain.

I held in my hand an amulet blessed by those who served the temple of Lucina, goddess of childbirth. My mother, Scribonia, was present, wiping my forehead with a wet cloth as I sat on the birthing chair. Marilla, the midwife, crouched at my feet.

I knew messengers were waiting in the atrium to leap on horses' backs and gallop off, bringing news of the birth to my father and to my husband. I knew also that word that I was in labor would have spread through the city of Rome, that good citizens would be flocking to temples, offering sacrifices to the gods on my behalf. Bringing forth a son was the one thing Rome asked of me—the one important thing I could do in my life.

Afterward, the midwife said I had an easy time of it, for a first birth, though truly it had seemed hard enough to me. "A son," Marilla said when the child entered the light of this world. Her voice sounded positively reverent. "Oh, my lady, a son."

Augustus's grandson, Agrippa's son. And he will rule Rome.

I do not remember who spoke these words—my mother? Marilla?—or if they just echoed in my mind.

Gaius. He was to be given the same praenomen as my father. Gaius Julius Caesar. My father would legally adopt him as his heir.

When I held the baby in my arms, I felt such intense love—and also such tender pity. I imagined the entire weight of the world one day coming down on this little boy's shoulders, and I wished I could save him from it.

"I am your mother, Gaius," I whispered to him, "and what I wish for you is not power or fame. What I wish for you is love and happiness."

Then I began to weep.

Did I weep for my son or for myself?

Cleopatra Selene

On our wedding night, Juba brushed back my hair and went to kiss my neck. Then he stiffened, seeing the mark where I had cut myself. "What is this?" he said.

"It's nothing. It's already almost healed."

"It's a strange place to come by such an injury. How did it happen?"

I sensed from his voice that he already suspected what had taken place. In any case, I did not wish to lie to him. I told him the truth.

"You would have gone through with it if Livia had not stopped you?"

"Yes."

He made a groaning sound deep in his chest.

"I thought what I did would move her, as nothing else could. And it was worth the risk to me. I wanted so much to marry you and for us to raise our child together."

Our lovemaking that night was different than it ever was before. He showed a new gentleness, a care—because I was carrying our child? Or because he realized how close we had come to losing each other?

We were married now, and we had the right to be together and need not fear being discovered. In the bedchamber of Juba's small house on the Palatine Hill, we truly consummated our marriage. I had thought before that I knew pleasure in Juba's arms, but now I realized that the acme of joy had eluded me. It did not elude me that night.

Soon we were off to our new home in Mauretania. The residents of Iol, the capital city, greeted us with great enthusiasm. We were carried through the streets in sedan chairs, and crowds shouted our names.

Many of the buildings we passed were made of sand-colored brick and rather shabby-looking. The architectural styles were a mixture of Egyptian and Greek, likewise the public statues. What we saw might be serviceable enough, but nothing was beautiful. I remembered hearing Augustus boast he had transformed Rome from a city of brick to one of marble. Could we do the same for Iol?

The North African sun shone down fiercely on the day of our arrival; I wondered if it was always hotter here than in Rome. I did not care for the heat. I focused on what I did like—the people's welcome. Everyone seemed so friendly.

"I hope you were not expecting this place to be like Rome," Juba said to me that night.

"Of course I wasn't."

"The people look poorer, don't they, than the people of Rome? Poorer and hungrier?"

I remembered people in rags and the gaunt faces I had seen among the welcoming throngs, and I nodded. Then I smiled. "They need a good king, and lucky for them, that is precisely what the gods have sent them."

He did not smile back. "I want to benefit the people of Mauretania and also satisfy Rome," he said heavily. "It will not be simple."

A Roman administrator, Porcius, had been sent along with us as an advisor and I suppose also a spy. We understood that Augustus's trust only extended so far. At a dinner party the evening after our arrival, Porcius suggested that since Juba was so fond of writing books about natural philosophy, he ought to devote himself to that and leave the governing to him.

Juba smiled. "Why, that would be too selfish of me—putting all that labor on your lone shoulders."

One of his first official acts was to give the city of Iol a new name—Caesarea. It was a gesture of loyalty, to Rome and to Augustus. "Maybe if he trusts me enough, he'll be willing to withdraw his nursemaid," Juba said. "One can hope." In the meantime he was pleasant to Porcius. In fact, he did his best to treat him as a friend.

Sometimes I forgot that Juba was ten years my elder. Indeed, our happiness together was so great that sometimes it seemed we were boy and girl, children together. But then he would do or say something that reminded me that he had seen war and far-off lands, things that I could only imagine. Patience and equanimity in the face of slights did not come naturally to me, especially now that I was a queen. But Juba was imperturbable. In many ways, in those early days in Mauretania, my husband was my teacher.

>>>>>>

Time passed. I grew used to being a queen and used to my new home while my pregnancy progressed. When I lay with my newborn son in my arms, I remembered again my mother's final word to me, *Live.* And I whispered this to the baby. Juba sat beside us, looking at the child, with wonder in his eyes.

We had not discussed a name before the child was born, for fear of tempting misfortune. But now with the living infant in my arms, I said, "Shall we call him Juba?"

My husband shook his head.

"It's a royal name," I said in surprise.

"I would rather my son bear a name from his mother's line—the royal house of Egypt."

A little thrill of pleasure went through me. "Alexander, then. After my twin."

"And after Alexander the Great . . ." Juba grinned. "I wish I could be in Augustus's presence when he reads my letter announcing the birth."

"You think . . . he'll see it as a threat?"

Juba kissed me on the forehead. "No, dear, just as a small reminder of who you are."

"Well, then he is Alexander." I felt a sudden sadness. "There are two names I know we must never give our children."

Juba nodded soberly. "You're right. Those two names Augustus truly would take exception to."

Mark Antony and Cleopatra.

>>>>>>>

I nursed the baby myself. I loved the sense of closeness it fostered with my son and the feeling I was directly nurturing his life. It was something no great Roman lady would do. But I was not a Roman lady. I was a Mauretanian queen.

When Alexander turned his face to seek my breast, the image came to mind of a flower seeking the sun.

"I think of the girl I was a year ago," I told Juba, "and I realize I am no longer that person."

"Of course. You are a wife and a queen."

And a mother, I thought.

I lay in bed, our child sleeping in my arms. Juba sat beside us. "How do you feel you have changed?" he asked.

"I have become the servant of life," I said. "I suppose I was without knowing it from the moment I knew I was carrying our child. But now it is much more real. I believe I would not act again as I did. It amazes me that I once held a knife to my own throat, even for so great a purpose as freeing the way for us to marry. When I look at Alexander, I see the value of life, and it is wealth beyond measure."

"I have often felt the same looking at nature's wonders," Juba said.

"You have seen battle. You have killed."

"Yes. I didn't much like it."

"The way my father and mother died has haunted me. I wanted to prove to myself that I had their courage—and I did prove I was ready to die by my own hand. But now, since Alexander's birth . . . I don't know if it is a good or a bad thing, but I think I've become less brave. I cannot picture myself ever again showing that kind of courage."

Juba kissed me. "You have me now to stand between you and any danger. I'll make it my life's mission to see to it that you never have to show that kind of courage again."

Livia

*T*avius and I were in Bithynia, a pleasant Romanized city on the Black Sea, when news came that a child was born who carried on the bloodline of the Caesars. I had rarely seen my husband so unashamedly relieved and happy as when we received news that Julia had given birth to little Gaius.

His daughter was well, the baby thriving.

"She'll be content now she is a mother," Tavius said confidently.

I thought of Agrippa, sober, stolid, and that bright flame of a girl. Contentment might be too much to expect.

At this time, our mission in the East was going splendidly, and my son Tiberius deserved much of the credit. He had already made a name for himself fighting in Gaul. He was strict, even harsh with the men under him, and therefore not especially popular with the troops. But he was universally respected for his courage, his skill with arms, and his intelligence. Tavius therefore gave him the huge responsibility of bringing Armenia to heel. He did it with little bloodshed, shrewdly enticing the rebel Armenian king's enemies to deliver the province into his hands.

My younger son Drusus, now eighteen, had meanwhile been dispatched to Spain with Agrippa. "I think he'll be hard to hold back," Tavius said. "He keeps saying there are territories in Germania that would fall easily to Roman arms."

"Easily!" I could feel my mouth twist. "And what does he know about it, child that he is?"

"He is not a child anymore," Tavius said. "He is a wonderful young man. Brave as a lion. Gods above, I wish he were my son."

I felt a prick of old pain, old longing; I would have given almost anything to present Tavius with a son. I also noticed that it was Drusus upon whom he lavished this warm praise, even as he loaded Tiberius with responsibility. This was an old story.

He had little affection for Tiberius, but real fondness for Drusus. It had been so since the two were small, when Drusus had easily taken to Tavius as a second father while Tiberius had treated him as an interloper.

I understood Tavius's feelings—truly I did. Drusus had a knack for wining hearts, while Tiberius did not. But I wished it were possible for Tavius to love both of my sons.

We lingered in the East for well over a year. Tiberius acted as Tavius's strong right arm as my husband tinkered with the government of the eastern part of the empire. Tavius grew to respect him more without warming to him much. Meanwhile we were feted by one minor potentate after another. I saw exotic sites, tasted foreign delicacies, and received rich gifts of silk, ivory, and gold.

Then we returned home with a wedding in store. Tiberius was to wed Agrippa's daughter.

Julia

I will be seeing your betrothed. Is there anything you would like me to tell him for you?" I asked the question mischievously.

My stepdaughter, Vipsania, averted her eyes and shook her head.

She had not been included in my invitation to Prima Porta, where Father, Livia, and Tiberius had arrived after their success in the East. Perhaps they did not think of inviting Vipsania, or maybe they considered it improper for Tiberius and the girl to spend time in each other's company before they married. Agrippa would come back to Rome—though only briefly—for the wedding. But he had not arrived yet. I felt a little sad about leaving Vipsania with just servants.

"Are you looking forward to your wedding?" I asked her curiously, just before I took leave of her.

She pressed her lips together for a moment, then said with a seriousness that belied her years, "I hardly know Tiberius. Why would

I be looking forward to marrying him? But I will do my duty and try to be a good wife."

It was probably the longest statement I had ever heard her make.

I had grown up with her betrothed, and if I had any stories to tell that showed his lovable nature or gentle character, I would certainly have shared them with her. But in fact I had always disliked him intensely, and my most vivid memory of him was anything but sweet. A little dog we kept in the garden had playfully leaped at him one day, and Tiberius, then about eleven, kicked him away so savagely that the poor thing ran off yelping. I might have called my stepbrother a brute—I had done it before, and I don't think Tiberius much minded. But instead I cried out, "What a coward you are! Did that little dog scare you?"

Tiberius's face had darkened.

"Coward," I said again.

He grabbed my hand and twisted my fingers back so pain shot up my arm. "You will never call me that again, or I swear by Almighty Jove I will break your fingers. And don't tell me you'll go crying to your father, because I don't care."

He meant it. I knew by the look on his face. He let my hand go and walked away, and I watched his receding back, hating him. I never again called him a coward. And truthfully he wasn't that, but I suspected he was something even worse. I pitied Vipsania, who must marry him.

>>>>>>>

It was summer, and the sky was bright as an azure jewel. I rode all the way to Prima Porta in an open litter, holding little Gaius in my arms. People who saw us stopped and waved, and I waved back at them.

For two years, I had not set eyes on my father, and we had communicated only in brief, rather formal letters. I still felt bitterness about my marriage, and yet my heart raced at the thought of showing Father his grandson.

I walked into the entrance hall of the villa, holding Gaius by the hand, and Father and Livia came forward to greet me. Father looked fitter and younger than when last I had seen him—bringing the eastern empire to heel evidently had improved his health. Livia too was glowing. Father embraced and kissed me, then swooped down and lifted Gaius in his arms, held him up as if he were some prize, his eyes glittering. Gaius kicked his little legs and cried, "Let me down!" Father laughed and lowered him to the floor.

"What a fine boy you have," he said to me. Then he and Livia began to talk about whether Gaius looked more like him, Father, or more like Agrippa.

"He has his father's eyes," Father said.

"Yes, but otherwise he could be you at that age," Livia asserted. Then she turned toward me and spoke kindly. "He favors you, Julia. You have a wonderful son."

Later, at dinner, I saw Tiberius. I had to admit that time had improved him. The cruel little boy seemed to have vanished. In his place I saw a well-built, self-assured man. Barely in his midtwenties, he already had a record of accomplishment behind him, and it showed in his bearing.

He was quiet, though. He said little to me in greeting, little to Father and Livia's other guests.

He and I reclined on adjoining dining couches. People around us were chatting. Tiberius sipped from his wine cup and ate a helping of the appetizer, not saying a word.

"The mullet is very good, isn't it?" I said.

"I prefer it with sauce."

We were silent for a while. Finally I made an attempt at conversation. "Our lives have taken an odd twist. I was your sister and soon I'm to be your mother-in-law."

"You're only my stepsister," he said. "And you will become my stepmother-in-law. That makes it a little less peculiar, I think."

"If you say so. Do you think we can be friends now?"

His expression became opaque. "Why wouldn't we be?"

"Well, we weren't friends growing up. Surely you remember that."

"I remember a haughty little girl who used to tease me."

I tilted my head, looking up at him. "Really? Was I haughty? As I remember it, you were the arrogant one. You seemed to think that because you were a boy, I should practically bow down to you."

"My memories are different. You were Augustus's daughter, and I the orphan graciously permitted to live in your house. You never let me forget it."

"Did it really seem that way to you?"

"Oh, no. After my father died, when my brother and I were taken into Augustus's house, you were the soul of kindness to us. You could not have been more welcoming to a boy in mourning."

I gave a little start, hearing the real bitterness in his voice. "Was that how it was?"

"It was exactly like that," he said.

I could have told him how it had been for me—feeling I already had so little of my father, and now must share him. I remembered the sense I had had that boys—even stepsons—could matter to Father in a way I never could. But it would be pointless to revive childhood grievances. "I am sorry," I said. "It seems I was even more foolish and selfish as a child than I recall."

He looked mollified. "It's all long past and best forgotten. I'm sure I was obnoxious. Small boys generally are." He gave me a smile that contained more warmth than I had seen from him so far. It was appealing, this sudden thaw. I smiled back.

I had never expected to feel in any way drawn to Tiberius, my stepbrother, who all through my childhood had repelled me. We were grown up now of course, and he had become not only an accomplished man but an attractive one. And something else drew me to him. He seemed so cut off from the people around us, even his own mother. He impressed me as being reserved rather than shy, and I supposed it was his choice to keep his distance. Yet he somehow struck me as lonely. I often felt alone too.

"You'll have a wife soon, and a family of your own before too long," I said gently.

He grimaced. "Yes, I'm fortune's darling. How would you describe Vipsania? It's ridiculous but I can't remember a thing about what she looks like. I saw her once at the betrothal ceremony. She didn't make much impression on me one way or another."

"Vipsania is . . . very sweet."

He leaned across the couches, so close that I could feel his breath on my cheek. "Is that what you think I want? A wife who is sweet?"

I drew back a little and glanced at my father and Livia, who were both at the table. They seemed to have noticed nothing improper. But I had flushed.

We were both quiet for a while. Then Tiberius spoke again. "You've changed—you're much more agreeable than I remember. Prettier too. It never occurred to me you'd grow up to be a beauty. You are, you know. Those eyes of yours . . ."

I looked away.

"Forgive me. I didn't mean to embarrass you. I'm not a smooth talker . . . The only thing I'm good at is being a soldier. I *am* very good at that."

"I've heard."

"Oh, but even there . . . there are men who have their doubts. I'm Augustus's stepson—it means every one of my subordinates is convinced I only outrank him because of nepotism. And now I'll be Agrippa's son-in-law too. So I'd better be perfect in all I do, or I'll get no real respect. It is a burden no one understands."

"I understand it only too well."

"You get tired of keeping up a public facade?"

"Yes," I said. "Oh, yes."

"Maybe now that we're grown up, we can understand each other better."

"And be friends?"

He looked at me for a long moment. "Why not?"

"Exactly my thought. Why not?"

I took a sip of wine. Tiberius was watching me, too intently, with an odd little smile playing around his mouth. My words— *Why not?*—echoed strangely in my ears. I had been speaking about a perfectly proper friendship with my stepbrother. Surely he understood that? Surely I had not meant something else?

>>>>>>>

Later, much later, I stood alone at the edge of the garden. My father, Livia, and most of the household had gone to bed. There was no moon but enough light from the oil lamp inside the house that I recognized the man walking toward me.

"Still awake?" Tiberius said.

I did not speak. I felt tension in the pit of my stomach, and yet also a pleasanter kind of excitement, as if I were on the brink of an adventure.

"We could be the last people on earth right now," he said, his voice husky.

"We're not."

"You didn't feel like sleeping, and neither did I. Would you call that a coincidence?"

"I don't know."

"I used to have a tutor who taught that coincidences don't exist. He believed in destiny."

"And do you?"

He shrugged. "I haven't thought much about that question. Still, it seems like more than a lucky chance that we both came out here tonight. What did you want to do—look at the moon?"

"There isn't any moon tonight."

"That's true. Lots of stars, though. Reminds me of how it was in Armenia. Beautiful starry nights."

"You enjoyed your time there?"

"Well, everything just fell into our hands. It's nice when that happens."

"You don't like war?"

"Actually, I do like it. But it's wasteful to fight when you don't have to."

"That's a reasonable viewpoint."

"I'm a reasonable man." He was quiet for a few moments, then said, "It's obvious we want each other. Let me come to your bedchamber."

The touch of arrogance in his voice reminded me of the cruel little boy he had been. I suppose I had been half expecting such an overture, but not for it to come so quickly and be so blunt. "No," I said.

"I've always desired you. All that hostility when we were younger—you do understand it was never . . . unmixed?"

I just stared at him. I could almost feel his big hands twisting my fingers.

"I'm not good at saying the right words. But I feel . . . as if this was bound to happen between us sooner or later. We have this chance now. Do you really want to let it pass?"

I imagined myself in his strong arms, and I felt a prickling in my skin. Some part of my mind said that Tiberius was right, that this was bound to happen, that in the end I would give myself to him. There was something between us, whose nature I was not sure of. A pull. It was powerful. Could it have been there since we were children, underneath all the squabbling? Hadn't we deliberately provoked each other when it would have been easier to walk away? Nipped at each other like two hound puppies who would grow up to mate?

He moved closer to me. I shook my head. But not because I thought our making love would be wrong. According to all I had been taught, it would be. That, though, was not stopping me. It was rather something about him—Tiberius. He attracted me very much, but at the same time, he made me feel I did not want to get too close; I had both feelings at the same time. "Forgive me—no. I hope you and my stepdaughter find great happiness together," I said and walked away.

Livia

When historians—all men—write their accounts of our times, I have no doubt they will emphasize the wars fought and won. For them, the battles are the fateful events. You could just as well say, however, that a series of marriages shaped our destinies. At least that is how it appears to me.

When my son Tiberius wed Vipsania, I had the feeling that this might be the last time our entire family circle would be together. Seeing Octavia brought this possibility home to me. Since the loss of Marcellus, she had become an invalid, keeping mostly to her bed. None of the expert physicians Tavius insisted she see could help her. She could barely walk and came tottering into Agrippa's house, leaning on the arm of her young daughter Antonia.

Tavius greeted her with a kiss on the cheek. "How are you feeling, Sister?"

"Oh, better," she said and glanced away.

In contrast to Octavia, there was Julia, dazzling, effervescent. Married to the bride's father, she acted the part of a hostess, instructing the servants on the final arrangements and welcoming guests. She did all this with grace and efficiency. At twenty, she was like a rose just coming into full bloom. She resembled Tavius more now than she had before—not so much the care-laden man in his forties as the boy I once had fallen in love with. I could see echoes of that boy in her fair coloring, her charm, her smile. I noticed the boldness, the challenge in her eyes, when she talked to this man or that. She seemed to be daring each one to amuse her. There had been a challenge in Tavius's eyes too.

I had noticed at the chariot races how much she enjoyed betting—just as Tavius did. They both liked giving themselves in to the hand of chance, confident that they would emerge victorious. I suspected that even after the sad loss of her first husband, Julia thought herself fortune's darling. I had never felt that way, even when I was young. I made no bet without calculating the odds.

Julia resembled Tavius—but she was different too. There was a touch of the exotic about the planes of her face, the tilt of her eyes. Especially now, as her beauty came into full flower, I saw a hint of some unknown ancestor hailing from a land far outside our ken. She had a lovely face, very changeable as emotion played on it, but always exquisite. Yet as I gazed at her, something gave me pause. Her very looks seemed to say, *Don't think you completely know me.*

Her husband, Agrippa, was present, though only sometimes at her side as he circulated, greeting guests. He had come home with the aim of conferring with Tavius, as well as to give his daughter away. No doubt he also had another purpose, which it would have been indelicate to mention. One little heir was not enough for the dynasty he and Tavius wanted to create. So before he went off again to tend to the empire's borders, he would do his best to get Julia with child.

Julia always treated Agrippa with the respect due a husband. He, for his part, used more courtesy with her than many men showed their wives. But I never noticed any particular rapport between the two of them. Agrippa seemed unmoved by her beauty, as if, soldier to his core, he was armored against her. There seemed to be only one way she mattered to him: to bear him sons.

The world is unfair to women. Only fools do not know this. And only fools beat their fists against stone, expecting it to yield like clay.

I had taken my son Tiberius aside before the wedding ceremony. "I hope you find joy in your marriage. A great deal depends on how you treat your wife. Remember that Vipsania deserves your affection and care. She is to be your partner in life."

Tiberius just nodded, as he usually did when I gave him advice. I had the feeling not a word penetrated.

"It's a question of your own happiness," I said urgently. "If she isn't content, you'll have an unhappy home."

"Gods above, Mother," he said. "Do you think I'm embarking on marriage intending to make my wife miserable?"

"Men generally don't intend to—but many of them seem to manage it just the same. I expect better of you."

On his wedding day, Tiberius did not seem a particularly happy bridegroom. But when did he ever openly display joy? Any young man whose heart was set on a military career ought to welcome a match with Agrippa's daughter, I thought. And other than Julia, he could not have looked higher.

The girl herself struck me as a placid little creature, neither pretty nor ugly, someone who would cause no trouble.

Her demeanor during the ceremony did not change my opinion of her. When Agrippa placed her hand in Tiberius's, I could view her face well enough through the diaphanous red veil she wore to see that she kept her eyes downcast. Proper, I supposed—but perhaps excessively so? Then she said, "Where thou art Gaius, I am Gaia," in so soft a voice I could barely hear her.

At the feast, Vipsania sat perched on the very edge of Tiberius's dining couch, her veil pushed back from her face so she could eat, but still modestly covering her hair. She avoided looking at Tiberius—exceedingly correct behavior for a bride. I began to wish I could glimpse some sign of spirit.

I approached and said, "May the gods bless your marriage." My son and Vipsania both rose, and I embraced them each in turn. The girl felt very slight and small in my arms. She stumbled over the words, "Thank you, Mother-in-Law." But when we moved apart, for one moment, Vipsania looked at Tiberius, and her whole face was transformed. Her lips parted; her eyes glowed.

Plainly, my son's little bride was ready to fall in love with him. And he—he did not glance at her.

I hoped that would change.

>>>>>>>

Jullus Antony and his wife, Tavius's niece Marcella, were at the wedding of course. Marcella had already borne Jullus a son and was visibly pregnant again. This only served to emphasize how Jullus had been absorbed into our family. His physical resemblance to his father could still jar me at times. But he was an appealing young man. It was as if Mark Antony had come back to life, still with his head of thick, curly black hair, muscular shoulders, and powerful stride, but temperate and thoughtful, with a touch of self-deprecatory wit. Jullus was the man his father might have been if the gods had removed all his faults—his impulsiveness, his cruelty, his crude manner of speech—refined and perfected him, and returned to us a being not even his worst enemy, Tavius, could dislike.

He and Tavius stood together talking, and I happened to overhear some of their conversation. It concerned troubles in Gaul, where Agrippa would soon be dispatched.

"Every time I think we've established peace, I turn out to be bitterly mistaken," Tavius said. "My grandchildren will be fighting there—worse, so will yours."

Tavius went on in this vein and Jullus nodded, commiserated, nodded some more. Then he said, "When Agrippa goes to Gaul, I'd like to go with him."

A moment of silence passed. Tavius had become very still.

"I believe I can serve you best in a military post," Jullus said. He sounded so young at that moment—and so ardent. "I promise you, sir, I'll acquit myself well."

And I will be loyal. These words were not said, and yet they were conveyed by Jullus's whole manner.

"Your eagerness does you credit," Tavius said in an expressionless voice. "But here we are at a wedding feast. You understand, it's not the best time for this kind of discussion."

"When can we talk?"

"I'll send for you." Tavius smiled and patted Jullus on the shoulder. "We'll have a long talk about your future."

Jullus studied Tavius's face and said nothing. The young man suddenly looked like someone who had just been given news of a death and was trying to hold in his grief, so as not to make an unseemly display. In that moment, I deeply pitied him.

"Soon. I promise you," Tavius said, and quickly turned away.

"I saw your little boy the other day," I said to Jullus. "He is very handsome—and so big for his age."

"Yes, everyone says so," Jullus said. He smiled.

It was like watching an actor don a mask. I think he had just realized there would be no military posting for him ever, and the knowledge crushed him. But he would not show it—at least not to me. So he spoke about his son, even told me an amusing story about the boy. He could not have been more delightful company. But I had seen his reaction when Tavius said no to him, the brief moment when he let his mask slip.

Later, after all the ceremonies and feasting were done and Tavius and I were alone in our bedchamber, the talk with Jullus preyed on his mind. "Did you hear him? He'd like a military posting."

"Yes," I said. "I heard."

"Mark Antony's son. I've given him my niece—and he has the wealth that goes with her. Now he would like me to hand him an army too?"

"He asked to serve you. He didn't ask for an army, but a posting. His father was a great general. Jullus might make a capable officer."

"And you enjoy the idea of Antony's son capably leading soldiers? Oh, you sweet, trusting soul."

"No one but you would ever call me a sweet, trusting soul." Why had I been speaking as if I were Jullus's advocate? Amazing, I thought, amazing that I had let myself be carried away by something as simple as human sympathy. I had forgotten for a moment who I was.

"You like the boy," Tavius said. "Strangely enough, I do too. But not enough to bare my chest and hand him a dagger. Do you think even if I could forget who his father was, Jullus ever could?" He let out a breath. "I understand his position much better than you do, Livia. It's not that I don't sympathize. I remember what it was like for me, when I had to pretend I would forgo vengeance for my own father." By his father, he meant Julius Caesar, who had adopted him. For many months, Tavius had acted as if he were reconciled with the assassins. "I had to bear the contemptuous looks of other men, and that rubbed me raw. The sense of being dishonored, of being viewed as coward—all that worked its way under my skin. If you think Jullus doesn't feel besmirched every day of his life, you're wrong."

"You believe he is only pretending to be loyal?" I said.

"No, he is loyal at this moment. I even think in some sense he loves me—I'm the man who raised him. But here are the facts. I killed that young man's father and his brother. It was necessary. Mark Antony set the whole chain of events in motion. He was at fault, not me. But blood is blood. You rear a wolf cub, you feed it by hand when it's small, you coddle it—it's still a wolf, not a dog, and one fine day it's liable to rip your throat out. You are a fool if you become so fond that you forget that. I am not a fool, Livia."

I could not argue with his reasoning. "And yet, the best way to make Jullus an enemy may be to treat him as if he is already one. To show distrust, and keep him idle, and make it impossible for him to fulfill any worthwhile ambition."

"I know that," Tavius said impatiently. He always became snappish when I implied I saw aspects of a situation he did not. "Of course it would be stupid to keep him idle. If he wants governmental posts, he can have them. I'm prepared to load him up with offices and honors. But a military command is out of the question."

Soon after we had this conversation, Tavius saw to it Jullus was chosen as a city aedile. He let him learn the ropes of governmental administration, took him under his wing, and even spent many hours personally instructing him. Despite all he had said about dogs and wolves, he had genuine affection for this young man.

Jullus threw himself into the administrative work he was given, and did it well. Tavius was pleased.

Julia

*I*n the little time that Agrippa was at home, I did my best to be a true wife to him. I longed for a man's love—and Agrippa was my husband.

I tried, and afterward, it embarrassed me to remember my own efforts. In bed I fondled him in a way Marcellus had found pleasing. And I took his hand and tried to show him how I wished to be touched. He moved away from me. This seasoned, gruff soldier—I truly think he was shocked. I do not know what his life with his previous wives had been like, but it seemed he believed that a good woman did not to feel much desire for a man or experience much pleasure in bed. Sometimes with a few muttered words, sometimes with no words at all, he made it clear what he expected. "Here, this way," he might say, positioning my limbs as if I were a poppet. I was to lie still, and he would use my body as he wished, with only the briefest of preliminaries, so as to get me with child again.

It would have been better not to know a man's touch at all than to be used the way Agrippa used me. For it whetted my desire without appeasing it. He would move away from me, fall asleep. I would listen to his snores, and would be burning, burning.

If he had been a man my own age, I think I might have screamed at him. I might have paraded naked as I had before Marcellus. But I remembered who he was—my father's lifelong friend, the greatest general in Rome, the winner of victory after victory, a man of ponderous dignity. How could I tell him he was a maladroit lover? I respected him too much. When I tried to speak to him on this subject, I might as well have been struck dumb. I could get no words out.

It was not just physical affection I wanted. That was not even the most important thing. I wanted a man to love me. I wanted a place in my husband's heart.

I imagined at times another woman—the woman my husband seemed to think I ought to be. She was one to whom the pleasures of the flesh did not matter, who wished only to serve Rome and her husband by bearing healthy sons. She did not ache to love and be loved. If I could have by some act of will transformed myself into that woman, I likely would have. But the best I could manage was an inept, crippled pretense.

I had one thing in common with that ideal Roman matron—I was fertile. In his brief time at home, my husband impregnated me again.

>>>>>>>

The next few years seemed spent in a dark mist, though I should have been happy. My little Gaius thrived. I had received a gift from the gods that many women would give their souls for. I conceived easily and gave birth easily too. My daughter Julilla was born nine months after Agrippa's brief visit to Rome. Agrippa came home again to consult with my father when Julilla was four months old.

He took pleasure in both his children and could be surprisingly tender with them. But after a short time, he left for Gaul again. Nine months later, I gave birth to my second son, Lucius.

My children all resembled Agrippa in the square shapes of their faces and their sturdy builds. Gaius's features were more like my father's, and he also had his fair hair, though not his blue eyes. As for the other two—anyone could tell at a glance they were Agrippa's children.

They were raised like royalty. They had the best wet nurses that could be found and the best tutors from the time they were very small. My father eagerly made plans for the education of the two boys. He legally adopted both of them soon after Lucius's birth.

Of course Agrippa had been delighted to give his consent. It was a common enough thing in Rome for prominent men without sons to adopt young relatives. My father himself had been adopted by his great-uncle, Julius Caesar. Natural fathers acceded to such arrangements when it would bring their children wealth or higher social rank. Gaius and Lucius, by becoming Father's legal sons, became heirs to the empire.

The adoption ceremony followed antique form—Father paid for the boys with two copper coins. I did not much like this; there was something ugly about the business, something too reminiscent of what happened at the slave market.

My boys would continue to live with me until they were older, but the important figure in their lives would be my father. I realized this would be true even for my daughter. Father would pick her husband. He doted on all his grandchildren; and I knew he had their good in mind. Yet I sometimes had a twinge of dismay about the way things were arranged—a realization of how little power I had. Even my children did not belong to me but to my father.

In gratitude, Father showered me with material gifts—jewelry, exquisite works of art, even a country villa right after Lucius's birth. From the time I was small, presents had been his favorite way of expressing affection for me. Just as I had as a child, I took what he gave, smiled, and thanked him. And wished for more, for a closer bond that was now further away than ever. I knew he did not want to hear my true thoughts, and so I did not offer them to him. He was pleased with me. And I think, because he himself was pleased, he never questioned whether or not I was happy.

I appeared regularly in public with my father and Livia. I went to the gladiatorial exhibitions as little as Father would permit—he did feel I ought to attend occasionally. But I never developed a taste for watching men hack at each other, let alone watching them die. I loved going to the chariot races with Father, though. Sometimes I bet more than I should—but Father would smile at this and even slip me coins, to make up my losses. I also attended religious observances, the dedication of new public monuments, and theatrical performances—but performances only of the most seemly kind, not the vulgar mime shows that Father disapproved of. And everywhere I went, people called my name and cheered me.

"These people have no earthly reason to love me," I said to Father once. "Why do they act as if they do?"

"Because the peace of Rome depends on you and on the sons you have brought into the world. Don't you realize that?" He spoke a little impatiently. Then his gaze softened. "And you are a beautiful young woman and you project—" He stopped and seemed to be searching for the right words. "The other day, when that poor woman in the crowd held out her baby to you—when you took it in your arms and admired it—I could not do something like that so naturally. Neither could Livia."

"But it was natural to me," I said.

"That's my point," Father said. "You have a . . . humanity. The people find you easy to love, and that is a fine thing."

I ought to have been pleased when he said this. But instead I felt a swirl of bitterness like a snake moving in my chest. Every gift I possessed—my ability to bear children, what Father called my beauty and humanity—*everything* was entered into Father's political account books.

He so enjoyed being seen with me—his dutiful daughter, whom the common people loved.

To me it all seemed bizarre. My own husband did not show the slightest sign of loving me. But when I appeared in public, the people of Rome went into transports of joy.

"Julia!" they would cry. "Julia!" People would say things like, "May the gods bless that sweet face!" They would even toss bouquets of flowers at my feet.

Father would beam at me. I would curve my lips into a smile that everyone took as real.

>>>>>>>

One afternoon, preparing to attend the theater with my father and Livia, I sat in a chair in front of my dressing table. I could see my own face in a copper mirror that stood on a stand. Phoebe stood behind me. She had learned to dress my hair the way I liked it. No, that would not be accurate. She had learned to dress it the way Father liked it, piled on the top of my head in a style almost as severe as the one Livia favored. I watched her long, pale fingers moving through my locks, arranging everything just so. The look of Republican simplicity took an hour to achieve.

Phoebe had already made up my face—applied a little rouge to my lips and my cheekbones, the barest touch of kohl to my eyelids.

If I wore more makeup than that, Father would not say a word, but I could always read the disapproval in his eyes.

I looked at myself in the mirror. I saw the eyes of someone drowning. Phoebe meanwhile fastened on my emerald earrings. They had been one of Father's gifts to me after little Julilla's birth.

I began to cry and found I could not stop. I wept with great wrenching sobs; it was shameful how I wept. And I loathed myself, even as the tears rolled down my cheeks. For here I was, the First Citizen's daughter, wearing those costly baubles on my ears. My three beautiful children, carefully tended by nurses, were at play in another part of this fine stately house, and I was about to go to the theater where strangers would greet me with adulatory cries. And yet I was so unhappy. I did not fit this life I had been given, or it did not fit me, and that surely was my fault.

What added to my sense of abasement was that Phoebe stood staring at me with dismay. She was a slave; she limped; she had no kin at all. But she was not the one weeping. She looked at me with true concern and said, "Mistress, what is it? Are you ill? Has something happened?"

"Nothing has happened," I sobbed. "I'm a selfish fool, and I want what I can't have and—oh, Phoebe, what you must think of me. I have never seen you cry, but here I am crying—all out of pity for myself."

She made a sound of commiseration, as one might tending a sick child.

"I can't bear my life. What is wrong with me, to feel such sadness, when everyone says I am so fortunate?"

"Maybe the ones who say it lack eyes to see, mistress," Phoebe said.

A choked laugh ushered from my throat. "*You* pity me?"

"There are more ways than one to be a slave."

>>>>>>>

At a poetry reading at my father's home, I met a woman named Aurelia. Her husband was a high-ranking officer serving under Agrippa's command in Gaul. She was young and had a vivacity I liked, and when she invited me to a dinner party, I accepted her invitation. Through her I made the acquaintance of several other women with husbands serving in far-flung corners of the empire. They often met at each other's houses to dine. Men attended their parties too, mostly unattached men with patrician names. I was twenty-two years old, but my life had been sheltered. I went to three of these parties before I understood that the people there came for more than company.

One evening I noticed a strikingly handsome young slave serving wine. He had a garland wreath on his head and wore a bright yellow tunic of some clinging fabric. He leaned over me too close as he filled my wine cup, then turned his head and gave me a hint of smile. I just thought this odd behavior by a waiter who was ill trained. But later I noticed him and a woman guest talking. He helped her to her feet. A statuesque woman, about thirty years old, she had a bright, hard look in her eyes. When she left, the young slave quietly followed her.

I was taken aback and must have shown it. A man on the dining couch next to me caught my glance and smiled, then, leaning over the space between our couches, whispered, "Aurelia likes to keep her guests entertained. But there will be a fee."

I could feel my jaw drop. I said nothing.

"You look like a little lost child. Are you truly the First Citizen's daughter?"

"Yes." I had heard other guests addressing this man, and I knew his name. "You're Sempronius Gracchus."

"I admit it."

In the Forum stood a statue of his great-grandfather portrayed as a handsome young paragon. This man had a pockmarked, plain face. I saw no resemblance except, when I looked closely, there was a cleft in his chin, similar to the one the sculptor had given the long-dead hero.

"You have a great name." *You have a great name, but you are a senator of very minor importance, and I know for a fact my father does not take you seriously.*

"That, my dear, is true enough, for what it's worth." He took a drink of wine. "You're shocked at Lucilla and that slave boy?"

"You're not?"

"I am the last person you would expect to find shocked by anything."

We fell into a prolonged and pleasant conversation—spoke of poetry and art. I found Gracchus to be a witty man with elevated tastes.

It had grown late when he suddenly said, "I don't give a fig for my name. But when I think about my great-grandfather, I long for what once was and could have been."

"I see. You're a democrat. You believe Rome has taken the wrong road."

He did not speak.

I smiled at him. "And now it suddenly occurs to you that you are talking to the First Citizen's daughter. You feel a bit uneasy."

He laughed. "Not really. I'm very sure that your father does not lose sleep over inconsequential people like me. While if Gaius Gracchus were alive"—he named his great-grandfather, Rome's dead democratic champion—"he would have to kill him."

"Actually, my father sees himself as carrying on your great-grandfather's work. All the public building and so on."

"Yes, indeed. I have heard him say as much."

"You don't believe him?"

"Gaius Gracchus was a democrat. One-man rule would be anathema to him."

"And to you . . . ?"

He did not answer.

Gracchus interested me. He was different from the usual run of people I met. He was in his midthirties, but still unmarried, and at the slightest provocation would proclaim his disinterest in marriage and family life. He did not revere my father, or even pretend to, and that set him apart from most people I knew. It occurred to me that perhaps that was what I liked most about him—he did not feel admiration for my father or even feign it.

We met at dinner parties and at poetry readings. We knew many of the same people. He was not rushed or crude. What happened between us came to fruition slowly.

"You ought to let me make love to you," he said to me one evening. He spoke lightly, without emphasis, the way one might say, *You ought to sample this new wine.*

A slave musician was entertaining us before the last dinner course was served. She plucked on a harp while singing of love in a high, flutelike voice. We were in an opulent dining room packed with guests, most of them wellborn, all of them rich. The mural on the wall showed Jupiter entering Leda's bedchamber in the shape of a swan.

"You know that I am married," I said.

Gracchus nodded toward Pompeia, our hostess, a matron of middle years, across the room, chatting with a young man who looked like he had only lately begun to shave. "Marriage doesn't stop her."

"You've made love to her?"

"I wouldn't speak of such things. It might damage the lady's reputation." He smiled because we both knew Pompeia had no reputation to lose. Then he began walking his fingers up and down my arm, tickling me.

Agrippa was in Gaul. It was the first time in a long while that a man had touched me. "Stop," I said, and he stopped.

"It wouldn't have to disrupt your life," Gracchus said. "I could give you pleasure. You deserve it."

"What makes you think I do?"

"You are a good person. Very kind, very sweet. You deserve some joy in life."

"And you could give me joy?"

"That is one area in which I am actually quite competent." He lowered his voice. "We would be discreet. I would never do anything to hurt you, Julia."

Strangely enough, I believed him. He did not support Father. Was he intending to use me against him politically? Planning perhaps to dirty our family name? It could be, but I didn't think it at all likely. There was a gentleness and a lack of guile about Gracchus that won my trust.

"And when I have a child and he bears no resemblance to my husband, but has a cleft in his chin just like yours . . . ?"

He laughed. "What a narrow experience of life you have had. It is terrible how you have been kept imprisoned."

"What do you mean?"

"Don't you know that there are many ways for a man to give a woman exquisite pleasure, without running the slightest risk of getting her with child?"

A little shiver went through me. I suddenly felt very warm. I looked away. "No more of such talk."

"As you wish."

≫≫≫≫≫≫

Of course there was more of such talk. Sempronius Gracchus never spoke of love as the poets did, never claimed to be in the grip of deathless passion. But I felt he liked and valued me. In appearance, he did not approach a sculptor's ideal. He had the soft body of a man who did no work, eschewed athletics, and did not keep himself fit for war. But my flesh came alive in his presence. And I felt the most elemental need. To be touched, gently, carefully, with understanding, by a man who wished to give me pleasure. Not rutted with for the purpose of giving Rome an heir.

Perhaps I did not want Gracchus, really. Perhaps I wanted Marcellus back, alive, wanted the man he might have become. I did like Gracchus, though.

I considered the danger—how could I not? I imagined bedding Gracchus, and my husband finding out. Or my father finding out. Their fury. Maybe a great public scandal. Many of the wives of the nobility had lovers, but almost all tried to keep the fact a secret. Cuckolded husbands almost never killed their wives or their wives' lovers as they sometimes had a hundred years ago—but there could be nasty divorces, the confiscation of the wife's dowry, and, worse, far worse, her separation from her children. For me, the ugliness of the scandal if it broke would be in proportion to my husband's fame and my father's power.

"Do you think it is wrong for a woman to let a man who is not her husband make love to her?" I asked Phoebe one night as she brushed my hair before bed.

She looked at me speculatively. "It depends on the circumstances, mistress."

"What kind of circumstances?"

"Well, for one thing, the love between her and her husband. Or the lack of love."

Of course she knew I was not talking about an abstract woman, but about myself. I almost told her everything. The truth was, she had become my closest confidante.

There are more ways than one to be a slave . . . Those words of hers often echoed in my head.

"If a woman has a chance for some little bit of happiness without risking too much, well, then I say why not?" Phoebe spoke vehemently. "Men always couple with women other than their wives—they do that and worse."

She did not like men. Most of the slave women of my household had husbands—marriages unrecognized in law but treasured just the same. Phoebe did not, and not because men did not seek her out. Something had happened to her—she hinted at it sometimes. My guess was that Roman soldiers had had their way with her when she was still a child—and she would never let a man touch her again, if she could help it.

She did not fuss much with her own hair, as some of the other slave women did, nor did she like to look at herself in the mirror. But she did enjoy helping me look pretty and appeared to find pleasure in seeing me beautifully dressed. Now she seemed to be encouraging me to find a lover. Perhaps she would take some vicarious satisfaction in that.

>>>>>>>

The first time I went to Gracchus's house, my heart pounded so I hard I could feel the blood pulsing in my temples and my throat. I rode my own litter to a backstreet off the marketplace, got out, and entered another, inconspicuous litter Gracchus had waiting for me there. My eyes darted around to see if anyone might be peeking out of the alleyways or the windows of the shabby three-story buildings. Would they recognize Caesar Augustus's daughter? My mouth was dry. I ought to have hated the sensation—the terror. But I did not. Not entirely.

There were moments at the chariot races when two chariots raced neck and neck, and the team I bet on was close to victory and yet also close to crashing at the finish line. My breath would come in gasps. It was awful—but I never felt more truly alive than at such times. That was how I felt when I rapped on Sempronius Gracchus's door.

He had been waiting for me, at the entranceway; it was he rather than a slave who opened the door. "Quickly, come inside," he said. When I was in, he embraced me. I clung to him.

His house was small but exquisitely furnished. There were couches with ivory fittings and red silk cushions in the dining room. We lay on one couch together and ate a simple meal of sliced chicken and dates, drinking wine out of a fine crystal cup we shared. From time to time, we would pause and kiss and caress each other.

When dinner was over, Gracchus asked, "Do you like being here with me?"

"Yes, I like it."

He stood up and extended his hand to me. "Come."

We walked hand in hand into a bedchamber, very bare-looking, with only a sleeping couch, a stool, and a small table holding a lit candle in a gold holder. He undressed me, slowly removing each item of clothing and depositing it on the stool, first my stola, then my under tunic, finally the linen cloth that covered my loins. We lay on the bed, and he proceeded to instruct me. With his hands, with his mouth. To touch me in ways no one had before.

"You see I do have certain talents," he whispered. "Would you care to learn about a man's body? I can teach you the things great hetaeras know."

I laughed. "Yes, make me into a great hetaera. My father would love that."

I felt bathed in a sea of pleasure. And yet later, deep in the night, I suddenly began to be afraid, to imagine eyes of judgment looking at me. I pulled away from Gracchus. "This way of coupling . . . might it be forbidden?"

"Who is here to forbid us? I delight in every part of you, every inch of your body."

I did not answer.

"I would never want to make love to you in a way you dislike."

"I do like it. I like all of it . . . It's as if I don't know myself anymore."

He nuzzled my neck. "You mean to say you're not your father's obedient daughter? Doesn't it feel good to defy him?"

"Yes," I said. "It does feel good." A thought occurred to me, a thought I did not like. "You're defying him too, aren't you, by making love to his daughter? Is that why you want me?"

"I would want you no matter whose daughter you were." I saw the glint of Gracchus's teeth—his smile barely visible in the candle-light. But after a few moments, he said in a different voice, "This is not an act of courage. The time for political courage is past."

"Poor Gracchus. Do you long to be a dead hero? Do you really?"

"Julia, right now I'm exactly who I want to be. The man who holds you in his arms."

Part II

Julia

For the most part, my life did not change. I watched my children grow. I exchanged polite letters with my absent husband, who was successfully subduing recalcitrant Gallic tribes and covering his name with ever more glory. I appeared with Father at public events whenever he wished me to.

And I had my own separate life. Gracchus and I were cautious about being seen together and would often meet not at his home but that of his most trusted women friends. Still, our love affair flourished.

I believed our bond transcended the physical. Gracchus was interested in what I thought. As time passed, he took to introducing me to the people who comprised his circle—poets, artists, philosophers with democratic leanings, people who walked on the edge of what was acceptable in Rome. I think some of them were intimidated by the fact that I was Augustus's daughter, but most seemed glad to spend time in my company. Maybe they suspected that Gracchus and I were lovers, but they pretended not to know. They were by and large disinclined to take life too seriously. Augustus's daughter in the arms of a man whose name was synonymous with Rome's lost democratic hopes—they were people who liked being amused, and if they did realize the extent of our involvement, it probably delighted them.

In the bedchamber, Gracchus was a skilled teacher, and I will say I was an apt pupil. I learned ways of performing the act of love that I had never before imagined, ways of prolonging ecstasy. How to make him quiver with desire and then come slowly, slowly to culmination. He took pleasure in bringing me again and again to a point of utter rapture. And as he promised, we did nothing together, ever, that could possibly have resulted in the birth of a child.

"This is freedom," he said once. "There is less and less freedom in Rome. But here in this bedchamber, we are free."

I laughed, snuggling up against him. "You mean what we just did was a political act?"

"Maybe it is," he said seriously. "Maybe all freedom is connected in some way. I'm not sure."

"Would your great-grandfather be cheering us on?"

"No, he would not. He was an exemplar of old-fashioned virtue. But that's gone, you know. That's a lost age."

"I will not bring up your great-grandfather again."

"Why?"

"Because when I do, it makes you sad."

He stroked my hair affectionately. "I'll tell you a secret. I wish it were possible to go back in time. To when it was possible to stand for something."

"Before my father came along."

"Yes, before your father."

"He ended all the civil strife. All that killing . . ."

"Yes. And most people value safety over freedom."

"Still, you think he is a tyrant?"

"Oh, yes, but I admit he is quite virtuous as tyrants go. He works like a galley slave to make the empire peaceful and prosperous. He does not seem to relish violence. But tyranny even at its best demeans us."

"Do you know I could go to my father—I would not do it, but imagine I did—I could tell him all of your opinions. And he would not care. So long as you did not actually whet swords for his overthrow, he would do nothing at all. Because he wants Rome's citizens to be free."

"He would not care what I think, because I am no threat. If I were, believe me, he would bring down a great booted foot and crush me like an insect. As it is, he'd consider it beneath him to squash a worm like me. But I think the man who succeeds him—whoever that turns out to be—will be less confident than your father is and therefore less benevolent."

"The man who succeeds him will likely be my son."

"You think so? You think your father will live that long—to see your son a man?"

I stretched and yawned. "I think my father will outlive his whole generation. There is not a disease deadly enough or a sword sharp enough to kill him. He is frail and sickly but somehow also strong. You can't imagine how strong he is."

"Then I consider myself put on notice—the next man we grovel to will be your son."

"You speak as if my father has enslaved his fellow Romans."

"My sweet, so long as one man governs us, and we can't rid ourselves of him by a free vote of the citizens, we *are* all slaves."

These political conversations, which often ended by disturbing me and putting Gracchus in a melancholy mood, at the same time fed our passion. I believe Gracchus felt brave as he uttered words he would never say in my father's presence—saying them to his daughter. And I—I felt as if I were defying my father just by listening. We were excited by our sense of peril. But really it was not the talk that was perilous—it was the lovemaking itself.

Our liaison becoming public knowledge was a constant danger. Gracchus and I never discussed what might happen, but I did consider the consequences of being discovered. I feared Father's rage and disgust more even than the anger of my husband. I tried to put thought of this out of my mind, but a chill would work its way down my spine when I imagined Father's reaction if he knew what I was doing. And yet when I considered ending the affair with Gracchus before disaster struck, I foresaw a descent into despair. What would there be for me but emptiness, a gray existence, nothing to look forward to but a dreary round of duty? I did not imagine myself in love with Gracchus, but I cared for him, and I felt so happy when I was with him. I owed him a great debt. He had shown me my own capacity for joy. I could not bring myself to give him up.

Cleopatra Selene

*F*ive years in Mauretania passed quickly. There was a time of great sorrow—our little Alexander died before he could walk. There was also great joy when our second son was born. He was given a royal Egyptian name, Ptolemy.

Livia and I corresponded during this time. For the most part, her letters to me were the kind I might have expected to receive from a favorite aunt. She was adept in the use of medicinal plants and happy to share her knowledge. When I told her the hot summer sun sometimes seared my skin, she sent me a recipe for a lotion that would help shield it. She also advised me to rub a certain ointment on my son's gums to ease his pain when he was teething. But mixed with this womanly counsel, I would find hints about statecraft: "Assume that none of your servants ever tell you the whole truth." "Everyone tends to think first of his own interests. In all your dealings, keep this fact in mind, and use it as a lever." "Nothing in government is perfect. All we can do is choose between imperfections."

She addressed me as an equal—or at least as if she were only my superior in experience and age—and she counseled me, as one female ruler might another. This was fitting. She was her husband's partner in government, and so was I.

Juba had the soul of a philosopher king. A great deal of his time was taken up by natural philosophy, his study of plants and animals. He published learned books that received wide praise. He also sent out surveying expeditions, for geography was another of his interests. His men mapped some small corners of the world for the very first time, even discovered islands no one had previously known existed.

Meanwhile at home, we encouraged the work of scholars of all kinds, and of artists as well. We also built roads and other public works; we strove to provide employment for free men in all our projects and limit the use of slaves. Augustus had made the city of Rome beautiful. We did the same with our capital city of Caesarea.

In governing Mauretania, Juba liked to set the broad direction. But he was so busy with writing his books that much of the mundane work of administering the country fell to me. I did not mind this. Porcius, our first "minder," eventually went home. But another, hardly more agreeable Roman came in his place. Controversy over how our tax moneys should be spent—what portion should go into Roman coffers, what part we could retain—constantly embroiled us. So in addition to my personal correspondence with Livia, we sent a stream of cajoling letters to Augustus. We tried our best to obtain favorable treatment for our country.

We had done only necessary renovations to our palace, except for the library. A huge room, far bigger than the atrium of a Roman house, it now had a colorful mosaic floor, and the walls and shelves for books were made of the finest cedar wood. We had indulged ourselves when it came to books—importing them from Italy,

Greece, and other places. We used the library for official work as well as for reading and research. One afternoon I sat there with Juba and our chief accountant, discussing allocations for building in the coming year.

"Obviously," I said, "we cannot make any definite plans until we know if Rome will remit some of our taxes this year."

Juba nodded. The three of us talked about small economies we might make if Rome insisted on receiving all the money we theoretically owed. Then a servant came rushing in. "Forgive me for interrupting you, my king," he said to Juba. "A messenger has arrived from Rome and brought this." He held out a leather case.

The seal showed the imprint of Alexander the Great's portrait. We had been expecting a letter from Augustus, which we hoped would grant us some remission of taxes. Yet my heart gave a jump when I saw the seal. I felt angry for myself then, for taking fright at nothing—angry that just the sight of Augustus's seal could inspire fear in me.

Juba took the letter and dismissed the servant. He slid a rolled papyrus out of the case and read it hastily.

"Will our taxes be remitted, sire?" the accountant asked eagerly.

"I'm afraid that's not clear. Would you leave the queen and me now, Corba? We have matters to discuss."

Juba spoke in an even, courteous voice. The accountant bowed his way out of the library; he plainly sensed nothing amiss. But I did.

"What is in the letter?" I asked as soon as Corba was gone.

"Augustus would like us to pay him a visit in Rome."

"A visit?"

"Here, read it," Juba said, and handed me the letter.

The wording was courteous, even friendly. Augustus and Livia would like to see us in Rome—perhaps within the next month?

And they hoped we would bring little Ptolemy too, so they could meet him.

It was a summons of course. I read the letter and felt a wave of nausea, very much as I had when I first met Augustus.

Juba patted me on the knee. "This is the best thing that could have happened. All these little annoyances we complain of, taxes and other things, can easily be resolved face-to-face when I see Augustus."

"He is reminding us that we are in his power. Surely you see that?"

"Of course I do," Juba said. "It's a kind of loyalty test. Will we come when he calls? I've actually expected that this would happen. We've become rather grand, you know."

Mauretania had acquired a new reputation throughout the Mediterranean world.

Our people had become more prosperous. Our capital was a desirable destination for scholars of renown. Juba was fast becoming a renowned scholar in his own right.

I thought of the people who cheered us whenever we appeared, the people of Mauretania, our people now. We must not fail them. Our actions could determine our kingdom's future.

Would we come when Augustus called? Walk back into the lion's mouth, baby and all?

I took a breath. I would not be a frightened child again. I reminded myself of who I was and what I was, Cleopatra's daughter, a queen.

"You're right," I told Juba. "We have much to be proud of. It will be a pleasure to tell Augustus and Livia about all we have achieved."

A galley, its sails decorated with the image of a bull elephant, which Juba had made his royal symbol, entered the Roman port of Ostia. We had been at sea for six days. Now Juba and I stood on deck, clothed in flowing purple robes, the garb of royalty. I wore diamond earrings and gold bangles. My hair was carefully arranged in crimped curls, my eyes made up in the Egyptian manner. My eyes sought Juba. He looked serious but unafraid. Just the sight of him bolstered my courage. I held two-year-old Ptolemy by the hand.

What was in store for us? A state visit, during which we would be felted as royalty? Or something else . . . an ugly fate I did not even wish to think of? Had we flown too high? Was this the end of our freedom?

I knew the answer to these questions as soon as our ship docked. For there, waiting for us, was a delegation of official greeters—all distinguished senators. They were exactly who one would expect to be sent to do honor to allied rulers who had come to pay a friendly call. And among them, smiling broadly, stood a newly inaugurated senator, distinguished in his purple-trimmed toga—my brother Jullus.

Once my husband and I had been brought to Italy to be paraded through the streets as captives. Juba had been a slave. Now we were greeted with honor, offered wine in great golden cups the moment we set our feet on shore.

After Juba and I had taken our sips from the ceremonial cups, my brother caught me in his arms and whispered, "You have done very well for yourself, little moon."

>>>>>>>

We went to stay with Augustus and Livia at their nearby Prima Porta villa—the very place where we had fallen in love. There we were treated less as visiting dignitaries and more as grown children returning to the parental home. Augustus had decided we had reflected great credit upon him—applying *his* principles of government to ruling Mauretania. There was no point in asking what view he would have taken if we had failed his test, not come running back at his first whistle. As things stood, we were granted a one-year remission of taxes. Little problems we had been having with the Roman administrator were swept away. Matters would not stay resolved forever, that we knew. But we could expect some special consideration for a time at least, a fine thing for our people.

We were told to make ourselves at home, stay as long as we wished. It was a great relief to know we could go back to Mauretania whenever we wanted to. That freed us to enjoy a holiday. Juba made full use of the cultural riches of Rome, spent time with scholars of many stripes. I was content to get reacquainted with the imperial family. It would be a stretch to say I felt these people constituted my own family—but what other kin did I have? And some indeed were related to me by blood. Antonia, Octavia's child by my father, Mark Antony, had recently become betrothed to Livia's son Drusus. We had never been close before—she was four years my junior—but now she seemed to regard me as her glamorous older sister. One day she asked me quite gravely, "What is it like to be a queen?" I told her about the weight of responsibility a ruler bore, and she seemed to grasp my meaning.

Octavia was unwell and had taken to her bed, but when I visited, she made an effort to welcome me, and was truly most kind. In general, people were cordial to me, who had never taken the trouble to be so before—even Jullus's wife, Marcella. When we had lived in the same household, she addressed me as you would a servant. Now she introduced her two little sons to me almost with a flourish, crying, "Here are your *nephews!*"

The person I had most missed when I was in Mauretania was my brother Jullus. His affectionate greeting and the sight of him in senatorial dress had warmed me as nothing else could. He had wanted to find a place in the world, and at first sight, it seemed he had certainly claimed an enviable berth. He, at that time, held a junior magistracy and played a responsible role in governing the city of Rome. He and Marcella had two handsome sons.

"You say I have done well. So have you," I said to him one day, as we sat alone in the gardens at his home in Rome.

He gave me a look that jarred me. What I thought I saw in his dark eyes was desperation. The change in him at that moment was so startling that I grabbed his arm and whispered, "Jullus—you're not in any danger?"

He gave a great hoot of laughter. "Danger? Gods above, Sister, I am likely the safest man in Rome. Why, Augustus himself is so concerned for my well-being that if I so much as hint he might want to send me to war, his face goes gray. He tells me how he needs me here, can't do without me."

I understood. As our father's son, he would never be truly trusted.

I did not say, *Is it so important to go to war?* for my brother was Mark Antony's son. Of course he wanted to be blooded on a battlefield. And it would have been one thing if some infirmity had held him back. But to be treated as a potential traitor . . . ?

"You have high governmental rank for a man your age. Perhaps in time . . ."

Perhaps in time Augustus would relent toward him?

He shook his head. Then he laughed. "The thought of Mark Antony's son with a sword in his hand is enough to make Augustus toss up his dinner. And can you really blame him? He is very kind to me. In the end he'll make me consul, maybe even give me a province to govern, as long as that province is strategically unimportant, and is very, very peaceful."

"Consul?" I said. Other than First Citizen, that was Rome's highest office.

"Certainly, I'll be consul. Even if Augustus doesn't think I quite merit that, Marcella will nag him into giving it to me." His face twisted. "Because she loves me so, so much. And she always had her heart set on being a consul's wife."

>>>>>>>

Juba and I planned to return to Mauretania in early May. A few days before we were to depart, Livia surprised me by inviting me to come with her to the ceremony honoring the Good Goddess to be held at the house of one of that year's consuls. I was amazed that she thought it fitting that I attend, for this was a most sacred and supremely Roman occasion. But she said, "You are a Roman citizen. It is required that the women who attend be wives or daughters of men of consular rank. You certainly qualify—your father held the consulship more than once."

I must have looked startled. A Roman consul's daughter—that was the least of who I was.

Livia smiled at me. "If you do not wish to come, that is perfectly fine. But I would very much like for you to attend."

So I went and, side by side with Livia, walked into the mansion on the Palatine where the event was to take place. The consul's wife, a plump little woman named Ravilla, welcomed me courteously. I saw other women looking at me wide-eyed, but everyone greeted me as if there were no question I belonged. The consul himself had been banished from the house, as had the male servants and even male animals. Even busts of male ancestors were hidden from sight. The house was bursting with women—the most high-ranking women in Rome.

This all-night ceremony had, in the waning years of the old Republic, fallen into disrepute. The women were said to get drunk, strip naked, do all manner of forbidden things. In Julius Caesar's time, a man in a woman's clothes—the lover of one of the celebrants—had been smuggled in, causing a great scandal. Livia, I knew, had taken matters in hand and now enforced a certain standard of decorum.

Steaming platters of food had been placed on tables set against the walls of the atrium. Women chatted happily, walking about, sampling the food. "Here is the honey pot," Ravilla intoned solemnly as female slaves carried in a huge ceramic jar and set it on a solid-looking oak table. "It is full of milk." The tradition was to call wine milk on this night. Soon, everyone present had a goblet of wine in her hand. Women who on any other occasion would not dream of drinking wine unmixed with water, on this night drank it unmixed.

Female harpists played. Girls beat cymbals. I saw Julia in the crowd. She came up to greet me with an embrace. "Oh, I am so glad you have come!" By then, many of the younger women had begun to dance. "Come," Julia said. "Dance with me."

We moved our bodies to the beat of the cymbals. All around us women—the most respected women in Rome—were dancing. I saw Livia doing a slow, graceful dance. She seemed to stand apart from the other women—she danced alone, keeping time not to the cymbals' beat but some other stately music only she could hear.

I was surrounded by women of my own age—young wives. They all looked giddy. Some were already a little bit drunk. "This is my husband!" one of them cried, and she moved her pelvis in quick, frantic thrusts.

"Oh, this is mine!" cried another. She moved her pelvis in a different, slower rhythm, gasping like a spent lover while she did it. Suddenly we were all laughing. It must have been the wine.

"And you, Cleopatra's daughter, how does your husband make love to you?" a black-haired woman whispered in my ear.

I moved my hips a few times—feeling rather shy—but the women laughed good-naturedly.

"Well, here is how a great general does it," Julia said, and she gave two hard thrusts of her pelvis and then stopped. She tittered. "And I burn—I burn when he does that, ladies. You cannot imagine the ecstasy—" Then she stood still and threw back her head and quoted a poem:

> *"At his merest touch*
> *My heart beats fast*
> *I am trembling with love*
> *Flame sears me*
> *And the taste of his lips*
> *Is honey*
> *Oh, Cupid, slay me now . . ."*

I had read this poem long ago and not thought it had much merit. But a rapt look transformed Julia's face. Her recitation was so full of feeling that I was flooded with emotion, listening. *Flame sears me* . . . I wanted to be in Juba's arms.

And then suddenly she was laughing—and we were all laughing and dancing together.

As the evening wore on, the music became louder and the dancing wilder. Julia remained in the thick of it all, whirling around, snapping her fingers above her head. But after a time I went to stand beside Livia.

She, not the consul's wife, was truly in charge, the arbiter of what was acceptable. She never once issued a rebuke; I had the feeling she did not have to; her presence was enough. I did not see anyone tear off her clothes; nor did anyone become falling-down drunk. But some of the women danced on and on as if purging themselves of pent-up feeling. Grief and rage played on some faces, joy on others. As the hours passed, some of the women kissed and caressed each other. This evidently was permitted.

Livia continued to stand apart, never interfering, but watching with an eye sharp as a hawk. She would certainly come away from these revels knowing far more about the attendees—mainly senators wives—than she had before the night began. Perhaps that was her intention. I, for my part, could not tear my gaze away from Julia. She moved with abandon, her eyes shut, a rapturous expression on her face; she was inexhaustible.

I stayed at Livia's side. As the night wore on, we opened our hearts to each other, more than we had before. Perhaps it was the atmosphere; perhaps it was the wine.

"This ceremony is more than it at first appears to be," Livia said. "We hold the world together, we women. In honoring the Good Goddess, the mother of all life, we acknowledge who we are." Livia spoke in a quiet voice, so only I could hear. "We bring life into the world. That shapes our perspective—or it should."

I remembered how I felt when Alexander was born, the new sense I had had of myself as a vessel of life.

"Today there is war, but it is confined to the fringes of the empire," Livia went on. "That is bad enough. I have seen what war does to people—from the humblest to the rich and powerful. All suffer. You of course can have little memory of what it was like when the empire was ripped apart. You were so young."

"I remember living in Alexandria when it was under siege," I said. "We inside the palace did not know hunger, but we sensed it when people in the city began to starve. My nurse told me I had no need to be afraid. But of course she lied."

"The gods allowed you and me to survive in that bitter time. Do you think we therefore owe them a debt?"

"Yes," I said. "I have long believed that."

We sipped wine without speaking for a while. It was stronger drink than I was used to. "I feel a bit light-headed," I told Livia.

"Eat something," she said. "The night is barely half over."

I munched meat-filled pastries. Around me, women went on dancing.

"Now, here it is—this is the most important part of the celebration," Livia whispered.

Maidservants brought in a sow. It was enormously fat. They prodded it along with sharpened sticks, but it remained ponderously slow in its movements, grunting with each step. Women moved to create a path for it.

"The Good Goddess rules," women began chanting.

Livia looked at me gravely. "Repeat the sacred words," she said.

We spoke them together: "The Good Goddess rules."

"On most occasions, women in Rome do not give animals in sacrifice. Only men do it," Livia whispered. "But this night is different."

Ravilla, the consul's wife, wielded the knife. Stranding in the crowd of women, Livia and I watched as Ravilla bent and slit the sow's throat cleanly. The creature sank to the floor, gave one long shudder, then was still. "The Good Goddess rules!" Ravilla cried, raising her bloody knife.

Slaves bore the carcass away. Others mopped up the blood.

Afterward, the feasting, drinking, and dancing continued.

"It was good you and Juba came back to Rome when Augustus asked you to," Livia said to me. "Being ruler of an empire works in an unpleasant way on even the strongest mind—it creates suspicions even when there is no cause. Sometimes Augustus needs soothing. Were you afraid when you received that summons?"

"Yes."

"I promise as long as you are loyal, there will never be cause for fear." She smiled. "I have heard you are turning Mauretania into a garden, a beautiful land out of myth, ruled by an exquisite queen and a philosopher king."

"People exaggerate. Mauretania is not a garden."

"Oh, but you have gone a long way toward making it one. And let us be honest—it is you who is doing it, more than Juba. I wish I could do as much for Rome. Sometimes all the choices we face here are ugly." She looked at me with grave eyes, eyes that seemed to contain infinite wisdom. "The past has us all in its coils. One has to accept certain limits."

"I know there are things I lost as a child that will never return to me," I said.

"Yes," she said. "Some losses can never be remedied. My father died for the Republic, and I married the man who, finding the Republic in its death throes, destroyed it for good and all. I will never have my father back, and I will always know he would feel the greatest shame if he saw the choice I have made. I live with that knowledge. I bear it. Can you guess what my justification is?"

"The fact that the empire has peace."

"You are precisely right." Livia's eyes shone. Without a pause, she went on. "I've heard that the people of Mauretania have never been so happy and prosperous as they are now under your rule. That must give you great satisfaction."

"It does," I said. Then I asked a question: "Why did you invite me to come tonight?"

"Why do you think?"

"To remind me that I am Roman. And, I believe, to make an ally of me in protecting Rome's peace."

"How perspicacious you are."

I thought I saw a glint of humor in her eyes. "Are you mocking me?"

"No," she said gently. "That I would never do. I am congratulating myself on the woman you have become."

Much later that night I told Livia I was pregnant again—news I had not yet even shared with Juba. I told her this as eagerly and happily as I might have if she had been my mother. She drew me close and kissed me on the forehead.

"If I have a daughter, I will name her for you," I said.

"For me?" Livia laughed. "That is a great honor. But really, it is not necessary."

"I want to," I said. My voice was a little bit slurred from drink. "I think . . . I owe you my life."

She looked thoughtful. "It was wise of you to name your capital Caesarea. Another loyal gesture can't hurt. Augustus sets store by names and symbols, as men do. But really . . . you had best think again, when your mind is clearer. This wine is very strong."

I smiled at her. "If I have a daughter, I will name her Livia."

"I am honored. In truth, though, I have never much liked the sound of Livia. My second name is much more melodious. Drusilla."

"It's a pretty name," I said.

The sow that had been sacrificed had been butchered and cooked. Everyone had a slice of the sweet meat.

When dawn came, most of the women had stopped dancing. But I saw Julia, her face flushed, still moving in time with the beat of the cymbals. "Oh, look at her," I said to Livia. "Everyone else is yawning, but she dances and dances!"

Livia did not reply. I glanced at her face and saw an expression that surprised me. She gazed at Julia as a mother might at a child climbing up too high on a tree or running onto a road where men raced their horses. She just shook her head.

Livia

While Selene was in Rome, she never set a foot wrong. She had a presence about her now, the elegance of a queen. And also, I thought, a sharp mind. I took pride in the decisions I had made that had helped to set her on her life course. She had grown into a magnificent woman.

Before she and Juba returned to Mauretania, Tavius gave them rich guest gifts. He also gave them what they surely wanted more than silver or gold, a freer hand to govern their kingdom. He felt great trust in Juba. So there were warm, affectionate farewells all around.

At this time, I did not think of my own family and the empire as two separate things but as completely intertwined. My son Drusus and Marcus, my foster son, were now serving with the army in Gaul. Marcus was a fine soldier; Drusus was extraordinary. I am his mother, and my word might be doubted, but I say only what is true. Drusus possessed an instinctive grasp of strategy and tactics rare for one of his years. He also had a gentleness, a kindness, that in no way detracted from his ability as a soldier. In Gaul, he had begun to make a name for himself, gaining not only the respect of the soldiers under him, but their affection. Unlike Tiberius, he had a knack for winning hearts.

Drusus had come home to Rome for a short time to marry Antonia, Tavius's niece. Looking at the two of them together, two glowing young people, one saw the flush of first love. After he left, Antonia, to her great joy and mine, discovered she was pregnant.

Tiberius, meanwhile, chafed at the bit. He had important administrative work to do in Rome but was eager to return to Gaul himself. I asked him one day, half mischievously, "Won't you hate leaving your wife?"

As expected, he looked at me as if I had uttered an absurdity.

"You are happy with Vipsania?" I persisted.

He shrugged. It would have been unlike him to admit to being happy with anything or anyone.

Vipsania admired Tiberius, and he enjoyed being admired. He gave orders, and she did what he told her to. Her pliant nature suited my son. If he did not praise her, at least in my presence, he never complained about her.

It mattered, of course, that their marriage was successful, not only for simple, human reasons, but because it was a knot that bound Agrippa close in alliance with our family. Agrippa had become, by this time, almost a full partner to Tavius in governing the empire. Of course this meant that the state of his marriage to Julia had an importance far transcending the personal happiness of two people.

Since their wedding, most of the time, weighty affairs had kept Agrippa from Julia's side. She—young, vibrant—could not be expected to live the life of a shut-in in her husband's absence. But as time went on, I became more and more concerned about the company she kept. I did not wish to alarm Tavius. Instead, at a time when I knew he would be absent, I invited Julia to my house for a little talk.

It was midsummer, hot in Rome. We sat in a shaded veranda in the midst of the garden. A slave served us juice in crystal goblets and plates of figs and dates.

"Gaius, Julilla, and Lucius are well?" I said.

Julia nodded. I noticed a tension in the set of her shoulders. Did she know what I had summoned her to talk about?

"Agrippa will be surprised, I'm sure, when he sees how big they have grown," I said. "It is a pity he has been away so much."

"Yes, a great pity."

"It's natural that you want to go out and enjoy the company of interesting people. I have heard that you have made a particular friend of Sempronius Gracchus and you socialize with the men and women in his circle. Now, I find that perfectly natural. I'm sure those people are very amusing."

I had done my best to speak in an easy, offhand manner. Still, I could see her bristling and then struggling to contain herself. "Oh . . . people bring you tales about how I spend my time?"

I looked her coolly in the eye. "People bring me tales about everything that happens in Rome."

It was true I had a network of informants. It was equally true that Tavius and I never punished people for their opinions or their private behavior. But we needed to know the popular mood.

"Am I to take it you do not fully approve of my friends?"

"Whether I approve or not hardly matters. I am concerned for your well-being. I am afraid your association with a man like Gracchus might lead to unpleasant talk."

I wanted to cry out to her, *Take care, you foolish child!* But instead I had to tread carefully, for fear of provoking her anger and defiance.

She eyed me warily. "You have not discussed this with my father?"

"I saw no need to."

She relaxed a little. "Well, Gracchus is a harmless, witty man. I enjoy his company, and that of his friends." She shrugged. "It's a question of keeping myself occupied, that is all."

"Yes," I said. "I am sure that with your husband away, life can be rather boring."

Was she sleeping with Gracchus? Nothing I had been told provided an answer to that question. I only had my suspicions, which I hoped were groundless.

I asked myself—of all men in Rome, why had she picked Gracchus to befriend? A memory flitted through my mind, Julia, at five or six, dressed in silk for a festival, her hair done up in curls, running to her father, crying, "Papa, look at me! Look at me!" I wanted to push the image away, but it persisted. Was she still that little girl and picking unsuitable friends in a bid to attract Tavius's attention?

I leaned toward her. "I want you to be happy and to be free to form the friendships that please you. But you are Augustus's daughter. For you to make a man like Gracchus your particular friend . . . could be misunderstood." *He is a libertine,* I might have added. *His reputation as a womanizer is well known. In politics, he is no friend of your father.* But surely Julia knew all this.

"Of course. I am supposed to act like a sort of clay doll that smiles and listens to the people's cheers while Father stands by beaming." She tossed her head. "As for talk . . . well, if people tell lies, let them. I am tired of being a clay doll. Do you blame me?"

"It would be better if you saw less of Gracchus," I said.

She did not answer me but just sipped some wine.

211

Are we rational beings? I would like to think of myself that way. But when I observe other people, I see how often they fail to be governed by reason. I have seen people plainly hold two intentions in mind that contradict each other, and so thwart and frustrate themselves at every turn. I have known them to pretend, even to themselves, that they are pursuing one course of action when it is plain as day they are doing the contrary thing. I have seen them love and hate the same person in equal measure. And I have seen intelligent people refuse to look at what is right before their eyes—or refuse to admit that they do see it.

Did Julia wish to provoke her father's anger? Who could say?

Perhaps it ought to have been obvious to me that my stepdaughter's behavior needed to be firmly checked. But there was no way to rein her in without involving Tavius. I imagined the most horrific explosion if Tavius heard of his daughter's doings. He would be injured, Julia would be injured—it seemed our whole family would suffer a wound that might never heal. So I did something unusual for me. I dallied, I equivocated. I allowed myself to hope that my warning to Julia would be sufficient to at least make her more cautious.

Julia

Of course Livia knew Gracchus and I were lovers. Was there anything that happened in Rome that evaded her all-seeing eyes?

I went back home, carried in a closed sedan chair, my nails digging into the palms of my hands. *Curse her,* I thought. *May she be banished to the lowest pit of Hades for spying on me.*

I was frightened as well as angry. She had not spoken to my father—but might she yet do so? I attributed her silence to protectiveness, but I did not believe it was me that she wished to protect. My father—his well-being came first and last with her. She would not upset him if she could avoid it. And he would be upset—terribly upset—if he learned about Gracchus and me.

At home, I sought out Phoebe. She was a freedwoman now. I had freed her because it was impossible to keep my closest female friend a slave. And she had become that—my close friend, my confidante.

"Will you be getting ready to go out this evening?" she asked me.

I shook my head. "I think I had better not."

"Oh, my lady, what is wrong?"

"You are free now, Phoebe," I said, "but I am still a slave. Maybe that is the gods' justice."

Sitting in my bedchamber, I told her what Livia had said. Phoebe knew all there was to know about me and Gracchus already. I knew I could absolutely rely on her loyalty.

"Perhaps you had better be circumspect for a while," she said.

I nodded. I would be careful and keep close to home.

The prospect made me want to weep. It was not only the thought of being separated from Gracchus. I felt as if I would be locked in a dungeon cell. It was so awful—as if I were about to be smothered. "Oh, Phoebe, why am I what I am? Why can't I be content with what I have? Do you think the gods have cursed me?"

"Of course not, my lady."

I sent word to Gracchus I would not see him for a while. In my caution, I only trusted Phoebe to carry the note to him. When she returned, she said he was saddened, but understood.

Almost two months after this, I was at the chariot races with my father and Livia. I had during this time been careful to avoid Gracchus and his circle.

The sun beat down fiercely on that particular day, and the heat made me uncomfortably aware of my body. Father and Livia were in a particularly cheerful mood. I remember her leaning close to him, whispering something in his ear that caused him to dissolve in laughter.

I caught sight of Appius Pulcher, one of Gracchus's friends, walking up to a tier above where we sat. A young poet, Ovid, and his wife accompanied him. All three waved at me, and naturally I waved back.

Later at dinner Father said, "That Ovid fellow—he writes obscene verse."

"Have you read what he writes?" I asked, a hint of challenge in my voice.

"Yes, a bit of it—but I wouldn't keep a volume of his work in my library."

"He is actually very talented."

Father nodded. "Which makes the use to which he puts his ability all the more regrettable."

"He writes about love. Do you consider that wrong?"

"What is wrong is the complete absence of morality in his work. You ought to reconsider some of your friendships, I think."

I said nothing. I felt two emotions: fear—what did Father know about my friendships?—and also anger. It seemed so unfair that when he controlled so much of my life, he must even control my friendships.

"Now Livia has her own artistic friends," Father went on. "Poets and sculptors. But she limits her friendships to people who are respectable."

"Father," I said, "be assured, when I am as old as she is, I'll have old friends too."

His face changed, as if I had slapped him. "I don't like your manner of speaking lately," he said. "I don't like the people you surround yourself with, and I don't like discourtesy."

I had seen Father look at other people as he looked at me now. One knew at such moments that he could pinch them out of existence like gnats. His reproachful gaze would fall on them and in due course—oh, no, he would not kill them, but if they were public men, their careers ended for good and all. Whoever they were, they were banished from his presence and his favor, which in Rome was a kind of death.

"It was a jest," Livia said in a strained voice. "I'm sure Julia did not mean to be discourteous."

"I misspoke. Forgive me," I said. "Forgive me, Livia."

She nodded. "It is forgotten."

Father gave me a thin smile.

But I knew what I had said would not be forgotten, not by him. When did he ever forget anything? And what concerned me most was not his anger at my barbed jest. How much did he know about the part of my life I endeavored to keep secret from him? *The people you surround yourself with.* Had it come to his ears that I was friendly with people he despised—or had more come to his ears than that? What had Livia said to him?

I loved Father, but I was angry, so angry at him. It was hard to always contain my anger in his presence. And perhaps this was how he had begun to feel toward me. Love and anger warred in him. If indeed, he loved me at all.

Livia

There were subjects Tavius and I did not talk about. We each silently understood that such discussion could only tear away at the foundations of our marriage. My feelings about the role he had played in the destruction of the Republic and the death of my own parents was one such topic. Another was the fact that he had not always been faithful to me in the years since we wed. The one time when we had spoken freely about these matters, the result had been a long estrangement. He had come close to divorcing me. Silence was better.

There were two other subjects we approached in a gingerly way and discussed only when we had to. The first was Tiberius, my son. He had great gifts as a soldier and an administrator, but Tavius did not like him. He used him, promoted him as an able man, indeed exhausted him with work, but had no affection at all for him. This always troubled me.

The second subject was Julia. Increasingly when I spoke of her to Tavius, I had the feeling I was touching an open wound. Did he know as much as I did about the life Julia was living? Did he know more? I never put any question to him. I was afraid of what my asking questions might let loose.

When Julia made her silly little joke about my "old" friends, I saw something frightening in Tavius's expression. He was not mainly reacting to the offense to me—though I doubt any other person on earth but Julia would have dared slight me in Tavius's presence. There was a much deeper emotion underneath the surface. I feared it—I feared a rage in direct proportion to his love for his only child. She was the mother of his heirs, the wife of his greatest general. A volcano erupting, an all-out conflict between Julia and Tavius could rain misery on all of us and threaten the empire.

A few days after the dinner with Julia, Tavius said, "The number of Roman citizens has fallen again. People avoid marrying and having children."

We were in the study, which he used for the sort of work that required privacy and concentration. It was up a long staircase, on the top floor of the house. Some of our most important conversations took place here, away from listening ears.

"Yes, I know it is a problem," I said.

"Young people today want to live just for their own pleasure."

The light from the single porthole window shone on his hair. It had gone white in places. I remembered a golden-haired young man confessing he had fallen passionately in love with me, saying he would divorce his wife as soon as their baby was born and that I must leave my husband and children. I almost could have laughed as Tavius went on, talking about the moral looseness of the younger generation. But looking at his grim face, I knew I had better not even smile.

"I doubt there is much we can do about contemporary morals," I said carefully.

"I have some legislation in mind."

He was enough of a politician to first tell me about the part of his new legislation I would like. Mothers of four or more children would be freed from the financial guardianship of men; this was a privilege I already had insisted on for myself and had obtained as the First Citizen's wife. They would have the right to enter into business contracts and dispose of their money without any man's permission. But there would be severe tax penalties for people—both men and women—who did not marry and have children. Even those who were widowed and did not remarry within a set time. It struck me at once that this law would greatly penalize men like Julia's unmarried, childless friend Sempronius Gracchus.

The legislation also set a penalty for both male and female adulterers—exile.

I said, "I think this legislation will be seen as intruding too much into people's private lives. You have protected Roman liberties, and people praise you for it. Tavius, this will not bring you praise."

His mouth set in a tight line.

I knew he would brook no argument. Still, I had to say, "Some of our own friends will take this ill. Even Maecenas . . ."

Maecenas was a major prop of Tavius's rule, an important and popular figure in his own right. When we happened to travel away from the city of Rome, he handled administrative affairs in Tavius's stead. Beyond that, he had presided over a new birth of Roman arts and letters. But his marriage was childless. His preference for male lovers was well known and little remarked upon by his friends. His wife freely slept with other men, married and unmarried. Tavius himself in the past had been one of her lovers.

"Maecenas?" Tavius said. "Gods above, I've made him rich enough that the fine for no children won't bother him. He'll realize this has nothing to do with my friendship and regard for him."

Would he? Perhaps. Or perhaps he was more sensitive than Tavius knew.

"And trials for adultery?" I said.

"There won't be many. And there will be legal safeguards. I doubt there will be many convictions in the end. It's mainly a question of setting forth an ideal—a monogamous ideal."

I still did not like this. "It will cost you popularity," I said.

"If it does, so be it." Then, quietly, Tavius said, "You're my ideal."

I tilted my head. "I?"

"Yes. A faithful wife. Faithful in body, faithful in soul."

He rarely said this sort of thing. I could not help being moved.

"Even if I am not as pure as you, at least I know such purity is to be revered," he said.

I found I had nothing to say. The truth was, such virtue as I had came easily to me. He was all I had ever wanted.

>>>>>>>

Tavius's new legislation was enacted into law despite widespread grumbling, particularly among the young. The tax penalties came under the most fire. As for the legal penalties for adultery—people saw that an eyewitness was required to make a charge stick and considered rightly that the law would have little impact on how people lived their lives.

There was one provision in the new law that Tavius had not mentioned to me and that gave me a chill when I read it.

A husband could not legally kill his wife or her lover if he discovered them in the act of adultery; he had to prosecute them in the usual way. But a man could execute his daughter out of hand in the same circumstances.

A father's right of life and death over his children is hollowed in our tradition—and almost never exercised. In theory, a father could execute a child at any time for any reason or none. Why, then, was this new provision needed? Was it a warning to straying daughters? Or to one straying daughter in particular?

I have wondered if it would have entered Tavius's head to pass any of this moral legislation if Julia's behavior had not troubled him. A peasant father in a like case, unwilling to directly confront his daughter, might have vented his frustration by railing about falling morals to any passerby. Rome's First Citizen imposed moral strictures on all of Rome.

Yet I think, despite the tenor of the legislation, Tavius never sought to find out definitely if Julia had a lover. He thought of her as having unsuitable friends, friends who needed to be pushed to live conventional lives. These friendships in themselves suggested a certain mode of living—but only suggested it. He did not want to know if Julia were truly an adulteress. And in truth, neither did I.

>>>>>>>

The naming ceremony for my first grandson took place on a clear June day, in Octavia's house, where Antonia continued to live, with Drusus away in Gaul. The child was strong and vigorous. He was named after his father.

I looked at the small, red-faced mite in his cradle and had a sense of the continuity of life. My father's life and my mother's were both continued in this child. At times, exhausted or discouraged, I wondered if existence had any true purpose. But gazing down at the baby, I did not doubt—here was the meaning I sought.

I was now a grandmother. It was a moment for looking backward, across the long sweep of years, and also for surveying the road ahead.

While the merrymaking was still going on in Octavia's atrium, I drew Julia aside. We sat in a small sitting room, alone. I wanted to reach her heart and her soul.

"I feel I am the same person inside that I was at your age, and even when I was an unmarried girl," I said. "But I know that is not so. I have changed. The years have changed me."

She looked at me warily, wondering, I suppose, where this conversation was tending.

"I regret the gulf that exists between generations. There are things I know, that I have learned from hard experience, that I wish I could teach my children and you. But perhaps those things can only be learned through the pain of living. And there may be matters I no longer understand. I believe I remember what it was like to be full of the passions of youth, but perhaps I am mistaken."

"What is it you would like to teach me if you could?"

I leaned forward in my chair. "That this world is a dangerous place. That it is more so for people in our position and even more so for women. One mistake can bring ruin."

Her face had gone tense, but I sensed a hardening in her. It was as if she were willfully steeling herself not to hear my words.

"You may think what I am saying is banal. Oh, the world is dangerous—who does not realize that? But you have not lost those you loved, as I have." I glanced away. "What do you think of your father's new legislation?"

"It is making him unpopular with everyone who is young and free," she said in a clipped voice. "I think that it is foolish."

"Yes. He cannot afford to do foolish things, but he did this. Why do you imagine that is?"

She gave me a long stare. "Are you blaming me?"

"There are debts you owe your children. There are debts we owe to future generations, to that baby in there . . ."

"Gods, all I want is a little space to breathe! I am harming no one."

We were both silent for a time.

"No doubt you're bored," I said finally. "It is a pity that you and Agrippa have been separated so much."

Her face was empty and blank.

"Before long, Agrippa will be in Greece. The eastern part of the empire cannot be left too long without a strong hand. You could hardly be with him while he was waging war in Gaul, but I see no reason you could not join on his new assignment."

She said nothing.

"Some travel . . . seeing new places, in company with your husband . . . it will be enjoyable, I hope. You will have some . . . fresh air to breathe. No doubt you will like that."

Julia still did not speak.

"I will arrange it," I said. I stood up and left the room.

Julia

$\mathcal{I}$ would not have admitted it to Livia, but I was relieved to be leaving Rome at this time. For I was afraid—afraid of my father. I took his legislation for the warning it was. It was hard now for us to be in each other's presence.

I pretended to others, and sometimes even to myself, that the prospect of joining my husband filled me with joy. I would take the children with me. For the first time in our marriage, we might all be together for more than a few months.

"Greece," I said to Phoebe. "Your own country. Will you be happy to see it again?"

She gave me a doleful look. "I will be happy as long as I can serve you, my lady," she said.

I took leave of Gracchus a few days before my expected departure. I wept a little, but those were light, easy tears. Sometimes I had tried to imagine we had a great love as Catullus had for his Lesbia. But I had always known something was lacking. In truth, we were good friends using each other's body for pleasure.

"Our friendship will always endure," I told him. The unspoken meaning of my words was that we had that and nothing more.

The parting that rent my soul came later, at Prima Porta. There I said farewell to my father, knowing I might not see him again for years.

My father and Livia escorted me and the children out to the gate of the villa, where a coach waited to take us to the port at Ostia, where we would depart by ship. The children clung to Father. He kissed and embraced them. They climbed into the coach.

"Have a safe journey," Father said to me. There was an emptiness in his eyes.

I nodded. Then suddenly, I cried out, "Father!" All at once, I was sobbing.

He took me in his arms, held me tight. "It's not forever, Julia. You'll be back. We'll be together again."

I looked up at his face. It was like stepping back in time. The father I had always loved and worshipped, the loving father of my childhood—he was there, he had returned to me.

"You'll have a wonderful time in the East," he said, speaking as one might to a child to soothe it. "You can't imagine what beautiful sights you will see. You must write me regular letters. I want to see it all again through your eyes."

"Yes, Father," I said. "Yes, I'll write to you."

He helped me into the coach. I trembled, gripping his hand, not wanting to let go. He kissed my cheek, then pulled away. And then the coach began to move, and we were separated. I hugged my children to me and continued to shed a flood of cleansing tears.

>>>>>>>

Our trip to join Agrippa was uneventful except for the last leg. We were to meet him in the city of Ilium, once the site of the city of

Troy. We had to cross the Scamander River and were assured it was safe to cross it at night. It was not safe. There was a storm. The boat almost capsized as we—the children, Phoebe, and I—floundered in the dark, water up to our ankles. I tasted terror—more for my children than myself. But the boat finally made it to shore.

We all stood on the bank, with no idea of what to do next. Nobody was there to welcome us. I sent a messenger to find my husband. Until he came, all we could do was wait in the dark and the rain.

Finally, I heard a clatter of hoofbeats, and Agrippa was there, surrounded by mounted legionaries. He threw himself off his horse and pulled me to him. "Are you all right?"

"Yes."

"The children . . ." He looked down at them, then glanced at me questioningly.

"They are fine," I said.

"I hardly know them, it's been so long," he said. Then, "I might have lost all four of you." In the light of sputtering torches, I saw his face contort with fury. "Lysis!" he barked.

A wizened man, some local official, came threading his way through the press of soldiers. "Lord Agrippa . . . ," he mumbled.

Agrippa began to berate him. Why weren't watchmen set to look for the boat in the storm? Why hadn't small rescue boats been sent out to meet us and guide us into port, for safety's sake? And why, in the first place, had our boat ever been permitted to sail at night while it was raining? On and on. I had never heard my husband shout in such a way, never seen him so beside himself. Before his rant was done, he seemed to be blaming the little man, and with him the whole city of Ilium, for the fact that the storm had happened at all.

Finally, he caught himself up short and remembered the children and me standing there drenched. At his order, a cart was brought up to take us to our lodgings. I climbed aboard, and then he lifted the children in beside me. A strand of Julilla's wet hair hung down across her forehead. He brushed it back, smiling at her. "You'll be in a dry house soon, little one."

I thought, *In his way, he cares for us—for me and the children.*

"Are you glad that we are to be with you now?" I asked.

"Of course," he said, as if that were a foolish question. I waited for him to ask me if I was glad too or to speak words of welcome. But instead he growled, "I will levy a fine on the entire city for this."

I looked blankly at him.

"Gods above, Julia, don't you realize their negligence almost got you all killed?" Then he added in a low voice, "Imagine bringing that news to your father. He would have gone insane."

I fought against the notion that the worst of it for him, if the children and I had drowned, would have been being held accountable by my father. Perhaps I was unfair to even consider if this was so—surely it was natural for him to think of having to tell my father such terrible news.

Agrippa did levy a fine on the city, a huge fine of one hundred thousand sesterces. Eventually, though, he was persuaded to remit it.

>>>>>>>

All the praise my husband received for his work in the East was surely warranted. He reorganized the governmental administration of Greece and Asia Minor, paying special attention to bringing a new order and efficiency to the collection of taxes. He rooted out corruption and allocated funds for useful public works. He worked ceaselessly, and as he did I traveled with him from place to place. I saw the Acropolis in Athens. I saw the sunrise in the Judean hills. I gave birth to our second daughter, Agrippina.

Everywhere we went, I was honored, as Augustus's daughter as well as Agrippa's wife. In Ephesus a special bronze coin was minted with my portrait as well as Agrippa's on it. Statues of me, standing beside my husband, were speedily erected in many cities and towns. I was feted, treated almost as a goddess.

In the core of me, I felt a darkness, an emptiness that only grew. I remembered Gracchus with yearning, remembered how it was to be touched by him. It was as if my skin itself could feel hunger.

Making love was like fighting a battle to Agrippa, a battle to be quickly won. When I had the courage to speak my desires to my husband, I expected him to be shocked—and he was shocked.

"I'm surprised you know of such things," he said to me. "Is it in that poetry you read?"

"Yes, the poets speak of love."

"I think those books are a waste of your time."

Nothing changed between us.

He was a good man. But it was impossible for him to be other than he was. And I . . . could I be other than I was?

There was a young officer serving on Agrippa's staff in Cyrene. Like Gracchus, he had a great name. Cornelius Scipio was a collateral descendant of those Scipios who brought down Rome's great enemy, Carthage. He sometimes dined with us, and I would find myself admiring his profile—he had a stern, pure look. At first he was too shy to even smile at me. But that changed. A word was spoken, out of Agrippa's hearing. Then another and another. Questions were asked, and answered, not only with words—the oldest questions on earth.

I would meet him in a small spare bedchamber, tucked away in a corner. Always, this took place after Agrippa slept. The shutters would be open—the night in Cyrene was hot. Some little insect, foreign to Rome, made music in the bushes outside, chirping almost like a bird.

Scipio's body was lean and hard. He was just my age. He was eager and ardent, and yet in bed I was teacher, he the pupil. Gracchus had taught me things Scipio did not know. I found it a delight to instruct him. I would never let him spend inside me. But I gave him pleasure and took pleasure from him.

I felt it would be doing Agrippa a great wrong if I bore a child who was not his. It would be such a violation of his dignity if I had tricked him into unknowingly giving his name to a child he had not fathered. I could not have done that to him. I could forgive myself for everything else I did as long as I was faithful in that one way.

Scipio and I never spoke of the right or wrong or the danger of what we were doing. The closest we ever came to that was when I said, "We ought to stop."

"But you don't want to, do you?"

"No."

"Neither do I."

I did not love him. I realized, as with Gracchus, that an element of love was missing from our passion. There was a yearning in me that he did not answer—and I had begun to suspect no man ever would. But the desire that I felt for him overwhelmed me just the same. When I imagined life without him, I saw a world drained of all color.

I was fond of him. Our time together would not be long—I knew that. I wanted in the moments we had to give him all the tenderness I was capable of—to give him that, in return for the gift he gave me. I had felt so barren, but he made me feel alive.

Meanwhile, at my husband's table, entertaining his guests, I exerted myself to be a good hostess, to say light, amusing things. Agrippa was proud of me, I think. I am sure I looked happy. Inside myself I puzzled over the nature of my own being. I would stand at Agrippa's side, welcoming guests, presenting a perfect surface, and know that very night I would steal away from our bedchamber for a blissful hour in Scipio's arms. I asked myself what sort of woman I was that I should do such a thing. I thought of stories of women sent mad by the gods—of Medea who slew her children, of Phaedra driven mad by Venus, unhinged by lawless desire—and in my darkest moments I wondered if such a curse could have descended on me.

"Do you think I'm mad like Phaedra?" I whispered to Scipio one night.

"Phaedra was cruel," he answered. "You are kind."

"Only too kind where you are concerned," I said.

He laughed.

Phaedra—she was the one who haunted me. Phaedra taking her own life. Phaedra willingly bringing down destruction on the man she loved.

I wanted to live. I wanted to hurt no one. I was not like her.

Livia

*J*ulia's absence from Rome eased my mind. I had feared gossip about her and Gracchus, and also people whispering that Tavius's moral legislation was meant to control his own daughter. In fact, there was little such talk. Julia's friendship with Gracchus had not become common knowledge in Rome.

Tavius seemed happier with Julia gone. She wrote to him about her visits to cities in the eastern empire. He showed some of her letters to me, and they were delightful—full of witty and colorful descriptions of people and places. He wrote her affectionate letters in return. At this point in their lives, he and his daughter loved each other best from a distance.

Meanwhile Tiberius was once more serving in Gaul. I wrote him just the sort of letters to be expected of a loving mother concerned for her firstborn who was at war, and he sent me kind messages of reassurance. Like Tavius and Julia, we seemed to get along better out of each other's sight.

Of course, my irritation with my son had never affected public policy. I hoped that now, with Julia gone and apparently happy, Tavius would ease off in his attempt to reform Roman morals. But he gave several long public speeches, reproaching noblemen who chose not to take wives. There were many such men who wished to avoid the burden of marriage and children. The thinning of the ranks of Rome's elite as a result did not bode well for the future. Still, the vehemence with which Tavius decried hedonists surprised people, and stirred up real anger.

He brought mockery on himself and me. People who for twenty years had been willing to forget the circumstances of our marriage—our shedding our respective mates—now joked about it. They talked about the love affairs Tavius had indulged in both before and after our marriage. A disgusting story started to circulate that had me selecting virgin slave girls for his bed.

In truth, his moralizing did no good at all. But he never abandoned it for long. And he would not consider dispensing with his taxes on those who were unmarried or childless. His rigidity about these matters was unlike him. I was left groping, trying to understand the man I had married, who I had believed I understood as well as my own soul.

>>>>>>>

One day he received a letter from Julia announcing the birth of her second daughter, Agrippina. "Another granddaughter, and Julia is well," he said with a rather subdued smile. He added, "I am sure the baby will look like Agrippa. All Julia's children do."

I said, without thinking, "Gaius looks more like you."

"Oh, come, anyone can tell that boy is Agrippa's son."

"Yes, but—"

"But?" he said sharply.

"I only mean Gaius has your coloring."

"My coloring but Agrippa's features," he said, as if this were a matter of the greatest importance.

"Yes, of course," I said. "He is very much like his father."

I had imagined that if Julia were really sleeping with Gracchus and the affair came to light, it might lead to a disastrous fissure with Agrippa. I had not given much thought to the shadow it would cast on the legitimacy of all Julia's children, including the boys who were Tavius's heirs. The two did resemble their father after all. But I realized that the slur even if false could taint them. Was a reputed bastard likely to become First Citizen of Rome?

I believe this aspect of things troubled Tavius deeply, though he would not speak of it. And it fueled his anger at Gracchus, and all men like Gracchus, who were the objects of his punitive laws.

>>>>>>>

The estrangement that occurred between Tavius and Maecenas at this time was sad but perhaps inevitable. No outright break occurred; Maecenas continued to be invited to our dinner parties and sometimes even came. But the old closeness between him and Tavius was gone.

"Do you know what I keep remembering?" Maecenas asked me once when we were alone. "How the three of us painted a kind of picture together, to augment Augustus's legend—a picture of old-fashioned virtue."

I could remember our painting that picture too. I was the faultless wife—devoted, chaste, and compliant. Tavius the ideal paterfamilias—all iron rectitude. And Julia—she was the perfect, obedient daughter, shyly waving at the applauding crowds when she wasn't home spinning wool. This was the politically useful portrait we sought to present to the world.

"We painted a picture," Maecenas went on, "and somehow Augustus took it for real and decided he ought to live in it. And to insist that everyone else live in it too. But I can't even pretend I fit in that painting. So if he feels he must dispose of me, so be it."

"He has no desire to dispose of you," I said. "He still desires your friendship. Be clear about it. He is not angry at you. You are angry at him."

Maecenas shrugged, as if to dismiss my words. "He says it won't kill me to pay his tax, and that much is true. I am disgustingly rich. But all the poets and artists I've induced to support and revere him are not so fortunate. There is an icy wind coming in their direction, where there ought to be a warm breeze. And they do feel it."

We sat in a garden. Larks sang overhead. I tried to think of comforting words to say, but they escaped me. I said in a low voice, "I have spoken to him about this matter. He is obdurate."

Maecenas nodded. "I ask myself—how can it be he doesn't know that the whole of humanity can't be like legionaries marching in lockstep? The poets, the playwrights, and sculptors, they have made the time of Caesar Augustus the golden age of Rome's rebirth . . . so many of them live lives that don't fit into his scheme for living any more than mine does. Augustus is the most intelligent man I know. Why has he become so blind to reality?"

I let out a deep, long breath. "He is not a tyrant. He will not actually harm any of the poets and artists you worry about. Oh, maybe their purses but—"

"He'll leave their heads attached to their necks? How kind of him."

"He has turned the world upside down, remade Rome for good and all. And I sometimes think the fact frightens him. So he harkens back to the world when he was young—how it was when you were boys growing up in that provincial town, before he ever walked the streets of Rome."

"Now his ideal is how it was in Velitrae? Then he's worse off than I thought."

Velitrae—where men took their pleasure where they would, but wives could be relied on to be chaste, where daughters obeyed fathers and accepted their choice of husband without a murmur. Where the world was unchanging for century after century. "I don't think either one of us can truly understand the burdens Tavius carries, or what that has done to him. There are so few people he can trust. He still needs your friendship."

"I doubt that," Maecenas said. "I doubt that very much."

Julia

We were staying in a villa on the Aegean coast. I had not seen my husband all day. When I entered our bedchamber that night, I found him sitting on the bed in the glow of the oil lamp, leaning down to rub one of his feet. He had been having pain in his feet for several months—sharp pain, though he tried to hide how bad it was.

"You must see a physician," I said.

"Physicians are idiots."

"But there must be remedies. You can't go on suffering."

"Sometimes the only thing to do is suffer. That's just the way life is." There was a note of muted anger in his voice. He stopped massaging his foot and gave me cold, level look. "I've dismissed Scipio from my staff," he said. "There'll be no scandal, no blot on his precious name. He is on his way to Gaul right now, no doubt glad of the opportunity to emulate his dead ancestors. Let's see if he can wage war like they did, or is only good for screwing other men's wives."

I looked back at him, saying nothing. I felt numb.

"Is Agrippina mine?" he asked.

"Yes," I said.

"No doubt in your mind?"

"I swear by all the gods, she is your daughter."

"Well, that's good to know."

I had an impulse to weep. But the tears did not come. And there was nothing to say. I just stood before him, still as stone.

"You've never believed I was good enough for you," he said.

"That's not true."

He actually laughed. "Oh, you mean it's not my low birth? It's more . . . what? I'm too old? I just don't suit you?"

I did not speak. I wanted to undo what had happened, but it was too late. Finally I got out the words, "What now?"

"We will go on as we were. There is nothing else to do."

"Because I am my father's daughter." It was not a question.

"Yes."

"Do you hate me?" The words surprised me even as I spoke them. I felt dread, waiting for the answer.

He shook his head and almost smiled—as if I had said something silly. "Do you have any idea who I am, what I've done and seen in my life? Do you have any notion at all of what it takes to get deep emotion out of me these days?"

I shook my head.

"I save hatred for the battlefield. It serves a purpose there. Hating you would serve no purpose at all." He let out a long breath. "You may be right about my needing to see a physician. My feet have gotten bad." He drew one of his feet up on the bed and massaged it with both hands, grimacing.

It felt as if my chest had filled with unshed tears. I knew that I would miss Scipio just as I had missed Gracchus. I even suspected that eventually I would long again for another man's arms. But at that moment, all I could do was walk over to the bed and say, "Let me."

Agrippa raised his head and stared at me. In the glare of the lamplight, his face showed deeply etched lines. I had never seen him look so old and tired.

"Let me," I said again.

He frowned and shrugged.

I sat on the edge of the bed, massaging his feet.

>>>>>>>

Previously, when Agrippa had been well and made love to me, I gritted my teeth. Yet now, with him ill and in pain, I hastened to minister to his bodily needs, doing everything I could to ease his suffering.

The physician said that the fact that the pain was centered on Agrippa's big toes meant Agrippa was suffering from the "unwalkable disease," a sickness that could be brought on by too much rich food or wine. Agrippa thought this was nonsense but grudgingly agreed to a change of diet. I made sure that simple food was prepared for him and that he took his wine diluted with three parts water. Every day I put ointment on Agrippa's feet and massaged them.

My maid Phoebe was amazed that I was such a devoted nurse. She, of course, knew the entire tale of Scipio and me. At this point, there was little about my life she did not know.

"I pity my husband. He is in terrible pain," I said. "And yes—I feel guilty."

"You didn't cause his illness, my lady."

"Who knows? With another wife, perhaps his mind would be easier, and perhaps he would be well."

A bitter expression surfaced on her face. I think she came very close to calling me a fool.

"You think your being with another man has brought this on him? You are not to blame. You've given him four fine children and catered to his every need. When has he ever accommodated himself to your wants? It's not as if he has been so pure in his life—he hasn't even kept his hands off the slaves in his own house!"

My mouth must have dropped open.

"Oh, my lady," Phoebe said, her eyes glittering, "surely you know. That little dark one, the second cook, he sold to his friend . . . ?"

It had been a small matter, the sale of a skilled slave three years ago, as a favor to an old acquaintance of Agrippa's. The slave had seemed happy enough to leave, to be head cook in a great household. The whole business had made little impression on me at the time.

"She was carrying Lord Agrippa's child," Phoebe said. "He wanted her gone. A usual thing for a man of his kind."

I shook my head. At this moment, I truly did feel like a fool. Had I really been so blind about the occurrences under my own roof? "Is this true?"

"He has had his women every place we've been."

A terrible thought came into my mind. "Have you . . . ?"

She gave a chuckle. "Me? Oh, no, my lady, he hasn't approached me. It may be the clubfoot or perhaps something in my eyes . . . I am not fond of men. And Lord Agrippa—I'll give him this—he does not rape. What need has he? A gold coin or a bauble is all it takes for him to get what he wants. But he has let his own child be born into slavery and left him enslaved."

"He has done that?"

"Oh, yes, my lady, more than once. And you feel guilty about a few tickles in the dark?"

>>>>>>>

Several days after this, Statius, Agrippa's body servant, came running to me. "Mistress, mistress, the master has injured himself. He is in the baths."

A large, elaborate bathhouse with hot and cold pools encompassed one entire wing of the house in which we were staying. Accompanied by Statius, I raced to the bathhouse. There I found my husband sitting on a marble bench, his fist jammed against his teeth, as if to hold back moans of agony. His feet were bright red. An overturned basin had spilled liquid on the tile floor. I smelled vinegar. "What happened?" I cried.

Agrippa shook his head, unable to answer.

"Oh, mistress," Statius said, "it is vinegar, heated on the stove. It is supposed to help the foot pain. But I think it was too hot!"

"Get the physician." I knelt beside Agrippa. "Why did you do this?"

"Why do you think?" he muttered. "For the pain."

Someone had told him hot vinegar was a remedy for his condition, and the pain had become so great he was willing to try anything.

The physician arrived and put salve on Agrippa's blisters.

When his blisters healed a little, I went to him and stated the obvious. He could not go on traveling incessantly and shouldering the mountain of work he did. "We should go home. There may be better physicians in Rome."

For once he listened to me. We went home.

Livia

"A re we old?" I asked Tavius one morning.

"You will never be old," he said.

"Flattery still rolls off your tongue very smoothly, I'll give you that." I was forty-five; he was fifty.

"Would you prefer I point out that the mausoleum is ready and waiting?"

Some years before this, he had constructed a grand family tomb in the Mars Field, big enough to accommodate our ashes and those of all our near relations. Sadly, the tomb's first occupant had been a mere youth, his nephew Marcellus.

"I don't feel ready for the mausoleum yet," I said. "And I don't think Rome will ever be ready to dispense with your services. You will just have to go on living."

"Do I look as old as Agrippa does?"

"No," I said, and this was true. Agrippa had come home from the East, hardly able to hobble on his feet and looking like his own ghost.

"He has worked too hard and too long. With rest, he'll be himself again." Tavius sounded as he were making an effort to believe it.

Agrippa, Julia, and the children had visited briefly with us in Rome. Then they had gone off to stay at his villa in southern Italy, where he could have a long holiday.

Seeing Agrippa with his glowing children, the two vigorous small boys, the sweet-faced little girls, one thought he ought to have been their grandfather. And Julia—she was at the height of her beauty and also presented a stark contrast. Just the sight of her with Agrippa—he so worn, she so vividly alive—had troubled me.

They had been away from Rome for more than three years. I wanted to believe Julia had matured in that time and returned home contented to be Agrippa's wife. But I worried about her.

"I suppose," I said, "it is natural at our time of life to be preoccupied with the younger generation."

Tavius's mouth tightened. I wondered if he knew I was thinking of Julia. But he seemed determined to keep the mood light. "Personally, I'm most concerned about Livilla. I predict she'll be a handful. Just look who she is named after."

Drusus's daughter was barely a month old.

>>>>>>>

At that time, both my sons were home. Tiberius had returned from Gaul for brief consultations; Drusus had been appointed urban praetor and, in theory at least, would be in Italy for an entire year. One evening they and their wives dined with me at my villa at Prima Porta. It was as if all the light in the room shone on Drusus. He and his wife, Antonia, shared a dining couch. I could see how glad Antonia was to have him at home. Tavius turned to Drusus and peppered him with questions about how he had left matters in

Gaul. Drusus answered volubly, smiling as he spoke of all the army had achieved.

Tiberius with his wife, Vipsania, was across the table from his younger brother. He too might have spoken knowledgeably of affairs in Gaul. But Tavius continually addressed himself to Drusus.

Tiberius's expression showed no jealousy. He looked resigned and even gazed at Drusus with rueful affection. I had to remind myself of the objective fact that Tiberius's achievements at that point in his life were greater than his brother's.

"Tiberius, take more of the lamb. It's prepared just the way you like it," I said.

The look he gave me was almost baleful, as if he suspected I was exerting an effort to act like his doting mother—and remind everyone else of his presence.

"Yes, dear, have some more of this delicious lamb," Vipsania said. "It has the most wonderful sweet sauce."

"Do me a kindness and don't badger me about the food," Tiberius snapped.

Vipsania looked down, her ears turning pink.

Marcus Ortho was also at the table. He was the son of a loyal servant of mine who had become my dear friend, and I had raised him as my own after her death. All through their childhood he had been Drusus's constant shadow; he had lately become his devoted military aide. I saw the look of dislike he shot at Tiberius.

Memories came back of Tiberius lording it over Marcus when they were growing up. Drusus had treated him as a brother; Tiberius never had.

Tiberius has reaped what he sowed with Marcus. He turned away Tavius's warmth, so now it is never offered. And he goes out of his way to browbeat his little mouse of a wife. Gods above, I am his own mother and even I find him hard to love.

This thought hurt me, for whatever his faults, Tiberius was my child.

>>>>>>>>

As soon as the dinner was over, Tiberius and Vipsania vanished. This was like them; they never seemed to relish time spent with the rest of the family. For his part, Tavius had work to do in his study. I remained at the table with Drusus, Antonia, and Marcus.

"I have to find a wife for you," I told Marcus.

He smiled at me, shaking his head. "I'm a soldier. A family can wait until I'm old."

"But a wife can be a fine thing, even for a soldier," Drusus said. He and Antonia were reclining close together, and his hand lay on her shoulder.

"Then you will be happy to be home for a while?" she said, smiling up at him.

"It's as if I am two beings—one who always longs to be home with you and another who wants to march into Germania."

I knew he wanted to push beyond Gaul, up into the regions still unconquered by us Romans. "I would rather we not speak any more about war this evening," I said.

"All right, Mother. But I have to tell you the only way to establish the peace you care so much for is to extend the empire's boundaries and bring the Germanic tribes to heel. And I will do it—" He smiled. "Well, Tiberius, Marcus, and I will."

He was not yet twenty-six and had already made his name as a great general. Who could help but be proud of such a son? But I feared for him. I feared for Tiberius and Marcus too, but most of all for Drusus, for he was the boldest.

"Germania is a savage place now," he said, "but it will not always be that way. Wherever we Romans go, we will make men civilized and free."

"You think the tribesmen of Germania will be fit to be citizens?" Antonia asked.

"In time. We are bringing enlightenment and peace to the world, great universal peace. But we must bring liberty too."

"Such lofty talk," I said, and took a sip of wine. "You are an idealist, my son."

"When Augustus first claimed power, order was what mattered most. There had to be an end to the civil wars. Now, however, the time has come to shape the future. We must think in terms of extending the rights of citizenship to all the subject peoples—and we must think of liberty at home."

Why did I feel a prick of fear?

Drusus seemed to sense my emotion. He smiled. "Mother, the love of liberty runs in our family."

He took after my kin. He had large dark eyes and hair with a hint of red. Moreover there was a greatness of soul about him that brought back memories of my own father—his grandfather who had died for the Republic. "Would you bring the Republic back again, if you could?" I asked in a strained voice.

"No, Mother," Drusus said gently. "The Republic failed. I would never bring that chaos back again. I only mean we must move gradually not in the direction of more authoritarian rule but greater liberty. Otherwise, our government might devolve into tyranny. All my friends—well, almost all of them feel this way."

"The young, you mean?"

"We are not all foolish, Mother Livia," Marcus said.

I gave him a stiff smile. "Yes . . . I remember feeling very wise indeed when I was young. And then life taught me I was not so wise after all."

"But you see," Antonia said, "Drusus is speaking of a gentle process that may take many decades. Nothing stays the same. We must move in one direction or another. And why not in the direction of greater rights for all?"

"Rome is no tyranny," I said.

"Of course not, Mother," Drusus said. "And it must not become one. Augustus's moral legislation was not a good precedent. What right has the state to intrude on people's private doings? I say none! I told Augustus that just the other day."

It was like Drusus not to withhold his thoughts but to speak boldly to his stepfather. "And what did he say?" I asked.

"He said we should agree to disagree about that. And then he said . . ." Drusus looked abashed and shrugged.

Antonia smiled proudly. "He said that given the way Drusus conducts his own life, the moral laws were hardly likely to irk him."

Informants brought me stories of my sons' doings, some I wanted to hear and some I could have done without. Tiberius and Marcus both had temporary liaisons while on campaign; it was a usual thing for a soldier. Drusus was the anomaly. He never touched a woman other than his wife.

"I told him that was hardly the point," my son said. "The point was that he was treading on people's liberty and ought not to."

"And was he angry at all when you said that?" I asked carefully.

"Angry? No. Why should he be at a friend who honestly speaks his mind? He just clapped me on the back and told me I was a better general than I was a politician." Drusus laughed. "Which I suppose is true."

>>>>>>>

Later in bed with Tavius, I whispered, "Drusus's talk of liberty—does it trouble you?"

"I brood and gnash my teeth over it from morning to night."

"Meaning you don't?"

"I know the boy's heart. The day I don't trust Drusus, put me out of my misery, please." After a few moments, he added, "The only real problem we will have is keeping him in Rome for a year. I want to teach him some things, and a term as city praetor is just what he needs. But he is burning to conquer Germania, and a young eagle has to fly."

In fact, it was impossible to keep my young eagle in Rome. After a few short months, he was back leading his army. This time, however, Antonia insisted on accompanying him, with her children in a tow, as far as the Roman city of Lugdunum in eastern Gaul, which was reasonably safe for civilians—a place where he could visit his family from time to time. For a wife to go trailing after a husband in this way when he went off to war was frowned upon. But she was Mark Antony's daughter as well as Octavia's; and beneath her calm surface she had a passionate heart, and a stubborn streak. I thought my son was wise not to say no to her.

Julia

*I*t was boring on Agrippa's country estate. There were times I could have screamed. I so wanted to be back in Rome, to see my old friends.

Yet I kept the bit in my mouth. I played the part of a good wife. I acted as Agrippa's nurse when his feet pained him and the doctor happened not to be in attendance. I also, of course, allowed him to make love to me when he wished. For many months, he had not wished to. Maybe the thought of a wife who had slept with another man repelled him; maybe it was just a matter of his weariness and the pain in his feet. But gradually, with rest, he began to feel healthier. Our marriage went back to what it had been.

My only real delight was my children. The boys, Gaius and Lucius, occupied themselves with their studies, taught by exacting tutors my father had selected. The knowledge of who they were and what was expected of them had already begun to weigh on their young shoulders. Their sister Julilla was quite different. She liked to laugh; she liked to read poetry. She reminded me of myself.

Our youngest child, little Agrippina, was unusually self-possessed, even as a toddler, carrying herself like a little judge. Agrippa fully accepted that she was his child—luckily there was a resemblance. He often would boast about how precocious she was.

When I looked back on the last few years, I saw that I was lucky to have skirted complete disaster. And so for months, I lived a quiet life in the country with my husband and my children. I was not happy, but I was tamed.

There was an outbreak of rebellion among the fierce Illyrian tribes in the Balkans. My stepbrother Drusus was fighting in Germania by that time; Tiberius was on his way to Gaul. My father's life could not be risked on campaign. Letters were exchanged. It was decided that Agrippa would go and quell the uprising.

I argued. For all my failings as a wife, I felt protective of Agrippa, who had recently been so ill. It was absurd, I said, for him to go to the Balkans—could no Roman but a member of our own family lead an army? Was there not another competent general in all our legions? Why should Agrippa of all men go to quell the rebellion when not long ago he had been barely able to walk?

"Have you never heard of duty?" he asked me curtly.

He went off to war once again. He went because he was Marcus Vipsanius Agrippa. He went because it would have been impossible for him to do anything else.

I, as soon as he had gone, escaped my bucolic life as though it were a dungeon cell and the door had suddenly been unlocked. I returned to Rome, where my old friends welcomed me.

I too acted in accord with my own nature.

Sempronius Gracchus understood our time as lovers had passed. As we reclined together on a dinner couch one night, he said, "I've always thought you were searching for something. And it wasn't me."

"Something?" I said.

"Well, no, someone." He smiled. "A great love. The sort Catullus writes about in his poetry."

I stroked his cheek. "You truly think that?"

"Actually I know it."

I shook my head. "Catullus was a very unhappy man. And he died young."

"What is it that you want really? Have you asked yourself that?"

"I want pleasure, as anyone does. And I want to feel . . . oh, I just want to feel. I want to be alive."

"Has it been terrible to you, being married to Agrippa? I've always thought he was a decent man."

"He is—he is very decent. At least, his flaws are no worse than that of most men in his position. But being married to him has been a kind of death."

I had been a captive, it seemed, for ages. And now with my husband gone, I broke free. I feared word of my actions reaching Agrippa or my father. But the fear was not enough to restrain me. I was so hungry—for life. There were men. More than one. High-ranking members of old Roman families. I took care, as always, to see they did not get me with child. But we gave each other pleasure. And I will say this—I never told them lies or made false promises. We always parted as friends.

I thought sometimes of what Gracchus said. Was I searching? Perhaps he was right. There was an emptiness inside me. And even at the pinnacle of pleasure, entwined in a man's arms, I felt some greater thing was forever out of reach. I did not even know the name of what I yearned for.

There is an old tale that we of the Julian line are descended from the goddess of love. I doubt there is any truth to it. I have also heard Greek stories of women who incurred Aphrodite's wrath by some awful trespass, and whom she therefore inflicted with inappeasable longing.

Was I one of these women? And if so, what had been my sin?

Cleopatra Selene

On a spring day I waited to welcome my brother Jullus and his family to Mauretania. It had been more than five years since I had seen him in Rome. The greatest disappointments those years had brought me were three miscarriages. My son, Ptolemy, was tall and thriving, but Juba and I had no other children; the daughter I longed for—who in my imagination had a name, Drusilla, and even a face—remained a hope and nothing more. And the hope was waning. I had begun to think I would never have another child.

The people shouted our praises when Juba and I rode through the streets of our capital city of Caesarea. The city itself was beautiful—thriving with commerce, graced by stately marble buildings and statues of the finest workmanship. It was moreover a magnet for scholars. Juba had acquired great fame throughout the Roman Empire not only as a patron of learning but for the books he himself authored.

Once he had merely funded geographical expeditions and compiled and published the information explorers brought back. But as time went on, he felt an itch to wander. I had gotten used to seeing him sail off to explore unknown territories. I missed him, but when he returned from these geographical expeditions, he was always exhilarated. "Do you know what it feels like to be the first man to look at an island that no human eye has ever seen before?" he asked me once. Of course I did not. I did not even fully understand the appeal.

Heaven had surely meant him to be an explorer. He did not relish the mundane duties that went with being a king. I, on the other hand, liked them very much. Some people say a woman is not meant to be a ruler. But I was a daughter of the royal house of Egypt.

I often distributed bread to the poor. I also looked into the eyes of murderers and rapists and sentenced them to death—I who had feared the executioner's blade myself did this, never with pleasure, but with the understanding that this was required of me. For it is a ruler's place to stand between the people and danger, and sometimes even to take life in order to protect life. I learned to make hard choices. I was a queen. And as a queen, I knew I had no more important task than to guard against hubris, particularly when I dealt with Rome.

One question recurred again and again: Could we in Mauretania govern our own land, or must we bow to Rome? A delicate diplomatic dance continued year after year. My personal relationship with Livia and our frequent exchange of letters played a crucial part in maintaining our independence. Because I had Livia's ear, Rome's representatives treated us with more respect than they might have otherwise. Several times I appealed to her for help when our latest "minder" impeded my actions. On each occasion she swept the stumbling block from my path.

Naturally, I was overjoyed when my brother Jullus ascended to the praetorship in Rome. This lifted him to an exalted rank in the Senate, second only to men who had held the consulship itself. His reply to my congratulatory letter struck me as rather restrained and dry. He had never yet been given the military command he had always longed for. Still, the praetorship was a great office, not an empty honor. He had become a highly influential senator. Of course his advancement had depended on his close family relationship to Augustus.

For some time, I had been inviting him to visit my family and me in Mauretania. Shortly after he completed his term as praetor, he accepted the invitation.

On a sunny day, Juba and I, in our robes of state, waited in our throne room to welcome this high Roman personage, my brother. He entered, accompanied by Marcella and their two half-grown boys and small daughter, as well as by a host of soldiers and retainers. Formal words of welcome were spoken, while my heart leaped with joy.

I remember Mark Antony, Jullus's father and mine, as a tall, laughing, boisterous figure who always seemed to be walking out the door. *Revered Father,* I told his shade, *take satisfaction from this at least—that your children live, that we remember you, that we have somehow each succeeded in living fruitful lives. And that we are here today, united.*

Juba and I held a great festive dinner that night to welcome my brother and his family. Marcella looked around the banquet room, at the tables with their gold fittings, the dining couches with their ivory frames and silk cushions. "Very fine," she said in a supercilious tone. "Why, we could almost be in Rome."

My brother said coldly, "I doubt there is a dining room in Rome as fine as this."

"Oh, dear husband, you are probably right. Except of course for the summer dining room at *my uncle Augustus's* villa. The murals there are extraordinary works of art. I doubt there is anything like them here."

The emphasis in her voice when she mentioned her uncle Augustus might have struck me as comical in another context. But I saw tension in my brother's face. How often, I wondered, did his wife speak of "my uncle Augustus"? How often did she remind him of all he owed to her and her kin?

I looked at my brother's two fine, handsome sons and lovely little daughter. I looked at his toga, with the broad purple stripe that marked him out as a former praetor. I tried to convince myself he was a fortunate man. Then I gazed again at his face, the tight set of his mouth. I knew he was not fortunate.

"Yes, I well remember Augustus's dining room murals," my husband said. Then he smoothly changed the subject.

My brother gave me a bleak smile.

He knew I had seen what his life was.

>>>>>>>

The next day we spent some time alone in the private garden where I received my most special guests.

"You will be consul before many more years," I said at one point to cheer him.

"Yes. And if I can help you in any way, please rely on me," he said. "But I think you have a better advocate in Livia, back in Rome. Whatever my position, I am kept on a tight leash."

Was he exaggerating the weakness of his situation so I would not expect great favors from him? I did not think so. But I was not sure.

He caught my look of doubt. "Believe me, little moon, I do not have Augustus's trust. What I have is his benevolence. And that is something quite different."

"I've heard that you are prominent in the Senate."

He brightened a little at that. "Really, that's come to your ears? Well, it's true I have many friends there. Younger men who are not so enamored of Augustus as their fathers were come to me with their grievances. I help them when I can."

"They come to you with grievances?" Something in that made me uneasy.

"Oh, sweet Sister, you needn't worry. We all know the bounds of free speech in the Senate. I for one would never be stupid enough to exceed those bounds."

There was a metallic taste in my mouth. I sensed danger. My brother was unhappy. He had attracted a coterie of unhappy friends. I told myself it was not as if he were speaking of a revolutionary cabal. Yet—yet—I did not like this at all.

"You must be careful, Jullus."

"Oh, please." He laughed. "I'm married to Augustus's niece. And you can see how we adore each other. No one's more secure than I am."

You ought to have left Rome, I thought. *You ought to have come to Mauretania with Juba and me.*

"I like the East, little moon," he said. "There's a pleasant scent in the air when you get this far from Rome. It is like the smell of freedom to me."

"The freedom is never complete. But there is much beauty here."

"You are content?"

"Yes."

"You don't think of what might have been? Our father was once ruler of the whole eastern empire, with your mother as his queen.

He hoped to conquer Parthia and equal Alexander. If one sea battle had gone a different way, he would have taken Rome. Don't you think of that?"

"Not often."

"It was because the crews on our father's galleys took ill. It wasn't better seamanship on Augustus and Agrippa's parts, certainly not because they were more brave. A strange trick of fortune—a sudden illness struck Father's sailors. They were all vomiting over the sides of their boats. And Augustus got the empire, and Father got a cold tomb." He gave me a mirthless smile. "Don't you find that funny?"

"I have heard that story many times, and it has never once made me smile."

"It rends your heart?"

I nodded.

"It rends my heart too."

The sense of our common kinship was palpable. I thought of my parents; I thought of my dead brothers. At that moment, I was no longer a queen but a child who had suffered incalculable loss.

"Oh, little moon," Jullus said tenderly.

I shook my head, lowering my gaze. I was close to weeping.

"And if not for that day at Actium, that woeful toss of the dice, I would not be who I am," Jullus said. "I would not have spent my whole life eating the bread of charity. I would be a great satrap in the East, I think—an emperor's son. And you would not be reduced to ruling over this small kingdom while your husband collects insects and samples of rock."

My head jerked up. I stared into my brother's eyes. "I do not consider Mauretania small. I consider it a bright jewel set in a sea of darkness. The people here are as happy and as free as Juba and I can make them. Learned men flock to us from every corner of the earth. And the knowledge my husband has garnered will be of great value to people in ages to come. His books will still be read when you and I are dust."

Jullus stiffened. "I am sorry," he said softly. "I have no wish to offend you. I have nothing but respect for what you and your husband have achieved. But do you know how quickly this jewel of a kingdom you have created could be destroyed, absorbed into Rome, governed like any conquered territory? Augustus would only need to snap his fingers."

"I hope that will never happen."

"You hope."

"In the end we may go down. But for as long as Juba and I can make it so, we will be what we are. We are a light, my brother. We glow like the sun."

>>>>>>>

"He does not know who you are," Juba said to me after Jullus and his family had taken leave of us and returned to Rome.

"What do you mean?"

We lay beneath a sheet of fine yellow linen. The shutters had been left open, for the night was hot. There was a faint breeze that smelled of lemons and hyacinths. My husband brushed my hair with his lips. "He forgets you are the descendant of the Ptolemies, a god-queen. I on the other hand am never so foolish as to forget that."

"You dislike Jullus?"

"I could do without him calling you little moon."

"It was his nickname for me, when I was a child. When I had no one else to rely on, he protected me."

"That speaks well for him. Still, I think he underestimates you. The little girl in need of his protection is now a great queen. A wiser man would recognize that." He leaned over me so our foreheads touched. "You are formidable, my love. If Jullus can't see that, he's blind."

Julia

When my aunt Octavia died, we all mourned. Father praised her in a public eulogy, lauding her as a model of womanly virtue. I am sure every word he said was sincere, but again and again he alluded to days far in the past. The pressures of ruling an empire had created a fissure between him and his sister. He had lost her, I think, long before she died.

The needs of the empire impacted all our lives. Tiberius had been in Rome for a time, serving as consul and garnering praise for how he performed his duties. During this time, Vipsania gave him a son. Within days of acknowledging the child—he named him after his brother—he was off to combat tribes in the Alps. Meanwhile Drusus fought along the frontier of Germania, beating back invaders who had forged across the Rhine.

I am sure Livia was proud at how Drusus in particular covered himself with glory. We heard that of their own accord, his troops gathered around his tent one day to cheer and acclaim him, and dub him an imperator. It was an extraordinary thing. He was only twenty-six years old. But looking at my own small sons, I imagined what her true feelings were. She was the mother of two fighting generals, one the young hero that all Rome idolized. But I suspected that given a choice she would have preferred both her sons safe at home.

My husband had been away fighting other battles. But a letter came from him saying he was returning to our villa in the south of Italy, that I should take the children and meet him there. Apparently just the sound of his name was enough to cow the Illyrian rebels. Their resistance collapsed as soon as his army entered their territory. He restored order with his usual efficiency and saw no need to stay in the province.

When I arrived, I found my husband sitting in a chair in the library. The little ones rushed to happily embrace him. I stood apart, stricken at how sick he looked. He had gotten very lean, his face almost skull-like. I asked him how he was, and he shrugged. "My feet are acting up again. And I've had some trouble keeping food down—there's a pain in my guts."

He wanted to couple with me that night. This surprised me since he hardly seemed strong enough for that. It was different from our usual lovemaking. He was slow, gentle, his hands lingering on my body. I thought of how one might dawdle, looking carefully at a familiar place one expected never to visit again, and spend time fixing it in memory. I somehow sensed that he was saying farewell.

In the following days, physicians danced attendance on him, but the pain in his abdomen only grew worse. "Write to your father," he said. "Tell him I want to see him."

I wrote, *Come to us here, Father. Please come immediately. Agrippa is desperately ill and asking for you.*

As Agrippa dozed, I sat at his bedside, wishing we had been able to love each other.

>>>>>>>

Two days passed. I knew Father would make haste. I wondered if he would be in time. Finally, he stood in the entranceway, flushed, his clothes splattered with mud from his journey. "I came the moment I saw your letter. Is he still alive?"

"He died not much more than an hour ago," I said.

Father let out a terrible groan. "Where is he?"

I showed him into the bedchamber. Agrippa's body lay stretched out on the bed.

Father stared at me. "Where are the coins for the ferryman?"

"There has been no time yet to think of that."

He took coins out of the purse tied to his belt, pressed two on Agrippa's closed eyelids, and slipped another between his lips. "Leave us alone, please."

In more usual circumstances, it would have fallen to him to comfort me, the new widow. But instead, dry-eyed, I reached out to Father and stroked his shoulder, trying ineffectually to ease his hurt.

He hardly noticed me. "Leave us. Close the door."

I stood outside the door. Inside the room came my father's voice choked with grief. "I am here," he said. Over and over, the same words. "I am here, I am here, I am here."

I did not discover I was with child until after the funeral. It made me sad to think that Agrippa would never set eyes on his last child, for he was fond of his children and took pleasure in them.

I was sorry Agrippa was dead, so sorry for him. He had deserved to spend some pleasant years at leisure, watching our little ones grow up. But I did not feel any great sense of personal loss. I tried not to think too much of the future, beyond giving birth to my child. I knew my father would expect me to marry again, and my husband would be determined by the needs of the empire.

Livia

*T*he only thing that makes sense is for Tiberius to marry Julia," Tavius said.

Eight months had passed since Agrippa's death. Julia would soon give birth. Tiberius had come home from Gaul to confer with Tavius. Drusus meanwhile was winning battle after battle as he carried forward the conquest of Germania.

"My son is married," I said. "He and his wife have a little boy."

"My older grandson is only eight," Tavius said. "If I were to die tomorrow—"

"You won't."

"I'm not young, Livia."

"You keep picking successors and they keep on dying, beloved. While you go on living. Have you noticed that?"

"That won't be the case forever." He reached across the couch, took my hand. "Oh, Livia . . ."

"What was I thinking of, when I married you? I must have been mad. One thing is sure—I had no earthly idea of what I was bargaining for."

"Look," he said. "Gaius is a boy. If I die in the next decade, there has to be a man to act on his behalf and hold the empire together. The only one who can do that is Tiberius. Drusus has a wife too, and besides that he is too young—a great soldier but naive when it comes to politics. Tiberius is not naive."

"No," I said. "He never has been that."

"So it has to be Tiberius. He must marry Julia. Otherwise, if I die, the moon and the stars will fall from the heavens and people will eat each other. You do see that?"

"Tiberius can't be forced. He must be allowed to make a choice."

"Of course," Tavius said.

>>>>>>>

Many would say later that the idea of Tiberius and Julia marrying came from me, that the impetus was my ambition for my son. This was a lie—and yet, like many false tales, it contained a grain of truth. For in fact I was ambitious for Tiberius, and I knew that the man who married Julia would be, after Tavius, the greatest man in Rome. Why, I thought, should that place of prominence not be filled by my son? While one part of me recoiled from the idea of Tiberius divorcing his wife and wedding Julia, another part did not recoil at all. This I admit before the gods.

Tavius had a conversation with Tiberius, put the proposal to him, and advised him not to answer immediately but to give the matter thought. Later that same day, I talked to my son alone.

"You are facing a decision that is bound to shape your future."

"I know that, Mother."

Sitting across from Tiberius, I felt confused about my own emotions, which was unlike me. "Vipsania is so quiet and self-effacing I hardly know her. But it seems to me that she suits you."

Tiberius's face took on a guarded look. "She has been a satisfactory wife."

"That is all? Satisfactory?"

"Mother, this conversation is not necessary. You can be sure I will do my duty."

His duty—what did that mean? That he would divorce Vipsania, marry Julia, and so discharge his duty to Rome? Or was he speaking of another duty, to his wife and son?

It struck me forcibly that my son was being asked to make an inhuman choice. And that I had placed him in this situation. On the day I decided to leave his father and marry Tavius, I had determined my son's path in life.

He sat before me now a grown man, a former consul, a general. Yet I still saw the three-year-old looking at me through his eyes, the child who had stood by helpless as I tore our family apart.

"I want you to be happy," I said.

He smiled faintly as if I had uttered an absurdity.

"Tiberius, do you know that Julia . . . ?" I groped for words, and finally said, "She has had unsuitable friends."

"Mother, I'm no fool. I know how Agrippa allowed her to behave."

"Then—"

"I really don't want to discuss all this with you, Mother."

I felt a prickling along the back of my neck. It was as if I saw a catastrophe taking shape and wanted to avert my eyes but could not. Suddenly, someone else seemed to be speaking with my voice. "Don't marry her. I am afraid of what marriage to Julia will do to your soul."

Tiberius looked startled and taken aback. He collected himself, then he almost snarled, "Well, thank you for your advice, Mother," and walked out the room.

>>>>>>>

That night in a dream, I saw a beautiful bird with bright purple plumage. It was in the sort of cage one often sees used for pet birds, tapered at the top. But this cage was made of pure gold. Flapping its wings, uttering loud, piercing cries, the bird threw itself at the bars of the cage. It did this again and again, until it was covered with blood.

I awoke in a sweat and lay in bed, shuddering.

The gods often send us dreams that carry messages. Was this a divine dream? I did not know. When I rose from my bed, the images from the dream faded in my mind. Strangely, since the dream had frightened me so much, I found it easy to put it out of my thoughts.

Later that day, Tavius informed me that Tiberius had agreed to marry Julia. "Perhaps eventually you and I will share a grandchild," he said lightly.

"Yes," I said, feeling a sudden fierce desire to hold that baby in my arms. I had not been able to give Tavius a child. But Tiberius and Julia's child would be like the fruit of our own love.

I was lost in the woods, pulled this way and that.

I had heard talk that Julia had been unfaithful to Agrippa. But I had seen her look at my handsome son with admiration. He was close to her in age, and in that respect a more suitable husband for her than Agrippa had been. It did not seem impossible that Tiberius and Julia would find contentment together. I prayed to the gods to make it so.

Julia

nother wedding. The scarlet veil, the sharing of the sacred
cake, the shouts of *"Feliciter!"*

My father gave me away, the first time he was ever
there to see me wed. A lucky omen? I hoped so.

Father at my side, holding my hand, whispering in my ear how
beautiful I looked. The way it might have been, should have been
when I was fourteen.

A new start? I imagined myself washed clean of all the troubles
of the past as I began life with my new husband.

I saw the logical necessity of this marriage. If Father passed away,
I would need a strong man to protect me and my children. Who
could fill that role but Tiberius?

I had to think first of the welfare of my children—of Gaius
and Lucius especially but also the little ones, including the baby
Postumus Agrippa, who had been born a few months before. If
Father died and they were left without a trustworthy protector, they

would all be like defenseless lambs surrounded by power-hungry predators.

I admit I thought of myself too. When I looked at Tiberius I felt a physical attraction that was primal and raw, but undeniable.

What gave me most pause was the thought of Vipsania, who had been my stepdaughter. My father said she would be generously provided for, kindly treated, even allowed to keep her son with her while he was small. "She is Agrippa's daughter—do you think I would let her be abused? Believe me, she won't lose by doing her duty and gracefully stepping to one side." Father gave me a look that brooked no opposition. "We must all do our duty, every one of us."

At the celebratory feast, my wedding veil thrown back, I studied Tiberius as he accepted congratulations. I saw his assurance. I heard the deference in other men's voices when they spoke to him. I knew he was the only man I could have married.

>>>>>>>

"Do you think we will be happy?" I asked him when we were alone for our wedding night.

He considered the question as if it were completely new to him, as if he had not given a moment's thought to it before. "I doubt it's in me to be happy," he said finally.

"Why?"

"It's my nature."

"Perhaps that can change."

"People never change."

"At least we can come to understand each other, you and I. We grew up in the same household, the household of the First Citizen. Few people can know the burdens it placed on us."

He did not speak but was listening intently.

"Maybe this marriage can be a blessing to both of us. I'll try so hard. Can't we at least finally become friends?"

"Friends?" He rolled the word off his tongue as if the concept amused him. But then he said, "I could use a friend, a true friend, that is. Most of my life, I've been surrounded by sycophants using me to get to your father. I despise all the honeyed words, the lying flattery."

"I won't lie to you, Tiberius."

"Good. See you don't."

"If we—"

"Enough talk." He untied the knot of Hercules around my waist with a few hard tugs, threw the rope of wool onto the floor. Then he was pulling at my muslin tunica.

"Wait," I said, not wanting him to rip it.

"Take it off."

I obeyed him. When I stood naked, he grabbed me. His kisses were hungry and fierce. I pulled away from him, wanting to catch my breath. "Don't do that," he said, and pressed me to him.

There was a savagery in the way he took me. He never said my name. He never gave a thought to my comfort or to pleasing me. And yet I responded to him. I did desire him—perhaps I had desired him without knowing it since we were children. I wanted to cry out, feeling his rough hands on me, kneading my flesh, cry out at his hard thrusts. But there was pleasure in the end. A piercing pleasure, more intense because it was mixed with pain.

So it began between us.

≫≫≫≫

"I want to make something clear to you," he said to me on the morning after our wedding.

I was still in bed, and he was standing over me. "Oh, what is that?"

"Gracchus and all that pack . . . you will stay away from them."

"Will I?" I got out of bed, stretched, and yawned.

"You will." He pulled me into his arms.

I twined my arms around his neck, studied his face. He was intent on what he was saying, almost angry. I could feel his heat, along the whole length of my body. We were both naked.

"You're my wife now. You'll act the way my wife is supposed to act." He gave a harsh laugh. "You won't need outside . . . recreation. I'll keep you busy."

Will you? Will you really?

"I'm not Agrippa," he said. "I'm someone else. You understand?"

"You're someone else," I said, smiling.

"Don't laugh at me."

"I'm not laughing. Truly, I'm not."

>>>>>>>

He was not gentle. And yet a mighty god smiled on our union. The name of that god was Eros. To be held in Tiberius's arms was to feel small and helpless, swept away by the mighty flood of a strong man's passion. He wanted me so much. But he used me as if I did not possess a mind or a soul.

After our lovemaking I would feel battered, cast aside like a damaged toy. Yet there was pleasure, dark pleasure, sweetness never overwhelmed by the bitter under-taste. During the hours of the day when we had to be apart, I longed for him. I wanted to feel that bitter sweetness again.

Phoebe would see the bruises and shallow bite marks on my body and stare.

"My lady, look how he has hurt you," she said once. "How can you—"

I laughed. "How can I? Do you truly want me to explain?"

"My lady . . ."

I felt a surge of annoyance. "If you wish to please me, you will not speak of this again."

When Tiberius and I were together, even in company, I would notice him watching me. Not with any obvious affection, but as if he could not tear his eyes away. When we were alone, he would unexpectedly touch me, fondle my leg, my breast. It was if he did this despite himself, as if he could not keep his hands off. I would smile at him. He would not smile back. I wondered if he disliked the fact that he desired me.

Once as we lay together, I asked, foolishly, "Was it like this with Vipsania?"

"Don't speak of her," he said, and pinched my arm.

"Tiberius, how dare you? Did you intend to punish me, as if I were a dumb animal? I am not one, and I resent it."

"Keep your tongue off her. She is a good woman."

What did he mean? That I was not?

He went on in a low voice, "She did not speak a word of reproach when I said I wanted to divorce her. She wished me good fortune, and she meant it. No one else has ever cared for me so unselfishly."

"Do you actually expect me to lie here and listen while you sing the praises of your former wife?"

"You were the one who brought up her name."

"Believe me, I will not do it again."

"Good." For a while he was silent as if thinking. Then he said, "I have always kept a check on my passions. I am not someone to let this business loom too large. Just lately, with you—oh, it has been pleasure, but . . ."

I laughed deep in my throat. "I think about you constantly during the day. Do you think about me?"

"Sometimes," he muttered.

"More than you would like?"

"Yes."

"Oh, do I obsess you?"

"I did not say that," he snapped. But in a moment, he whispered, "Yes, yes, I am obsessed."

"How lovely."

"You think it's a lovely thing, for a man like me to be always thinking of a woman? Believe me, it is not."

"Poor Tiberius," I said and kissed him. "Poor, poor man."

>>>>>>>

He gave me instructions about how to dress and wear my hair. I obeyed him. Why not? I adorned myself mainly for his eyes anyway. His taste was old-fashioned like my father's. He did not like to see much of my skin uncovered before the eyes of others. Nor did he like it when I wore much jewelry. "Simplicity is the mark of a lady," he said.

"Are you planning on turning me into your mother?"

He scowled. "What an idiotic thing to say."

What troubled me most about Tiberius, early in our marriage, was the harsh, commanding tone he took with my two older sons. Agrippa had been a kind father. Now in his place my children had a stepfather who ignored my little girls and the baby but barked military commands at Gaius and Lucius.

Once, after I came home from my dressmaker, I heard sobs coming from Gaius's bedchamber. I found my son lying facedown across his bed, weeping. As I approached, I saw a small red stain on the shoulder of his tunic.

"What happened?" I asked. Though of course I knew.

My son turned a red, furious face on me. "Your husband, Mother."

"Sit up. Take off your tunic. Let me see."

I gave a little cry when he bared his back. From shoulder to waist it was crisscrossed with welts.

"What did he beat you with?"

"A birch rod."

"What did you do?"

"Nothing!"

"Gaius, love, you must have done something."

"He said I was impertinent. I don't know who he thinks he is."

"He thinks he is your stepfather, Gaius." And you are Augustus's heir, and well you know it.

"Mother, I hate him. Send him away, will you? I was playing in the courtyard, and he said not to do it there. All I did was ask him why. He said I shouldn't ask questions, just obey. Then he beat me."

I was sure Gaius's tone of voice when he asked the question had been less than respectful, that Tiberius had beaten him for disrespect. I realized most people would highly approve of such an action on the part of a father or even a stepfather. Boys needed the rod if they were going to amount to anything. Still I hated seeing my son's back covered with welts. I applied a soothing balm, my feelings in turmoil.

"Mother, he whipped Lucius too the other day. Lucius didn't want to tell you."

"What did he whip him for?"

"For nothing!"

"Gaius, you want to be a soldier, don't you? Well, soldiers must obey their superior officers. You have to learn to be obedient, darling. Obedient and respectful." I finished putting the balm on his welts. "Does that feel better?"

He shrugged.

"Watch what you say to your stepfather, and how you say it."

I could not keep myself from remonstrating with Tiberius, telling him he was too harsh with Gaius. He told me I was a fool. "The boy needs discipline," he said. "In fact, I'm very much afraid your coddling has already ruined him."

"Ruined him? There is nothing wrong with my boy."

"Julia, open your eyes. You've made him a weakling. Him and his brother both."

Over the next few days, I paid close attention to how Tiberius spoke to my sons, the expression on his face when he looked at them. It was clear to me that he disliked them both, disliked two children.

After Agrippa's death, my father had said that the two boys must come to live with him. He wanted to take personal charge of their education. I had resisted this. I did not relish the idea of them living under another roof from me, at ages nine and six, and had been postponing the move. But now I acquiesced to my father's wishes. Father might sometimes be stern with the boys and demand too much of them, but he loved them.

We—my father and Livia, Tiberius and I—now lived in adjacent houses on the Palatine Hill. I told myself I would still see my sons regularly when they were in my father's care, and I did. But I would have preferred to keep them with me.

My passion for Tiberius did not ebb away. But it began to be mixed with resentment.

And yet I tried. I tried to be a good wife to my husband, and to help and understand him.

We regularly appeared in public with Livia and my father. Tiberius disliked these occasions and was often in a bad mood afterward.

"Why do the people shout your name?" he said one evening after he came home from attending the theater with Father and Livia.

I shrugged. "They've always done that."

"My mother spends her money succoring the poor. She feeds orphans. She gives poor girls dowries. You'd think the people would love her—but they don't, at least not the way they love you. And what have you ever done? Smile at them?"

"My sons represent Rome's future," I said.

"Your sons. But your sons are not you." Tiberius was frowning. "You remind me of Drusus. He has a way of dazzling the eye. Everyone loves him. Hades take it, even I can't help loving my brother. But the truth is, I've always worked harder than he does and accomplished more. And who knows it? Who cares?"

"My father appreciates—" I began.

"Your father!" Tiberius snorted. "Drusus can insult him to his face, and he smiles. I treat him with reverence and get sneers in return."

"You're not serious." What he was saying seemed so extreme and silly I actually giggled. "You're in an awful mood today. 'Poor me, poor Tiberius. Nobody gives me the appreciation I deserve.'"

He suddenly gripped my arm. I felt his nails biting into my flesh. "Are you mocking me?"

"For heaven's sake, stop it, you're hurting me. What are you talking about? Everyone admires you. Other than my father, you're the most important man in Rome."

"But did you hear one person shout my name today? Even one?"

I had been wrong to laugh. There are people who require continual assurance of love but don't know how to seek it. Tiberius was one of these. I saw the need at the core of him, and that made it possible to forgive a great deal. "Smile at the crowd a little," I said. "That's what I do. That's all it takes. Everyone knows how much you've accomplished."

He made a sour face, but looked slightly appeased.

He did not take my advice about smiling, however.

>>>>>>>

Our marriage was not the sweet melding of souls that I had dreamed of as a girl. Still, Tiberius had only to look at me in a certain way, and I would feel an inward thrill of delight. He never spoke flowery words, but I knew he wanted me as much as I desired him. There was a spark between us, which I had never felt in the years I was Agrippa's wife. I thought if I was affectionate and gentle, in time Tiberius would become gentler too. I told myself sternly that I must fight down any impulse to tease him and must try to look at the world through his eyes. My previous marriage had been a desert. Now, in Tiberius's arms, I knew passion. And if it sometimes burned too hot . . . well, fire is better than ice. I wanted with all my heart for our marriage to succeed.

Did I love him? I did feel a kind of love. And I wanted him to love me.

Livia

When I noted how my son Tiberius and Julia gazed at each other, in the early days of their marriage, I felt enormous relief. My fears about their marrying seemed absurd. It was as if my love for Tavius was being carried forward into the next generation, with the marital felicity of our children.

"I am glad you and Tiberius are so happy," I said to Julia one day as we sat together at the chariot races. There were unstated questions in my mind: *You are, aren't you? Hope hasn't tricked me into seeing what isn't there?*

She turned a glowing face to me. "Tiberius is exactly the husband I needed. And I want to be the wife he needs."

I patted her knee and was even moved to confide. "I hope there will be a child in time. It will mean something very special to your father and me."

She smiled. "I hope there will be several children. We both want them."

Julia, the ideal daughter-in-law? *Oh, Diana, let it be so.*

The crowd cheered. A charioteer driving a team of pure-white horses won his race, the other competitors bunched up three lengths behind.

>>>>>>>

Meanwhile my son Drusus carried on the war in Germania. He had been chosen consul and went from victory to victory. But he managed to snatch time to be with his wife, Antonia. We received news that a second son had been born to her in Gaul. The little one was called Claudius.

I took care to make the proper sacrifices to all the gods and in particular to my tutelary deity, Diana. I have always been suspicious of life at those times when the world accords too well to my own wants.

A small event cast a tiny shadow on my happiness. Tavius and I were dining with Tiberius and Julia one evening when a messenger arrived from Drusus. This soldier had first left official dispatches and personal letters for Tavius and me at our house, then preceded to bring Tiberius a letter from his brother.

Tavius said, "Open the letter now, Tiberius. You might read us some of what Drusus has to say. I'm hoping for good news on the military front."

Tiberius obeyed and started to read the letter out loud. What came first was word of the campaign. All was well. "'The new province of Germania is secure for now. Our frontier has been pushed back from the Rhine to the Elba. Your plan to begin another military action in the spring I heartily approve. I look forward to your being back here, Brother. The time is ripe for us to act in concert again.'" Tiberius looked pleased. He glanced at Tavius. "You see, we are in accord on that." He planned to leave to rejoin his army in only a few days.

Tavius nodded benignly. "Is there more to your brother's letter? Read us the rest."

Tiberius went on reading aloud. "'I'm happy to be at actual war, rather than fighting political wars at home. I think you vastly underestimate the feeling against Augustus in the Senate. It's mainly men of our generation . . .'" Tiberius paused, looking embarrassed.

"No, don't stop," Tavius said coolly. "Please read us the rest."

"'It's mainly men of our generation who groan because of his . . . high-handed approach.'" Tiberius stopped again.

Julia, reclining beside Tiberius, looked as taken aback as I felt. "Father . . ."

"Read it," Tavius said in a hard voice.

"'The bad feeling among younger men of the most illustrious birth causes me great concern. I wish they wouldn't write me to complain, but they do. He does not consult with the Senate nearly as much as he should, nor does he pay sufficient attention to the views of the common people. We will have to get him to alter his dictatorial methods. Really, it's for his own good.'"

"Haven't we heard enough?" I said.

Tavius gave me an icy smile. "I'm touched that Drusus is concerned for me."

"My brother may be a great soldier, but in some ways he is a fool," Tiberius said angrily. "This tripe he writes me is utter idiocy. If there is opposition to you in the Senate, you must stamp it into the ground."

"In your view I've been too soft?" Tavius said.

"Yes!"

"You and your brother seem to have diametrically opposed views. But you both agree I don't know what I'm doing. And yet somehow I am where I am. Isn't that odd?"

The antipathy toward Tavius among certain younger senators that Drusus alluded to was only mildly worrisome. What I feared more was a serious falling-out over politics between my husband and my younger son. It might have come about in time. The gods decreed otherwise.

Julia

J hated the thought of Tiberius leaving for war. I asked him if I could go and live in Gaul as Antonia did. He shook his head.

"Don't you want me there, where you can come and visit me?"

"Of course I'd like it," he said. "But I happen to believe a man should pay full attention to business when he is dispatched to a province. Don't you see it's absurd—a general constantly leaving his troops to go running back to see his wife?"

Actually, I did not see the absurdity at all. But Tiberius was adamant. "I am not a fool like my brother," he said. "And I won't have my soldiers laughing at me."

"Do they laugh at Drusus? It is the first I've heard it. I thought they worshipped him."

He walked away from me without another word. I had committed two faults—arguing with him over a decision he had made and praising his brother. His orders, once given, had to be the law in our household. Even if you showed him clearly why he was wrong, he stuck rigidly to his original dictate. This was strange to me because my father was not that way, at least not with Livia, and my two previous husbands had never been that rigid either. I had also erred in mentioning how Drusus's soldiers adored him. Tiberius's feelings toward his younger brother were complicated. He would smile telling me about things he and Drusus had done together as boys. Yet he envied him.

In any case, Tiberius left for war without me. I did not care for his farewell words. "Behave yourself while I'm away."

I just looked at him quizzically.

"Be careful whom you associate with. What you do reflects on me."

I began to miss him as soon as he was gone. Yet I felt freer without him. I realized I had been expending a great deal of effort just to avoid displeasing him.

Since my marriage, I had stayed away from Gracchus and his circle. I hoped they understood the cause and did not hold it against me. I continued to keep clear of them after Tiberius left for war. But there were many people whose company I enjoyed who Tiberius had no special grievance against but never wanted to spend much time with. With him away, I was able to see them more often. One of these, whom I'd known well since I was a little girl, was Maecenas.

I attended a dinner party at his house. He was an attentive host, talking to me of this poet and that. "Have you read Ovid's latest book of poems?" I asked him. I had yet to get my hands on it.

"Yes, it is wonderful."

"I wish I could get my father to appreciate Ovid."

"I'm glad I wasn't drinking wine when you said that."

"Why?"

"Because I would have choked."

I don't think there had ever been a quarrel between Maecenas and my father, certainly not an open break. They had, however, come to look at certain important matters differently.

Maecenas looked perfectly healthy that evening. He seemed to enjoy the honeyed peacock his superb cook prepared as much as or even more than his guests did. We all laughed a great deal. Certainly he did not complain of any illness. Therefore, it was a great shock to me to learn that the next morning when his servants went to wake him, they found him dead in his bed.

Poets who had received his patronage vied in writing poems in his memory. They were the greatest writers in the Latin tongue; Maecenas had set our literature on a new, glorious path. In regard to sculpture and painting, his accomplishment was only slightly less. I only truly understood the extent of his achievement after he was gone.

I wondered, when people to come remembered my father's time, would they remember mainly the order he had brought to the empire? Or would they think first of the great flourishing in the arts that owed so much to Maecenas?

Maecenas's wife, Terentilla, had died the previous year, and he had no close relations. I had imagined he would bequeath his money to the same needy artists he had made it his calling to help. But he did not do this. He left every bit of his vast estate to my father. This was a grand gesture, an affirmation of friendship that surprised many in view of the recent strain between them.

Father plunged into deep mourning, as shattered as when Agrippa died. He had many allies, but I think that his whole life long, he only had two close friends. With Maecenas gone, who was left?

"We were boys together," he said. "I never expected Maecenas to die."

He and his friend were almost the same age. And Maecenas's death had come so suddenly. I imagined losing my father in an equally abrupt fashion. It seemed a real possibility in a way it never had before. The thought filled me with dread.

Livia

*I*t devastated Tavius that he had seen so little of Maecenas in the years directly preceeding his death. I think he had been telling himself that they would revive their friendship in good time. Now that would not happen. As for me, I felt the loss of an irreplaceable friend and also another loss, harder to define—I felt as though our sun had passed its zenith. It was as if Maecenas took the last bit of our youth with him.

The war in Germania continued to go well. If Tavius had not forgotten Drusus's criticism of him, he had largely shrugged it off. I imagined a luminous future for my younger son. He was happy in his marriage and family life, happy in his many victories. He was idolized. And then, suddenly all was lost.

It was not the result of war, but a mere riding accident. Drusus, on horseback, accompanied his marching troops on the way to a new encampment. Something startled the horse, which threw him. The fall broke Drusus's leg. He developed a fever. As his condition worsened, he got word to Tiberius, who was camped a considerable distance away. Tiberius raced to reach Drusus's side. People would talk of this ride as an incredible exploit. He exhausted horse after horse, rode for a day and a night without pause.

Can one speak of comfort in such a circumstance? It was some slight balm that Tiberius did reach Drusus in time, that my younger son died in his brother's arms. He was twenty-nine years old.

The Senate voted him posthumous honors. Statues would be erected in his memory. They gave him the name Germanicus—conqueror of Germania—which would be passed on to his sons.

Drusus's troops at first refused to let Tiberius take his body from them—they claimed the right to conduct his funeral themselves. He had difficulty quelling what amounted to a near riot, but he gave a speech in which he reminded the soldiers of their duty to uphold discipline, even in their general's absence. He also told them they must show manly restraint even in grief. They demanded the right to erect a monument to Drusus there in Germania, which Tiberius granted.

Tiberius, Antonia, and the children accompanied Drusus's body back to Rome, and Tavius and I traveled to meet the procession at the town of Ticinum in the north of Italy. All along the way there and back, people stood on the sides of the road, weeping as they watched us pass. They kept great pyres of wood burning in Drusus's memory.

In Mars Field in Rome, I stood listening to the eulogies both Tavius and Tiberius delivered. I was dry-eyed, beyond tears. Tavius said that his greatest hope was that his heirs, Gaius and Lucius, would grow up to emulate Drusus. It fell to Tiberius to light Drusus's funeral fire; his elder son, who would afterward be called Germanicus, was only five years old. We placed the urn with his ashes in the great mausoleum Tavius had erected for our family.

Afterward, for many days, I wished to be alone. I would sit in a small room with the shutters closed. When darkness came I did not bother to light a candle.

One night Tavius came to me and took my hand. "I am going to write an account of Drusus's life," he said. "A book recounting not only his victories but how he was loved by his troops—indeed how he was loved by everyone. I will have it copied and widely distributed. I promise you, he will always be remembered."

I said nothing. I could not see his face in the darkness. But I heard the grief in his voice.

"You know our political disagreements were all wind and air."

I did not speak.

"He was a pure spirit. I already miss him."

Not as I do, I thought. *You did not carry him in your body. You do not feel this unspeakable pain that only a mother can feel.*

I felt angry at Tavius—angry that he had sent my son away from me. I realized the injustice of my anger, but I did not care. In some awful way, I was punishing Tavius with my silence. It was as if I needed to hurt someone, because of the great hurt I had received.

"Antonia wishes to stay here in this household with us. It will be good to have the little ones living here, don't you think? She told me she will never remarry. 'Who will I find who will ever equal him?' she said. I will never ask her to take another husband, not as long as she feels as she does. I understand. Theirs was a great love."

I listened, as if from a great distance. I wanted to be alone.

"Oh, Livia," Tavius said finally, "I can't lose you the way I lost my sister. Please, have some pity on me. This is more than I can bear."

In his concern for me, Tavius insisted I speak with a Stoic philosopher named Areius. This man, who had long been a personal friend of Tavius's, was supposed to be greatly skilled in helping people through times of grief. "Do not hesitate to talk about your son with others," he told me. "Don't avoid mentioning his name. Keep busts of him in places where you will often see them."

This philosopher meant well, and most of his advice was sensible enough, so I followed it. But in any case it was not in me to permanently turn my back on life, as Octavia had. For there were people who depended on me—Tavius above all. I loved Tavius too much to desert him. A part of me died with my son. I suffered. But I went on.

Julia

After Tiberius's return, my marriage seemed more and more like a kind of servitude. Tiberius disapproved of my friends. They were only friends—not lovers. But I had to see them behind his back. Otherwise I would have to suffer his black looks and listen to his criticism.

If he did not find me home when he expected me to be there, he would ask me afterward where I had been. In reply, it was easier to lie than to tell him the truth.

I saw the downhill slope we were on, but felt powerless to resist the slide. Then fate intervened. I discovered I was with child.

When I told my husband, it was late in the evening and our bedchamber was illumined only by a single candle. The change in Tiberius's face seemed to light up the room.

Had I never seen him happy before?

He pulled me into his arms and kissed me. "A son—oh, gods above, let it be a son."

He had a son already, by Vipsania. He rarely spoke of him, never saw him, had left him completely in the care of his mother.

This child I would bear, however, seemed to matter to him in an entirely different way. As my pregnancy progressed, Tiberius treated me with anxious solicitude.

He does care about me, I thought. *Perhaps he even loves me.*

We were reborn—or at least our marriage was. No baby can heal all its parents' wounds. And yet my pregnancy worked a great healing.

A son, a son, I prayed. *Oh, gods, let me give Tiberius the boy he wants.*

True happiness never seemed so close, so possible as it did at this time.

>>>>>>>

My baby was born on a rainy spring morning. I had a long labor, harder than with any of my other children, perhaps because I was now past thirty. I saw worry on the midwife's face—and that only served to frighten me. *Oh, thank you, gods,* I thought when I at last heard her exultant words: "A boy!"

Later, I lay with the swaddled infant in my arms, and my husband came and sat on the edge of the bed and looked down at the baby with shining eyes. "My son. Caesar Augustus's grandson. He will be a great man. I have had a sense of it, ever since you told me you were pregnant. This child will be nothing ordinary. I am sure of it."

He said he would name the boy Tiberius.

I waited for a loving gesture from him, a caring word, some acknowledgment of the pain and danger I had been through. That did not come.

"I am tired," I said, and turned my head away from him on the pillow. After a moment, he got up and left.

>>>>>>

I found a good wet nurse for my new baby, just as I had for my other children. He was never alone; a trusted maidservant sat by his cradle day and night.

When I held my little one in my arms, often I could not help pitying him. I saw my two older boys, Gaius and Lucius, weighted down by their grandfather's expectations. I suspected that it would be worse for little Tiberius growing up. He had an exacting father to please and was the carrier of Father and Livia's joint dynastic hopes. "I will love you no matter what," I promised my son. "You don't have to become a great man for me to love you."

I whispered many endearments to him every day, as if to fortify him for what lay ahead. It was as if some god prompted me. I wanted him to fully know a mother's love.

In late afternoon, I came home from looking at the work of a new sculptor. It was a staid occasion, an opportunity to see some of my women friends who liked art.

The moment I entered the house, Phoebe came rushing to me. "Oh, my lady, we did not know where you were, but we fetched the physician right away. The baby . . ."

I rushed into the nursery. Tiberius stood over the child's cradle with Brocius, a physician we often employed. My husband stared at me. "Where were you?"

"Is the baby sick?" I directed my question at Brocius.

"He has a fever."

"Where were you?" Tiberius repeated. He added accusingly, "The servants found me at Mars Field. They couldn't find you."

I shook my head. "I was at an exhibit . . . a sculptor . . . What does it matter?" I went to the cradle. I looked at the baby. His little face was flushed. His eyes were shut. I watched his small chest rise and fall, to be sure he was breathing. "Oh, gods above, how sick is he?"

"Now you care?" Tiberius said.

"Of course I care!" I cried. "I was only gone for three hours."

"You're lying. You said you wouldn't lie to me, but you've been lying all along, haven't you? Being where you shouldn't be?"

"It was three hours!"

"You left him."

"Am I a captive? Do you think you carried me to Rome in chains?"

The physician averted his eyes.

>>>>>>>

So many people have suffered the horror of seeing a laughing, happy baby in his cradle one day and the next day losing him. But are human souls constituted to bear such a loss without descending into madness?

In my mind, I see a kind husband comforting his wife on the death of their child, she comforting him in turn.

But Tiberius had no kindness in him, no pity.

When we turned away from the cradle that held our dead child, Tiberius spoke to me. "You had be out with your degenerate friends."

I could do nothing but weep.

"How can a mother desert her own son?" He asked this question with such pain and grief that anyone who did not know would have imagined he spoke of something real.

"I did not desert him," I said.

"I know now exactly what you are."

I walked back to the cradle, looked at the baby. He could have been sleeping, he seemed so peaceful. Above his head, attached to the cradle, his golden bulla hung. Before he was born, like every mother, I had filled the locket with objects meant to bring good luck, a little charm in the shape of a dolphin, a tiny bronze phallus, a new gold coin.

"Oh, maybe this is the gods' mercy," I sobbed. I turned on Tiberius. "Better the baby died than to have you as a father. All you ever do is make the people around you suffer. Even as a boy you were that way, and you haven't changed. You are evil—evil."

He grabbed my arm in a crushing grip. "Shut your mouth."

"Or you'll do what? I am Caesar Augustus's daughter. And who are you? The son of some fool no one even remembers?"

He did not strike me. But he let loose a torrent of all the vilest words that could be applied to a woman.

"Coward," I said.

He stood perfectly still, hatred transforming his face. He said nothing, but I felt I was looking at the face of a murderer.

All this took place while our dead baby lay in his cradle.

Livia

Our whole family suffered a terrible loss with the death of little Tiberius. Many years ago, Tavius and I had lost a son who had been born months too early and lived only for a few hours. Now it was as if we once again had to suffer the death of that child whom we had wanted so desperately. Our grandson's death cut us to the heart. But Tiberius and Julia's response to the death exceeded all human bounds. Somehow their grief was transmuted into anger. They looked at each other now with silent loathing as if each blamed the other for the child's death—a death that was an act of the gods no parent could prevent.

I had often worried that Tiberius seemed to lack the capacity to find great joy in life. But I never before knew him to be as deeply troubled as he was at this time.

An informant brought a story to me that soon all of Rome knew. On the street one day Tiberius happened to meet his former wife, Vipsania. By then, Tavius had arranged a good marriage for her with a senator named Gaius Gallus. She seemed contented enough with her new husband. I do not know if meeting Tiberius stirred deep feelings on her part, but she greeted him in a seemly way, saying she had been sad to hear he had recently lost a child.

He, in a voice loud enough to be heard by passersby, told Vipsania that every day of his life he regretted the decision he had made in divorcing her and marrying Julia. He begged her forgiveness for the divorce.

Vipsania acted very well, speaking soothing words and telling Tiberius that of course she forgave him, or rather, she saw nothing in his actions that required forgiveness. When they parted, Tiberius stood in the street, gazing after her, eyes full of tears.

>>>>>>>

I summoned Tiberius to me later that day. We met alone in my private sitting room, with the doors closed. He looked haggard to me, as if he had not slept well for a long time. "I think you are under great strain," I said.

"Did I embarrass you today, Mother?" He half smiled. "I am so sorry."

My son had a knack for turning away compassion. But this was my child. "Has something more happened between you and Julia?"

"More? What more could there be? She is vile. I know I can't end our marriage. You don't have to tell me that. There won't be any more scenes in the street, Mother, if that's what you're worried about."

He refused to discuss the subject further.

That evening I learned that Tavius too had been informed of Tiberius's encounter with Vipsania. He felt no sympathy for my son but was furious with him.

There could be no recurrence of Tiberius's meeting with Vipsania. An administrative position in Rhodes was found for Vipsania's husband. This was the kind of comfortable post senators liked—where they could bring along their wives and children. Tavius and I wanted Vipsania where she and Tiberius would never meet.

And soon afterward, trouble in Gaul called Tiberius away. He was glad to go. He could not bear to be with Julia.

Julia

J, heard about him accosting Vipsania on the street, asking her forgiveness, saying he wished they had remained married. Did he do it to humiliate me? I do not know. But I felt the sting of a public insult.

I could not keep from upbraiding him about it. "Can we at least keep our misery to ourselves? Must you make it public knowledge?"

He looked at me as if he hated me. "I gave up the only woman I ever loved, for you and for Rome. And see what I have received in return for my sacrifice."

"I don't believe you loved her," I said. "I don't believe you have ever loved anyone."

I had thought we could be happy together. I had imagined for a few moments that I had found love. What an ugly joke that was. I had been taken for a fool.

When he left for Gaul, I was glad to see him go.

My father never had any great affection for Tiberius. But he valued his competence and loyalty. After Tiberius left, I saw unspoken blame in his eyes. It was my task as a wife to please my husband, and I had failed in that task.

>>>>>>>

"I am sorry to see you so unhappy," Gracchus said to me when we met at a dinner given by one of my women friends. "I am not surprised, though."

"You have no liking for my husband."

"The wrong brother died."

"You were Drusus's friend?"

He nodded. "He might have been a bridge between me and my friends in the Senate and your father. Tiberius, on the other hand, will reinforce your father's worst tendencies. And heaven help us if he succeeds him. He has the character of a tyrant."

"Tiberius will never succeed my father," I said. "My sons will."

"Julia, I truly hope so. But your father is growing old, and your sons are still mere boys."

"You believe there will be an interval between my father and my sons, when Tiberius will hold power?"

"I think so."

I took a sip of wine. I remembered the fear I had felt after Maecenas died, the terror of Father being suddenly taken from us. But I said, "I think you are wrong. You don't know my father. He will live to be a hundred."

"I would prefer that. Because if Tiberius ever gets power, I don't see him yielding it. To your sons or anyone else."

I felt a chill at these words.

Later, at the same dinner party, another old friend of mine, Aurelia, sought me out. "We have been missing you. Where have you been hiding?"

"No place you'd want to hear about."

"Perhaps you'd like to dine with me tomorrow? An old friend of yours will be there."

"Oh? What old friend is that?"

"Scipio."

>>>>>>>

It began again. I do not mean my love affair with Scipio, although within days of this conversation with Aurelia, I was in his bed. Rather, the life I had led before my marriage to Tiberius.

I had lost the dream of marriage to a husband who loved me. I had lost a child. There was a void in me. Being in a man's arms filled it for the moment at least. I longed for . . . something, someone. It was as if I were lost in the desert searching for water.

It surely was that thirst that drove me to attend what Aurelia called her special celebrations. Much laughter, much wine. Rooms lit by candles. In the half darkness, people coupling. Sometimes we dressed as gods and goddesses. Often we wore masks. We became tigers, lions, creatures that existed only in the ancient tales. Men, women, what did it matter? Flesh was flesh, flesh was sweet. There was too much wine, too much heat.

Sometimes I wanted to flee. I knew I was in a place where I should not be. But at the same time, I wanted to stay—to feel something, anything rather than the bleakness I knew at home. And there was that terrible need in me, that ache to be touched.

Is it you? Is it you? Is it you? Are you the one I am looking for? My head swimming from all the wine, sometimes I voiced my question aloud. Men would laugh. "Oh, yes, darling, it's definitely me."

Phoebe nursed me when I came home sick, saw to it that I did not show myself to my children when I had had too much wine. She was the message bearer when I needed to send notes to my lovers. Phoebe, faithful Phoebe. She was my truest friend. She knew about all my doings, and yet I never saw disapproval in her eyes. On the contrary. "Why shouldn't you live your life as you see fit?" she told me. "Why shouldn't you be happy?"

I would wake up in a strange house, sick from all the wine. Sometimes I forgot to be cautious at all. There were months when I was relieved when my courses came.

"No one will ever stop me again from doing just as I wish," I told Phoebe.

But how empty my life seemed, how loveless.

>>>>>>>

One day Livia came to see me. Her severe manner instantly put me on guard. She dispensed with all niceties in a way that was unlike her and said quite bluntly that unpleasant tales about me had come to her ears. "I have not repeated them to your father. I do not want to hurt him . . . or you. But if things go on as they have, these stories will reach your father's ears. And they will reach Tiberius's ears as well. You are courting disaster."

I felt a prickling up the length of my spine, but I said coolly, "I don't know what you are talking about."

A few days later my mother visited. "I am so worried about you," Scribonia said.

Incredibly, it was Livia who had persuaded her to come and talk to me. Just the same it was a source of comfort to me to weep in my mother's arms. I told her I would be cautious in what I did—much, much more cautious. I wanted to ease her mind.

She was aghast. "You must be faithful to your husband," she said. "My dear child, it is not a matter of right and wrong but of who has the power. You cannot set yourself against your father and your husband."

"Mother," I said in a low voice, "there is something that drives me. Even against my will. I wish you could understand. But I hardly understand it myself."

She gave a kind of keening wail. "Oh, Julia, Julia . . ."

I continued on the same path. For months, nothing changed.

And then Tiberius came home from Gaul.

>>>>>>>

He would not let me live my life as I wished to live it.

There were terrible arguments. Nights when we were both hoarse with screaming at each other. We had no dignity. We had no restraint. The passion that we had once shared was dead, dead with our baby, and this is what we had in its place. This rage.

Once he blocked the entranceway when I wanted to leave the house. "Where are you going?" Tiberius said.

"Out. To see my friends."

"You're going nowhere," he said.

"I go where I like," I said.

He grabbed me by the shoulder.

"Do you want me to scream? Shall I scream to the world what I think of you?"

He raised his clenched fist. "Go ahead."

I smiled at him. "Oh, hit me. Please do. I would so like bruises to show my father."

He let out a stream of curses, vile barracks obscenities.

"Why don't you hit me, you brave man? Hurt me, kill me, what does it matter? Just as long as you're ready to face my father."

He lowered his fist, let go of me. "Why get filth on my hands?"

Livia

S houldn't someone tell Augustus what his daughter is?"
Tiberius asked me the question between clenched teeth.

"No. And if you are the one to do it, believe me he will
hate you for it."

My husband would never forgive the person who made him
directly face the reality of Julia's promiscuity. I knew the man I had
been married to for the past three decades. If he had been able to
confront Julia's behavior, he would already have done it. He loved
her too much to punish her for what she was doing. It was all so
painful, so shaming. So he had chosen not to see.

Tiberius stood, leaning back against a balcony railing. It was
a sunny summer day at Prima Porta. Behind him, I glimpsed an
expanse of countryside, everything verdant and in bloom. His face
was congested with anger, his eyes burning. "So I am expected to
tolerate this?"

"Come inside. Sit down." No one would hear us, and yet it
felt wrong to be having this talk out in the air. We entered a small

side room and closed the door. I sat. Tiberius stood. He stared at
the mural on the wall, which showed Jupiter coming to Danae in
a shower of gold, looked at it as if it were a vision of surpassing
ugliness.

"If you could win back her affections—"

"Mother!" His shout made me jump. He stood over me. His
hands were clenched, and for an instant I felt almost a sense of
menace. "I wonder how much shame you would like me to bear."

*Do you think I wished for this? Do you not remember I counseled
you not to marry Julia?* I knew these words from me could only do
harm, and so I kept silent.

"I will never touch her again," Tiberius said. "She has dishonored me."

"She does not have that power," I said. "Only you can dishonor
yourself, my son, by your own actions."

"This is not the time for Stoic platitudes."

"It is the time for you to show strength."

"Yes. There you are right."

We were silent for a few moments.

Then Tiberius spoke again. "I have done everything you and
Augustus wanted. I have fought, I have worked, I have sacrificed
my own happiness. And what I have out of it is this dishonor, a wife
I cannot discipline and cannot divorce, who behaves like a common
prostitute. I am tired, Mother. Sick of it all. Sick of the army, sick of
the sycophants who pretend to be my friends. There is not an aspect
of my existence that gives me any pleasure."

I let out a long breath. "Oh, Tiberius . . ."

"There's only one thing to do, and that is walk away. So I'm
leaving."

"You have been under great strain," I said. "You are not yourself."

"Then who am I?" He gave a harsh laugh.

"Dearest, think. You are the second most powerful man in Rome after Augustus."

"After Augustus," he echoed. He laughed again. "I am no one, Mother."

"You can't just leave," I said.

But he could.

>>>>>>>

In the end, it proved impossible to get Tiberius to stay in Rome, or to continue a career of public service. Tavius asked him to reconsider, offered him every inducement. He would hear none of it. In their conversation, neither of them mentioned Julia.

Tiberius left for Rhodes—ironically just where I had wanted him to go to continue his studies when he was seventeen. Rhodes was a pleasant place, a center of learning. It was also where Vipsania now lived with her husband. Tiberius said he wanted to be close to his son, whom Vipsania was rearing. But of course people whispered he wanted to renew his acquaintance with his former wife.

Tavius was furious at Tiberius for what he called his "desertion." But at the same time he harbored the hope that he would return, a hope that I also nurtured. "He is exhausted," I told Tavius. "We should give him time to rest."

"He is exhausted? What should I say? How can a man simply walk away from his public responsibilities?"

There was now a great silence in the heart of our marriage, subjects we did not talk about. It was understood between us, of course, that Tiberius and Julia's estrangement had contributed to Tiberius's leaving Rome. But we did not discuss the precise dimensions of their estrangement. I believe we were both afraid of what might be said. We were parents of a son and daughter who were married to each other but could not bear to even dwell in the same city. I feared

that the collapse in our children's union might do irreparable damage to our own. Perhaps Tavius feared that too, or perhaps he was
more afraid of what I might in a moment of anger tell him about
Julia. So we were silent.

One year passed and then another and still one more. It was as if
we were all frozen in a great block of ice: Tiberius in Rhodes, living
the life of a gentleman of leisure, engaging in scholarly study in
accord with his passing interests; Julia in Rome, living the life she
chose; Tavius and I carrying the burden of ruling Rome's empire.
Sometimes it seemed we were absolutely alone in carrying that
burden.

Time passed and little changed.

I accepted matters as they stood. For it seemed all too likely that
any change would be for the worse.

Part III

Julia

One afternoon, I attended a poetry reading at the house of my friend Varilla. The reading was well attended because Varilla's friends were numerous and diverse. The poet himself was a new friend of Varilla's. He had auburn ringlets and milky white skin. "Poor boy," Varilla said to me when the reading was finished. "His verses aren't very good, are they?"

I shrugged. Of course, Varilla had chosen him for talents that had little to do with literature.

"The poetry was execrable," Jullus Antony said, coming up beside us. "But your hospitality, Varilla, is as always superb."

She smiled at him. Smiled the way a gourmand smiles at a sumptuous banquet.

Jullus was nearly forty; the gloss of youth was gone. Time had etched world-weary lines under his eyes. But he was attractive in a way I could not remember him being as a boy.

"You should give a reading of your own poetry sometime," Varilla said.

"You write poetry, Jullus?" I said.

He averted his eyes, just for an instant. I sensed a shyness that seemed not to go with his tall, strapping physique. "Oh, I dabble."

"Really, you ought to give a reading," Varilla said.

My cousin, Marcella, Jullus's wife, stood beside him. "Jullus would never give a reading. He has published a few volumes, just among our friends. But he has never wanted to draw much attention to his work."

"Some poets never publish their poems while they are alive because they write about such private themes," I said.

Jullus gave me a small, deprecatory grimace. "My poetry is not all that private. It's just not very good."

"You never admitted that before," Marcella said with a laugh.

"I felt no need to state the obvious, my dear," Jullus said.

Later that evening, after we had all dined, a few of us lingered before going home. I stood alone admiring a statue of a nymph, a recent addition to Varilla's house, by an artist just coming into his full powers. I loved the pride conveyed in that nude carved figure, how the girl stood with head up and an open gaze, despite her nakedness. I studied the statue for a few moments, thinking I must make a point of buying a work by this new sculptor.

I seemed to feel rather than hear someone coming up behind. There was an impression of warmth. Then I heard Jullus's voice, low and mellow. "Gorgeous, isn't it?"

I turned. "Absolutely beautiful." I noticed how the tan of his skin contrasted with the white wool of his toga and that his eyes were not quite brown, not quite green. "Varilla has good taste in art," I said.

"If not always in poetry."

We discussed poetry for a while and discovered we were both fond of the work of a poet named Aulus. "But," I said, "I wish his poems were more cheerful."

"How could they be, given the theme he has chosen?"

"I would say he has taken love as his main theme."

"Exactly."

"You think love must always be painful?"

He shrugged.

"Aulus's poems are almost all about tragic lovers," I said. "Really, you would avoid falling in love at all costs if you took him as a guide. He seems to be deliberately warning us that love is more dangerous than war."

"I don't think he intends to lead or warn anyone," Jullus said. "He is lost in the woods, and supposes everyone else is too. What use is a guide where there are no paths?"

"That's how you think of love—being lost in the woods?"

He nodded.

"It's been like that for you?"

"No," he said. "I have been very good at avoiding . . . getting lost. I've always been afraid that if I did, I might never find myself again."

"Oh, you have too dark a view of love."

"Well, my father's experience you know . . . How many people had to die because he fell in love with the wrong woman?"

"A great many, I would think."

"A great many," Jullus repeated. "And the world we live in was altered because of that."

We were standing very close to each other, too close. I found I did not want to move away, but remembering that others were present, I did.

I was suddenly looking at Jullus differently, as if I hadn't known him all my life.

He had been a boy on the fringes of our family, someone my aunt Octavia cared for, but no one else took much notice of. I thought of him as an object of my aunt's charity and then my father's. He had long been married to Marcella—my cousin whom I disliked and avoided when I could. He had become consul and had spent the last few years as the governor of Asia Minor—a post that sounded much more important than it actually was, for it came empty of independent power.

He had muscular shoulders and arms and a handsome face with the most sensual-looking lips. Some men have an aura. He did, and it was strongly masculine and magnetic. How had I not noticed this before?

"Is the theme of your own poetry love?" I asked him.

"My poems aren't worth talking about. Marcella could tell you that much."

"I'm not sure I would consider her an authority on poetry."

"She believes she is an authority on me."

"Is she?"

He shook his head.

"What a pity," I said.

"And you—how well does your husband know you?"

"Did no one tell you? I scarcely have a husband. He's fled to Rhodes to get away from me."

"Tiberius always did strike me as a fool."

"He is not that. He is something else entirely."

"If you say so. Well, enough of that unpleasant subject. Do you write poetry?"

"No. I have no talent in that area. Or in any other."

"Oh, I think you do," he said.

Somehow we were standing close together again. And we were speaking in low voices, almost in whispers. I wondered if Marcella noticed and what she would make of it. I realized I did not care.

"Suppose you did write poetry," he said. "What would you choose as your theme?"

I tossed my head. "Haven't you heard about me? My theme would be passion, of course. Passion and all the delights of the flesh. If I were a poetess, I would write odes to pleasure."

"I doubt that," Jullus said. "I think your theme is loneliness."

He spoke gently, with compassion. Suddenly, I had to fight back tears. "Most people who heard you say that, to me of all people, would want to laugh."

"Most people don't see what is before their eyes," he said.

I could not remember a time I had not known him. Even in my earliest childhood, he had been there—the orphan boy who lived in my aunt's house. Yet until this moment we had been strangers to each other.

Now we stood so near each other I could feel his breath on my cheek.

I said, "Maybe your father thought it was worth it . . . worth altering the world."

"To love Cleopatra? Maybe it was."

>>>>>>>

We met alone for the first time in an inn on the Appian Way. I borrowed an inconspicuous, plain litter to get there, went by a circuitous route. He was waiting for me in a small, ugly room. I had been in rooms like this before, rooms that served only one purpose.

"It's tawdry, I know," he said.

I felt a thickness in my throat. "What does it matter?"

He tipped up my chin, looked into my eyes. "It matters. I will remember everything about this moment. For the rest of my life, I will remember this shabby room, but also true beauty. The beauty I see when I look at you."

I glanced away.

"You don't like to hear your beauty praised?"

"Not especially."

I was used to having my looks extolled by sycophants and men who wished to bed me; it had no meaning for me. And what I saw when I looked in the mirror these days was a woman who had begun to show her years.

"Most people don't even see me when they look at me," I said. "They see Augustus's fortunate daughter. Or they see . . . shall I say what they see?"

He shook his head.

"They would say these are the perfect surroundings for me," I said, glancing around the chamber. "I am just where they would expect to find me—in a room in a cheap inn with a man who is not my husband."

"Shall I tell you what they see when they look in my direction?" Jullus said. "A fortunate man. Lucky beyond all reckoning. Because of the great benevolence that has been extended to me, and which I have accepted, from the man who killed my father and my brother."

I found I had no words to say.

"Not many men forfeit all claim to honor when they are ten years old. But I did."

I shook my head, disbelievingly. "How? How could you possibly think you did that at such an age?"

"Your father told my older brother Antyllus and me that he was going to war with my father. Father had left us with Octavia to raise, but now he demanded that we be returned to him. I have always told everyone—even myself—that my father completely forgot about me on the day I was born, but that is not true. He remembered Antyllus and me, at the last possible moment. Now if your father were a dishonorable man, he would have slit both our throats. But he didn't. He said we could go to join our father or remain with him and his sister, Octavia, according to our wish. And if we stayed with him, he would treat us as his kin, so long as we stayed loyal."

"That choice was left up to you? At the age of ten?"

"It was Octavia's idea. I believe left to himself, Augustus would have just sent us to our father. But Octavia thought we would choose to stay, out of attachment to her, and she, kind heart, thought that would be best for us."

"So you made that choice—at ten."

"Yes. My brother surprised Octavia—he did not surprise me—by demanding to be sent to Father. He even spoke defiant words to Augustus's face. I, on the other hand, threw myself into your aunt's arms and cried out that I wanted to remain with her."

"Of course you did that," I said. "You were a little boy, and she had been the closest you had to a mother."

Jullus looked at me in silence, a cynical half smile on his lips.

"Do you blame yourself . . . for a choice made as a child?"

"I think the person we are at ten is the person we will always be, Julia. I certainly loved your aunt, but when I threw myself into her arms—was that an uncalculated action? Do you truly think so? If you do, I'll tell you this—I distinctly remember thinking your father was going to win."

"Win the war between him and your father, you mean?"

He nodded.

"You believe you deliberately picked the winning side at ten years old?"

"Does it seem so unlikely to you?"

"Yes, it seems extremely unlikely. You were a child, Jullus, faced with a terrible choice, and you chose the only love and shelter you had ever known."

He moved his shoulders negligently.

I reached up, touched his cheek. I could feel the stubble of his beard, his cheekbone.

"All I'm sure of is this," he said. "I am alive and my father and brother are long dead."

"Why blame yourself for what you cannot help?"

"Yes, why blame yourself. Some women can live without love, but you cannot, Julia." He drew me close and kissed me on the lips.

Forever afterward, I would remember his strength and his tenderness, the hard and the soft of him. His mouth on my lips, on my breasts, on my thigh, the fire where he touched me. I became a well of need, and then the need was met. I cried out when he entered me. I gasped again and again clinging to him.

Later, as night drew on, we lay pressed heart to heart. "I have wondered if there is love anywhere in the world for me," I murmured. "I have searched and searched. And you were there all the time. Why did I not see you?"

"Forget the past. Isn't it enough that we are together now?"

"Will you love me, Jullus? Or am I fool to expect that?"

"I will love you. I love you now."

"Truly?"

"Yes, truly." His lips brushed mine.

We were two wounded and unhappy creatures who found each other. He was what I wanted. I knew it from that first night. He was what I had wanted all my life. And I was what he wanted.

It would have been better if we had been members of the nameless Forum crowd. Then nobody would have cared what we did.

But he was a former consul of Rome, Mark Antony's son; I was Augustus's daughter. And still nothing mattered as much as what we felt for each other.

>>>>>>>

Everything changed for me. I wanted no other man but Jullus. As long as we could have our stolen hours together, that was enough. It was a time of bliss for me, a time of perpetual spring.

Once after we made love, I asked, "Do you love *me*? Just me, the woman I am. Not Augustus's daughter. Not . . . a way of getting something else. Do you understand what I am saying?"

"Yes, I understand what you are saying, and I love you." He spoke in a grave, measured voice.

"I'm not who they think I am, Jullus. I'm not . . . some kind of filthy joke."

"No one thinks of you that way."

"Oh, but they do. Even many people who pretend to be my friends do. Jullus . . . do you know how many beds I've been in?"

He nuzzled my neck. "Why are you talking about this now?"

"I don't understand how you can love me."

"I've lived off the charity of my own father's killer all my life. *All* my life. Can you love me?"

"I do love you," I said.

We came together with a tenderness I had never known before. I thought, *Oh, this is what it is to make love. This. This man's touch.*

At the end, there was pleasure that was almost unbearable to me, a pleasure that was almost pain.

I whispered,

> *"Suns can set and rise again;*
> *For us, once our brief light has set,*

There's one unending night for sleeping.
Give me a thousand kisses . . .'"

He gave a low laugh and whispered back, *"'Then a hundred,*
Then another thousand, then a second hundred . . .'"
We slept clasped in each other's arms.

>>>>>>

"It is so strange," I told Jullus once. "I have been looking for you all
my life. And you were there but I didn't see you. Did you see me?"

"Yes and no. I saw your beauty—how could I not? You daz-
zled me. But it would have been foolish of me to raise my eyes to
Augustus's daughter. So I looked away."

"Foolish? Why?"

"You know why. Your father would never consider me as your
husband."

Of course.

He asked in a low, hesitant voice, "Would you marry me if you
could?"

"You need to ask me that question?"

"You are Augustus's daughter, and I'm who I am. Not much of
a prize for you."

I embraced him. "But you are . . . you are a prize. You are everything. Of course I would marry you. Of all the men in the world, I
would marry you."

"If that were possible," he said in a leaden voice.

"If only it were."

Livia

*T*avius and I both had our deep unspoken griefs at this time, related to our offspring. I mourned—I would always mourn—my son Drusus. And his youngest child, little Claudius, had developed a palsy in his limbs. He learned to speak later than his brother and sister had, and when he did talk, he stammered, which made it hard to understand him. Antonia's older boy, called Germanicus, resembled his father at a similar age—a handsome, promising boy. My granddaughter, Livilla, was pretty and playful. But Claudius's sad condition was a great sorrow to Antonia and me.

Tavius's grandsons Gaius and Lucius continued to thrive, and he had great hopes for them. They lived in our household, and he made a point of spending time with them every day. The boys worshipped him. Their younger sisters and small brother who remained in Julia's care seemed to be doing well. It was Julia herself who was the great weight on Tavius's heart.

His dealings with his daughter were extremely cool and distant. I don't think he ever saw her alone at this time. He spoke of her only when necessary; he preferred not to hear her mentioned.

I heard rumors that Julia had taken up with Jullus Antony. They were both married to other people—and Julia was my son Tiberius's wife. Certainly I did not celebrate. But I felt relief—an indication of how much I feared imprudent actions on Julia's part. A quiet love affair with a man known for caution, who all his life had carefully cultivated Tavius's good opinion . . . well, it could have been worse. Better this, I thought, than a stream of lovers, or the kind of entanglement that would result in public scandal.

The people of Rome gossiped about our family, and I suppose they even laughed at us. Maybe they would have done so whatever we did, but the gods know we gave them reason. Vipsania, still in Rhodes and married to Gallus, bore a son. Malicious tongues dubbed Tiberius the father. Tiberius and Gallus got into a public quarrel, and Gallus went about telling people that not only was Vipsania's last child his, but her first son, Tiberius's boy, Drusus, was also. This was an utter absurdity. But Tavius told me flatly that he had been informed that Tiberius and Vipsania had become lovers. I did not probe for details. It seemed likely that both of Vipsania's boys were actually my grandsons.

"Matters are far from ideal," I said to Tavius one day. "But I think our best course is to live with what we cannot alter."

He gave me a sour look and did not answer. Still, he did not contradict me. I don't think he had drawn the same conclusions from recent events that I had, though. Our children were the people they were. We could not reshape them to suit our convenience. I accepted this. But I doubt Tavius ever accepted this bitter lesson. Rather he had thrown up his hands in disgust. It was hard and painful for the man who ruled the Roman Empire to feel unable to govern his own family.

Julia

For a long time, it was enough for Jullus and me to have our
times together. Many months passed before we dared speak
of having more, and then we did it only wistfully.

"If I were married to you . . . ," I would say.

"If you were my wife . . . ," he would whisper.

He broke with his wife, Marcella, and took lodgings in a quiet
district of the city, distant from the Palatine. A humble place, but
we could meet there—though not without risking gossip. But where
could we be safe from wagging tongues?

I dreaded to think about the future, but I had to. I had to think
not only of myself and the man I loved, but of my children and
especially my two older sons.

"If my father were to die . . . what would happen?" I asked Jullus
one night.

"I think we ought to offer sacrifices for your father's long life and
good health."

"But if something did happen to him now . . . ?"

"Tiberius would come back to Rome and assume power," Jullus said. "He has great credit with the army. And he is your husband."

"My husband . . ." I gave a little rueful chuckle.

"There's been no divorce," Jullus said.

"It sickens me to still be bound to him." For a while we were silent. Then I said, "My father is supposed to be so wise and all knowing. But he imagines that if he dies tomorrow, Tiberius would be content to hold authority as a kind of placeholder and then turn power over to my sons when they are old enough. Do you think Tiberius is capable of such generosity of spirit?"

Jullus did not need to answer. He just pulled me closer to him.

I imagined Tiberius as ruler of Rome. It was a terrifying thought. What would he do to me? What would he do to my children? I knew him in a way no one else did, and I felt he was capable of great cruelty.

The shutters were half open, and outside I saw the waning crescent moon. I turned my head, pressed my face against Jullus's shoulder. *If only this moment could last forever.*

"Tell me truthfully," Jullus said, "would you trust me to look out for your boys' interests, if I were in Tiberius's place?"

"You are the only man I would trust."

If only I were married to Jullus. If only he were my husband and Tiberius were not.

Cleopatra Selene

I actually want to go. Isn't that strange?" I said to Juba.

"Times have changed," he said.

There had been a flurry of letters between Livia and me, touching on the possibility of our visiting Rome again. Several matters of public policy could best be settled by meeting in person. Also, Livia had yet to see Drusilla, the child named in her honor. Two years ago, I had finally fulfilled my hopes, bringing my bright-eyed little girl into the world. "I'm sure it will warm Livia's heart to meet our daughter."

"And what warms Livia's heart has a way of translating into . . . advantage for Mauretania."

"Oh, you cynical man." I kissed him. "Tell me the truth, though. You don't have any craving to visit Rome, do you?"

He shrugged. But I knew him. He was happiest either engrossed in scholarly work in our library or off exploring unknown territories. "Poor Cleopatra Selene," he said. "You have a lazy husband who finds the whole business of kingship a terrible chore."

"Poor Juba," I said. "You have a wife who delights in being queen and would rule the entire world if she could."

He smiled, a bit ruefully. "Do you remember how after our first child was born, I swore I would always protect you? It seems you don't need any protection from me. In fact, the person who has been protecting this kingdom is you."

"That is a wild exaggeration," I said. "But we have . . . taken unexpected paths in our marriage. Does that trouble you?"

"I married exactly the right wife for me. I know better than to complain about good luck."

"What if I go to Rome myself—just take the children? Would you prefer that?"

"Deal with the Romans without me there? How will you ever manage?"

"It will be a struggle." I raised my chin. "But I actually have some slight skill at dealing with the Romans."

We laughed.

Julia

*J*ullus and I began to speak as if taking action were possible.
But at first, I drew back, as if from flame. It was momen-
tous, this thing we wished to do. To push Tiberius aside,
not only as my husband, but as a future guardian of my sons and
of the empire. For Jullus to replace him. For Jullus to divorce
Marcella and marry me.

As we spoke about it again and again, it began to seem less like
a fever dream and more like something that could actually come to
pass.

Jullus was a former consul and provincial governor. He had
given great thought to politics and government; he could weigh his
own strengths and weaknesses against Tiberius's. "I am popular in
the Senate, while Tiberius has made more than his share of enemies
there. If Tiberius had stayed in Rome, it would probably be impossible to undercut his position. But he is far away and has thrown
over his responsibilities. He still has great standing with the army
that I lack. But the people love you, Julia. If the people rally to us

and I muster enough support in the Senate, we might bring enough pressure on your father for him to let us marry. And then I would be the natural choice to assume leadership after your father dies."

We went away together, to my country house, the one Father gave me after Lucius's birth. Our staying there together would fuel the talk about us, but I was beyond caring. We sat in the garden one morning. Jullus talked on and on about the politics of our situation—whether this senator and that one ought to be considered a friend or an enemy. I glanced away from him and watched a bee circle a flower.

"I wish we could just be a man and a woman," I said, "just two people who love each other and long to wed. But you wouldn't wish that, would you?"

"What do you mean?"

I looked back at him. "You're ambitious, aren't you?"

His mouth tightened.

Whenever he talked at length about the politics of our situation, I felt an inner uneasiness. Was our relationship a means to an end for him? "Is it power that you want? Or do you want me?" It was the first time I voiced my doubts.

His face froze for the space of a heartbeat. Then he smiled faintly. "I want both."

A breeze from the garden blew a strand of hair over my face. I brushed it away.

"Would you rather I lied, Julia?"

I shook my head, but did not speak.

"I would love you if you were a peasant woman. I love you—you alone. You call to my soul."

"Oh. Your soul." I was on the verge of bitter laughter, or perhaps tears.

"Julia . . . I want to leave my mark on this world. Is that wrong?"

"No." My voice was flat.

We sat at a small oak table. He reached across it, grasped my hand. "If you wish us to go on just as we are, we will. You call the tune, Julia."

"I would like for once in my life for someone to look at me and actually see me, myself, not a means to get something else. I thought with you . . ."

"But I do see you. Of course I do."

"You can't. And I have no right to blame you, do I? No one ever manages that trick. I can't escape being my father's daughter."

"Julia, you can have me any way you want. As just your lover. Or as your husband. You are my queen, and I am your servant when it comes down to it."

"What a nonsensical thing to say. You are no servant."

"Can't you understand?" His voice was rough with feeling. "I have no way of defending myself when it comes to you. I wish I felt less, but that's impossible for me. I have never loved another woman. In all my life, I will never love another. I will take you on any terms. Just tell me how it is going to be."

"That's a very pretty speech," I said.

His face hardened. "We won't speak of marriage, then. We'll forget all this business, all the politics. We'll go on as we are. Do you want that, Julia? Just tell me what you want."

"I am not a fool," I said. "I understand that you want to make use of me, Jullus, to have a place in Rome that is worthy of you. And I want to make use of you too—to prevent Tiberius ever ruling over me and my boys. I am so frightened when I think of my children falling into his hands. So it's mutual, isn't it? But I wish it were different. I wish we were different people—pure people. Because I love you—I love you—"

"I *am* in love with you, Julia."

He was not made of flawless white marble, and neither was I. But I took him as he was, as he took me. That night, I whispered in his ear the same pledge he had made to me. "In all my life, I will never love another."

"And you do trust me?"

"Yes," I answered, and it was true.

A life with the man I loved suddenly seemed possible. I could almost taste it. And for the first time I felt I might shape my own fate. All the follies of the past seemed just that now . . . follies. Almost the actions of another woman.

What Jullus and I wanted was right, not just for us, but for my sons and for Rome. And we had friends, supporters, among them senators from some of Rome's most illustrious families.

A circle of men in the Senate believed Tiberius had the makings of a tyrant and feared the destruction of Rome's ancient liberties. Scipio was now a senator and prominent among these men. There were several other young senators who, like him, came from leading aristocratic families, had at one time or another been intimate with me, and were ready to back me and Jullus. "You are an unusual woman, Julia," Gracchus said to me one evening over dinner. "Rather than nursing old wounds, most of the men you have been with like you and wish you well."

I smiled at him. "Actually, this has been my aim all along—to form a faction in the Senate composed entirely of . . . oh, I can't say it. It's too silly."

"A political faction led by men with kind memories of you," Gracchus said.

We both laughed.

If my father could only be made to understand how matters stood, he might acquiesce to my marrying Jullus. Mightn't he?

A part of my mind told me that Father would never agree to our marriage. But I remembered that he had never been fond of Tiberius. There had been a coolness even when Tiberius was a boy; Drusus was the stepson Father loved. Later he came to respect Tiberius's ability but without ever much liking him personally. He had advanced him as far as he had mainly because he was Livia's son. Now Tiberius had abandoned all his public duties. That had shaken what regard Father had for him. *Could I make him see Tiberius as I saw him? If I found the right words, could I persuade him to put Jullus in his place?*

"I will speak to Father," I told Jullus. "I will tell him I wish to marry you."

"Do you want me to go with you?"

"No," I said. The bedchamber was lit only by a single candle. As I sat beside him on the bed, I could barely see Jullus's face. "I want to do this on my own. I feel strong. And I think it is better that I speak to him alone, that I remind him . . ."

"Remind him of what?"

"Sometimes I wonder if he cares for me at all. But when I was a child, he could be so affectionate. Some of that must remain, mustn't it? Don't you think so? Could you ever stop caring for one of your children?"

"No."

"I couldn't either. I've disappointed Father, and he's disappointed me. Still . . . I am his child—his only child—and he *is* my father. I have to remind him of that."

Father had no affection at all for Tiberius. That mattered; it mattered terribly. But what mattered most was that I was his daughter. All my happiness depended on my being freed to marry Jullus. Surely that would carry weight with him. It must.

>>>>>>>

I sent Father a note by messenger. *May I please talk to you soon, alone and in private? I wish to discuss a matter that means everything to me.* I soon received a brief note back. *Tomorrow, at the fourth hour. Come to the house.*

The next day, I dressed carefully, in the traditional style Father preferred. My stola was perfectly draped, and I wore the simplest of jewelry. When I set out to see Father, my heart hammered. So much depended on the words that would soon be said.

When the slave at the door indicated I was to go up to Father's private study, I felt pleased that Father would see me there. We would be totally alone and undisturbed.

I hoped to somehow reach the man I had seen little of in recent years—the father I used to laugh with, who was so human and approachable. I remembered being ten or eleven years old and standing next to Father at some ceremony. An official went on and on at pompous length about Father's greatness, practically calling him a god. I recognized the speech's utter absurdity even at that young age—and I glanced up at Father to see if he took it seriously. The moment our eyes met, it was as if we read each other's thoughts. I knew he was exerting all his effort to keep from laughing, and an instant later I was biting the inside of my mouth, fighting to keep from laughing too. After the ceremony was over and the official took his leave, Father hugged me, and we laughed so hard in each other's arms that it brought tears to my eyes. Surely the man I had felt so close to then still existed?

I found Father sitting at his long oak writing table. Neat piles of writing tablets—sealed letters from every part of the empire—covered most of the table's surface.

I went to Father and without a word bent and kissed him on the cheek.

He looked like what he was—a man past his sixtieth year who worked from dawn to dusk every day of his life and was beset by a thousand cares. He had saved Rome, united the empire. He was a human, he made errors, but even his enemies had to admit he had governed us well. He was Caesar Augustus. He was my father. How could I not love and revere him?

"Sit down, Julia," Father said, indicating a chair next to his. "Now what is this grave matter you wish to discuss with me?"

In my mind I see—I will always see—a conversation between a father and daughter who love each other deeply. I tell Father I love Jullus and wish to marry him. That my marriage to Tiberius has been a mistake from the start, and now it is a painful sham. That I feel I can trust only Jullus with my sons' futures. Father hears me out, not without discomfort, but with compassion. He expresses understanding—there were false starts in his own life before he married the woman he adored. He is glad I have finally found love. Of course he will allow me to divorce Tiberius and marry Jullus. I weep in Father's arms—weep tears of gratitude.

This phantasm lingers in my mind, a bitter mockery. The reality was quite different.

I said, "Father, you know Tiberius and I live apart and have no marriage. I have found the man I wish to marry—the man I will love all the rest of my life."

Father's face lacked expression. I knew that this did not mean he was indifferent. He had a well-practiced look of contained feeling, a look that gave nothing away. "I see," he said. "And what exactly do you want from me?"

"Your permission to divorce and remarry."

"Remarry whom?"

"Jullus Antony."

He did not look surprised. "Are you by any chance with child by him?"

"No."

"Well, that's one small piece of good fortune."

I became very still. "I don't trust Tiberius as guardian for my children. We loathe each other, Father."

"Julia, do you understand that if I die tomorrow, your husband must rule this empire, hold it for your sons? Tiberius could do it. Jullus never could."

"But that's not true, Father. Jullus can. And I would trust him to protect my boys."

"You would trust him? Mark Antony's son?"

"Father, the civil wars are past."

"The past lives in us. It's right here with us in this room today. Julia, the only man prepared to take up my burden is Tiberius. No one else could begin to do it."

"If you heard how Tiberius has spoken to me—the vile things he has said—"

"Perhaps you provoked him."

I took a deep breath. "Tiberius is not a good man. I think deep down you know it yourself. You have never had any warm feeling toward him, and there is a reason. He is hard and mean and—"

"Do you think a soft man can lead armies? He is not charming, I give you that. But he is competent."

"He is not to be trusted. Not with my sons' futures."

"Are you thinking of your sons? Or are you thinking of Jullus?"

"Oh, Father," I said, "I need a husband I can love. Is that so wrong? But if you would only open your eyes, you would see that Jullus is a better man than Tiberius."

Father shook his head impatiently.

I felt a spurt of anger, of panic too. I wanted desperately to reach this man, my father, and I could not. "Father, Tiberius is Livia's son. She can't see him clearly. How could she? She is his mother. And you look at him through her eyes and don't see him clearly either. He was harsh with my boys. He has no kindness for them. He has no kindness for anyone. How can you trust him to carry on for you, to be a steward for your life's work and for your grandchildren? He is merciless, Father. Rome should not be in his hands. He doesn't value liberty. He has no feeling for our best traditions."

"But Jullus Antony does," Father said, his voice ice-cold.

Had I made a mistake, suggesting that love for Livia had blinded him? Had that mere suggestion closed his eyes to anything else I might say?

"Tiberius is vicious," I said.

"I cannot let your . . . whims injure Rome. Even if Tiberius is vicious as a wild cur—and he isn't, unless you've made him that way—better him to hold an empire together than a man who is weak."

"Jullus is not weak!"

"He has lived off my bounty all his life. He would now like power—and his way to get it is to seduce my foolish daughter. I find it utterly despicable that he stoops to such means. I thought better of him. But now I see he has no moral character at all."

"He loves me."

"He would like to push Tiberius out of the way and become my son-in-law. Gods above, Julia, open your eyes. He does not love you. He loves what he imagines he will gain if he marries you."

"That is not true!" I cried. "Jullus does love me."

Father gave me a look of icy contempt. "He wants the power his father sought. You are letting yourself be manipulated by a scoundrel."

For a moment I asked myself if Father could be right. I felt the most horrible despair thinking that he might be. I almost hated him for causing me that instant of doubt. "It's not true! Just because I'm nothing but a tool to you—just because you can't love me—don't think Jullus can't. Don't judge him by yourself. He is not like you. He is not all cold calculation. He has a heart!"

"You utter fool," Father said. "How dare you take that tone with me? How dare you raise your voice in my presence?"

"You are defaming the man I love."

"Love? That is the word you use?"

"I love him."

"You do not know what love is. You know lust. Do you think I have not heard for years of your wildness, your lewdness? Do you think I have not been shamed?"

I grasped something that I had been blind to before—how angry Father had been at me, how long he had been holding his anger in check. Now what I saw in his eyes was rage. I knew his power, knew that he held my very life in his hands. I wanted to flee. And yet, I had to go on trying to reach him.

"Oh, Father, please forgive me. How can I make you understand? Jullus is different. We care for each other. When we marry, you will see how we conduct our lives together. I promise I will never give you cause for shame. Never again. Jullus is a strong, honorable man—"

"If he were honorable, do you think both he and I would still be breathing?"

I stared at him. "What are you saying?"

335

Father spoke in a voice that grated. "When I was a powerless eighteen-year-old, Julius Caesar, whom I called father, was assassinated by a cabal led by Marcus Brutus. Within three years I had gathered an army and fought great battles, and I had Brutus's head on a spike. If I had acted differently, I would have been unworthy to govern Rome."

"You fault Jullus for not killing you?"

"I understand what sort of man Jullus Antony is!" Father shouted. "Gods above—he thinks he can gain an empire just by seducing one foolish woman. By seducing my daughter!" He took a deep breath and eyed the material on the table. "Do you see all these letters here? They come from all parts of the empire, sent by people who look to me—me!—to hold back violence and chaos, to tame the world for them and make it civilized. The burden I carry crushes me to the ground, but I carry it, the whole miserable world requires that I carry it. And you—when have you given me a bit of help? You have lived a wild life and have consorted with irresponsible fools who hate me, and I have been too fond and done my best to turn a blind eye. But even I have my limits. I warn you—do not push me any further. You have exhausted my patience and my paternal feeling for you. That well is dry."

"'That well is dry,'" I repeated the words, trying to comprehend what he meant. I felt a severance, deep in my being. It was as if Father had already died.

"Enough of this," he said. "Enough, you hear me? Stay away from Jullus Antony. I will never let you marry him."

Livia

Tavius was physically sick after his talk with Julia. Even in his youth, he had been prone to fall ill when the burdens of life proved too great. Now the cough that had troubled him from time to time since his boyhood recurred with a vengeance. I mixed him up a hot medicinal brew that had helped him in the past, but he impatiently told me to take it away. He refused to summon a physician or to rest. He sat in his study, coughing and working.

I felt great anger toward Julia. *War couldn't kill Tavius. Neither could the great fevers that have swept through Rome, carrying away stronger men. But he may not survive his daughter.*

I was angry at Tiberius too, Tiberius who had deserted us. I had always felt sure he would eventually return to Rome. He was a man of enormous talent for generalship and government. When the gods bestow a great gift on you, they also drive you as with a lash—drive you to use it. But now it seemed he had left the field to another man—and of all men Mark Antony's son.

The idea of Jullus Antony ever stepping into Tavius's shoes was too foolish to seriously contemplate. The only one I could even begin to imagine filling Tavius's place was my son.

Julia

"**M**y father has demonstrated time after time that he has no love for me," I told Jullus. "But as quickly as I learn the truth, I forget it again. He called me an utter fool, and I think he is right."

The bedchamber in his lodgings was small and devoid of any beautiful decorative touch—decent enough, but to me it looked like it was a place for illicit coupling. I expected Jullus to take me in his arms, to comfort me. Instead he looked at me with a grave, set face and said, "It is not over. We are in a political battle now. I always suspected it would come to this."

"A political battle . . ."

"Do you have the nerve for a fight, Julia? It is the only way we'll ever be able to marry."

"You think there is still hope?"

"Yes. But do you have courage for this?"

"Yes," I said. "I have the courage for anything now." But after this bold declaration, I pulled back. "When you say fight . . . you don't intend to use force? You mean to use pressure and influence to get Father to accede to our marrying."

"Yes, exactly. No one will be harmed." Jullus was thoughtful for a moment. Then he asked, "What did he say about me? What reason did he give for rejecting me as your husband?"

I looked away. "He said you have no love for me, that all I am to you is a means to power."

"It is not true."

He spoke with such simple sincerity. Surely he was telling me the truth. Surely he did love me? I gazed up into his eyes. "You don't have to tell me that."

He made love to me then. Later, when he was asleep, I gazed at him. The dim candlelight smoothed and burnished his face. He looked decades younger, almost like a boy, and he was beautiful. I stroked curls of his black hair back from his forehead—careful to keep my touch light so I did not wake him. I had feared he would surrender when I told him my father forbade our marrying. I should have known he had more strength than that. And I would be strong too. I would stand by his side.

A small bitter smile settled on my face.

I have the courage to fight you, Father. Don't underestimate me.

>>>>>>>

"I have to talk to Augustus myself, put my case to him," Jullus said the next morning.

"Don't," I said.

He smiled. "Are you afraid he'll chop off my head?"

I did not return his smile. "Yes, I am afraid for you."

Despite my remonstrating with him, he did seek an audience with Father, and the audience was granted. Waiting in my house on the Palatine for Jullus to return from this talk, I paced like a caged leopard. *Father, you say Jullus lacks honor. It is precisely because he is a man of honor that now he is going to face you. Because it is the decent thing for him to do.*

When I heard Jullus's voice in the atrium, I sobbed with relief. I ran to him. Then I saw the ravaged look on his face.

"What did my father say?"

"Nothing I would repeat. But I tell you this. Up until today I revered him almost as if he were my own parent. In spite of everything, I revered him. That is over." I saw grief and loss in Jullus's eyes as well as anger.

"Did he—"

"Do you know why Augustus won't let us marry? What the impediment truly is?" Jullus gave a wild, mirthless laugh. "He can't forgive me for the fact that he killed my father and my brother."

>>>>>>>

We dined the next evening with one guest—Gracchus.

Some people might have found this an amazing sight, and even one to provoke lewd suppositions—a woman, still legally married to a distant husband, dining with her former lover and her current one. But I might have been another man, reclining there on my dining couch. There was no flirtatious talk. Our minds were fixed on the politics of Rome.

"As matters stand, if Augustus were to die, Tiberius would come back from Rhodes and attempt to take his place," Gracchus said. "If he succeeded, that would mean further erosion of our liberty."

"If I were in his place," Jullus said, "I swear to you I would lead our country in the opposite direction."

Gracchus gave Jullus a long, appraising look. "I'm no seer when it comes to the future. I am content to let your role—and the role of Julia's sons when they come to be men—be determined by the

Senate and the people at the appropriate time. I know only this, that the prospect of Tiberius assuming power should make all lovers of liberty shudder. We must prevent that."

"Jullus will respect the rights of the Senate and the citizens," I said. "Oh, Gracchus, you were the one who taught me to revere the liberty that your great-grandfather fought for. It can be reborn. And if my love for Jullus can contribute to that—to a rebirth for Rome—then it is doubly blessed."

Gracchus took a sip of wine. "I believe in fairness to Augustus, we must attempt to open his eyes to what Tiberius is."

"I doubt that it is possible to open them," I said.

Gracchus let out a long breath. "You know, for many years I have dreaded this moment. I feared it, I hoped to avoid it. But it has come."

"What moment is that?" Jullus asked.

"The moment when I finally take a risk. It's ironic that it should come now. When for the first time I stand responsible for the welfare and happiness of another human being."

Several months before, he had astonished all his friends by marrying, a thing he had loudly proclaimed he would never do. Gracchus had long been saying that tax on the unmarried was nearly ruining him, but in the end my father's law played no part in his decision. It seemed he had glimpsed a girl—a maiden, closely kept by her family—and was smitten. Wedlock was the price of having her. I had doubted he was capable of falling deeply in love, but his little bride had snared him, heart and soul.

"And now Metella is with child . . . It's not even that I fear your father so much, Julia. But over the years I have come to know Tiberius a little. I know his autocratic tendencies—and also his venom. If in the end he wins and we lose, I am sure he will remember my name."

Once, for Rome's sake, Gracchus's great-grandfather had gone out unarmed to face his enemies' swords. What Gracchus did was write a letter. It was a private letter to my father, though a copy circulated among our friends and was widely read. He coolly dissected Tiberius's character and said he had the makings of a tyrant. By contrast, he called Jullus a lover of liberty. He said Jullus was the right man to act as protector of my boys, if my father passed away, the right man to lead Rome. Jullus was liked and trusted in the Senate, as Tiberius was not. Gracchus advised that I be permitted, even urged, to divorce Tiberius and marry Jullus. Concluding he wrote, "I ask this because the blood of my ancestors impels me to do it. I appeal to you not out of personal affection or animus, but for Rome's sake."

Livia

*T*iberius was my son. I recognized that he had faults, as all
men do. But he was my son.

Tavius showed me the letter he had received from
Gracchus and sat watching me while I read it. The letter called
Tiberius cruel in the treatment of the soldiers he had commanded,
contemptuous of the people, and arrogant and rude in his dealings
with ranking senators. It said he was dangerously power hungry. I
went hot and cold reading it.

"My son is a patriot," I said. "He has fought for Rome, bled for
Rome. Gracchus is a man who lives only for pleasure. In his entire
life he has accomplished precisely nothing. Will you pay heed to his
words when he defames my son?"

"No," Tavius said. "Of course I will not."

He wrote Gracchus a note drenched in sarcasm, thanking him
for his kind advice. Another man in his position would have punished Gracchus for his effrontery. But Tavius did not do that. He

always said we should let people say what they wished. The moment
to intervene was when thoughts became actions.

Julia

The icy indifference with which my Father greeted Gracchus's letter surprised neither Jullus nor me.

There was another letter—sent from Father to Jullus. It was brief. It contained no insults and no threats. Yet it chilled me.

As I made plain to you when we spoke, I regret that you and my niece are now living apart. I do not insist that you and Marcella reconcile, though I would take it as a favor if you did. If you wish to keep my friendship, you will make no further proposals to my daughter. In the circumstances, it is best that you completely avoid her company. I am sure I can rely on you to respect my feelings as a father.

"He wants you to go back to Marcella," I said. "From his point of view, that would solve everything."

"I won't give you up."

"We can defy Father," I said. "But he won't forgive us. There will be no further governmental posts for you, and don't tell me it doesn't matter, because I know it matters terribly to you. And what will happen when Father dies? I think Tiberius will come back to Rome as Father's heir. Tiberius hates you and he hates me and he will revenge himself on both of us." Deep fear gripped me. "Oh, Jullus—I don't want my children at his mercy."

"Your father could live a very long time yet."

"Even he cannot live forever." I heard the ice in my own voice.

"Maybe we should run away," Jullus said with a sad smile. "Live together in a forest hut. I would hunt game and you could pick berries."

"There is no place on earth where Father could not find us if he wanted to," I said. "Or Tiberius could not find us if he sits in Father's seat. The only way we can ever marry is if Father were to—" I almost said "die," but I stopped myself. My thoughts were going in an unspeakable direction.

"If he were removed from power," Jullus completed my sentence, his voice level.

"Yes. Just that. Oh, Jullus, I don't want harm to befall him. I just want him—removed. And you to take his place, not Tiberius."

For a few moments, Jullus did not speak. He seemed far away from me, a man soberly contemplating the possibilities on which his entire future rested. I did not want to interrupt his thoughts. Finally, he said, "If he were removed and I led Rome, then we could be free—and Rome would be free too."

"But is it possible to remove him?"

"There are many men in Rome who long for the return of our old liberties," Jullus said. "They would back us."

"Then you think . . . ?"

"To topple your father from power would be hard and risky, but not impossible."

I saw that Jullus wanted this—truly wanted it. The unwelcome thought came to me that perhaps for years he had harbored a hope of seeing my father overthrown. He was Mark Antony's son. But I loved him. And I saw that as long as Father was in power, we could never have a life together. I wanted that life with all my soul.

Still I recoiled. My mouth felt dry. "Oh, gods above. Oh, gods, what are we talking about, Jullus? Can we really be talking about this?"

>>>>>>>

Was there a moment when we stopped toying with the idea of overthrowing my father and started to plan it? I think that moment passed by, without us marking it.

Jullus and I had gathered around us a circle of senators who disliked my father's rule and feared the prospect of Tiberius as his successor. Some of these men had been my lovers. Some had long been Jullus's friends. They were now our allies.

The heart of this group was Gracchus. His was the calm voice encouraging the others. It was as if his great-grandfather's noble spirit had revived in him. He spoke of democratic reforms he hoped Jullus would institute in Rome's government.

"You trust me," Jullus said, gratified.

Gracchus smiled. "Not completely. But at least with you there is hope. With Tiberius there would be no hope at all."

A secret member of our group was Quinctius Crisponus, a former consul. I did not particularly like this man, who plainly was driven by jealousy of my father. But his active support was vital to us. Father almost never turned down a social invitation from such a high-ranking member of the Senate. And he trusted Crisponus, whom he considered a close political ally.

"When we are ready to act, Crisponus will invite your father to dinner," Jullus told me. "My friends and I will be waiting for him."

I drew in a sharp breath. "Waiting to do what?"

"Take him into custody. It won't be hard. Your father has grown careless in recent years about the matter of bodyguards. He'll only have a couple of them, and we will surprise and overpower them."

I felt an inward recoil, a shrinking in the marrow of my being. It seemed impossible at that moment that I could take part in such a scheme, deposing my own father, taking him prisoner.

Jullus put his hands on my shoulders. "Is there another way for us?"

"My father must not be hurt."

"Of course." Jullus's voice was gentle. "He will be allowed a comfortable retirement."

It was as if at that instant a dark pit swallowed me up. *Jullus is lying to me,* I thought. *He knows it would be too risky to let Father live. I am here plotting my own father's death.*

I shook my head. *No, that is not true.* I thought of how during the civil wars, a general named Lepidus had made himself my father's enemy. Father had defeated him. This was shortly after his marriage to Livia, and she had moved his heart to mercy. And so this man Lepidus, already past middle age, had been allowed a peaceful retirement. He withdrew from public life to his own villa on the southern coast of Italy. Father stationed guards all around to keep watch, but the man was left alone to live as he wished on the grounds of the villa. He had had a long, peaceful old age and never caused any trouble, finally dying of natural causes.

"We'll allow Father to retire as Lepidus did," I said. "Jullus, we will do that?"

"Yes. Of course."

Caesar Augustus in his country villa . . . making no trouble for those who deposed him . . . Was that an impossible vision? I told myself it was not, that Father was a man who accommodated himself to reality and would accept what he could not alter. Of one thing I was certain, though. He would never forgive me for stripping him of power. If he lived to be a hundred, he would go to his grave cursing me. And if Jullus and I tried to overthrow him and failed, his vengeance would be terrible.

>>>>>>>

We had to avoid alerting Father and yet in some way prepare the people of Rome so they would assent to his overthrow. They had to rally to our side when Father was deposed.

"They love you, Julia," Jullus said. "They will rally to you."

Rome had a spot where ordinary citizens went to discuss public affairs, the open space in front of the statue of the satyr Marsyas in the Forum. To the common people, the swaggering Marsyas—a creature with a goat's ears and legs and a tail—was a symbol of liberty. He was said to have boldly risked the wrath of Apollo, the Olympian who vastly outranked him in the pantheon of immortal beings. Since Father worshipped Apollo above all other deities, the statue of Marsyas had taken on a special meaning for those who did not care for Father's imperium. People had for years adorned the statue's base with bits of papyrus on which they wrote criticisms of Rome's ruler, often in obscene language. Father permitted this and could point to it as proof that he had not deprived Romans of their right to speak frankly. I think he even believed it made his rule more secure when citizens vented complaints against him this way, rather than silently nursing anger.

For Jullus and I to simply make an appearance in front of the statue of Marsyas was no crime. But I knew it would infuriate Father. A tinge of fear kept me from going there with Jullus during the day.

So we went at night and stood beside the statue in the torchlight. Gracchus came with us the first time we did this—an act of friendship I would never forget.

A few men stood talking near the statue, but they did not seem to notice our presence.

Jullus and I smiled at each other. No harm done. But our course was set.

We visited the statue night after night, staying for the better part of an hour. Gradually people began to realize who we were, and to greet us. At first there were just a few people, but bit by bit, the number grew to several hundred. People grumbled about politics, in the way they were prone to do at this particular spot. They said elections were no longer free but invariably won by Father's puppets. Young men of rank spoke with special vehemence about how Father financially penalized those who did not marry and father children. They called Father a hypocrite. And the poor spoke about how all the wealth we won in our wars somehow never found its way into their purses but only those of the rich, though their sons did the dying. Jullus and I said little but listened to all of this sympathetically. I actually did feel sympathy for these people who always greeted me kindly, often with a touch of awe.

"The people want a change in government," Jullus told me confidently.

As more and more people took to gathering in front of the statue of Marsyas at night, Father surely heard of it. He took no action.

I heard from Gracchus and other friends that Jullus and I were more and more spoken of, as two who were bound together in love of each other and of Rome. Those who wished to see a change in how Rome was governed viewed us as sympathizers, allies, even leaders.

"Maybe Father will realize that we are loved by the people, and he will give way to the people's will. He will let us marry."

"Don't count on it," Jullus said.

"But even he must see that people do love us."

Jullus kissed me and, holding me tenderly, whispered, "It's not us they love. They love you."

Livia

*A*s expected, Cleopatra Selene arrived in Rome for a visit and came to stay with Tavius and me. Her son, Ptolemy, a darkly handsome youth of eighteen, and her little girl, Drusilla, accompanied her. As soon as they were ushered into our house, I embraced Selene and the boy affectionately. Then my eyes sought the little girl—Cleopatra's granddaughter—named in my honor.

The child wore a little red silk dress and had her hair arranged in curls. Her eyes in their darkness and depth were like her mother's, surely like her grandmother's too. "Greetings, Drusilla," I said. I bent and kissed her and imagined her grandmother's shade standing by, wearing an enigmatic smile.

That evening over dinner, Tavius turned to Selene and said, "Let's postpone arguing about tax policy and Mauretania. Put it off at least until tomorrow—all right?"

"I would never dream of arguing with you at any time, Augustus." She smiled at him, and he smiled back.

"You get my wife to do your arguing for you," he said.

"Lady Livia has been most kind. But we both know that it is your best interest and Rome's that is always closest to her heart."

How at ease she seemed, reclining across from us, sipping the finest wine from a jeweled goblet. She wore her hair up, which showed her high cheekbones off to advantage. Her dress was purple silk—the royal color—and she wore amethyst earrings and a torque of worked gold.

I had wondered if I ought to cancel her visit, for in a sense it came at an inauspicious time. The actions of Julia and Selene's brother had become increasingly troubling. They were obviously seeking public support—wishing the people to press Tavius to allow them to marry. This had only served to infuriate him and reinforce his conviction that Jullus was unworthy of marriage to his daughter.

Tavius and I did not wish to offend Selene by asking her not to come, and I, at least, had some notion she might provide her brother with wise counsel. They were close, and she had the prudence I had come to see he lacked. I therefore hoped—perhaps foolishly—that she could talk sense to him.

He should stop the nonsense with Julia. That was how I thought of what was occurring—as nonsense. Irresponsible people meeting around a satyr's statue to complain; it put me on edge. But I knew how power was gained and lost in Rome. I could mourn the days when it was a matter of counting votes—but those days had ended years before my birth. I had long since faced reality, understood that power was won with a sword. The people around Marsyas's statue had no weapons. Tavius had an army. I admired his self-control in tolerating Jullus and Julia's doings, much as he seethed.

That first evening we spent with Selene, we did not speak her brother's name, and neither did she. I doubted if she had heard about the gatherings around the statue, though probably she did know about her brother's affair with Julia. The studied avoidance was the only indication that anything at all was wrong.

Julia

s the day approached when we would carry out our plan
to overthrow my father, I felt terror, but also exhilaration
at the thought of having a life with Jullus, exhilaration at
finally being free.

"I want to bring one more person into our circle of friends,"
Jullus said. "One more person, with a great name not only in Rome
but in the entire empire."

"Do you mean Selene?" She had recently arrived in Rome as
Father's guest.

"We will need supporters beyond the borders of Italy before
we are done, and she can bring us that. She is a queen, the only
descendant of the royal house of Egypt. She commands loyalty
beyond Mauretania. Just the mention of her mother's name will
work magic."

"Are you certain she can be trusted?"

A tender smile appeared on Jullus's face. "She is my little sister,"
he said.

⪢⪢⪢⪢⪢⪢

The festival of Liberalia came on March 17, a day on which gods associated with the common people were specially honored. On that day, it was a custom to crown the statue of Marsyas with a laurel wreath. "Who better to do the crowning than you?" Jullus said.

And so that morning I appeared in daylight in the Forum and approached the statue with a wreath in my hand.

A crowd of people had gathered. There must have been hundreds of them, and they shouted, "Julia! Julia!"

Jullus walked beside me, smiling. "See how they love you?" he whispered.

I made my way slowly through the crowd. People all around me continued to cry out my name. Their faces were so eager and hopeful. They were ordinary people, many of them poor, and I felt they truly believed in me, that somehow I would make things better for them. Then I was looking up at the statue. The satyr was depicted with his right arm raised, as if to rally some unseen army, and with a wineskin slung over his left shoulder. He had the horns and ears of a goat but a human face, thick lips curved in a smile.

I told myself it was a small thing I was doing, participating in a yearly rite, crowning a statue. This could even be seen as a pious deed. But I realized it would be reported to my father—and he would view it as an act of utter defiance. My heart raced. I knew I had lied to myself. This was no small thing.

A narrow ramp stood in front of the statue for me to walk up so I could reach to place the laurel wreath on the head of the statue. But I did not use it. I looked at Jullus, saying nothing, rested a hand on his shoulder. A light came into his eyes; he understood what I wanted, understood we must do this together. There before the crowd of people, he lifted me in his arms.

There were more cries of "Julia! Julia!" and cries of "Antony!" as well. I also heard shouts of "Liberty!" and I felt that for this one moment, I embodied something greater than myself. I looked down at Jullus's shining face and smiled at him. "Liberty!" the crowd shouted. I reached up, set the laurel wreath on the head of the statue. I had never felt so free.

Cleopatra Selene

My brother had not been among those who welcomed my children and me when we arrived in Rome. In Augustus's house his name was never mentioned. I found this understandable.

In Mauretania I had my own, albeit limited, sources of information about what was happening in Rome. I knew that my brother was carrying on a love affair with Augustus's daughter. Though Augustus had apparently tolerated this for well over a year, I did not suppose he was pleased with the situation.

I would have much preferred it if Jullus had stayed clear of Julia. But I knew he was not her first lover, and I imagined that before long Jullus would be replaced in Julia's bed, just as other men had been. I was woefully ignorant about the political implications of the liaison.

Early in my stay in Rome, I received an invitation from Jullus to come and see him in lodgings he had taken in a humble part of the city. He had an important matter he wished to speak to me about in private, he said. Naturally I went to see him at the earliest opportunity.

I had heard he and Marcella were estranged and living apart from each other. Still when he greeted me, I did not expect Julia to be standing there at his side, as if she were his wife.

"Selene, I am glad to see you again." Julia's cheeks were flushed, and her eyes sparkled. She was exactly my age, thirty-six years old, but when I looked at her, I thought of a girl on her wedding day.

Jullus was tense and grave. He and Julia led me into a small sitting room with a sturdy oak door. Jullus closed the door firmly.

"Your husband and children are well?" he said. "All is well with you?"

Julia remained largely silent while Jullus and I spoke for a while of ordinary family matters. His side of the conversation seemed strained, forced. I felt as if he was trying to make sure I was still the loving sister he remembered. And I was of course. We could be apart for any length of time, live in different countries, yet never be estranged.

"I have missed you," I said, meaning it.

"I've missed you too," he said. "We can rely on each other, can't we?"

"Yes, we always have."

My brother grew more at ease with me. He leaned forward and said, "I have something to discuss with you. A very great matter." Soon after, I understood that I had reached a crossroad in my life, and a moment of extraordinary peril.

>>>>>>>

I listened with a feeling of dread as Jullus told me that he planned to overthrow Caesar Augustus. He said that the very next evening, Augustus would be induced to visit the home of a senator pledged to Jullus's conspiracy and Jullus and his friends would seize him there.

I stared at him in shock. "And you will become First Citizen?"

"Yes," he said, his eyes burning.

I turned toward Julia. "You have agreed to this?"

"Yes." She gazed at Jullus. "We will marry."

A look passed between them. It made me think of my parents—political allies united in a quest for power but also more than that. Did love outweigh politics? I thought it did with Julia, from what I knew of her as a person. With my brother I could not be sure. But there was affection, even passion, in his glance.

Jullus turned his attention back to me and said, "The story of Mark Antony, Cleopatra, and their children will have a different ending. Instead of spending his life groveling to the man who destroyed them, Mark Antony's son will rise to power, with Cleopatra's daughter as his respected ally. Don't you like that ending better, Selene?"

I said quietly, "You wish revenge? You will put Augustus to death?"

"No!" Julia cried.

Before she made this utterance, I had seen assent on my brother's face.

However when he spoke, he said, "Augustus's death is not necessary. He is already old. He can retire to one of his country villas. Under guard of course. But in comfort and dignity."

Yes, of course, Caesar Augustus—Caesar Augustus!—could be nullified as a threat and yet still be left alive. I think Jullus read disbelief in my expression, because he quickly changed the subject and began to tell me the names of senators who had rallied to his side.

"I need you beside me, little moon," my brother said. "You and Juba as well. I will restore what is yours. You will have Egypt as well as Mauretania and even more lands. You and Juba will govern the eastern empire as Father and your mother did."

The offer took my breath away. I felt a stirring in my blood. But I said, "You do not plan to . . . neutralize Tiberius?"

It was Julia who answered. "We do not wish to kill our opponents. We wish to be just."

"That is admirable," I said. "But surely you do not think you will seize the empire without opposition? Tiberius will come against you with an army at his back. And even if he were eliminated, that would not mean you would be unopposed. There are other men whose standing with the army is nearly as great as his, and they would not simply submit to your rule."

"I have allies in the army too," Jullus said. "Men who will support me once I show there is a chance of success."

"But it will mean war," I said.

"If it comes to a battle, then so be it," Jullus said. "We will win."

I turned to Julia. "You say the same?"

She raised her chin. At that instant she was more her father's daughter than I had ever seen her before. "Yes. We will fight and we will win."

"We will win with your help and Juba's," Jullus said. "You and those who are tied to you by bonds of loyalty must come over to us, right at the beginning. You must show you are on our side from the start, little moon."

He spoke with assurance that this aid would be forthcoming. I wondered at that moment—and would wonder ever after—why he was so sure and so willing to confide his plans in me. I think it was a testament to the strength of the bond we had formed when we were two orphan children, surrounded by those who had destroyed our parents. I felt it too—that tie that grew out of shared pain and loss.

Julia said, "Selene, we want you with us. There will be a new day for Rome. You will see. The people will bless this day."

The people will bless this day. How many noble hearts had said that, not so far in the past when the Republic was ripped to shreds and Romans took up arms against each other?

There are people who can tell themselves great lies and believe them. But I . . . even as a child, I had not had that option. I had had to face the truth unvarnished in order to survive at all.

If Augustus was overthrown, he would be killed. What followed would be a civil war that would engulf the whole empire; I knew it in my bones. Tiberius would never accept the rule of his wife and her lover. Neither, I thought, would other leading generals who aspired to power themselves.

I imagined Mauretania's peace destroyed by war. My husband leaving his scholarly work to lead out an army, my son forced to become a soldier before he had time to truly learn what it was to be a man. Ptolemy and Drusilla perhaps one day suffering the same terrible losses that Jullus and I had suffered.

I could feel in my viscera the agony of a child, deprived of mother and father, a captive at the conqueror's mercy.

I might avenge the blood of my parents and my brothers. I might become as powerful a queen as my mother had been. But first I would have to risk all. And win or lose, many would die.

"There will be blood and more blood," I said. "Jullus, do you remember what civil war has already cost us?"

"I remember many things."

I took a deep breath. "My brother, don't do this. You are gambling with your life, and more than your life. There is still time to turn back from this path. Please, turn back."

He had never expected me to say this, and he recoiled as if slapped. It took him a moment to collect himself. Then his expression hardened. "My path is already set. My decision is made. Understand, Sister, there can be no going back for any of us."

I just stared at him. The taste of death filled my mouth. I saw he had the ruthlessness to carry through his plan, whether or not it meant unleashing civil war. I knew he could not be turned aside by any words of mine. And I understood also that at this very moment, I was in great danger. *There can be no going back for any of us.*

He said in a low voice, "You and Juba cannot be neutral. Situated as you are, that is impossible. This is a matter of life and death. You must be either with me or against me."

If I said I would not join him, would Jullus let me walk out of this house? How could he, after what he had already told me?

He hadn't believed that I, his younger sister, his little moon, would not follow him. I sensed it had greatly surprised him when I did not at once embrace his cause. Even now he scarcely believed it possible that I would say no. But if I hung back, he would view me as a traitor to our shared blood. My mother had executed her own sister who had betrayed her. If one is to rule, one must know how to deal with traitors. Jullus understood this, as did I.

When I was young, the need to survive had shaped me. I was able to look at danger and keep a calm countenance. I had learned to coldly weigh odds and do what I had to do.

Jullus spoke. "It is blood that calls to blood now, Sister. Remember our father, remember your mother. I am your older brother. I am calling on you in our father's name. Will you not answer in loyalty?"

"I love you, Jullus," I said. "I have never loved you more than I do at this moment." And it was true. I understood the causes that were impelling him forward, and I did love him.

"Then you will you join us?" Jullus said. "You will prevail on Juba to join us too?"

"Yes."

He smiled. I imagined our father smiling in just that way, on the battlefield of Philippi before he won his greatest victory. And I could suddenly see Jullus succeeding, avenging our father, and making himself ruler of the empire. Surely it was possible? Then all the shame of our parents' defeat would be wiped away. Cleopatra and Mark Antony would triumph in the end.

Jullus, Julia, and I spoke for a long time of plans and contingencies. The sun was setting when Jullus asked if I wished to stay the night at his lodging. He asked it almost casually. Why then did I think it was a test? Why did I wonder if he would let me leave?

I said, "Augustus and Livia expect me to remain with them as their guest. I don't want to create suspicion. And my children are there."

My brother looked at me for a long moment. Then he shrugged and said, "As you wish," and gave me a lopsided smile. It was an expression I remembered from my girlhood.

He was Jullus and I was Selene. There was old love, old trust between us.

Something clutched at my heart as I embraced him.

"Don't worry so much, sweet Sister," he said. "All will be well."

Livia

J was in my study, reading correspondence when my secretary
came in. "Excuse me for interrupting you, mistress," he said.
"But the queen of Mauretania says she must speak to you
at once."

I felt a small fluttering in the pit of my stomach. I did not know
why Selene wished to see me right at that moment, but I sensed it
could be nothing good. I said, "Of course. Show her in."

I stood as she entered. For a moment we looked at each other,
and I remembered another talk we had had in this room, so many
years ago. I saw the shadow of a frightened fourteen-year-old girl.
But that image quickly vanished. I saw a queen, her face so grave
and still it might have been carved in ivory.

"Please sit down," I said, and we sat on the couch. "Is there some
trouble?"

She looked at me levelly. "Julia and my brother Jullus are plotting to overthrow Augustus."

All the air rushed out of my lungs. "Julia and Jullus . . . ?"

"And others." She named several senators.

It would have been impossible to look into that somber face and not believe the truth of her words. "You must tell me all you know," I said.

She did, quietly, never hesitating.

"When will all this be set in motion?"

"Tomorrow." She added, "They said Augustus would not be killed. He would be allowed to retire."

It would not happen that way. We both knew it.

Where was Tavius? At the Temple of Castor and Pollux, inspecting some recent repairs, I believed. "My husband is in no immediate danger at this moment?"

"No."

I rose and dispatched a messenger, one of his bodyguard I particularly trusted. "Tell him he must come home immediately. The matter is extremely urgent." I went back into the study, sat down beside Selene. "You did the right thing coming to me. Thank you," I said.

"I kept my oath to you."

"Yes. Is that why you told me? To keep your oath?"

"It was a terrible oath I took. But I am not sure I believe in it. I am not sure I believe in my mother's gods. Still, one's word should be sacred, should it not?"

I listened for Tavius's steps in the atrium. But that was foolish. It would be a while yet until he came home.

Selene and I went on talking. "I do not want war. Not for Juba or my children. Not for the people of Mauretania." Her voice was edged with grief. "I saw what was coming. I could not permit it to happen."

I imagined for a moment what Tiberius would do if his wife and her lover seized power. I knew he would gather an army and battle against them, wage a savage struggle to the death. "Your action will spare many lives," I said. "That should comfort you."

"And my brother's life? Is there a way to save it?"

I said nothing, but she read the answer in my face.

The answer did not surprise her, but her features tightened. "I hope at least he will be permitted to die with honor."

For a while, we were both silent. She sat motionless, her head raised. I imagined her mother sitting on a throne in Alexandria, just as still, just as erect, waiting for the serpent's bite.

>>>>>>>

A lifetime seemed to pass by the time Tavius came home. We entered a room alone, and I told him what Selene had told me. His eyes went wide, and for a long time he said nothing. I think it took him that long to make himself believe what I was saying was true. He spoke finally in a hollow voice. "Once long ago you reproached me for the blood I spilled during the civil wars. You swore the gods would have their revenge. Perhaps you were right. If this is intended to pay me back for wrongs I have committed, then believe me, the gods know how to punish."

I shook my head. "This is not the gods' work." What god was cruel or malicious enough to craft this punishment, wreak vengeance on Tavius through Julia's betrayal?

That night Tavius did what was necessary to protect the peace of Rome.

The impact of soldiers' boots echoed on paving stones. The most loyal troops from Tavius's private guard moved through the city, making arrests.

Julia

A flare of torchlight woke me from my dream.

"Get up!" a harsh voice shouted.

I lay beside Jullus and pressed closer to him, blinking at the light.

Three soldiers, armed for war, stood over us. Each held a torch, and the insane thought came to me that they intended to burn the house down around us. I could hear shouts from the corridor.

"Get dressed," one of the soldiers said.

"I am the First Citizen's daughter!" I cried.

The soldier who had spoken had a square face and small, close-set eyes. He looked at me with utter contempt.

"You can't just drag us off in the middle of the night . . ."

"Julia." It was Jullus's voice.

I turned and saw his face illumined by torchlight. He did not look surprised or desperate or even afraid, but like a gallant soldier, bleeding from many wounds and waiting for the deathblow. The fact that he had already despaired sent a tremor of terror through me.

At that moment, I allowed myself to fully understand what was happening. I looked at Jullus, and I died inside. I threw my arms around him. "I can bear anything, but we must not be apart."

His eyes were full of pity for me. "The gods spin a web, and we are caught in it," he said. "Better to believe it was fate. Better to believe this is the only way it could have ended."

"What is ending?"

"Our time together. My life."

"No!" I cried.

He tightened his arms around me, and he kissed me. He kissed me with a fierce hunger, as if just by this act, he meant to meld our two souls together. So we would never be apart. At that instant I knew with utter certainty that he loved me. Whatever trespasses we had committed, the bond of love between us was real and true. Facing death, he proved it to me by his action. Then soldiers pulled him away from me. I saw by their faces that they thought we should be ashamed, two naked people, caught in adulterous embrace, being dragged from bed.

Fools, I wanted to say, *there is no shame. I love him!*

They pulled Jullus out of the room. "Where are you taking him?" I cried.

The only way it could have ended. Our time together. My life.

I screamed, "No!"

>>>>>>>

The soldiers let me dress. Then the officer in charge said, "Come." He put his hand on me, gripped my arm.

"Where are we going?"

He did not answer.

Soldiers packed the hall. A knot of Jullus's servants stood huddled together. I realized they would be interrogated. Would my father have them tortured to get them to tell Jullus's secrets and mine? Three of my own servants had come here to serve me. I saw Phoebe in the group, and we exchanged a glance. Her eyes were full of terror. Then I was taken away, one soldier shoving me from behind, another who had hold of my arm pulling me.

I felt an inward shock—that common soldiers should deal with me this way, with no courtesy at all.

"Where are we going?" I said again.

Again my question was met with silence.

"I want to see my father! I demand to see him."

The soldier who had hold of my arm gave a chuckle. "Oh, never fear, you will see him."

I was not afraid for myself even then, not physically afraid. My fear was for Jullus, for Jullus above all. And then for the others—Gracchus and the rest who were privy to our plot. I thought of Phoebe's face, the awful fear I saw there. She was a freedwoman now, not a slave. I told myself that meant they could not legally torture her. But I knew laws could be broken.

At the road, the officer stopped as if startled by his own thought. He turned to me and said, "Do you have any weapons on you?"

"Weapons?" I said stupidly.

He ran his hands over my body, felt my chest, my waist.

"Are you searching for a dagger? What do you imagine I would do with it? Attack your soldiers?"

Maybe he was afraid that I would slash my throat and escape him, I thought. Or maybe—yes, of course, since he was bringing me to my father—it was Father he feared I would attack.

I could almost have laughed at the absurdity. "I would never harm my father," I said.

The officer looked me hard in the eyes, the way you would look at a criminal or perhaps a lunatic. Then he lifted me into a cart that was waiting and pushed me roughly into a seat. He sat on one side of me, and another soldier sat on the other side.

Overhead, I could not see the moon or any stars. The sky was pale gray. The cart began to move. It went up the Palatine Hill, in the direction of my father's house.

Inside myself I cried out, *Jullus!*

>>>>>>>

Father's steward darted a nervous glance at the soldiers and then at me. "Take her in there, please," he said, and he gestured toward Livia's sitting room.

The homely familiarity of this room leant a sense of unreality to what was happening. I had sat in here so many times with Livia. But now she was not alone. Father was with her. He stood facing away from the door, looking down at the brazier that heated the room. Staring at nothing. Livia meanwhile sat on a couch. She rose when I entered. I saw how tense her face was—as if someone had pulled the skin back more tightly over the bones. She stared at me with her great dark eyes.

Father turned around. His face was pale, and his eyes glittered with rage. "Leave her here," he said to the officer who had been standing by uncertainly. "You wait outside."

"Father—"

"Don't call me that. You are no longer my daughter."

I felt a tightening in my guts.

"I know all your plans," he said. "Don't bother to lie. I know everything."

I shook my head, as if with wonderment. "Has someone been speaking against me to you, Father? Against me and Jullus?"

He did not answer.

"Selene had the good sense and the loyalty to come to me," Livia said.

I found I was not truly surprised. I remembered how she at first had tried to sway Jullus from the path he was on.

"And you believe her accusations, Father? Against your own daughter?"

"All the fools you drew into your conspiracy, Sempronius Gracchus and the rest, are being rounded up even now," Father said. Then he asked coldly, "Who initiated this scheme? Jullus, I suppose? Or was it Gracchus's idea?"

We stared at each other. A great deal of time seemed to pass; seas could have turned to desert in that time. My voice finally broke the silence. "I was the initiator, Father. The others went along with me out of love and friendship."

"I don't believe you. It was Jullus, wasn't it?"

Jullus and me. We thought of the plan together. Because we are one. "I had to persuade him. He only agreed because he loves me."

"Are you informed of what the penalty for patricide is, Julia? To be tied up in a sack with crazed beasts and thrown into the river. Do you understand why the punishment is so horrible? Because to kill a father—the one who gave you life—is the epitome of ingratitude and disloyalty. No other act is so base."

"But you're alive, Father." I felt my lips twist into a semblance of a smile. "You would have been alive in any case. If we succeeded, you never would have been harmed."

Livia spoke next, her voice as I had never heard it before, charged with cold fury. "Can you possibly believe that?"

My eyes were still on my father's face. "You would have been allowed to retire—to return to Velitrae." I desperately wanted him to believe me, to know I had not planned his death. But there was no change in his expression. I might as well not have spoken.

"Your friends would have slit my throat," he said. "And I can almost forgive that now, for the gods know at this moment I am sick of living. But what you would have done to Rome is beyond all forgiveness."

"We would have saved Rome from Tiberius. Even if we had to fight, it would have been worth it."

Livia took a step toward me, her face full of anger and fierce pride. "My son would have rallied the army. He would have met you in battle. And I assure you, he would have won."

"How could you do it?" my father burst out suddenly. "My own daughter. How could you?"

"You never saw me," I said. "I never mattered to you except as a tool."

"Have you lost your reason? I gave you everything."

"You gave me nothing I wanted." I took a breath. "What will happen to Jullus? And the others?"

"You are like a malignancy," Father said, "something that grew out of my own body and sought to kill me. You are a cancerous growth, and I must cut you off."

I felt he was pronouncing my death sentence. My life was over. I was not afraid, though. Not at all afraid for myself. I remembered being held in Jullus's arms. What mattered was our love; what mattered was that he should live. "Do what you want to me. I don't care. But spare Jullus."

"That's who you think of now, Mark Antony's son? Not your children? Not the shame you have brought upon us all?" He walked to the shut door, opened it. I had a glimpse of glinting armor, of soldiers—the atrium was packed with soldiers, and they all stood stiffly at attention, waiting to do my father's bidding. "Take her away," he said.

Livia

*J*ulia was gone now. We were alone, Tavius and I.

"What will you do with her?" I asked.

He answered in a flat, emotionless voice. "I will put her to death, and I will put Jullus Antony to death, and Gracchus and the rest of them—everyone who had a part in this treason."

"We do not know who is involved," I said. "Not with any certainty. Gracchus and the other senators should be interrogated."

He nodded. "And Julia's servants. They must tell all they know. Then all those who had a part in this madness must die."

His voice was ice-cold, but I knew him too well. I did not believe the coldness.

"Dead," he repeated. "I want them dead."

"Don't give the order yet. Wait until we know the full extent of the conspiracy. That is only wise."

"I want her expunged from the earth," he said.

Not them, all the traitors. *Her.*

He took a step back toward the door, I suppose to give some order, and he staggered. I caught him in my arms. For a few moments I felt I was propping him up, that he would collapse if I let him. Then he straightened. We stood still, me with my arms around him. I saw the expression on his face, the look of horror. "Oh, gods above," he said. "Oh, gods above."

"Come sit down." I led him to a couch, my hand under his elbow as if he were an invalid. He sank down and sat leaning over, his head in his hands.

I caressed his back and shoulders. The bones felt sharp and fragile under my hand.

He turned his head and looked at me. "I will make them sorry. I will have their blood."

"Yes, yes," I said.

My mind was already working out how to limit the destruction. Not for the sake of Julia and the rest, not even so much for Rome's sake. For Tavius.

The execution of Gracchus and other senators will only breed more enemies. But that is not the worst of it.

He will kill his daughter. And then one day he will awake to what he has done, and he will go mad.

"I must go out—I must be seen to be in charge."

"But please, wait with the executions until we have talked again." I spoke as if this were an ordinary thing, some routine decision I did not want him to make without at least giving my views a hearing.

He leaned against me for a moment like a little child. Then he rose, and he was not a child and not a tired old man either. He was who he had always been, Caesar Augustus, and he went to take command.

Julia and Jullus in a sense had many backers—many people who wished them well, even many who would have liked to have seen them seize power. Some were malcontents and paupers; there were always such people who longed for any change, hoping it would better their lot. Others, mainly aristocrats, yearned for what they called our ancestral liberties—in other words, they wished for the Republic to be restored. Finally there were the young libertines who hated Tavius's moral laws, resented his tax on the unmarried and the childless. All these individuals together added up to—what? A horde of discontented people, not quite discontented enough to bear any real risk. They grumbled and waited for someone else to take the lead and right the world for them. The conspiracy itself was small. It consisted of a few senators, most of them with names redolent of past glory. Gracchus, Scipio, Pulcher. Men whose ambitions had been frustrated, men who dreamed of undoing history.

The core came down to fewer than a dozen people. Would they truly have seized Tavius when he came to Crisponus's house for dinner, seized him but not killed him? I did not believe it for a moment. Even if some of them had intended to spare Tavius's life, wiser heads would have prevailed.

I could have forgiven the fools who dreamed of restoring lost liberties. Some tiny corner of my heart even sympathized with them. My own father had died for the Republic. I could even have forgiven Julia and Jullus for their unwise passion and their ambition.

But they had committed acts bound to lead to my husband's death. That was what I could not forgive.

>>>>>>

As a new day dawned, Tavius and I sat exhausted. A soldier entered the atrium to report on new developments. I noted the tension in this man's face, and the back of my neck prickled.

The soldier saluted Tavius, then said, "I regret to tell you, sir—one of the traitors we have in custody managed to hang herself."

All the breath was expelled from my lungs. My first thought was that he meant Julia.

"Who?" Tavius demanded.

"One of your daughter's servants. A freedwoman. Her name was Phoebe."

Expressionlessly, Tavius said, "She should have been better watched."

"Yes, sir."

"Is that all you have to tell me? Then you're dismissed."

The soldier saluted, looking relieved. I supposed he had expected there would be punishment for carelessness, allowing a prisoner to escape our clutches. I wondered why the woman had done it. Fear of a worse fate than hanging? Or did she act out of loyalty to Julia—did she possess secrets she feared she would reveal under torture?

Interrogators even now were doing what they were expected to do in such cases. There would be pressure applied to get at the truth. No one would lay hands on Julia—but who knew what would happen to the others? I did not want to know.

"I wish I were Phoebe's father," Tavius said. They were the bitterest words he had ever spoken. He wished Julia dead with some scrap of honor. But was he drawing back from the thought of executing her himself? After a moment, he answered the unspoken question in my eyes. "Yes, I am still resolved that they must all die."

Once as a young man, he had sat in judgment on those who had taken part in the assassination of Julius Caesar. I had been told of the savagery of his demeanor, how he had pointed to men who begged for mercy and said, *You must die.* That was long ago. The young man who had slaughtered his enemies had been regarded by many as a brute. The Roman people would have grown to hate that young man. But the wise and merciful ruler he had become—that man they called Father of His Country.

It would be absurd arrogance for me to claim that wise ruler was my creation. I had merely helped him to bring forth the qualities that were there in him all along. There at his side with a love and a loyalty that never wavered, I had been like a midwife at a birth.

My love for Tavius and my love for my country had mingled, so I could not separate one from the other. At this moment I saw the wise ruler who was my beloved destroying himself with his own hand. There would be bloody executions—executions of scions of Rome's foremost families. Worse, he would kill his own daughter. That act, whatever its justification, would leave a black stain on his name through all the ages to come.

Who would he be after all the killing was done? The man I loved or some other being?

I said carefully, "It is possible Julia did not foresee any physical harm coming to you."

He gave a derisive snort. "She is my daughter. Do you think I bred a fool? She is not stupid. She knew."

And maybe he was right. Somewhere, if perhaps not in the forefront of her mind, the knowledge had surely lurked. I could imagine that anger had grown over the years, as again and again her desires for happiness were thwarted. I could imagine her wanting to shed the burden of being this man's daughter. Perhaps resentment had grown in her like a tumor, eating away at her restraint.

I could not forgive her. And yet . . . and yet . . . how desperate she must have been to do what she did.

Maybe some people, situated as they are in life, can never be happy. Perhaps because of this, their doom is preordained. I was enraged at Julia. She had set in motion a conspiracy sure to lead to the death of her own father, the man I loved. But I felt . . . not precisely guilt but responsibility. I had played my role in creating the circumstances of her life.

I spoke to Tavius in a low, gentle voice. "Do you truly want her dead?"

"Yes. I want her finished, done with. I want her removed from the world."

I had learned some things in the years of our marriage. I knew how great power could work on you, and destroy everything human in you. Always separate and above other people, able to confer great benefits or do great harm with a word, fawned over, you started to believe the false praise. It was easy to imagine yourself as godlike, to regard the common run of humanity with contempt. In such circumstances it took strength not to become a monster. Add to this the responsibility for everything that happened in a vast empire, and one could easily lose one's reason.

Something diamond hard in Tavius had until this day kept him sane. But if he killed his daughter, he would be destroyed as a human being.

I tried to speak in the dispassionate voice of a political advisor. "Please think a moment. Now the people of Rome will be on your side. They will see Julia as a traitor. But if you execute her, the people will blame you. They love her and they will pity her."

"Do you think I care what the cursed people think?"

My self-command broke. "You can't do it," I said. "Oh, gods above, we created her, don't you see?"

"You are speaking foolishness. You ought to be thanking the gods you are not her mother."

"You don't want her dead. You want her gone, obliterated, never to have been born. But she was born. She is your only child. If you cause her to be put to death, you will never recover."

"You think I'll recover from this now?"

"No." My voice shook. "Not entirely. But you'll be the ruler you were. You'll move past this for Rome's sake. But not if you kill her. I know you, beloved. We know each other. You are not the man they think you are, not entirely. They only see the shell of power. I see you. I've always seen you and you've seen me. Tavius, if I have ever given you reason to trust me, trust me now. Kill her and you will destroy your own soul."

"She deserves death. That is justice."

"I do not care about justice now. I care about you. You love your daughter. Whatever she has done, you will never stop loving her."

He shook his head. I thought he was rejecting my words, that he was intent on executing Julia. But then he began to weep, his body racked by great wrenching sobs.

I knew that he had battled all his life not to reveal himself in this way, not to weep in front of another. It occurred to me that perhaps I should walk out of the room. I was not sure if he would ever forgive me for seeing him like this.

"My daughter . . ."

I took him in my arms. I could not abandon him.

He had conquered an empire to prove to himself and to the world that he was not small, vulnerable, and sick, not the boy he had been. But who was this trembling being I held in my arms if not that child? I hated Julia in that moment as I had not before then, hated her for what she had done to him.

I kissed him on the head as I might have my boys when they were small.

His weeping gradually subsided. He did an unusual and tender thing then. He took my hand and kissed it, a sign of love, and reassurance.

"Beloved," I said, "remember who you are. You are Caesar Augustus, Rome's revered one. Nothing that has happened can touch that. Nothing ever will."

After a little while he said, "I will banish her to a far island. I will never see her again."

I nodded.

"That pack of fools—Gracchus and the rest—they are not worth killing. I will exile them to lands across the Mediterranean. They can live out their miserable lives far from Rome, alone and forgotten."

"I think that is magnanimous and wise."

"But Jullus Antony—he dies."

"Let him die by his own hand," I said, thinking of Selene.

"If he has the courage for it," Tavius said, his mouth twisting. "See to it."

>>>>>>>

It was the first time I played a part in ordering a death, and I had a strange vision of the girl I had been watching me with large, grave eyes—the girl who believed in a free Republic, the girl who was so soft. She grew up in a terrible time, saw her parents take their own lives. She learned what civil war was. That girl was my silent witness.

I wrote the words *"Redeem your honor"* on a waxed tablet. My hand did not tremble. I ordered a centurion to bring the note and a dagger to Jullus Antony in the cell where he was kept.

I remembered the intelligent, charming man I had always liked, remembered how he had struggled lifelong with the burden of his father's name. I remembered also that he had meant to kill Tavius.

When the centurion had gone, Tavius said, "Mark Antony botched it and was a long time dying."

I nodded.

>>>>>>>

Jullus did not botch it.

The centurion returned inside an hour. Tavius had gone to lie down, overwhelmed by fatigue. I had waited to see that the order was carried out.

"Is it done?" I asked.

"Yes, my lady," the centurion replied.

"He did it himself?"

"Oh, yes. He smiled when he saw the dagger and read the note. I left him alone. He didn't waste time. A brave and honorable death, my lady—I'll give him that much."

"Yes, we have to give him that much. You're dismissed."

It was late morning, and all I wanted to do was sleep.

Julia

*I*t was only when I was about to be put aboard a galley at the port at Ostia that I was told my fate. A military officer informed me that I had been exiled for life to a tiny island called Pandateria. "It is less than a mile wide," he said. "But there is a villa. You will be comfortable."

"Will my children be allowed to visit me?" I asked.

The officer's face was expressionless. "I very much doubt it."

So I had lost my children. Lost them forever. I ached at that moment to hold each of them in my arms, but I would be denied even a chance to say farewell. I said nothing, but inside myself I cried out for my five beautiful little ones.

"There is something that your father, the First Citizen, wished me to tell you."

"What?"

"That he will accept no communications from you in the future. And he will never set eyes on you again."

I almost smiled. "That is no punishment. I lost my father long ago."

The officer was silent and stony-eyed.

I finally forced the words out of my mouth that I hardly dared to speak. "And the men arrested for plotting against my father? What is their punishment?"

"They are to be exiled."

Not death, life. I was amazed. Inwardly I rejoiced. Because Jullus would live. I could bear all else, if only Jullus was allowed to live.

Then the officer said, "All but one, Jullus Antony."

I managed to get out the words, "Has he been condemned to death?"

"The First Citizen showed him great mercy and let him take his own life."

"Jullus Antony is dead, then?"

"Quite dead."

Darkness surrounded me. It seemed to me I had been born into darkness and lived in it all my life. Now all would be darkness until the day of my death.

>>>>>>

The boat moves through the water, toward the cursed island of Pandateria. I stand on deck with my mother beside me, my mother, Scribonia, she who bore me in her body. She has volunteered to share my exile and spend her last years on the island for my sake. I cannot begin to grasp yet the full meaning of her sacrifice—to fathom such love.

I stare out at the gray Mediterranean. One memory comes back again and again. I hold a laurel wreath in my hands, and I look up at a carved head with horns and goat ears. Jullus lifts me in his arms. When I gaze down, I see his beloved face, full of fearless exultation.

All around me, people are shouting, *Liberty! Liberty!* Jullus lifts me, higher and higher. I reach up and place the wreath on the statue's head. The warm sun caresses me. *Liberty!* I cry.

Cleopatra Selene

I will return home with my children. I will return to Juba, and to our kingdom of Mauretania. I have won the concessions from Rome that we hoped for. Caesar Augustus himself took my hand and told me I have his everlasting gratitude.

I, daughter of Mark Antony and Cleopatra, had to choose whether Rome would know peace or be plunged into another civil war. It fell to me of all people to ensure that Caesar Augustus, my parents' great enemy, would continue to rule. I acted as I did to protect the well-being of my family and of my kingdom; I chose peace for the empire. At least for now, Mauretania is safe, and my husband, and my children also. I protected my own.

There is a scar on my heart. I will carry for the rest of my life the knowledge that I sacrificed my brother, whom I loved.

I do not know if my mother would approve my decision. But I believe she would understand me. I carry her blood and perhaps some fragment of her spirit. This world is a hard and unforgiving place. She commanded me to live in it. I have obeyed her.

Juba and I, who were brought to Rome in captive bonds, will leave behind a noble legacy. That is my comfort.

May the gods forgive me.

Livia

I have never had a daughter. But in some sense, Cleopatra Selene has been a true daughter to me. Yes, I admire her. I wish she were the child of my own flesh.

I will never see Julia again, and I will try not to think of her.

My son will come home sooner or later. Not when Tavius or I call, but when Rome does. In this regard, I know him better than he knows himself. If one day he becomes First Citizen and I still survive, I will do my best to make his rule merciful. I believe a woman who walks on the stage of history should devote herself to peace and the preservation of life. I will strive to do so as long as the gods grant me breath.

The End

Author's Note

The Roman histories that are our chief source of knowledge about Caesar Augustus's time are incomplete and were written by men—never women—who had political agendas and, more often than not, misogynistic attitudes. It's hard to be certain about people who lived so long ago, but recent biographers have made a convincing case for Livia's innocence of the murder charges that have darkened her reputation. The stories of her poisoning some of Augustus's heirs and ultimately him have been largely discredited. Historians also have revised their view of Augustus's daughter, Julia, once seen as merely a promiscuous wild child. Many now believe that she and her lover Jullus Antony led a political faction that aimed at substituting Jullus for Tiberius as Julia's husband. This would have made him guardian of her sons (and of the empire) in the case of her father's demise.

All the ancient sources speak of Julia's multiple lovers, but beyond that, there are varying accounts of her behavior. I find it hard to give credence to tales of her prostituting herself on the Rostra (speaker's platform) in the Forum, but it does seem highly likely she was unfaithful during her marriages to Agrippa and Tiberius. Historians point to the irony of Augustus criminalizing adultery and campaigning for Roman "family values" when his daughter was promiscuous and he had committed adultery himself. (It should be kept in mind that adultery in ancient Rome by definition involved a free, married woman; other sex outside the bonds of marriage did not count.) This campaign was not very successful, and it certainly alienated some citizens.

The details of Julia and Jullus's plot are veiled in mystery. Augustus officially accused the two, as well as their accomplices, of adultery rather than treason. But Julia's crowning of the statue of Marsyas was clearly a politically subversive act. Romans commonly believed that Julia had plotted to overthrow and kill her father. Augustus, who had closed his eyes to her sexual escapades for years, suddenly exiled her and politically prominent men who were her friends and lovers. This included Sempronius Gracchus, a member of the family that a few generations earlier had produced Rome's heroic democratic reformers, the Gracchi brothers. Antony committed suicide, as an alternative to being put to death.

Julia is described in the ancient sources as kind, humane, and greatly loved by the Roman people. (After her exile, a crowd in the Forum begged Augustus to forgive and reinstate her.) If we assume she was a would-be murderer, of her father no less, this adds up to a contradictory portrait. My biggest challenge in writing this novel was to portray her as a psychologically comprehensible human being.

Jullus Antony (the first name is alternately spelled Iullus) was the son of Mark Antony by his wife Fulvia, who died before Antony's marriage to Octavia. He was raised by his stepmother and ultimately married her daughter. Augustus denied him military commands but on the whole treated him surprisingly well and is said to have liked him personally. He was allowed to become a senator and fill high governmental posts. Intelligent and capable, he was also a prolific poet, though unfortunately his poems have not survived. Julia also had literary interests, and that may have been a bond they shared.

Cleopatra Selene, daughter of Cleopatra and Mark Antony, is an especially fascinating historical figure. She arrived in Rome as a captive, a young child at the mercy of the man who destroyed her parents and executed her two teenage half brothers. We might expect her to have lived a miserable life in the event she avoided an early death. Somehow or other she wound up queen of Mauretania, married to King Juba, an admirable man with a formidable intellect. Augustus even provided her with a huge dowry. We really don't know how in the world this came about, but she must have attracted one or more powerful patrons. I find the fact that she apparently named her daughter Drusilla in honor of Livia suggestive.

She and Juba were enlightened rulers who beautified their capital city and made Mauretania a magnet for scholars. It is recorded that she exerted great influence as queen. Given that Juba authored numerous books and went off on voyages of exploration (he discovered the Canary Islands), it seems fair to suppose that much day-to-day government was in her hands. Unfortunately, many of the specifics we would like to have about her later life are impossible to come by. Even the year of her death is a matter of controversy, with reputable scholars arguing for widely differing dates.

In the novel, Cleopatra Selene gives away Julia and Jullus's plot to overthrow Augustus. Actually, no source tells us how the plot was thwarted. Cleopatra Selene made several visits to Rome as queen. Unlike her brother, she remained at least outwardly loyal to Augustus all her life. She could have played the role she does in the novel, though I would never try to prove that she did. It is certainly true that she and Jullus chose opposing ways of dealing with a tragic family legacy.

Acknowledgments

Both my literary agent, Elizabeth Winick Rubinstein, and my first editor at Amazon/Lake Union, Terry Goodman, provided feedback and encouragement as I developed the proposal for this novel. Without these two brilliant and creative people, I doubt that I'd ever have fulfilled my dream of becoming a published novelist, much less be bringing out my second book. I owe each of them a huge debt. Liz, thanks for combining business smarts with empathy. Terry, I wish you the happiest retirement imaginable. It was a joy and an honor to work with you.

A writer is probably lucky to find one extraordinary acquiring editor in her career. I somehow found two. My thanks to Danielle Marshall for stepping into Terry Goodman's shoes, contributing valuable insights that improved the novel, and shepherding it to publication. Thanks also to my amazing developmental editor, Charlotte Herscher, for her sensitivity and acumen and for making my work better than I ever thought it could be, and to the meticulous Laura Petrella, my copyeditor.

I've relied on the behind-the-scenes efforts of two extremely capable teams, one at McIntosh & Otis, America's second-oldest literary agency, and the other at Amazon, publishing's leading innovator. My special thanks to Amelia Appel and Alecia Douglas at M&O and Thom Kephart, Tyler Stoops, Dennelle Catlett, Susan Stockman, and Gabriella Van den Heuvel at Lake Union.

Finally, I'm deeply grateful to the fellow writers who gave me kind support and astute feedback during this latest journey: Bruce Bowman, Susie DeFord, Henya Drescher, Cynthia Dunn, Frances Northcutt Green, Mary Hoffman, Noah Lederman, Vicky Oliver, David Rothman, and Norm Scott.

Questions for Discussion

1. Julia saw herself as motherless even though she had both a mother and a stepmother. Were Livia or Scribonia to blame for this? Do you think if Julia had had a closer relationship to one of them growing up her life would have been different?

2. Did Augustus (Tavius) truly love his daughter? How did their relationship impact Julia's life?

3. Cleopatra Selene managed to survive and prosper after an adverse start in life. Why do you think that was?

4. Each of Julia's marriages were political arrangements, but she reacted differently to each one. Why?

5. Augustus (Tavius) tried to legislate morality in Rome. Do you think governments can successfully foster morality? Should they try to?

6. Why do you think Tiberius turned on Julia when their baby died? How do you imagine their relationship would have evolved if the baby lived?

7. Jullus says he wants both Julia and political power. Which do you think was most important to him?

8. In arguing with her father, Julia says Livia can't see Tiberius clearly because she is his mother. Was she right? Thinking of the three central women characters, Julia, Livia, and Cleopatra Selene, would you say they have accurate views of the people close to them?

9. Was Julia right to revolt against her father? Do you think she was willing to have him killed by those who plotted to overthrow him?

10. Livia says that some people are unable to be happy in the situation they are born into. Was this true of Julia? Do you think it is true of some people today?

11. How are the women in the novel used by men to help them keep or obtain political power? How do Livia, Julia, and Cleopatra Selene exercise power themselves, openly and/or behind the scenes? Have the political roles of women completely changed in the modern world—or only in some respects?

About the Author

Photo Credit © 2013 Rachel Elkind

Phyllis T. Smith was born and currently lives in Brooklyn, New York. After obtaining a bachelor's degree from Brooklyn College and a master's degree from New York University, Phyllis pursued a practical career in computer applications training, yet found herself drawn to writing fiction and to the history, literature, and art of the ancient world. Her first novel, *I Am Livia*, was a #1 Kindle and Digital Book World bestseller. She plans to write more novels set in ancient Rome.